"LESSON NUMBER ONE IN ADVANCED BUSH SURVIVAL: LOOK FOR WATER."

Kat shoved at the cockpit. It gave with a sudden jerk that threw her off balance and flailing into the control panel.

Kat made the awkward climb out of the cockpit. She jumped onto the wing checking the area for specific landmarks. The sun made a fiery ball due west. Not much better landmark than that. It turned the area under her aircraft into an inky morass.

An inky morass that moved and slithered.

Kat scrambled back up the wing toward the cockpit in a hurry. She fished an emergency light out of the kit and shone it down into the shadows.

Hundreds of black snakes covered the ground—all moving. Wedge shaped heads with venom pits and viper heat sensors lifted and tasted the air with rapidly moving forked tongues of blood red.

And then one particular dark knot lifted to become a giant snake. Bigger than the biggest snake she had ever heard about. Its head was bigger than hers.

As the monster rose up to stare her in the eye, it fluttered six pair of black bat wings.

She could not run from it. She could not climb high enough to get away from it. She could not hide from it. . . .

Be sure to read these magnificent
DAW Fantasy Novels by
IRENE RADFORD

The Stargods:
THE HIDDEN DRAGON
THE DRAGON CIRCLE
THE DRAGON'S REVENGE

The Dragon Nimbus:
THE GLASS DRAGON
THE PERFECT PRINCESS
THE LONELIEST MAGICIAN
THE WIZARD'S TREASURE

The Dragon Nimbus History:
THE DRAGON'S TOUCHSTONE
THE LAST BATTLEMAGE
THE RENEGADE DRAGON

Merlin's Descendants:
GUARDIAN OF THE BALANCE
GUARDIAN OF THE TRUST
GUARDIAN OF THE VISION
GUARDIAN OF THE PROMISE
GUARDIAN OF THE FREEDOM

The Dragon's Revenge

THE STARGODS #3

IRENE RADFORD

DAW BOOKS, INC.
DONALD A. WOLLHEIM, FOUNDER
375 Hudson Street, New York, NY 10014
ELIZABETH R. WOLLHEIM
SHEILA E. GILBERT
PUBLISHERS
http://www.dawbooks.com

Cover art by Luis Royo.

DAW Book Collectors No. 1344.

DAW Books are distributed by Penguin Group (USA) Inc.

First Printing, November 2005
1 2 3 4 5 6 7 8 9

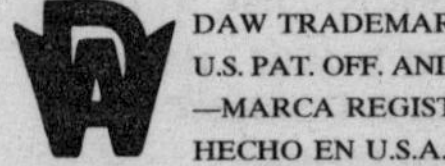

DAW TRADEMARK REGISTERED
U.S. PAT. OFF. AND FOREIGN COUNTRIES
—MARCA REGISTRADA
HECHO EN U.S.A.

PRINTED IN THE U.S.A.

This book is for Karen, Deb, Connie, Mike B., Bob, Mike M., Eric, Sheila, and Di Anne, the friends from "Digging Deeper" who reinvigorate my writing and keep me going when the books muddle in the middle.

PROLOGUE

THE NIMBUS OF DRAGONS has found a way to eliminate the foreign ship that orbits our home. We manipulated forces as a group that would elude any single one of us. Together, we have ensured the safety of our nimbus and those we protect. No more foreigners will plague us with their machines and their diseases. The rest of their vices we can manipulate or eliminate as we did their ship.

A dragon dream is a powerful tool, and a dangerous one. We all agreed that this one must be given. Only if we all agree will we use one.

If only eliminating the threat of the Krakatrice were just as easy. The snake monsters are resilient and more resistant to manipulation. Perhaps we should pit the humans against our enemy since we may not kill them ourselves. All life is sacred.

One of us has gone rogue. We have no way of controlling the one called Hanassa. The purple-tipped dragon has developed a taste for human blood, human power, and living within a human body. He changes bodies at will until he finds a host strong enough of body and weak enough of will to destroy or imprison him. The dragon nimbus is out of options. We may not destroy one of our own any more than we may destroy the Krakatrice.

There is one among the humans who needs our help.

Which of us shall we dispatch to guide her in finding what she truly quests for and not what others tell her she must quest for? We have promised the God of All that we would aid the humans. We have promised to maintain the unity among every living thing in the universe. The Krakatrice add nothing to the unity. The one called Hanassa threatens unity with his every breath.

CHAPTER 1

LIEUTENANT KAT TALBOT, Imperial Military Police, wrestled the massive hydroponics tank through the listing shuttle bay doors. The six-meter-by-two-meter apparatus weighed nothing in zero G, but its bulk and mass were awkward. She couldn't see around it and kept bumping into bulkheads. Commander Amanda Leonard, captain of this derelict ship, had chosen Kat because of her bushie height and strength as well as her experience in and affinity for zero G, more than anyone else among the scattered crew.

Since *Jupiter* had stopped spinning two months ago, gravity had evaporated aboard. Atmosphere had leaked away before that. Unless Kat could find and replace the stolen crystal array and get the ship operational again, all she could do was salvage as much as possible.

She paused in her struggles. The air in her EVA suit tasted stale. "Nothing for it but to get this thing aboard a lander so I can fire up some atmosphere," she grunted.

A flicker of movement off to her left made her stop and look around. Nothing.

She shivered. Just her imagination running wild. Ghost ships were notorious for evoking atavistic fears.

Jupiter was very much a ghost ship. Derelict and drifting in space.

Nine months ago, the three outlawed O'Hara brothers had stolen the crystal array from *Jupiter.* Without the star drive the ship was doomed, her crew stranded in the back of beyond.

For nine months she'd been salvaging essentials for survival and still life dirtside resembled a tribal hunter-gatherer society more than civilization.

"How long, Kat?" Lieutenant Commander Jetang M'Berra called over her helmet comm.

"Ten minutes," she panted. She'd spent too much time dirtside breathing real air. Getting used to recycled oxygen mixtures again would take time.

The hydroponics tank tilted and jammed in the partially open hatch. No power to open the doors further.

"S'murghit!" she borrowed an epithet from the planetary locals. "You could have made this easier by assigning me an extra crewman." She didn't care if M'Berra heard that comment or not. She didn't care if Commander Amanda Leonard heard it either.

Her superior officers had gotten too used to her initiative as well as her bushie height and muscle mass for doing their dirty work.

"My sensors read you are running low on air, Kat," M'Berra advised her. "You have less than ten minutes to get that tank aboard a lander and fire up life support."

"Acknowledged." No wonder her air tasted stale. Her EVA suit's monitors hadn't operated properly in months. But the suit worked. That was more than she could say for most of the high-tech equipment they'd salvaged.

She heaved and levered the tank free of the obstruction. A gentle shove sent it gliding toward the open bay doors of a lander.

She wished for her more maneuverable and sleeker fighter. But she needed the extra cargo space and fuel efficiency in a lander.

"Kat, what did you do in med bay?" M'Berra's voice contained an edge of worry.

"Didn't go near the place," Kat grunted as she shoved the tank into the hold of the lander. It was a small lie. She'd passed the med bay on a private errand to her own quarters, but M'berra didn't need to know that. Besides, she hadn't actually gone into that med bay.

She climbed in after the hydroponics tank and closed the hatch. Still eight minutes to spare on her suit air. She reached the cockpit and keyed in comm system and life support before settling into the pilot's seat.

"What's wrong in med bay?" she asked. Good thing she'd set the entire lander's systems on standby before going after the tank and her own personal memento. She'd have air and heat before her suit emptied.

"Get out now, Kat." M'Berra didn't mask the anxiety in his voice.

"Can't. I need two more minutes to fire up all systems."

"Don't wait!"

"What's wrong?"

M'Berra's panic was contagious. Kat skipped the usual safety protocol in favor of faster engine ignition. Life support would come on faster that way, too.

"Something sparked in med bay. The volatile chemicals . . ."

"No air to support a spark," Kat reassured herself and M'Berra.

That flicker of movement had been in the direction of med bay at the center of the ship.

"Still some air in med bay. It's sealed better than the rest of the ship. A spark. Kat, the whole ship is going to blow with you in it."

"Not if I can help it."

In the background she heard a dull roar. Something flashed on the periphery of her vision.

Without thinking, she tapped an override sequence into her interface. Before she could inhale one last gulp of rancid artificial air, she launched out of the shuttle bay.

The explosion rushed through the confined passageways seeking an exit and expansion. The force behind it propelled Kat's lander through the open bay doors faster than safety dictated. Her tail fins nicked the edge.

More flashes of light sent her adrenaline surging. With a teeth-grinding screech she broke free. A hard bank to starboard brought her looping around the mass of the space cruiser and back within view of the planet below.

Large chunks of cerama/metal hull followed her and greeted her. Another sharp veer, this time to port. A flying mass just barely missed hurtling into her viewscreen.

Was one of those chunks a fighter headed dirtside? No way to tell. No time to think.

Kat exhaled and realized she had nothing left to inhale. Quickly she ripped off her helmet and gasped the first faint traces of atmosphere generated by the lander.

"What did you do to my ship?" Commander Leonard's voice screamed through the ship comm. "We saw the explosion from here, Talbot. What did you do? I'll court-martial you here and now."

"A lot of good that will do you, Capt'n Leonard,

sir," Kat grumbled. "We're three sectors off the star charts and no way to communicate with civilization."

Friction from the planetary upper atmosphere began to glow around the nose of the lander. Kat hit the control to extend the rudimentary wings to slow her descent. She overrode the command just as quickly to avoid having the wings torn off by another burning chunk of debris that flashed past her.

"Simurgh take you, Konner O'Hara, and both your brothers. Once again, you've destroyed my home," she cried. Unwanted tears touched her eyes. She blinked them away and concentrated on keeping her trajectory shallow. Kat's curse, while not exactly accurate, reflected the emotions welling in her chest.

Somehow the outlawed brothers had something to do with that stray spark. They had to have. Just as they had stolen the crystal array. They had given the ship and its crew a death sentence, stranding them on the primitive planet below, without possible communication with the rest of the galaxy.

Atmospheric stresses screamed through the lander.

"M'Berra, this lander steers like a garbage scow. I'm having trouble keeping to flight plan." She turned as tightly as the ship allowed, trying to bring the big vessel back to the proper coordinates. Three G's of pressure pushed her against her restraints and flattened her face. At the end of the tight turn, Kat breathed heavily. Sweat dotted her brow. She checked her sensors.

Chunks of *Jupiter* still fell around her, just a small percentage of the ship. The explosion had directed most of the debris out of orbit and away from the planet.

As the stray pieces hit the upper atmosphere and encountered friction, they became various sized fireballs, shedding bits in their wakes. The westering sun added red brightness to the mass.

"Report, Lieutenant Talbot," Commander Leonard barked over the comm unit. "How much of the ship is lost? Can we make it spaceworthy once we reclaim the crystal array from those thieving O'Hara brothers?"

Kat grimaced and dodged another piece of glowing debris from the once-proud vessel. She checked her rear visual screen. "Not much left, sir." She flashed the sensor view of the scene to ground communications.

Commander Leonard wasn't going to like it at all.

"Salvage?" Leonard said. Her voice lost none of its bite.

"Unknown," Kat spat back. In the last nine months her captain had lost her sense of reality in her obsession over restoring *Jupiter* and, with it, her command.

Kat pictured Amanda Leonard in the back of her mind as she had last seen *Jupiter*'s captain: a black patch over her left eye, pacing Base Camp with the comm pressed closely against her face, her uncovered eye looking black and sunken from lack of sleep. The uniform she insisted upon wearing was clean and pressed, but it hung on her wasted figure. More than lack of sleep and poor appetite ate at Leonard's once buxom and robust body.

"Not good enough, Talbot. I need a clearer picture. I need evidence to condemn the O'Hara brothers for sabotaging my ship," Leonard sneered. As if she didn't have enough evidence already.

To convict, first they had to capture the outlaws.

At the moment Loki, Konner, and Kim O'Hara, though outlaws, virtually owned the planet except for Base Camp.

What's more, the locals revered them as Stargods.

"May a Denubian muscle-cat scratch the balls off all three of the O'Hara brothers," Leonard cursed. "They cost me an eye and now they've cost me my ship."

Kat smiled. She'd wished similar fates for the O'Hara's—as well as their infamous Mum—many times herself. She'd sought revenge upon them for twenty years, long before their sabotage had stranded the crew of the *Jupiter* on this forgotten planet three jumps beyond nowhere.

She fingered the bracelet of braided hair she had retrieved from her own quarters on this trip. The detour had cost her time and air. But she was glad now that she had this last memento of her mother and the family she had lost at the age of seven.

"Get that hydro tank back here, Talbot, then report to me. Directly to me. Not to First Officer M'Berra, not to your buddies in the flight pool, and definitely not to any enlisted personnel."

"Yes, sir," Kat replied in her briskest military voice. If she'd been face-to-face with the captain, she'd have snapped a salute. She discommed and returned her focus to her sensor screens.

Pieces of *Jupiter,* large and small—too many big ones—descended toward the surface at a steep angle. Cerama/metal flared brightly against atmospheric friction. Kat's viewscreen darkened automatically. The afterimage of flames streaking across the sky lingered on her retinas.

"I will never forget this," she said to herself through gritted teeth. "Nor will I forgive you, O'Hara brothers, for causing this."

"What is happening, Talbot?" the captain's voice demanded through the comm unit.

"What you see is what you get, Captain," Kat muttered.

"Will any of it hit Base Camp? Do we need to seek shelter?" Leonard continued her barrage of questions.

"Looks like most of the larger pieces are east of you," Kat reassured her captain.

Silence from Leonard.

"Captain, you still there?" Kat dreaded silence from her commanding officer more than she would a string of curses.

Proximity alarms blared. A sensor array flew directly toward Kat. She banked the lander to port and barely missed the aerial.

Her path took her into the backwash from a larger glowing piece. She fought the shuddering controls of her lander.

"*Dregging* stupid computer interfaces!" She cut off her complaint to punch in a new command before she collided with the next piece of debris.

Something large and hard smashed into her starboard wing. The lander careened off at an odd angle, north over the uncharted ocean rather than back to Base Camp.

"*S'murghit!* The starboard proximity alarm is gone." No maintenance and few spare parts these last nine months in the land of the Coros had caused the breakdown of more than one plane. Kat was lucky they had enough fuel cells operating to get this lander back with the precious hydroponics tank. None of the crew knew how to grow food in dirt. Few wanted to experiment with the distasteful and unknown medium.

She fought the lander for control. It shuddered and listed more with each maneuver. Finally, in frustration, she kicked at the underside of the control panel.

The plane righted and resumed the last course she had commanded.

"Lieutenant Talbot, your recording has lost resolution," Commander Leonard yelled. "Your sensors are facing directly into the sun. I can see the sunset with my own eyes. I don't need to see a recording of it."

"Correcting now, Captain," Kat replied. She said some more things, but not out loud. *I just hope that M'Berra is with you, Amanda, to keep you calm. Hard enough to convince the troops you are sane under normal circumstances.*

Amanda Leonard wasn't sane. That didn't matter, though. She commanded the Marine contingent. They followed her with blind, almost worshipful loyalty. They delighted in punishing any infraction of the rules or suggested slur against their captain.

The ocean receded behind Kat. She spotted a small port city on the primary continent north and east of the small land mass where they'd set up Base Camp. Gray-black-red desert stretched endlessly ahead of her.

Kat fought to return to her proper flight path. The ship resisted. It shuddered and vibrated right through to her bones. A crack appeared beneath her feet and widened with every attempt to turn the lander.

"Talbot, I'm still not getting coherent pictures of the breakup of *my* ship," Leonard said. She sounded frantic. "I see a heck of a lot of desert beneath you and not much else."

"I've lost navigation. Sensors going fast," Kat reported. She gulped back her momentary panic. She could do this. She could land the vessel safely. She'd just be delayed getting the tank back to Base Camp. M'Berra would send someone after her.

If he had enough fuel cells.

If he could find anyone brave enough to fly across the uncharted ocean after dark.

If he survived the crash . . .

She switched to real-time view out the windscreen rather than trust the sensor-transmitted image.

A network of spidery, silver-blue lines showed just beneath the surface of the desert. Kat had seen them once before. She'd used the power in the lines to extend her senses and perceptions.

Her lander plummeted. She fought to get some air under the wings, get the nose up, fight the gravity that pulled at her and her craft.

"Transmit your coordinates, Kat. Tell me what you need to land safely," Lieutenant Commander M'Berra's deep voice came over the comm. He broadcast an aura of calm.

"You got the evidence to convict the O'Haras of sabotage, treason, and murder. Use it," Kat demanded. If she accomplished nothing else in this life, she had to know the tyranny of the O'Haras would end.

"Talbot, you do not sound reasonable." M'Berra always sounded calm and reasonable.

"I'm going to crash unless I can conjure up a lot of magic. Promise me to use the evidence to convict the O'Haras."

"Eject, Talbot," M'Berra ordered. "Eject."

Kat pushed on the manual eject button. The canopy remained closed, her seat intact.

CHAPTER 2

LUCINDA BAINES, Cyndi to her few friends, granddaughter of an emperor, daughter of a planetary governor, and niece to a galactic senator, shifted uneasily from foot to foot. She watched carefully as Kim O'Hara, the youngest brother, performed his arcane ritual to allow her through the force field.

No matter how many times she watched each of the three brothers, her captors, she could not figure out the process for opening the way into or out of the family clearing.

"Loki is going to be very upset that I let you in to use the hot spring pool," Kim said grimly as he gestured Cyndi through the barrier.

"I wouldn't give a microgram of stardust for your brother's opinion," Cyndi replied haughtily.

Two years ago she did. Then she'd cherished her engagement to Loki, the oldest O'Hara brother. Legally, he was Matthew Kameron O'Hara, but no one called him that without getting a black eye and bloody nose.

Since then she'd seen how inconsiderate, self-centered, and amoral he was.

That was why she'd broken her engagement to him and secretly married a nephew of the emperor. Then she'd thought perhaps she should tell Loki to his face about her altered plans.

But he and his brothers had sabotaged *Jupiter,* her unofficial transport back to Earth, and had stranded her and the entire crew on this benighted planet.

"I have to admit, I understand your need for a real bath in the hot spring," Kim said. He nodded his head toward the path to the bathing pool. His bright red hair clubbed back into a queue and scraggly beard reminded her too much of Loki. She looked away from him.

"The hot spring will be pure luxury after a winter of sponging off with a bucket of cold seawater." Cyndi shuddered. Not that water could truly cleanse a person. She needed a sonic shower. Nothing else was civilized.

When would these people—namely the three O'Hara brothers—learn that their so-called freedom wasn't worth the inconvenience of primitive living! Any life outside the Galactic Terran Empire was no life at all.

But the hot spring would feel good. Besides, it gave her an excuse to get into the clearing alone.

Kim closed the portal into the clearing and left.

All Cyndi could see was a slight distortion in the landscape if she peered too closely directly into the force field. She reached a tentative hand to check its integrity. Her palm met a burning wall of energy.

Good. She checked the confines of the forest clearing for any signs of habitation.

For once, all of the family—the three brothers and the two wives—had decamped from the clearing. She'd watched Konner, the middle brother, and his local wife Dalleena take off in a hurry toward the shuttle *Rover* about an hour ago. Loki was out fishing with the village men, Kim and his wife Hestiia had been in the village this morning. Cyndi hadn't seen

Hestiia since, but the woman was hugely pregnant—positively indecent of the woman to show herself in public in her condition—and wouldn't walk uphill for an hour to get to the clearing alone. So if Kim was working in the village, his wife was there, too.

She didn't bother checking the lean-to where Taneeo the priest lay comatose. He hadn't so much as blinked his eyes without prompting let alone spoken or moved in the nine months Cyndi had lived—been held captive more like—in the nearby village.

Cyndi couldn't remember what Taneeo had looked like when conscious and vigorous.

Initially, he had sided with the Imperial Military Police from *Jupiter* against the O'Hara brothers. Then, in the battle for the crystal array, the priest had been injured in some manner. Cyndi had endured most of the battle tied to a tree and gagged, bait to lure the IMPs farther uphill.

Once the IMPs lost the battle and Konner O'Hara closed the force field, the Imperial troops had retreated to Base Camp and left Taneeo with the O'Hara brothers.

They had no use for the man now that he was comatose.

Satisfied that no one eavesdropped, Cyndi pulled out a handheld communicator. "Are you there?" she whispered. She heard only static.

"Psst. Are you there? It's nearly sunset, the time you said to call."

"What . . . who . . . Oh, yeah, Lady Cyndi," a rough voice issued from the communicator with a yawn.

Cyndi shuddered as she imagined her contact stretching and scratching in indelicate places.

"What am I supposed to do to the power cells?" Cyndi crept toward the open half acre the O'Haras had designated as the "power farm." The spare fuel cells sat in orderly rows with maximum exposure to sunlight; they were filled with dragon wine distilled from a local berry. The berry was inedible, and she assumed the liquor was too, at least based on the stench.

She wrinkled her nose and placed one dainty foot next to the first cell.

"Do you see a seam along the top?" her contact asked.

"Yes," she replied hesitantly. Not much of a seam, more like a long dent in the casing.

"Run your fingernail along the seam and press hard."

Cyndi stared at her broken nails and jagged cuticles. Once upon a time her manicure had been impeccable, with nails all the same length, beautifully shaped and painted in delightful colors to match her pretty outfits. Using them to open a fuel cell couldn't hurt them much more than any other of the disgusting chores the locals forced her to perform. Not at all suitable for the wife of one of the Imperial heirs to have to clean *fish.*

She placed the outside edge of her right thumbnail in the groove at the top of the cell and ran it the full length of the meter square top.

"Nothing's happening," she cried into the handheld.

"Press harder. You've got to get the fuel cells open. If you don't, they win. If they win, they'll never let us leave. We'll be stranded here all of our lives, all of our children's lives. They'll register themselves as sole owners of this planet and close it to all outside influence."

"If you say so." Cyndi repeated the operation on the fuel cell, pressing as hard as she could without straining her arm. She hated the look of all the muscles she'd developed working for her keep. If she never washed a dish, peeled a tuber, or carried a water bucket again, she'd be happy.

The groove widened. She reported her success to her contact.

"That's good, Lady Cyndi. Now do it again. You have to make the groove wide enough to stick your fingers in it and pry it open."

Cyndi tried again and again. Finally, she could push the tips of her fingers into the crack and pull it apart.

The lid of the fuel cell slid open. A nauseating red-and-yellow mist whooshed out at her as the pressure released and the fuel dissipated.

Cyndi laughed.

"How many cells they got?" her contact at Base Camp asked.

"A full dozen." She counted the blocks.

"They only need four in that shuttle of theirs. You've got to open some more cells or the brothers'll be flying outta here tomorrow."

"We can't have that," Cyndi agreed.

"My commander wants to know if you can steal one of the recharged cells and put it where one of our flyboys can pick it up."

They'd tried to find the clearing many times. Cyndi had heard them fly over. But the force field that kept nonfamily out also cloaked the clearing from observation.

Cyndi looked askance at the heavy blocks. "I don't think so. The path down to the village is pretty rough and these things are too heavy for me to carry alone."

"Just a thought. If we had those extra cells, we might be able to locate the brothers' ship in orbit and call for help. You'd be one of the first ones evacuated."

Cyndi sighed in disappointment. She so wanted to go home and claim her rightful place at court.

"Maybe I can get some help next trip up here." She mentally checked off which of the men in the village she could convince how important she was so they would help her betray their Stargods. Not a single one came to mind. Men on this planet married early and remained faithful. What kind of civilization was that?

She had two more of the cells open and reclosed when she heard someone singing. Hestiia, Kim's wife. She sang all the time in a husky voice. One of the few decent voices in the village that, with some training, might serve some smoky jazz joint on the edge of civilization where the clientele had little taste and no exposure to better.

Cyndi straightened from her chore and stepped away from the power farm. She listened more closely.

No, it wasn't Hestiia. The voice was deeper, raspier. And it sang a sad dirge, not the happy little ditties Hestiia favored.

Cyndi crept the two dozen paces to the central fire pit. From there she followed the sound of the mournful song that sounded as if the singer's heart would break.

At the edge of the clearing, nearly half a kilometer away, she stopped short of the lean-to where Taneeo lived. He lay unmoving as always, eyes staring directly at her as if he knew what she had been up to.

The singing continued in his accusatory tone. But he did not move his mouth. He still stared into nothing.

Help me, someone whispered into the back of her mind. *Help me cast off the demon who possesses me.*

Cyndi tried to step away from the lean-to.

Taneeo's unwavering gaze kept her rooted to the spot.

Please, help me. The words came separately from

the tune. Both sounded as if they came from the same voice.

Cyndi's knees shook.

"I . . . I don't know what you want."

Taneeo's clawlike hand snaked out and grabbed hers.

Blackness swirled through her mind, clouding her vision and upsetting her balance. She locked her knees and fought to remain upright. All the while she pulled desperately on her arm, trying to free it from Taneeo's firm grip.

He shouldn't have that much strength after nine months in a coma.

Jolts of electric energy coursed from his hand to hers, up into her shoulders and down the other arm.

For one brief moment she knew everything about Taneeo: how he'd apprenticed under another priest named Hanassa; how Hanassa had used his priestly power to satisfy his bloodlust; how Hanassa had enslaved Taneeo.

She relived in a flash the scene where Loki and his brothers had freed Taneeo and killed Hanassa in the tunnels beneath the blown-out volcano.

And then—nothing. No memory of the months that followed, of the coming of the IMPs, or of the battle for the crystal array. Nothing.

She had to grit her teeth to keep from crying out.

Just as suddenly as the alien feelings engulfed her, they disappeared.

Taneeo's hand relaxed. He fell back upon his pallet, eyes closed, body limp, and memories contained in his own body.

She jerked free of his grasp but had to cling to a tree for several moments to regain her balance and her composure.

"What just happened?"

Silence. Even the singing had ceased.

Heart racing and mind whirling, she ran headlong toward the place where Kim had let her into the clearing. She bounced off the force field with a stinging jolt. Desperate to escape, she pounded on the invisible barrier until her hands ached and burning pain lanced up her arm.

Crying and desperate for the company of another human, another *sane* human she ran down the path to the hot spring. The force field ended just beyond the pool, making it very private for the O'Hara family. It also trapped Cyndi in with Taneeo and that strange swirling blackness of the mind.

Hestiia looked up from where she sat at the edge of the pool dangling her feet in the water. "That's no way to get a bath. The water won't hurt you," she said lightly. She levered her bulky body off a rock and shed her leather wrap. Totally nude and unembarrassed, she waded into the pool between two small waterfalls and began splashing the water over her uniformly tanned body.

"Was that you singing?" Cyndi asked, still looking over her shoulder toward the clearing and Taneeo. He knew what she'd done to the fuel cells. He'd tell Loki.

"Of course I was singing. Who else?" Hestiia replied in that aggravating drawl that took forever to pronounce just a few words.

"I don't know. I thought maybe Taneeo had awakened."

"I wish he would," Hestiia said as she splashed warm water over her gravid body. "Will you wash my back? I can't quite reach anymore."

Bleakly, Cyndi shed her threadbare clothing and

boots, resigned to the fact that she would have to wait a while longer to finish her job of sabotage.

And for explanations.

* * *

Hanassa hovered over the collapsed figure of Taneeo, one clawed foot embedded in the man's brain. Long had he fought to regain total control over the body. Long had he struggled to keep his get from throwing him out completely.

The tight confines of the lean-to kept Hanassa from fully stretching his purple-tipped wings, even though his spirit body remained small and silvery; as he had been in the flesh before he invaded his first human. That person had only been two years of age, the same as Hanassa at the time. That conquest had been easy. The child had been weak, on the brink of death, without a fully formed identity. Hanassa's dragon strength had flooded the body and allowed it to heal.

Dragon strength had given Hanassa power within the human community. Dragon cunning had given him control over the lives of many. Dragon appetites had made pitiful humans quake in terror of him.

Let the dragon nimbus keep their winged bodies and their rules and their traditions.

Hanassa made his own rules and traditions among humans.

Until the Stargods came and ruined everything. They had finally managed to kill Hanassa's human body, but not his spirit. He had taken over the body of Taneeo without the Stargods suspecting. He had dwelled among them for many moons without their noticing.

But Taneeo was stronger in will and mind than Hanassa had suspected. He fought Hanassa every day. Even after the Stargods had nearly killed him again with their weapon of murderous sound, Taneeo had continued to fight Hanassa's control, until he finally lapsed into a coma rather than accept defeat.

Hanassa needed another body.

He thought he had to wait for one of his own get to happen by. Only one of his own blood would provide the unique combinations of compatibility of mind and flesh.

But now he knew differently. The woman Lucinda had shown herself strangely vulnerable to his presence. And strangely resistant at the same time.

How close did she have to be to accept him? Physically touching? Within the confines of the clearing? Or anywhere on the planet?

CHAPTER 3

"TWO POINTS TO starboard," Loki O'Hara, sometimes known as Stargod Loki, called to the rudder man and the oarsmen behind him. The sound of the waves crashing over the rocks nearly drowned his words. He dug his paddle deep into the next trough. The little fishing boat responded. His companions must have heard him.

The next wave pushed the boat sideways to port.

Loki could see his youngest brother, Kim, waving frantically to him from the shore. The setting sun turned his dark red hair into a halo of fire. Early summer and his usually fair skin was already deeply tanned. He'd shed his shirt in favor of a leather vest. He wore that and knickers—like the locals; only the locals called the men's pants trews.

"*Starboard,* you muscle-bound sulfur worm!" Kim's words drifted to Loki. "Paddle starboard."

"I'm going to starboard, my starboard, you brain-deprived lumbird," Loki called back. A big grin split his face as salt water sprayed over him, further soaking his sweat-drenched shirt. He sank his paddle deep and corrected course around a pillar of water-carved volcanic rock.

Yaakke, Kim's brother-in-law, acted as rudder man on this fishing venture. He muttered something incomprehensible to their two comrades in the boat.

None of them seemed to appreciate the grand adventure of pitting wits and muscle against the sea.

Loki fended off the rock to port with his paddle. He caught a glimpse of a clear path to the cobbled beach.

"Come on, men. We're close and I smell dinner cooking!"

Submerged portions of the jumble of broken volcanic rock scraped the bottom of the boat.

Loki bit his cheeks. "Stay afloat. Just a little longer," he pleaded with the boat and whatever gods might listen.

They had lost three boats and six men over the course of the winter. His people needed the small catch flopping in the bottom of the boat. They'd lost more people to disease and cold than to the sea.

"Simurgh take every last one of the Imperial Military Police. If they hadn't stolen our stores and confiscated our village as their Base Camp, we'd have had enough to get us through," Loki grumbled a familiar litany as he dragged his paddle through the water. A few more strokes, a couple of good waves to push them landward . . .

The boat scraped bottom. Pebbly bottom this time. They'd made it home with minimal damage to the last boat and no loss of men.

Loki jumped into the surf to drag the boat higher onto the beach. Frigid salt water soaked him to his thighs. His calloused bare feet barely felt the rounded rocks.

Kim waded toward him to help.

Yaakke and the other men leaped free and added their strength to the task.

"What troubles you, little brother?" Loki grunted while tugging on the bowsprit. "Your face is nearly as long as this boat."

"Pryth. She's taken ill."

Loki gulped. Not Pryth, the ancient Rover woman, midwife, and bard. Sometimes Loki thought the old wisewoman was all that held the villagers together. His own leadership qualities seemed minuscule compared to hers, his status as a Stargod notwithstanding.

"Can't you do anything to help Pryth?" Loki asked Kim. "You're the healer in the family."

"Not alone. I need you and Konner to support the spell," Kim replied. He gave one last tug and the boat was high enough for the villagers to begin unloading the fish.

"Where is Konner?" Loki looked around at the gathered villagers. Light and dark hair, tanned and pale, they all wore combinations of leather and woven red cow wool. None of them had the red hair and deep blue eyes of Loki and his brothers.

"Konner's favored dragon, Irythros, commandeered him and Dalleena. *Jupiter* exploded," Kim said. "The dragon is flaming debris in the atmosphere to minimize damage when it falls." He began walking up the cliff path to the plateau and the village.

"Good, they aren't wasting fuel in *Rover?*" Loki shouted as he followed Kim.

"Why fly a shuttle when you have your own pet dragon?" Kim turned a big grin on Loki.

"I gather that other dragons are also flaming debris, but without passengers," Loki asked.

The villagers began unloading and cleaning the fish. They were better at it than any of the three brothers. They wouldn't waste a bit, turning innards into bait.

"Konner and his wife seem joined at the hip to that red-tipped monster Irythros." Loki sighed, almost jealous. Kim and Hestiia communicated often with Ilanthe, the purple-tipped dragon. Konner and Dalleena had Irythros. No dragon had come forward to befriend Loki, or his lover across the sea, Paola.

But he had *Rover.* He'd rather control the shuttle than be a passive passenger on a dragon any day. He just couldn't take the shuttle up often enough to suit himself and, therefore, saw very little of Paola.

Efforts to manufacture enough fuel for *Rover* so they could return to their mother ship *Sirius* and depart this primitive planet had proved slower and more difficult than expected. But then, accomplishing anything on a world that had just barely embraced iron-age technology was slow and difficult.

A wave of homesickness engulfed Loki as completely as the waves in the cove had nearly capsized the fishing boat. He hadn't seen Mum in almost two years; hadn't had boots or new clothes in a year; hadn't eaten a meal that didn't taste of smoke and copper, or listened to recorded music, or . . .

He swallowed the despair that threatened to swamp him.

Soon. He and his brothers would leave the land of the Coros soon.

Kim stopped Loki with a hand as soon as they were out of earshot of the locals. "Now that *Jupiter* is gone and the IMPs can't divulge the coordinates of this planet to the civilized world, perhaps it's time to make peace with them."

"Never," Loki spat.

"They have antibiotics, medical equipment, a trained medic. Our magic may not be enough to help Pryth. Pryth may not have enough skills to help Hestiia when she delivers our baby. We need their help. We need to expand our gene pool . . ."

"We need to get off this planet without interference from IMPs. We do that and we don't have to worry about the gene pool," Loki shouted. His face grew hot and his hands itched to hit something.

Qwarlian swamp slime for brains! he thought, being careful not to project telepathically to his receptive brother.

A year ago, when the brothers happened upon this hard-to-find planet while running from the IMP cruiser, none of them had considered that magic, a.k.a. psychic powers, might work or that dragons were real. This planet had shown them otherwise.

He took a deep breath for calm that never quite reached his hands. "You know that now that *Jupiter* is gone the IMPs will try to steal *Sirius,*" Loki surmised. "Kat Talbot has the right DNA to break into the ship and override command locks. All she has to do is figure out how we cloaked the ship and hack through the programming. She's smart enough to do it. In fact, I'm surprised she hasn't done it already."

"We are going to have to learn to live with the IMPs eventually, Loki," Kim said, altogether too calm and rational.

"No, we don't. *We*—you, me, and Konner—are leaving as soon as we have enough fuel." Loki pressed forward, angry at his brother for bringing up the forbidden topic. Again. "I'm packed and ready to go as soon as Konner finishes up on the fuel cells."

"I am not leaving my wife and child, Loki. Konner and Dalleena are coming back as soon as they get his son away from his first wife. We and our people have to live with the IMPs. I will not abandon them or betray them."

"Will you keep Cyndi Baines here, too? We can't take her with us. You know she'll blab everything to everyone she meets if she ever sees civilization again. You want to live with that woman?" Loki sneered.

Kim blanched.

Loki chuckled.

"I can't see why you ever thought yourself in love with Cyndi, Loki." Kim shook his head. "Nor can I imagine who was stupid enough to make her a diplomatic attaché. She's the most undiplomatic person alive."

"Cyndi got her appointment because she's related to royalty. I fell in love with the idea of stealing her precious self right out from under the nose of her important and officious father. Why she hopped aboard *Jupiter* rather than a luxury liner for a quick trip home, I can't begin to guess."

Loki turned and stared at his brother. "We have to leave here soon, Kim. We have to report back to Mum. We have to help Konner retrieve his son. You have to come with us." He tried to force his brother's compliance with a mental probe.

The power bounced back to him, stabbing him between the eyes, instantly generating a fierce headache. He stumbled and pressed a hand over his eyes, blocking the light of the suddenly too bright sun. He reached his other hand to steady himself against whatever rock or shrubbery was nearby.

Kim grabbed hold of Loki's arm and held him upright.

"Will you at least consider an expedition to steal some drugs from the IMPs?" Kim asked.

"I have no problem with stealing from the enemy. Why don't we kidnap their medic Lotski while we're at it," Loki tried to smile around the pain in his head. He was always up for an adventure. Well, almost always. Right now he wanted only a cold cloth over his eyes and complete darkness.

Kim pressed his hands to Loki's temples.

The pain faded.

"Remember this next time you try to manipulate me with magic, Loki."

"I'll remember."

CHAPTER 4

(USE THE LEY LINES,) a calm voice whispered into the back of Kat's mind. *(Find their power and make it your own.)*

"Yeah, right. Want to tell me how to do that?" she sneered at the invisible voice.

(Remember.)

"Remember what?" Last time she had seen the spiderweb of blue power lines beneath the surface of the land, a dragon had guided her to place her feet atop a junction of two lines. She could not do that now. She was still several hundred meters above the rapidly approaching ground.

The lander nosed down.

"Ley lines." She closed her eyes and thought about how the power had tingled up her legs, along her spine, then into her mind. She pulled on the memory and forced the nose of the lander up with all of the considerable strength in her arms and shoulders and will.

Her shoulders ached. Her face ached. And her head ached when she finally got the nose up.

"I shouldn't have been able to do that!" Had her psychic powers actually overridden the laws of physics?

Nonsense. Loki O'Hara had filled her head with

nonsense. No one had enough psychic power to force an out-of-control aircraft to break the laws of physics and defy gravity.

With enough air under her wings to glide, she took a deep breath and a quick look around. She was low, too low. No wonder the cockpit wouldn't eject, she didn't have enough altitude for a parachute to open or a jetpack to engage.

Breathing deeply, half wondering if she were already dead and only dreaming, she guided the fighter down in large swoops, first starboard then port, shedding altitude gracefully and gradually. The setting sun cast long shadows, disguising the true height of obstacles in her path. She took a chance and selected what appeared to be an almost level landing field. Her VTOL jets were history and unable to steady her drop.

She had to do this the old-fashioned way, by the seat of her pants. Very few pilots in His Majesty's fleet knew how. She was glad her father and brother had taught her more tricks than the official manual allowed.

The lander bounced and kicked and rolled over the rough desert floor. Kat rolled and bounced and kicked all over her seat, despite the tight safety harness. The hydroponics tank broke free of its restraints and slid forward, blocking access to the hold from the cockpit.

Finally, the cumbersome lander came to an abrupt halt, nose crumpled against a rock, one wheel off the ground. The other tire was slashed to ribbons by the rocky ground. Both struts were mangled.

Shaken and shaking, Kat released her harness. She tested her limbs and head for obvious injury. No bleeding, a few aches and bruises.

"I've survived worse in simulation," she muttered. But in simulation she'd always had a cup of hot coffee and a medic awaiting her.

Out here in the desert she had only herself for comfort and solace.

"Saint Bridget, I hope Brewster packed the emergency kit to regulation before I took off." She pulled out the bin from beneath her seat. It felt suspiciously light.

"Simurgh take his hide!" No water, no food. Only a basic first aid kit.

The thought of being without water suddenly made Kat extremely thirsty. Her throat thickened and tasted sour. She wanted a long cool drink now. *Right now.*

"Now what am I supposed to do?" Kat wondered out loud. Commander Leonard did not know if she'd survived or gone up in a fireball. The captain would be unlikely to cannibalize three planes to get one in the air to search for Kat. She had not passed any sign of civilization beyond the coastline a thousand klicks west. The rest of the continent was largely unmapped.

"Lesson number one in Advanced Bush Survival, look for water." Kat shoved at the cockpit. It remained clamped into place. Muttering enough curses to exhaust her extensive vocabulary, she banged on override switches, released manual clamps, and finally heaved with her back pressed into the canopy. It gave with a sudden jerk that threw her off balance and flailing into the control panel.

A blast of desert heat rose up from the gray-green sands. She almost ducked back beneath the smoke-colored canopy. But this was desert; without a cloud cover, the land would lose heat rapidly the moment the sun dropped below the horizon. She guessed she had about a half hour for a preliminary search, then back to the plane for shelter.

Kat made the awkward climb out of the cockpit, cursing that she couldn't get past the hydro tank to exit through the main hatch in the hold. It now weighed half a metric ton in full gravity, well beyond her capacity to shove it aside without mechanical help.

She jumped onto the wing, checking the area for specific landmarks in case she got turned around and lost sight of the plane. The sun made a fiery ball due west. She wouldn't find a much better landmark than that. It turned the area under her aircraft into an inky morass.

An inky morass that moved and slithered.

Kat scrambled back up the wing toward the cockpit in a hurry. She fished an emergency light out of the kit and shone it down into the shadows.

Hundreds of black snakes covered the ground. Thick ones. Skinny ones. Long ones. Short ones. All moving. Wedge-shaped heads with venom pits and viper heat sensors lifted and tasted the air with rapidly moving forked tongues of blood red.

And then one particular dark knot lifted to become a giant snake. Bigger than the biggest snake she had ever heard about. Its head was bigger than hers.

As the monster rose up to stare her in the eye, it fluttered six pairs of black bat wings.

She could not run from it. She could not climb high enough to get away from it. She could not hide from it.

* * *

"Yaakke!" Loki called to his friend from the path. "Join me in the bathing pool." A good soak in the hot springs ought to loosen some of the tight muscles in Loki's shoulders and ease the remnants of his migraine.

"Never try to read someone who can backlash the probe," he reminded himself. Kim was a talented healer, but even he couldn't cure everything. The tight and tired muscles in his neck and shoulders only aggravated the psychic pain of the backlash.

Maneuvering the fishing boat was hard work. Satisfying work. He deserved a soak in the pool.

The only work he'd rather do was outsmarting customs patrols with a high-profit black market cargo in the hold of *Sirius.*

"Thank you, Stargod Loki. My wife appreciates me more when I wash the stink of fish off my skin before I come home to her," Yaakke announced as he caught up with Loki and Kim on the path to the village. The man might be Kim's brother-in-law, but he still deferred to them as if they truly were gods and not just men.

"Enjoy your bath. I'm going to check on Pryth." Kim hastened ahead of them to the plateau and the village.

Loki and Yaakke proceeded more slowly, bypassing the village for a second uphill path that skirted a cliff, wound around a few ravines, and leveled out near the family clearing. Loki hummed a few phrases of his mother's favorite lullaby, but to a lively march tempo and touched the force field surrounding the clearing. The programming responded to the harmonic vibrations of the tune and his DNA to open a portal.

"I do not see how you do that. How you know when the barrier is up and when it is down?" Yaakke shook his head.

"Magic," Loki replied with a huge grin. He loved

having control over the secret to the force field. He loved the amazement he created in the locals.

A screech that made the hairs on his arms rise sent Loki running toward the bathing pool. He grabbed an ax from the woodpile as he passed.

Another bone-chilling feminine cry. Shudders ran up and down his spine. He hurried his pace down the path, careening into trees and undergrowth as he rounded each bend.

He had nightmare visions of Hestiia going into premature labor and Kim being in the village, nearly an hour away.

"Yaakke, check on Taneeo. Make sure he's still in a trance." Another nightmare. The village priest's body had been taken over by a rogue dragon last autumn. Now he lay comatose, capable of moving if led, capable of eating if fed, otherwise Taneeo's young body seemed empty of mind and soul.

Loki and his brothers knew that the spirit of Hanassa had possessed Taneeo, had ruled his body for months until the battle for the crystal array. A sonic blast from *Rover* had felled the enemy and disrupted Hanassa's control over Taneeo's body.

Disrupted but had not ousted.

If the alien spirit of Hanassa should rise again in him, there was no telling how much murder and mayhem would follow.

"Stop it this instant, you silly child!" another feminine voice commanded, followed by a resounding slap.

Loki came to a heel-skidding halt one layer of shrubbery away from the bathing pool. The second voice, calm and musical, belonged to Hestiia, Kim's wife and Yaakke's sister. The strident screecher could only be Cyndi, Lucinda Baines.

"The bane of my existence," Loki moaned.

"What's wrong now?" he called out. He needed to stay back from the natural hot spring while the women made use of it. Hestiia was not terribly body conscious, but Cyndi certainly was. No sense borrowing trouble.

"What's wrong?" Cyndi stormed through the brush. A damp tunic in her favorite deep teal clung to her body, outlining her lush figure.

A year ago, Loki would have nearly fainted with desire at the sight of her body. Since coming to this planet he had no interest in this spoiled socialite.

"I'll tell you what's wrong. A fish tried to eat me in that cursed water." She shuddered. "How can you expect me to get truly clean without a sonic shower? My hair is a mess. My skin feels like cerama/metal. I have no makeup or proper shampoo. Not even a decent hydroponic diet. I'm certain my body is withering into premature old age open to every disease imaginable without the proper nutrients."

Loki had to turn his back on the woman before she saw him chuckling. Actually, her skin glowed and her hair gleamed from the natural cleaners of water and a soapy root. The lack of makeup allowed her natural beauty to shine through the mask of sophistication. She'd put on a little weight, replacing sharp planes and angles in her figure with natural curves. But she would never see that. She would never accept life in the bush, despite the evidence of how she thrived.

"How dare you turn away from me, Mathew Kameron O'Hara?" Cyndi grabbed his arm and spun him around.

Loki cringed at her use of his full name. No one called him that—not even Mum.

She trembled with anger. Or was it more? Cyndi was arrogant and spoiled, but she usually had more control over her emotions. She could strip a soul to the bone with a sarcastic tongue. But anger? Fear? Not the Cyndi he had once loved.

"Eric Findlatter will have you mind-wiped for such an insult to his wife!" Cyndi continued. Instantly she clapped her hand over her mouth as if to take back the words.

"Eric Findlatter?" Cold washed through Loki at the name. "Nephew to the emperor? Mostly likely among the heirs to be elected next emperor by the GTE Parliament? That Eric Findlatter? And you married him without telling me?"

Anger flooded him after the cold dread. Boiling hot anger that turned his vision red and made his hands itch to hit someone.

Cyndi straightened and assumed a regal post. "Of course. I wouldn't settle for anyone less."

"Meaning me."

"Especially you, you filthy outlaw."

"I am tired of baby-sitting this woman. Her hysterics accomplish nothing," Hestiia snarled. She waddled up the slight slope from the pool. She'd draped a long sarong around her body, covering the bulk of her pregnancy and her engorged breasts. She pressed her left hand against the small of her back as she moved. She moved very slowly.

Loki did not think she could get much bigger. No wonder Kim was anxious for her.

"Hysterics?" Cyndi screamed. She didn't seem to have any other volume to her speech lately. "Hysterical is what I should be after Taneeo tried to invade my mind and fill me with darkness. I'll show you hysterical." She launched herself at Hestiia, fingers extended like dragon talons.

"No," Loki said firmly as he grabbed Cyndi about

the waist. "Have you lost your mind, Cyndi? Attacking a pregnant woman is frowned upon in domed cities. Here, it will get you burned at the stake. New life is precious. Nothing and no one endangers it! Not even the wife of an Imperial heir."

He took a deep calming breath. "Now what is this about Taneeo?"

"Unhand me," Cyndi ordered. She continued to squirm and kick. Her fingers remained extended, ready to scratch whatever she could reach.

"Stop it!" Loki turned her to face him with a hard twist.

"You can't do this to me!"

Loki slapped her.

Instantly Lucinda Baines sobered. She grew rigid. Her eyes turned icy.

Loki knew a moment of fear. Then she shoved herself away from him.

"I'll kill you for that, Matthew Kameron O'Hara. I've had enough of you. I never want to see you again."

"Good. Because I don't want to have to see you again either. You are banned from the hot spring and this clearing. If I could, I'd exile you from the village, I would, but that's not up to me." He marched back to the circle of lean-tos and cabins in the clearing.

"Yaakke, take her back to the village. Now."

"Gladly. Maybe I can talk some sense into the primitives. You won't be a god to them when I get done. You'll be their next sacrifice." Cyndi's voice turned deadly cold.

"The happiest day of my life will be the day I leave you behind on this planet while I enjoy the freedom of space." Loki took a deep breath for calm.

A moment of panic crossed Cyndi's face. She

looked almost vulnerable. For half a femto Loki considered softening his edict. What had she said about Taneeo?

Then he remembered how she had betrayed him—marrying another without so much as a good-bye to him first. And not just any other man, an Imperial heir. A man who could push through Parliament a Bill of Attainder, the hated edict that could condemn an individual to incarceration and mind-wipe without trial or other due process of law.

"You can't leave me behind," she whispered. "You have to take me with you, Loki. I'll die if you leave me here. I'll shrivel up into an old woman and die. Alone. Filthy and starving. Do you want that on your conscience, Loki O'Hara?"

"We all die sooner or later." He shrugged and leaned casually against a tree. At least he hoped his stance was casual. His nerves felt as tightly strung as one of Hestiia's bowstrings.

He suddenly wished he had Hestiia's bow and her expertise with it to use on the coming raid against Base Camp.

Maybe he should take Cyndi along instead and let the IMPs deal with her hysterics and pouting demands. *S'murghit,* he would do just that.

"Why did you hop aboard *Jupiter* for transport, Cyndi?" Loki asked, suddenly exhausted from the day's exertions and trying to figure her out. "You could afford faster and more comfortable ships. Did you manipulate them to come find me and my brothers? Did you want to watch them arrest me, mind-wipe me, and throw me in prison?"

"I do not have to explain my actions to you," she said haughtily. She tried to fix him with a withering gaze.

He yawned and looked away.

"May I escort you, Lady Cyndi, to the village?" Yaakke asked. He sounded meek, totally unlike his forthright, adventure-seeking normal self.

From the vacuous look in his soft brown eyes, he was in for quite an adventure.

"If she tries to escape, let her. I'm done with her," Loki called after them.

"This primitive barbarian has more manners than you, Loki." Cyndi stalked toward the portal. Loki hummed, making the lullaby into a dirge, to let her through.

"You have made a formidable enemy, brother Loki," Hestiia said quietly. "I hope the backlash of her hatred does not destroy more than herself."

"Me, too. Did she say anything about Taneeo to you?"

CHAPTER 5

(I DO NOT LIKE this place, Stargod Konner,) Irythos said into Konner's mind.

"I don't like it either, Irythros," Konner replied to the red-tipped dragon as they flew tight circles around the crash site of a large chunk of debris from *Jupiter.*

Dalleena, Konner's wife, clung tightly to him from behind. They were both wedged between two of the dragon's red spinal horns, but they were also both aware of their altitude and the very long fall should they slip off Irythros' broad back. Each hair acted like a crystal or mirror deflecting light and casual glances around the dragon.

Glass globules littered the impact crater below them. The heat from the ship's reentry had melted sand into glass. A tall column of dust rose high into the atmosphere.

"We must land, no matter how much we dislike this place. We have to see what we can salvage. There might be an intact fuel cell or two."

"This place reminds me of the volcano crater," Dalleena whispered. "The place where the IMPs tried to capture you." Her eyes grew wide with wonder. She never showed fear, even if she felt it.

That was only one of the reasons Konner loved this woman from a primitive planet. She embraced new experiences.

Many of her people cowered in fear at the least hint of change. The IMPs and a lot of politicians in the Galactic Terran Empire had the same attitude; anything different had to be bad.

"At least you did not have to listen to the crystal array scream in agony as the ship exploded. The crystals are safe." She hugged him. After only nine months together her vocabulary nearly matched his own, even if she did maintain the slow drawl of the locals.

"The crystals seem quite happy maintaining a confusion field around our clearing," Konner replied absently. He didn't want to remember how the king stone had screamed in his mind when he removed it from *Jupiter.* All of the crystals had protested disruption of their harmonic unity until he built a new home for them beneath the clearing and gave them the task of protecting his family.

He'd had to disable the crystal star drive aboard *Jupiter.* If any of the IMPs left this planet, ever, they would be obligated by law to reveal the location of a pristine planet ripe for colonization and exploitation. The incredible beauty of the place, the culture of the natives, everything they valued would be destroyed under the onslaught of droves of new people, mechanization, pollution. And for what? To feed a bloated empire that valued industry and money more than people.

He focused on the tailpiece of *Jupiter* where it stuck above the impact crater.

"I wish we'd seen this piece soon enough to flame it into smaller pieces," Konner muttered. He did not like the amount of dust reaching toward the jet stream. It could cause all kinds of climatic damage in the next year.

(If we land, we must leave as the sun touches the horizon,) Irythros said ominously.

Konner checked the level of the sun. It lacked only a few degrees to the deadline imposed by the dragon.

"Perhaps we should return another day, when we have more time," Dalleena suggested. She bit her lip as she watched the sand. "Salvage will not get up and walk away on its own."

The lengthening shadows moved as if a wind scattered them.

The only wind Konner could find was from Irythros' passage through the air as he circled.

An eerie sensation crawled up his back, like a chill or a dozen tiny snakes slithering over his skin.

"We can come back when the crater has cooled," Konner said. He didn't want to know what awaited him down there tonight.

The eerie feeling intensified. He suddenly knew he was needed elsewhere. Where?

(Home,) Irythros said.

"Not home. Somewhere else. Somewhere close." The crawling along Konner's spine made him want to twitch and scratch. He forced himself to still his body and breathe deeply.

Something to the north and west tugged at his senses.

Dalleena's right arm shot up, level with her shoulder, palm out. She rotated her body slowly, tracking something lost and in trouble. "There." She pointed northwest.

A scream rent the air. Konner felt the distress behind it like a knife along his spine. The crawling sensations ceased, replaced with a sharper, scarier feeling. He was surprised he didn't start bleeding.

Irythros thrust his massive translucent wings downward, once, twice, a third time. They rose a hundred meters in the air and shot forward.

Konner clung more tightly to the red spinal horn in front of him, and clamped his knees against the dragon. Dalleena wrapped her left arm around his waist, her right hand remained extended over his shoulder. Her tracking talent was fully engaged.

"Who?" Konner asked.

Neither Dalleena nor Irythros answered.

"Anyone we know?"

Dalleena nodded her head against his back.

"Kat," he said flatly. He'd seen an Imperial Military Police lander gliding out of control amongst the debris. Only his sister Kat Talbot or his brother Loki had the skill and spirit to risk maneuvering among the flaming chunks so closely.

Who else would be out in this dangerous desert so close to sunset?

"Kat?" Dalleena sounded as if she tasted the name on the wind. "Kat is there, but she is not the one who screamed."

"I'd hate to be on the receiving end of her temper if I was foolish enough to attack her. She may have been adopted and raised by Governor Talbot when she was seven, but she has all the stubbornness and ferocity of an O'Hara," Konner said. He dug his knees into the dragon's side, urging him to more speed.

Irythros snaked his long neck back to glare at him. Dragons flew at the speed they determined, not at any urging from a mere human.

Konner sighed and hunkered down, making his position on the dragon's back more aerodynamic. Dalleena bent with him.

Very shortly, another crash site came into view. An Imperial lander lay canted to one side, supported on the broken strut of one wheel. The stubby wings on the cigar-shaped vessel looked partially retracted. One dipped into the rocky ground, the other stuck up at a twisted angle.

A few more wing flaps from Irythros and Konner saw a figure balanced precariously upon the thrusting wing. The setting sun caught the red of her hair and turned it into a corona of flame.

"Kat," he said again.

His sister held a stun pistol out in front of her and blasted away at something moving around the lander. Long tendrils snaked up out of a dark mass and struck out at the gun. Kat blasted it.

It screamed in pain, almost in a human voice.

Konner heard the electronic pulse of the gun and watched the tip of the tentacle, or snake head, explode in a spray of red gore against the black mass.

Deep inside the moving shadow, red eye-shine blinked and twisted, constantly moving. Constantly watching for an opening in Kat's defenses.

Another downward thrust of Irythros' powerful wings and Konner knew that a thousand snakes besieged his estranged sister. One of them crept up behind her.

"Flame, now, Irythros," he called.

The dragon obliged, shooting a long tendril of fire into the midst of the snake pile beneath the wing with pinpoint accuracy.

"Good shot, Irythros. I couldn't have done better myself!" Kat called as she loosed another blast. That stream of energy seared the coil of snakes moving behind her.

"Need some help, Kat?" Konner asked belatedly.

"Is that you, Konner?" She shot another beast trying to climb over the wing of her downed lander.

"Who else would be riding Irythros in the middle of nowhere?"

"Dalleena might. Or I will." Kat hopped atop the nose of the aircraft, shooting snake after snake. Some of the monsters withered and died on the spot. Others—the biggest ones—merely jerked out of the way and continued their siege.

Her gun dribbled less and less energy with each shot.

Irythros blasted the center of the mass.

The odor of burning meat and fried venom rose up, nearly choking Konner.

Kat doubled over, coughing.

A particularly large black snake with a head the size of Konner's two fists combined sneaked up behind her.

"Behind you, Kat," Konner called, wishing he had a weapon of his own.

Dalleena peered over his shoulder. "That's the matriarch, Irythros. Kill her and the entire coil dies," she called.

The dragon obliged with another stream of flame at the wedge-shaped head and darting tongue. The fire swept past Kat's feet, nearly igniting her flight suit. Kat jumped onto the other wing, away from the shooting fire just as it scorched her ankles.

"Shite!" she yelled.

The mother snake reared back and away. She hissed and bared her fangs. But she dropped back into the coil.

Another viper wrapped itself around Kat's good ankle. It lifted its head and prepared to plunge fangs into her calf.

"Keep flaming the mother snake," Konner called. He crawled up the dragon's back to balance on his head. Before he could reconsider he jumped atop the nose of the lander and stomped on the tail of the attacking snake. He held his breath as he stretched across the aircraft and grabbed for the head just behind the eyes. He wrenched the beast away from his sister.

The snake twisted and fought. It spat venom. It hissed. Its red eyes blinked and looked at him with malevolent intelligence.

Kat reached into the open cockpit. She came up with a tube of wound sealant. She sprayed it into the snake's face.

In a single heartbeat, the beast went limp. Its eyes closed. The fangs withdrew.

Konner threw it as far out into the now dark desert as he could.

The mother snake detached from the coil and slithered after her wounded knight.

In seconds it was over. Kat sagged with relief. Konner draped an arm around her shoulder, as much for his own need to know they both had survived as to offer her comfort.

"Is it safe for you to land, Irythros?" Konner called.

Without answering, the dragon circled once and touched down lightly a short distance from the IMP craft.

(There is room for one more upon my back, if you wish a ride, Kat O'Hara,)" the dragon suggested.

"I am not an O'Hara!" Kat spat.

Konner remained silent for a moment at the false insult.

"We lost you when you were seven, Kat. But we are still family. Will you accept our hospitality for a short time?"

"Will you return me to Base Camp?"

Irythros blinked. His multicolored swirling eyes glowed a shielded white when he opened them again. *(If that is what you desire in your heart of hearts.)*

"What is that supposed to mean?" Kat asked. She tested her weight upon her burned ankle. It nearly crumpled beneath her.

Konner put his arm about her waist and held her up. "Never expect a direct answer from a dragon. But think about what he says deep in the night when you have only yourself to answer to. You'll find truth there." Konner remembered some of his other encounters with dragons. They exhibited wisdom with each carefully chosen telepathic word and each action. They'd saved his butt more than once.

"I don't expect to find truth with you or your brothers. You are outlaws, smugglers, saboteurs," Kat spat. She tried to pull away from his supporting arm.

He held her tighter, knowing she'd crumple if he didn't.

"That may be. But we are still your brothers. Let me help you, Kat. I promise we'll let you go back to Base Camp."

"Why would I believe you?"

"Because I have a dragon and my lady to answer to if I break this promise."

"I'll believe the dragon when I walk into Base Camp. But not you, Martin Konner O'Hara. I'll never trust an O'Hara again."

"Then you will have to learn to trust yourself as well as your brothers. For you are an O'Hara by birth. We never deliberately abandoned you when Governor Mitchell firebombed our home, Kat. You have my solemn oath for that."

Kat snorted.

Konner continued to beg her with his eyes to reconsider. Maybe she could learn to believe and trust him if she ever spent any time with her brothers, rather than cerama bonding herself to Base Camp. In the nine months since the IMPs had landed she'd spent perhaps ten hours in the company of her family.

Prior to that the O'Haras had not seen their prodigal sister in twenty years. Nor had they known for certain that she lived.

But she, apparently, had made it her mission in life to find out all she could about her missing family. She'd tracked them to the weird jump point that led to this planet with the intention of arresting them. The Imperial judicial cruiser *Jupiter* had a judge and attorneys aboard, all the facilities for bringing captured outlaws to trial. They even had mind-wipe equipment for carrying out sentences.

He drew a deep breath. "Got any fuel cells aboard the lander?"

"All of them are nearly spent," she returned. Her saucy air told him that she was pleased to deny him even one fuel cell.

But she allowed him to lift her free of the plane and she leaned heavily upon him as they climbed aboard the dragon.

CHAPTER 6

MARTIN FORTESQUE PACED the VIP salon at the Aurora Spaceport. A hologram of the landing facility in the wall mimicked a window. It remained empty of any craft, large or small. The shuttle from the orbiting space station was late. Three hours ago his best friend Bruce Geralds had called to say that he, Jane Quenton, and Kurt Giovanni had arrived. They'd be down as soon as they cleared customs. The trip should only take an hour. What was keeping his friends?

They'd been planning this reunion for nine months, ever since Martin's fourteenth birthday. All their parents had agreed to allow the four to meet on Aurora rather than go to summer camp.

Melinda Fortesque, Martin's mother and owner of Aurora, had denied Martin the right to attend the camp where the four teenagers had met every year for eight years. Melinda didn't want her son to leave Aurora at all.

At last, a small transport came into view. It circled twice before finding an approach vector and landing. It rolled to a stop beside an awning protecting a private entrance. Not his friends.

Then a woman stepped out from the awning to greet the three men and two women who disembarked from the shuttle.

Martin would never mistake the woman's blond hair, trim figure, and stylish suit that cost a year's salary for most of the workers on Aurora.

Melinda Fortesque.

His mother, sole stock holder, president, and CEO of Fortesque Enterprises, the corporation that owned and operated Planet Aurora.

"Melinda, you had better not have interfered with a visit from my friends," Martin growled. "If you've ruined our plans, I'll find a way to ruin yours." Never before in his fourteen and three quarter years had he been as angry with his mother as he was now. Nor as frightened of her.

He pulled out his handheld and called up the latest bit of information he'd dug out of Earth Archives. It was still there. Melinda had not managed to steal it from him. Yet.

If he showed this to a judge on any planet belonging to the Galactic Terran Empire, combined with other bits and pieces he and his friends had gathered, Melinda would end up in prison, mind-wiped, and rehabilitated over a long period.

But at the first indication of trouble with GTE law, Melinda would transfer membership of Aurora from the empire to the Galactic Free Market—or the black market as some referred to the loose alliance of planets. She'd done it before for economic advantage. She'd do it again for legal safety. In the GFM, she did not have to obey any law but her own.

But markets were fewer and trade profits were lower within the GFM.

Money always dictated Melinda's moves.

If Melinda would not allow Martin off planet to attend the most exclusive summer camp in known space, then she would not even consider allowing him to go where he could present damning evidence to the authorities.

He needed his friends' help for that.

Until they landed safely, and then departed safely, he had to hope his mother had no idea he knew so much about her.

At long last a shuttle appeared in the distance.

Martin breathed a sigh of relief as it taxied into position outside his waiting area.

"Marty! You've grown." First off the shuttle, Jane Q—as opposed to Jane Zelany, her roommate at summer camp—rushed to hug him.

"So have you, squirt. But I'm still taller than you." Martin returned her hug while extending his hand to Bruce and Kurt.

"Not taller by much, flagpole." Jane put him at arm's length to survey him more closely. "Something's different." She frowned.

"Two years' difference," Martin hedged. "You gave up braids for curls."

"Like it?" Jane pirouetted showing off her cap of loose brown hair that bobbed with every move. She highlighted the rather plain color with subtle red-and-blue streaks.

"Yeah. I like the dress, too." Martin admired her legs, which he'd never noticed before, even when she wore shorts. At summer camp they were all just buddies; gender never played into their schemes and daydreams.

"There is something else different about you, pal." Kurt Giovanni peered over the top of his spectacles—purely an affectation. Implants at the age of two had cured his myopia. Always the tallest and skinniest, he topped Martin by only a few centimeters now.

Martin exchanged a glance with squarely built

Bruce. He disguised his true weight and form with flowering particolored shirts and baggy pantaloons.

"Not here, *mes amies.* We'll talk later in a more secure location." Bruce took charge of them and herded them away from the mass of people exiting the shuttle.

Martin had divulged a few bits of information about his plans to Bruce under strict oath of secrecy. Even among Kurt and Jane.

Luggage trolleys began appearing on the far side of the waiting area. One man came out of the hidden recess with the trunks and suitcases. He stood squarely in front of a massive pile. Tall with light brown hair and medium coloring, he could pass for any bushie who'd had the rough edges honed off and pasted on a veneer of civilization. His stance and alert awareness defined him as a bodyguard. Bushies had more muscle mass than civils and therefore tended to drift into security work. Martin had put up with his fair share of private security personnel over the years. His own lurked in a dark corner to the right. He easily spotted them in any crowd.

Kurt made his way over to the bodyguard and the assorted luggage. "Sorry guys, my dad insisted he come with me." Kurt shrugged and began sorting his soft sided fold-up and duffel from the three trunks.

"Why?" Martin asked. He surveyed the area as warily as the bodyguard.

"Dad's up for reelection this year." As Prime Minister of Neuvo Italia, Giovanni Padre commanded almost as much power as Melinda, but not nearly the wealth. "He's made some enemies. His political advisers suggested that taking me out was a good way to force him to drop out of the election." Kurt shouldered his own bags.

"Have there been attempts on your life?" Martin asked. This could put a big crimp in their plans.

Kurt shrugged again.

"Only one," Jane said. She handed Martin two large suitcases and flagged down a skycap for an antigrav trolley to manage her trunks. She certainly had changed since her days of showing up for three Standard Months at camp with only a backpack.

"What happened?" Martin added the suitcases to the trolley. He wanted his hands free if things got messy. He didn't trust his bodyguard—Melinda had selected him and signed his paychecks, not Martin.

"Bomb in the limo that takes me to school. Good thing I decided to take my ped-cycle that day." Kurt half grinned. His eyes told a different story; one of fear. His casual traveling suit looked two sizes too big rather than his usual saggy off-the-rack outfits, like he hadn't been eating much.

"The good news is that the bodyguard is also a rated pilot. We don't have to hire another one," Kurt whispered as he tried to put on a bright face.

"What's your rating?" Martin asked the guard. This was all just too coincidental.

"Ace solo on everything up to fifty million tons. And call me Quinn." The bodyguard remained alert, only briefly making eye contact with Martin.

"License?" Martin wasn't taking the man's word. He already had his handheld ready to search six databases for the man's identity and credentials.

Quinn fished in his inside jacket pocket, still keeping his eyes on the moving crowd. He handed a smart, synthleather wallet to Martin.

Martin flipped it open to find the man's ID and license up front. "He's a Sam Eyeam," he told his friends. Part private investigator, part bodyguard, part freelance agent and courier, the coveted SE license exams were tough to pass, tougher to find an administrator for the test. Only the best became SE (officially Security Executive but the nickname from an old children's book was more popular). The best of the best commanded huge salaries and bonuses for "delicate" work for the politicians and corporate executives that ran the Galactic Terran Empire. Some SEs were known to move outside the law as often as in.

Bruce nodded with an "I-told-you-so" grin.

Jane rolled up her eyes and snatched the wallet away from Martin.

Martin's handheld beeped. Three pages of credentials, references, and résumé scrolled past him. Full name: Adam Jonathan Quinnsellia.

"Why'd you quit being the emperor's private pilot, Quinn?" Martin asked suspiciously.

"His Majesty got his own licenses and didn't need me anymore. I decided I could make more money freelancing than flying for the major liners."

Martin refrained from commenting on that. The story was just a little too pat.

"May I suggest we get out of here," Quinn stated. "We are too noticeable in this crowd." He shouldered the last bag and gestured them through the hidden door into the bowels of the spaceport. "Inform your driver to meet us at entrance D12," he said quietly to Martin as they trundled past baggage handlers and runway guides. Servobots scanned and read luggage tags, routing them to various waiting areas.

"Some Earth diplomats came through the space station just after we did," Kurt said. "They had to clear customs and get their private transport well away before they'd let us out of customs. That's why we were late."

"Any idea who they are?" Bruce asked Martin.

"I watched my mother meet them. Figured they had to be important for her to come all the way out here. Usually dippos and distributors have to go to her."

"I have heard rumors that the daughter of a planetary governor and a judicial cruiser are missing," Quinn added. "The daughter is a diplomatic attaché and she hitched a ride on the cruiser for a fast trip home. Rumor also places her in frequent romantic company with the emperor's nephew."

Martin raised his eyebrows. Maybe this guy's presence wasn't such a coincidence after all. "Don't see why they need to talk to Melinda about missing personnel," Martin shrugged. Maybe they had something to do with Bruce's father, another Sam Eyeam. Also missing.

Quinn ushered the four teenagers into the armored flitter that would take them to Martin's home for their reunion. The bodyguard took one look at Martin's regular pilot and guard. After a whispered discussion and exchange of credentials, Quinn dismissed them. Then he took the controls of the craft. Once they were in the air, he fiddled with the communications ports. A band of static emerged from the speaker.

"Now that we have some privacy, you kids care to tell me what this is all about?"

Martin looked at Bruce. Bruce looked at Jane. Jane looked at Kurt. Kurt looked at Martin.

Since no one else seemed interested in spilling the truth, Martin decided he had to be the one.

"We are mounting a search for my father. A search my mother will go to some lengths to stop."

"Fair enough. Now tell me how you expect to do this. I am at your disposal. My loyalty is to Kurt. His father paid me very well to keep him off planet and safe until after the election. This sounds as good a project as any to do that."

"I'll pay you, too, to keep your mouth shut and keep my mother from following us," Martin added.

Life was suddenly looking brighter than the overcast day portended.

(Be careful what you wish for,) a voice said into the back of his mind. A voice that might have been his conscience but did not sound like it.

CHAPTER 7

KIM O'HARA SAT in the cockpit of *Rover,* the family shuttle. He watched through the magnified viewscreen as Yaakke waited patiently on Cyndi. He fetched a hot drink for her, refilled her trencher with fish stew, and spoke attentively to her throughout the long evening.

The rest of the villagers went about their routines, finally settling in to a session of quiet storytelling. Without Pryth, their midwife, bard, and matriarch, to lead them in spirited song and dance, their mood was subdued and cautious.

Cyndi listened politely, then moved off to the women's quarters, a cave set into the soaring cliff.

Yaakke's gaze followed her with longing. Then he returned to the evening's activities. But his eyes kept straying back to the entrance of Cyndi's cave.

Kim shook off his speculation on what had happened between Hestiia's brother and the village hostage.

He had a chore tonight. A chore which neither of his brothers would approve.

Loki was nowhere in sight. Konner and Dalleena had not yet returned. He had time and privacy to break every rule his family adhered to.

For Hestiia, his wife, and Pryth, the midwife, he had to do the unthinkable.

He fingered the comm unit.

Before he could talk himself out of his plan, he keyed in a common IMP frequency. "*Rover* to Base Camp, come in please. Over." His signal seemed to take forever before the diagrams showed it had bounced off his mother ship *Sirius* and returned to ground.

A lot of dead air was his only response. He changed frequencies three more times before he found a static-interrupted voice at the other end. "This is Base Camp. Identify yourself. Over."

Kim couldn't tell if he had contacted a male or female, someone in authority or just someone playing around with the comm units.

"This is Mark Kimmer O'Hara." He gulped, then proceeded with precious information. "Citizenship number Alpha George Cat Zero niner eight two seven Omega Prime niner eight two seven." If any of the IMPs got off the planet, they could cancel his citizenship knowing that number. Without the number they had no power over him. "I want to strike a deal."

Did they have any databases left to show that his number was legal?

"O'Hara? This is Captain Amanda Leonard. What kind of deal? Will you take us off planet? Will you reconnect your king stone and allow us to communicate with home?"

"Baby steps, Commander Leonard." He wouldn't give the woman the honor of calling her captain. She had no ship left to captain. Only her rank and name identified her now. And she would not have her rank long when her corps of followers had to hunker down and start working for survival.

Kim had never truly approved of stranding the IMPs in Coronnan. That amounted to imprisonment under conditions worse than what the IMPs would do to the three brothers if they were captured and returned to the GTE. But he recognized the necessity of keeping the GTE out of Coronnan. The exploitive policies would pollute and ruin the ecology. The GTE would totally destroy the unique and beautiful culture of the people. Hestiia's people.

His people.

If any of the IMPs ever returned to the GTE, they must by law reveal the location of this planet.

"What do you mean by baby steps?" Leonard nearly screamed.

Kim instinctively reared away from the shuttle's speaker. "I mean, Commander Leonard, we start learning to live together with small concessions to each other."

"Who said we agreed to live together?" The former captain sounded nearly hysterical.

"Mr. O'Hara," a deep voice injected into the conversation. "This is Lieutenant Commander Jetang M'Berra, First Officer of the Imperial Military Police Judicial Cruiser *Jupiter.* What do you propose?"

Kim wished he could see what was going on at Base Camp—the village he had helped build last year. He'd left communications on voice only. He could not take a chance that Leonard or M'Berra would recognize the landscape around *Rover* in the background of the messages. If they found the shuttle, then Kat could break into it and fly it up to *Sirius.* Giving any one of the IMPs access to the mother ship would destroy everything he and his brothers had fought for. Giving Kat access to anything in their lives meant instant danger to their persons as well as their liberty.

"Lieutenant Commander M'Berra, I have a hostage that you want very badly. You have a medic with drugs and knowledge that I need. Can we talk a trade?"

"I will settle for nothing less than your complete surrender, O'Hara," Leonard screeched in the background.

"Consider this, M'Berra." Kim gave up trying to reason with Amanda Leonard. The stress of losing her ship and surviving a winter on a primitive planet had obviously unhinged her mind. "In the optimistic view that you might get off this planet and back to civilization, think of the report Diplomatic Attaché Lucinda Baines will be giving her father, a planetary governor." Kim almost chuckled at the look that must be crossing the big African's face.

"We will get off this planet, O'Hara. And when we do, you will be grateful to come with us." Menace dripped from M'Berra's tone.

"Now why would we do that, M'Berra?" Kim asked, not at all intimidated. "We know how to survive on this planet. We know how to plant grain, fish the seas, and hunt for food. We know how to build shelters that keep out the cold wind and rain. You should know that. You lived in my house all winter. Now it's past time to start planting grains and vegetables, to repair winter damage to houses. Have you done that?"

"If you are so successful, why do you need a medic and medicines?" M'Berra asked coldly.

Kim almost choked out the painful confession that Hestiia was eight months pregnant and not doing well, that their midwife had taken sick, and that Lucinda Baines was a pain in the ass. He wasn't about to reveal his vulnerability.

"Winter brings aches and pains and chills and fevers to my people. I have over fifty locals to tend. They depend upon me and my brothers. We are their Stargods," he said instead.

"Barbarians!" Amanda Leonard called. Her voice sounded muffled, as if M'Berra had removed her from proximity of the comm unit.

"Think about your options, M'Berra, and get back to me on this frequency at midnight." Kim discommed and sat back in his chair in the cockpit of the shuttle. For so many years *Rover* and *Sirius* had been his home. Now he could not imagine living with recycled air, tanked food, and cramped quarters. He could not imagine living without Hestiia.

He'd go on Loki's raid if he had to. But he'd rather do this peacefully. He did not want this world to dissolve into civil war between the "civilized" few who needed to go home and the bushie many who embraced life on this planet.

That had happened once before, three hundred years ago among the first human colonists. Scientists had unleashed a bioengineered plague as a way to settle the dispute and reduced the population to the barbaric stone age. The plague went dormant for a few decades at a time and then bloomed with new intensity.

Kim and his brothers had found a cure. The locals had honored them as Stargods because of that. They had no guarantees they could help should something more disastrous erupt from a new war. Kim would not risk his wife and child, nor the villagers who depended upon him as their Stargod.

* * *

Kat limped painfully as she climbed off the dragon. She *would* walk the two hundred meters to Base Camp. In the dark. Alone.

"Sorry I can't help you, Kat," Konner said. At least he had the decency to sound regretful. "I risk capture by your friends."

"You cannot risk capture, but I can," Dalleena said. "I'm just a dumb bushie who came to her aid. Wait for me. I *will* be back in an hour." She slid off the dragon and landed easily.

She paused at the dragon's head and stroked his muzzle. "Will you wait for me, Irythros?"

(As long as we safely can.)

"Will you keep my man safe?"

(As safe as he will allow.)

Kat heard a definite chuckle behind the monster's telepathic voice.

Within a few seconds Dalleena had an arm around Kat's waist and a shoulder under her arm. She was nearly as tall as Kat, only a decimeter or two shorter than Konner. The position must have been uncomfortable for her.

"Dalleena, you don't have to . . ."

"Yes, I do. You are family."

"I don't claim . . ."

"You are family." That stated, she began walking, dragging Kat along with her.

Kat had to admit walking was easier with her sister-in-law as a crutch. Much easier. Almost too easy.

"Can you see in the dark, Dalleena?" Kat asked when they had traversed only a few meters.

"No. But my tracking talent guides me along the easiest course."

"More magic," Kat replied with a modicum of disgust. She'd had a few strange experiences on this lonely planet. Not enough to convince her of her brother's claims of psychic powers beyond imagining.

The fact that she had fought off giant serpents and ridden on the back of a mammalian dragon that appeared nearly invisible, except for his red spinal horns and wingveins and -tips, was not enough to convince her that on this planet magic worked.

(You will learn soon enough the extent of your own power,) Irythros spoke into the back of Kat's mind. There were other voices accompanying his bright tenor, deeper voices, more melodic voices, an entire choir of voices.

Kat stumbled under the onslaught of alien thoughts inside her head.

Dalleena kept walking, as if she had not heard the dragon's prophecy.

They covered nearly the first hundred meters to Base Camp slowly but relatively smoothly. Just as the torchlight—electric illumes had worn out moons ago—around the cluster of cabins became visible in the gloom, Dalleena stopped short. Kat stepped awkwardly upon her burned ankle. Fiery pain shot up her calf into her thigh. The leg wanted to crumple.

She dropped her grip on Dalleena and sank to the ground, grateful to get her weight off that leg.

Dalleena still did not move.

"What is it?" Kat whispered. As much as she needed to sit, she wanted more to be back at camp with Medic Lotski spraying cooling sealant on her wound. She'd used up the scant supply in her med kit deflecting the snakes.

"Th . . . there." Dalleena pointed hesitantly toward a darker lump against the dark meadow, then turned her palm up in that direction.

Kat peered into the darkness, barely able to discern the shape let alone the substance against the backlighting from the torches. "It looks like a rock to me."

Then the lump moved.

Both women yipped and skipped, or scooted, back a pace.

The lump lifted one end, extending a tail. Then it rocked forward and stretched, revealing a head.

"It's just a cat," Dalleena sighed. She sounded a bit chagrined by her earlier fear.

"Biggest cat I've ever seen," Kat said on a long exhalation. "Almost as big as a Denobian muscle-cat, and they are reputed to be huge, closer to a lion than a cat."

The cat wandered closer, stropped Dalleena's ankles, then butted its head against Kat's hand and purred.

She obliged it with scritch behind the ears. "Do you have a name, kitty?" she asked. The purr soothed her frazzled nerves. Knotted muscles relaxed. She wanted to gather the animal into her lap but didn't quite dare. Would the beast even fit? It must weigh eleven kilos at least.

(Gentian.) The beast spoke into her mind just as the dragon did.

Kat yipped and scooted again.

The cat followed her, insisting upon more scritches and pets. It even tried to climb into her lap, sprawling awkwardly across her legs.

"We cannot stay here, Kat. I have to get you to your people and return to Konner."

"Tell that to Gentian," she replied a little breathlessly. Something strange was happening.

"Shoo." Dalleena pushed the animal off Kat's lap and helped her to her feet again.

Gentian's eyes glowed in the dark. He looked particularly sullen as he shook and ruffled wings.

"Wings? The cat has wings?" Kat choked.

Dalleena crossed her wrists, right over left, and flapped them.

Kat didn't have time to puzzle out the origin or meaning of that particular superstition.

"Y . . . you have been honored, Lady Kat," Dalleena stammered.

"Honored? By a cat?"

"A cat with wings. A flywacket. Such creatures are rare. They bestow their affections on very few humans."

"We stumbled over it. It purred."

"He gave you his name."

"I was just getting used to dragons who speak telepathically and insist upon names," Kat moaned.

"You must introduce yourself. It is the proper protocol." She spoke the words carefully, as if still uncertain of the vocabulary. "Gentian, I am Dalleena Farseer, a Tracker, mate to Stargod Konner."

Kat sighed heavily. She waited a long moment. The winged cat just kept looking at her. Expectantly?

"Gentian, I am Mari Kathleen O'Hara Talbot. Pleased to meet you."

Gentian meowed and detached himself from Kat. He ambled forward three steps then stopped to look back over his shoulder. *(Are you coming or not?)*

"I think we are supposed to follow him," Kat said. "I just hope he takes me to Base Camp. I really need a medic right now."

"Gentian knows that. I've heard rumors that flywackets begin their lives as purple-tipped dragons. One of a set of twins, but there can only be one purple-tip in the nimbus at a time. So the redundant twin must become a flywacket. They know everything the dragons know."

"And what one dragon knows, they all know," Kat finished. "This world gets weirder every day. I really wish I could go home."

(Be careful what you wish for.)

CHAPTER 8

CYNDI WAITED IMPATIENTLY at the top of the steep path to the cove. She pretended to watch the phosphorescent waves crashing around the broken volcanic rock. Every once in a while she glanced over her shoulder toward the evening gathering around the village's central fire pit. The voices had become subdued as more and more people drifted toward their huts or caves and their beds. Someone sang a quiet ballad in a fine tenor. She thought the voice belonged to Yaakke. She hadn't paid much attention to him until today.

Now he presented her best opportunity for recruiting an ally to her cause.

The village fell into silence. Even the waves seemed quiet at slack tide.

Then she caught the whisper of a footstep behind her. She turned slowly, a gentle smile upon her face.

"You should be abed," Yaakke said. His tone was gentle but wary.

"I don't get many moments alone."

"Alone?" he asked as if the comment was alien to him. In the communal atmosphere of village life he'd probably never developed the concept of privacy.

Another reason Cyndi so desperately wanted to go home. No one here ever left her alone with her thoughts, or bathed in private. They wouldn't even allow her to launder her undergarments without ten other women marveling over elastic and silk and counter-levering.

"I cherish moments when I can watch the waves by myself," she replied simply. She sidled closer to him until they nearly touched. The hairs on her arms fluffed under the heat of his proximity.

He did not back away.

"Alone is not safe," he said. He watched the shadows for signs of predatory animals or marauding humans. But his eyes returned to her often. In the dim backlighting from the dying fire and few torches she caught glimmers of movement from the patrolling guards. They passed through and around the village silently.

Star-frags, she wasn't as alone as she thought.

"I feel safe with you organizing village defenses." She touched his arm with one finger.

He smiled at her and locked his gaze on hers. "I am second to the headman. Protecting you is my job."

Was there a slight emphasis on the word "you?"

Emboldened by his attention, Cyndi placed her palm against his chest. He'd definitely puffed it out a little.

"No one would dare attack this village with you in charge."

"Thank you, Lady Cyndi. I am proud to serve my village. The village gives us all life, purpose, security."

Give me a break! Cyndi thought. *The village is a political unit, and needs to run politically. No one serves unless they are angling for more power.*

"You should be headman," she whispered drawing tiny, sensuous circles on his chest.

"I have not the age or experience . . ."

"But you have the talent, the wisdom, the," she

paused for a deep breath, "the strength." She let her hand move in larger circles, cupping his bicep firmly.

His hand captured hers. "My time will come."

"Not soon enough. I could help you become headman."

He pushed her away. "I do not need a woman's help. I will not betray Raaskan, a good man and trusted friend. Go back to the women's quarters, Lady Cyndi. I will go back to my wife and child."

He pushed her toward the upper cliff and the series of small caves where most of the village dwelled communally. She felt the heat of his anger in his tone and his touch.

"Now how am I supposed to steal those fuel cells!" she fumed.

Simmering at her failure to seduce this . . . this *primitive,* Cyndi marched back to her uncomfortable pallet more determined than ever to find a way to escape these people and their Stargods. She would do anything to help the IMPs get off this planet with Loki and his brothers in custody—preferably bound with force bracelets at hand, ankle, and neck.

* * *

Hanassa fluttered around the village on ghostly wings. He watched in amazement as people looked directly at him and did not see him.

Strange that he had not thought to separate from Taneeo before. This afternoon he had found that he could move about the clearing and still keep a tendril of his mind connected to the man's body. Now he ventured farther, still maintaining his hold on Taneeo.

The villagers continued to ignore him, not even

stopping to shiver when he brushed past them. Anger boiled in him.

He would change their disrespect for him to terror and awe when he found another body. The right body. Someone with the potential to take control and gain power.

Then he saw her. The woman who had come with the IMPs. The woman who had become vulnerable to his touch for a moment. With her compelling beauty and ruthless ambition, she would make an admirable host.

He watched as her temper loosed her control over her will. She, too, had been rejected. She knew what Hanassa felt.

She was vulnerable!

He loosed his hold upon Taneeo and prepared to sink into the woman's body.

* * *

Martin angrily threw Kurt's suitcase on the large bed in a medium-sized guest suite of his mother's palace. Then he moved into the living room where Kurt sprawled on a long Lazy-former®. His long arms and legs dangled over the furniture as if it couldn't shift to accommodate his entire body.

As usual, Melinda had done her best to isolate Martin from his friends, from the world of Aurora, from the galaxy, and from his quest to find his father. She had housed his guests and Kurt's bodyguard in suites at the far end of the wing most distant from Martin's own rooms.

They were also in a separate wing from the Earth dippos Melinda had met at the spaceport.

Jane had the corner suite across the hall from here

and Bruce the one immediately to the east—at the end of the corridor and thus theoretically marginally more vulnerable than this one.

Quinn had made the decision on who slept where once the rooms were designated. The bodyguard now prowled about with various devices looking for hidden monitoring equipment and points of vulnerability. He had already put overrides on the locks.

"We'll be private here. House guards and monitors can't open those doors without Kurt's or my permission and the password you four agreed upon," he assured them. "And, Kurt, don't open the door to anyone without that password even if the voice sounds like one of you friends or me."

"I have to call my dad," Kurt said. He fished in his pockets for his handheld.

Martin politely turned his back, an illusion of giving his friend privacy.

He could have left. But he knew that the moment he stepped into the hallway his mother would summon him away from his friends. He didn't dare disobey.

Someone pounded loudly upon the door.

Martin looked to Quinn for permission to open it.

The bodyguard nodded, indicating that his equipment recognized the person demanding entry with a second loud round of knocks. Then Quinn moved into the bedroom, still concentrating on his equipment.

"Password?" Martin whispered into the sensor at the doorjamb.

"Crystal blue quantum six to the sixth power," came an anxious reply from Jane.

Martin opened the door.

"Have you heard the news?" she asked.

"My mom says the search for the missing dippo is really heating up," Bruce added, right on her heels.

"My mom says the same thing," Jane hastened to give her version before Bruce could trump her scoop. "Eric the worthless Findlatter just announced his betrothal to Lucinda Baines, the missing dippo. The emperor has asked the Imperial Military Police to aid in the search for her and for the missing judicial cruiser."

"Seems the last anyone saw of Ms. Baines, she hopped a ride back to Earth aboard *Jupiter.* Now they are both missing." Bruce barely let Jane finish before adding his own two credits of information. "And *Jupiter* is reported to be hunting three unnamed outlaw brothers. The news is speculating that the only outlaws on the official hunt list are named O'Hara."

Martin forgot to breathe. O'Hara. "My dad?" he asked on a whisper, hoping Quinn didn't hear. "My dad has brothers?"

"My dad just confirmed the same thing," Kurt added, closing his handheld. "*And* he says that there is some mysterious connection between the O'Haras and your mother, Marty."

"A big connection. Like me."

"Something I should know?" Quinn wandered back into the living room. His eyes looked vague as if he'd been in deep concentration, not noticing anything else that went on around him.

Martin wondered if it was an act. Could anyone be that fine an actor?

Melinda could.

He decided to hold back the trust he had been on the brink of giving the bodyguard. He needed to know more. To do that, he needed to search several databases only his personal computer could access. That computer was back in his own suite where Melinda could find and track him.

CHAPTER 9

"KONNER!" SEVEN-YEAR-OLD KATIE O'Hara screamed for her brother.

Mum had taken four-year-old Kim, the youngest, to the landing strip. Loki, at fourteen the oldest brother, prepped a shuttle for them to escape.

Twelve-year-old Konner had been assigned to watch over Katie. She'd left him here just a moment ago while she ran back into their burning house.

"Konner, where are you?" she whimpered, hugging Kim's teddy bear Murphy that she had rescued from the flames. Smoke made her eyes water more than the frightened tears she already shed.

Maybe she'd left her brother in the west courtyard. She couldn't tell where she was anymore. The smoke was too thick, the night too dark. Maybe she'd gotten turned around.

"Konner!" she yelled again. She darted from one corner of the courtyard to the other. Her breath came in panicky gulps. No way out. No sign of Konner.

The fire crackling around the windowpanes of the family home reached long tendrils upward. Katie watched it, wondering if she dared go back in to try to thread her way around to the other courtyard. Maybe Konner was in the house, searching for her. She buried her face in Murphy's fur. Her little brother wouldn't sleep without it. Especially in a strange bed as the family made their escape from the men who had set fire to the house.

An explosion erupted from the center of the house. The blast knocked Katie into the courtyard wall. She hit her head with a smacking sound. Black stars burst before her eyes.

Then there was nothing but blackness.

"Konner?" Kat awoke with a start. She lay absolutely still until she figured out where and when she was. Her eyes remained sealed shut with the aftermath of sleep and a gummy film. Her chest felt heavy. She had as much trouble drawing a deep breath as she did that terrible night nearly twenty years ago when smoke had filled her lungs and the family had abandoned her.

A deep rumble in her ear chased away the last of the dream fog. "I am not seven years old and alone. I am twenty-seven. I have a career in the Imperial Military Police. I am Kat Talbot, foster daughter of a planetary governor." She repeated the familiar litany over and over, banishing the ghosts and nightmares of her childhood.

Then she opened her eyes. A huge black cat perched upon her chest, staring unblinking into her eyes. He must weigh twelve kilos.

(You went home,) the flywacket whispered into her mind.

"That is not home. It is only a memory of a nightmare," she insisted to the cat.

Gentian's eyes crossed while looking at her. His velvet-green eyes begged her to confide the truth to him.

She had spoken the truth. She had. Benedict Talbot was her dad. His two daughters were her sisters. They were family. Their home was her home.

The cat shook his head and heaved himself off her chest and off her bed.

Or was it a bed? Kat looked around for the first time since awakening. She lay on a cot in a dimly lit cabin. Ranks of vials on a crude shelf, a medical monitor in the corner, and baskets on the floor filled with clean bandages revealed her location. "Lotski's med cabin," she muttered.

Kat's ankle began to ache. It felt hot and swollen where the dragon's flame had scorched it.

Medical Officer Chaney Lotski poked her head around the door curtain. "Oh, good, you're awake. Sorry to leave you so long. We had a lost crewman wander in. He's so starved and dehydrated he's incoherent." The lieutenant babbled on as she fussed with some of the vials on the tilted shelf.

"Who is he?" Kat asked, hoping conversation would take her mind off the burning ache that shot up her calf to her knee.

"Funny, I thought I knew everyone aboard. I didn't recognize him," Lotski replied. She selected one of the little gourds strewn among the vials and bottles.

"There were three hundred assorted crew and judicial personnel aboard the *Jupiter.* Judiciary tended to keep to themselves. Same with the Marines," Kat replied.

"But Judicials tend to have more ailments in space—mostly boredom—than anyone else. And the Marines are always getting hurt doing excercises in heavy grav. They all trooped through my office at one time or another. I should know this guy."

"How do you know he's one of ours? The locals are human, and without a uniform . . ."

"His teeth are too good for him to be a local. Ah, well, we'll sort it out as soon as he's absorbed some fluid and nutrition. Looks like he walked a long way. His boots are worn through and his feet are badly bruised and cut beneath the holes. Now let's look at this. How did you get a burn this deep on your ankle? Fall into a bonfire?"

"Something like that." Kat didn't want to explain her adventures to Lotski. No one sane would believe that she had ridden on the back of a nearly invisible dragon with crystal fur that directed the eye around it, and yet challenged the watcher to look for him among the clouds and mists.

The one other time she had ridden dragonback seemed more like a half-remembered dream than reality. Irythros had taken her to an open area and shown her the ley lines. Using them, Kat had reached out with her senses, far beyond this star system, all the way across the galaxy to her mother. For a brief moment, she had tapped into Mum's thoughts, her *obsessions,* and flinched away in disgust in less than a heartbeat.

Lotski touched Kat's burn with a tentative finger.

Kat jerked her leg away from the delicate probe.

"Hurts a bit, I see," Lotski said. "I have to clean it and apply an ointment, then I'll bandage it."

"Can't you just spray a sealant on it?" Kat propped herself up on her elbows to survey the supplies. She peered into the gloom, looking for the familiar can of universal first aid remedy.

"Sorry. Ran out of it weeks ago. Our crew have had to learn to use live fire and cook over it since we ran out of fuel for the burners and lights. They aren't familiar with how flames reach out for victims." The medic chuckled at the image of sentient fire.

Kat kept her mouth shut. On this planet the green flames just might be sentient, like the dragons and her flywacket.

Where was the beast anyway?

A quiet purr told her the cat was beneath her cot,

hiding in the shadows. He would not leave her alone with this talkative woman.

"This is an ointment some of the local women swear by for everything from burns to diaper rash—not that we need that yet—and insect bites. It goes on quite cool and should feel good on the burn."

"Whatever. Just do something so I can walk back to my bunk." Kat lay back on the cot.

"Oh, you won't be walking for a day or two. That burn is quite deep. I'll keep you here with our mystery crewman. You are my only two patients for the moment. You're lucky; I can fetch and carry for both of you."

"Great." Kat turned her head away from the medic and dangled her hand over the side of the cot. Gentian butted his head into her palm. She scratched his ears.

I want to be alone, Gentian, she thought. *Away from other humans.*

(We know. But now you can solve the mystery of the stranger and prevent him from doing any harm to you and yours.)

This mental conversation took some getting used to.

By "me and mine" do you mean what's left of the crew?

(And others.)

My outlaw brothers.

(And their families.)

* * *

A rush of air, like wind in the treetops, told Loki that the dragon Irythros returned long before he could see the beast.

"About time you showed up," Loki growled as

Konner and Dalleena walked the short distance from their landing place at the edge of the village.

"We got delayed by a coil of black vipers in the desert," Konner growled back at him.

"Vipers? Do you suppose that is what keeps the city from expanding beyond its walls?" Loki turned away from his preparations to raid Base Camp with new interest.

They'd discovered several small port cities on the big continent. All of them huddled behind protective walls, preferring crowds, housing shortages, and inadequate sewage systems to venturing beyond those walls after sunset. Yet no one in any of those cities spoke of what they feared.

"Could be the vipers that keep them confined," Konner said on a shrug. "The beasts are aggressive. Huge. Seem to be nocturnal. And they are led by a matriarch who can direct their actions." He pulled Dalleena close to his side, as if drawing comfort from her presence. For the past nine months he rarely allowed more than a meter of space to get between them.

"We'll do another recon after we finish the current project," Loki said with a big smile. "I'm looking forward to expanding the trade network and opening up those ports. We need to advance this planet to provide surplus food for us to sell on the black market back home. Trade is the best way." He sheathed a hunting knife at his hip, grabbed a sledgehammer and a spear. Then he surveyed his crew of handpicked village warriors.

Yaakke was missing. Loki shuddered at the thought that he lingered with Cyndi.

"What are you up to?" Konner asked. He and Dalleena retreated one step.

"Pryth is sick," Kim said flatly. His eyes looked bleak. "And Hestiia does not thrive with this pregnancy. We need to liberate medical supplies from Base Camp." He looked grim, hefting a spear.

Loki knew his little brother had never enjoyed brawls as Loki did. Kim was the first among them to refuse to eat meat because a carnivorous diet deprived animals of life; always the first to suggest compromise; always the last to pick up a weapon to defend himself and his loved ones.

"We might even need to bring back the medic," Loki added. He gestured for his crew to gather around the family shuttle *Rover.*

Konner and Dalleena exchanged a strange look.

"What?" Loki demanded.

"Not tonight," Konner replied quietly.

"Why not? We're ready. *Rover* has enough fuel for the trip, even though three of the cells up at the power farm seem to be duds. They have no fuel at all . . ."

"We ran into Kat in the desert. She got hurt and we returned her to Base Camp," Dalleena said hastily.

"And?" Loki stared at her, uncertain how to respond; his mind still on the problem of the fuel cells. They'd been nearly full this morning. What had happened to them?

"While I waited for Dalleena to return from delivering Kat, I prowled the perimeter of the camp," Konner added, more slowly "A lost crewman wandered in. He was in really bad shape, starving, dehydrated, raving."

"What was he raving about?" Kim dropped his spear and suddenly took an interest in something beyond Hestiia's health.

"Cannibals. Lotski couldn't get him sedated fast enough, though. The crew heard him. They are jumpy, doubled the watch. If we go in tonight, even using magic, it's suicide."

"Cannibals?" the village headman Raaskan asked. He and his fellow warriors all crossed their wrists and flapped their hands in a ward against evil. "The man has been west of the mountains. No one returns from there alive."

"I do not think this man was a member of the crew," Dalleena whispered.

A superstitious shiver ran up Loki's spine. "Who is he, then? We are the only outsiders on this planet other than the IMPs."

"The Sam Eyeam we met last autumn, across the ocean. The one with fine teeth," Dalleena explained.

"The one who had my ex-wife's distress beacon broadcasting our location to the IMPs," Konner finished.

CHAPTER 10

KAT WATCHED through slitted eyes as Medic Lotski helped one of her corpsmen carry the stranger into the medical cabin.

Lotski tried to be quiet and not disturb Kat's slumber, but the new patient thrashed and moaned and screamed in delirium.

He fought some internal demon. Each jerking movement threatened to dislodge the IV that dumped precious liquid and nutrients into his system.

Kat opened her eyes further, trying to find something familiar in the man's features. The light from the oil lamp was too dim. Just another man, tall for a civil, barely medium height for a bushie, with shaggy hair that hung too long against his shoulders. His beard appeared to be streaked with blond, or possibly gray. If he had indeed met with cannibals, the trauma could have induced a premature stripping of color from his hair.

Civilized men shaved regularly and kept their hair trimmed above their ears. Most of the crew that had found their way to Base Camp after escaping from *Jupiter* nine months ago, had managed to keep up that indicator of civilization. Her brothers and this stranger had not.

Eventually, Lotski finished fussing over her patient and withdrew to the fire in the common area at the center of the Base Camp. The night was mild and many of the crew gathered around the fire pit for a last cup of herbal tea and a bit of gossip. Kat wished she could join them. Being stuck with a raving stranger bothered her.

The fact that he was a stranger bothered her more.

"Get away, you devils!" the stranger screamed. He punched at imaginary enemies. His thrashings tangled his IV.

The machine let off a quiet beep of alarm. Medic Chaney Lotski did not respond. She'd had a long hard day after a longer and harder nine months. Setting off a plasma cannon beside her ear might not wake her.

Kat thought the alarm should have been louder. They had seemed to shriek the last time she heard one. Apparently, the solar batteries of the machine had not fully recharged.

"I'll kill you all before I let you eat me," the stranger said. He thrashed again.

Still Lotski did not appear in the doorway.

What if the man died because of the tangled IV? Kat had to do something. She couldn't allow him to die.

Gritting her teeth against the pain in her ankle, she swung her legs over the edge of the cot. One test of her weight upon her foot sent jolts of pain and weakness up her entire leg. Dizziness spun her perceptions. Too like losing control of the lander and spiraling toward the ground.

Kat did not like losing control.

"Stand back or I'll shoot!" The stranger sat bolt upright, eyes wide open, arms flailing. "Where am I? Darkness. Oh, so dark. What hell have they dropped me into? Good Lord save me. Somebody, please help me."

Kat dropped to her knees and crawled over to the second cot. "Wake up, Mister," Kat ordered in her best military voice. "That's an order."

The stranger continued to moan and pray, still trapped in his nightmare.

"It's okay." Tentatively she touched his back.

He slammed his fist into her jaw. "Women are the worst. Most vicious. Most hungry." He tried to hit her again.

She scuttled away from him. "Settle down, soldier."

Gentian mewed quietly. He stropped Kat's legs where she sat on the floor. His purr rumbled through her. Then the large cat hopped onto the stranger's bed, still purring. He stepped into the man's lap, circling and butting his had into his chest.

Gradually, the patient ceased his raving. He breathed deeply and closed his eyes. "So scared," he murmured. A tear leaked from the corner of his eye. "So many of them. So scared." He trembled all over.

"Easy now," Kat whispered, suddenly uncomfortable with a man's tears. But she rubbed his back, kneading the strong muscles of his shoulders and the leanness of his waist.

With her free hand she untangled the IV and anchored the pole in the packed dirt floor.

"Sorry," he whispered and laid his head upon her shoulder. "Not manly to cry."

And then he nodded off. Kat shifted gently until she leaned against the wall at the head of the bed. She raised her dangling legs to rest beside his. Then she settled in for a long vigil with a stranger in her arms.

Eventually she, too, slept.

* * *

The Krakatrice, the venomous snakes, are our cousins. Still, they menace us as well as the humans. They keep the desert from blooming with their hatred of water. They have built dams to divert streams out of their territory. They have joined together to shift air masses so that no rain falls where they live. They have fed upon or driven off the game that we would hunt. Our numbers cannot increase, nor can we dwell in the lands across the seas as long as the Krakatrice thrive.

Now we must find a way to equip the humans with weapons that will end the predation of our cousins the Krakatrice. We may not kill one of our own.

At the same time we must direct the humans toward Hanassa so that they can negate his influence. We may not kill one of our own, no matter how much damage he inflicts; no matter how much he threatens our existence.

* * *

Konner pulled Dalleena back from the hasty conference his brothers convened with the village warriors. "Let's walk patrol," he said quietly.

"What troubles you?" Dalleena held her right hand out, palm up, seeking danger better than her eyes or Konner's handheld could.

"I do not like this business of the fuel cells. They are not duds. I checked them myself, thoroughly, before setting them out to recharge. Sunshine and dragon wine have worked well enough to bring them up to full capacity, even if it has taken a long time."

"What emptied them?" Dalleena stopped her prowl of the perimeter of the village to face him. She kept her left hand on his arm.

Konner mimicked the contact. This way they could sense each other's body language without visual clues and without him resorting to probing her mind—his least effective psi power.

Since their marriage—little more than pledging themselves to each other before their gathered friends and family—they had become attuned to each other, rarely needing to speak other than the most complicated thoughts.

As the tension in his body rose, she tightened her grip, reminding him to gather calm in order to think clearly.

"I don't know. And I don't have time to walk up the hill to check the cells before my brothers call us back to the conference."

"Then you must bring the cells here, where we have the light of many torches reflecting off cave walls, almost as good as daylight for your inspection." She grinned.

He kissed her lightly and ran his fingers through her long dark hair. She knew him well. They had truly become two halves of a whole that was bigger and better than either one of them alone.

"Let's find a few Tambootie leaves. I need some help in levitating the cells."

"Right behind us. I can smell them. The sap is running strong now."

"Those trees do have a rather pungent perfume." He wrinkled his nose at the aromatic scent in the warm summer night air.

Within a few moments they had plucked two fat leaves dripping with essential oils and taken a fresh torch into one of the smallest caves. Konner had to crawl into the low opening and sit with his back against the far wall. He folded his long legs to make room for Dalleena beside him and the two cells to nestle before them.

He licked the oil from the green leaf with pink veins. Warmth and energy surged from his mouth throughout his body and into his mind. Before he could hesitate and ruin his concentration with doubt, he closed his eyes and breathed deeply, gathering his mental powers.

Dalleena placed her hands upon his thigh, adding her physical strength to his as he had taught her.

Bit by bit, he pictured in his mind two fuel cells, each a cubic meter, one bursting with energy, the other spent and lifeless. Then he built the image of the gray cerama/metal cubes resting between himself and his wife on the rough dirt and rock floor of the cave.

One more deep breath to center himself and he opened his eyes.

The two cells rested upon the cave floor, a few centimeters apart with only a bare half meter between their tops and the ceiling.

Konner ran his hands over the full cell, sensing the energy within waiting to be tapped. All it needed was a few fiber optics connecting it to an engine and the direction to activate. It felt normal, like every other fuel cell he had ever worked with.

Then he shifted his hands to the other cube. His fingers felt the roughness along the top seam. He bent over to peer more closely.

Dalleena moved the torch a fraction, giving him a better, unshadowed view.

His eyes confirmed what his hands had told him.

"Someone opened the cell and released the pressurized energy. But they didn't close it properly."

"Who would do such a thing?"

"Who could gain access to the clearing to do such a thing?"

"Could your sister Kat levitate it out and then back?"

"I don't know." Konner looked into Dalleena's pained eyes. They reflected his own distress. "Would she, though? She would more likely keep the full cells for her own use."

"Kat is straightforward, honest in her hatred, honorable as are you and your brothers." Dalleena confirmed Konner's own assessment of his sister.

But he had not known her for nearly twenty years. He did not understand the people and events who had shaped her during those years.

"Let us look closer to home before we condemn my sister."

"How close? Hestiia does not want Kim to leave with you and Loki. Kim does not want to leave, though you and Loki both insist he must."

"I hate to think it, but they are the most logical suspects. No one else could enter the clearing without our knowledge and supervision." Konner closed his eyes. "I won't think that of my brother and his wife. I won't."

* * *

Something strange on the wind disturbed Hanassa. He lifted his attention from the Cyndi-woman's less-than-orderly mind to sniff the air.

What ruffled his dragon senses? An emotion rather

than a scent. An emotion strong enough to reach across long distances.

A mind more vulnerable than the Cyndi-woman. A mind in distress.

"Later, my lovely," he whispered to Cyndi.

She did not hear him. Or, if she did, she ignored him, locked in her own obsessive anger.

He flew upward, seeking that other. Now that he knew he could separate from Taneeo and live in spirit form for a time, he needed to investigate and find the best candidate to host him.

A chuckle rumbled up from his belly. Yes, this might be fun. He'd sample many before he chose the best. And while he sampled, he would wreak havoc among the humans.

He might even try to temporarily give some courage to the flywacket. But only temporarily. He wanted a human body, not a miniaturized and transfigured dragon body.

CHAPTER 11

MARTIN CHECKED the readings on his hand-held. Two meters ahead of him, a security sensor read body heat and movement. Anyone or anything generating more heat than a servobot, or moving more than half a meter above ground would be recorded. Melinda's flunkies monitored everything in the palace except Melinda's office and private quarters. She could alert them to record there, too, but that required her voice and thumbprint override.

On top of that, Melinda and her crew moved the sensors every day.

Finding ways around them had become a daily exercise for Martin.

He did not want Melinda to know where he and his friends were every femto of the day. Especially since she had lodged them in the far guest wing, kilometers of corridors and staircases away from Martin.

He ducked directly beneath one of the sensors, trusting that his black leather pants and dark skin shirt, both woven with deflection threads, would mask his body heat. In this position, with the sensor angled toward the other side of the corridor, security should not be able to detect his movement.

A servobot came along, sweeping the edge of the corridor. It bumped against his feet, backed up, and scooted around him. Martin held his breath, praying that nothing internal to the machine reported the obstacle back to security.

Hopefully, the thing was programmed to ignore stationary pedestals and free-standing art. Melinda indulged in new decorations in binges. She hadn't bought any new artwork in almost a year. Time for things to start showing up in different places again and new ones filling odd gaps.

Melinda never discarded anything. Art she no longer wanted in the palace ended up in warehouses or servants' quarters until she craved change once more.

Martin dropped to his belly and scooted along in the wake of the servobot. Within a few meters he found the next space of dead air beneath a sensor on the opposite wall. He slid upright, back against the wall. So far so good. No blips in the sensors that his handheld could detect.

Just a few more meters and then he could round a corner into the guest wing. Melinda hadn't updated security there quite so recently. He could bypass it all with one loop of fiber optic cables.

"Martin, there you are," Melinda called out from the opposite end of the guest wing where she had lodged the Earth dignitaries.

"Melinda." Martin stood stock-still, wondering what lie he could come up with to mask his movements.

"I see you are on your way to visit your friends. I just saw them in the pool. That Quinn gentleman is most charming and Kurt Giovanni has wonderful manners. I must commend him to his father."

Martin nodded, not knowing what to say. He shuffled his feet awkwardly.

Melinda checked her chrono that sufficed as a handheld. She removed an electronic pencil from her earring and tapped something into it. Then she returned the pencil to her ear jewelry where it attached with a molecular bond.

"While I have you, perhaps it is time to introduce you to your new bodyguard and driver," Melinda said brightly.

Something was up; she was giving Martin her full attention.

"What happened to Miles and Jim?" Martin asked. He hadn't really liked the pair, but he'd sort of gotten used to them, knew their weaknesses.

"I decided they were more useful elsewhere." Her eyes narrowed. They had left Martin in Quinn's care yesterday without her permission.

Two men, nearly identical in height, breadth, and dark suits marched into view. They moved in step and swung their arms in time to their synchronized movements.

Ex-military, Martin decided. Or mercenaries. Not to be trusted.

"Martin, meet John and Karl." Melinda nodded to the two men as one, not differentiating between them. "Until this mess with the Earth diplomats is cleared up, I want these men with you at all times. All times."

"But, Melinda, I had hoped for some time alone with my friends. I haven't seen them in over two years." Martin hated that he sounded like a little kid whining.

"I'm sure we can dispense with the dippos by tomorrow. Then you can have some privacy back."

"I don't see what threat they can pose to us, Melinda." He almost called her "mother" just to annoy her.

"They seem to think I should know something about this missing judicial cruiser and their passenger.

I don't and that bothers me." She paused a moment tapping her toe and her fingertip against the chrono.

"They have nothing to do with us, do they?" Martin tried for wide-eyed innocence.

"Not that I know of. But I'd better find out what they suspect quickly. Martin, return to your room and that map of yours. See if you can plot where that ship disappeared and where it might have gone. I'll begin researching that girl—their passenger. Lucinda Baines. Does the name mean anything to you?"

"Baines?" Martin had to think a moment. Melinda must be running scared if she included her son in her plans and research. "Didn't a Carolyn McArthur marry a planetary governor named Baines, reuniting the former royal house with a cadet branch, thus forming a possible dynasty?" he recited a history lesson, and gossip that Jane had given him.

"Ye . . . es," Melinda said. Now she tapped her teeth with her fingernail, a true sign of her agitation. "But our current emperor's father won the election in Parliament and proceeded to begin major reforms in the bureaucracy. The Baines faction couldn't skim off nearly as much in profit from taxes as they had."

"Sounds like Lady Lucinda is off somewhere planning a *coup d'etat.* I heard her name linked romantically to Eric Findlatter, the emperor's nephew."

"I need to know more about this woman. Go do some research and report back to me before dinner."

"But my friends . . ."

"Will still be here when you finish. More incentive for you to get right on it and stop testing the new security upgrades."

"You knew what I was doing?"

"Of course I knew. And you did very well. Security shows you still in your room. If I had not spotted you with my own eyes, you might have defeated the system completely. We can't allow that. I'll fire a few layabouts in the monitoring room and demote some others. That ought to bring them up to speed in plugging the holes."

"Yes, Melinda."

"And thank you, Martin. Now I know where the weaknesses in the system are. We will make a formidable team." She turned abruptly and headed back to her own wing, doubtless to figure some way to use the ambitious Lucinda Baines. By dinnertime, Melinda would likely know the woman's shoe size, color preference, and the names of her last six lovers.

"Don't suppose I could postpone that research until after a swim with my friends," Martin mused.

"No," his guards, jailers, replied in unison. They each grabbed one of his elbows and marched him back to his own quarters.

* * *

"Searcher, this is Jester, come in, please," Loki whispered into his handheld. He watched his screen anxiously for any flicker that might indicate a response.

With Konner and Dalleena off on some private errand—probably more lovemaking—and Kim checking Pryth, now was the best time for Loki to contact his own lover.

He hugged the cliff face near the path to the beach. A freshening breeze nearly blew him back into the heart of the village.

After interminable moments the screen on his handheld went from gray to black and then brightened enough to reveal the shadowy outline of Paola Sanchez, formerly a corporal in His Majesty's Imperial Military Police.

"Searcher here," came her crisp reply. The static of distance and a lack of satellites created a delay between the movements of her lips and his hearing the words.

"Searcher, I have new intel on the monster in your backyard," Loki said. He couldn't help the smile that crept across his face. Short and stocky, with dark hair, and an authoritative air, Paola represented everything he disliked in a woman. But she was the best lover he had ever been with. Cyndi's wild moans and thrashing paled in comparison to Paola's intensity and true passion.

"Is this just another excuse to drag me back to Coronnan for a face-to-face debriefing?" she asked with a big smile.

"I wish," Loki replied on a sigh.

"Then you have honestly found someone who will talk about the monster I'm chasing?"

"More than that. Konner and Dalleena encountered a coil of huge black snakes. Very venomous, very aggressive. Dalleena said the dominant matriarch had a head as big as a man's and a tongue as long as an arm. She also has six pairs of batlike wings. The rest of the snakes are ground huggers."

Paola let out an extended curse that taxed even Loki's vocabulary and imagination.

"That's the best intel I've had in six months. No one in the port city seems to know why they can't stray beyond the wall after dark. Digger—er, Ross Duggan—up north is having similar problems in his city. I think I need to come there and talk directly to Konner and Dalleena," Paola finished.

"Want me to bring the shuttle to pick you up?"

"Yeah. Unless you've got a dragon handy."

"They don't answer my calls like they do my brothers'."

"Probably 'cause they know you don't want to stay here. They love this planet."

"As do you and your Amazons, and Digger and his troop of rogue Marines."

Nine months ago, when Loki and his brothers began the plot to trap the IMPs on this planet, they had found unexpected allies among the first landing parties. Paola, a corporal with ten years' experience, would never rise higher in the ranks because of her bush origins. She had gladly sided with Loki, after bedding him, for the chance to command her own troops. Thirty other women from *Jupiter* had joined her for similar reasons.

Ross Duggan, or Digger, had been an IMP sergeant with a grudge against GTE politics. He'd sided with the O'Haras for the opportunity to earn more money in order to free his family from indentured servitude. Now he commanded his own troops north of Paola in a different port city hoping to carve out some land and a place to bring his family once Loki sold some surplus produce on the black market and purchased the Duggans' indenture.

"Yeah, I love this place, bush backwater that it is. When can I expect you?"

"I'm on my way. Dawn your time." The port city on the big continent was close to a thousand klicks east and another thousand north of Coronnan.

"Good. I can catch an hour of sleep. Searcher out."

The handheld went dark again.

Loki sighed on a smile. He did that a lot when he talked to Paola. He needed Paola's vibrancy to remind him that not everything about his life was one dismal trial after another.

He hadn't used the shuttle to raid Base Camp, so he might as well use it to consult with the chief Amazon on the big continent. He stepped away from the shadows that hid him.

"Wasting fuel again?" Konner asked. He stood between Loki and the shuttle, hands on hips, feet firmly planted.

"Why aren't you making love to your wife? Back in the clearing," Loki replied. He'd not get around his brother easily, judging by the deep frown on his face.

"It's not a waste of fuel, if we can defeat the monster serpents and expand the port," Loki continued his defense. "We need a thriving port city to increase trade. Can't do that if the snakes keep everyone behind walls." They'd known for months that some monster preyed upon the populace; they just had not seen or heard about the nature of the beast.

"Agreed. But we need fuel to get back to *Sirius*. Someone sabotaged three of our cells. We haven't got any fuel to spare. If you haven't forgotten, I need to get back to Aurora to claim my son."

"I haven't forgotten. What good is claiming your son if we haven't got enough of an economy on this planet to support ourselves?"

"Later. You aren't going to take the shuttle again."

"Try and stop me." Loki pushed past Konner.

"I've rekeyed the ignition in order to keep Kat from stealing *Rover*. It only responds to my DNA now. Either I approve the mission or the shuttle goes nowhere."

CHAPTER 12

"SINCE WE AREN'T GOING raiding tonight, I propose you two assist me in a healing spell," Kim said to his two brothers. He had several hours until midnight when M'Berra might return his call.

Since he was the tallest of the three—by three centimeters over Konner and five over Loki—he did his best to command them by staring down at them. They each outweighed him by several kilos—most of it muscle—so if it ever came down to a physical fight among them, Kim would, and usually did, lose.

They shouldn't have to exchange blows to cooperate on this chore. Their fights were usually just an opportunity to vent anger and frustration at problems they couldn't easily solve. At the end of these bouts, all three of them came up laughing.

"For the good of the family and this village we have to try to heal Pryth," he urged.

"Do you know how to do this?" Loki asked. He stood with his fists on his hips and his feet braced for a fight. But then he was always braced for a fight.

"None of us have done this before, but we have to try. We are running out of options," Kim insisted.

"This won't be like the last time," Konner reminded them.

"Last time with Raaskan, a seven-metric-ton rock dropped on him," Loki reminded him. "After Konner levitated it off him, we had to push bones back into alignment and stop internal bleeding. What do we do with Pryth? We don't even know what is making her sick."

"She has all of the classic symptoms of pneumonia," Kim said. "We have to clear her lungs of fluid and bring her fever down."

"The locals swear by willow bark tea for fever," Konner mused. "I've seen it work. But how do we drain fluid from the lungs? Bringing it up might gag her. Or if we do it wrong, we could drown."

"A little bit at a time?" Kim suggested.

His brothers remained silent, shaking their heads.

"Too dangerous," Loki finally decided.

"We have to try! This village, my wife, depend too much on Pryth. We have to try!" Kim cried.

"Maybe we should read up on this before . . ."

"I have read up on this. We are running out of time. Pryth is so weak she might die tonight if we do nothing."

"If she's that weak, maybe we should leave well enough alone. What if she dies under our hands?" Loki said.

All three brothers shuddered. Each had a memory of another person dying either by their hand or by their negligence. None of them wanted a repeat performance of their spirits trying to follow another into death.

"If we don't do something, then who will deliver my baby? Who will know what to do if Hes has trouble delivering? Are either of you willing to take the chance that my wife and son might die in childbirth without Pryth?" Panic edged Kim's voice.

Both Konner and Loki looked at the ground.

"With or without you, I have to try to heal Pryth."

Kim turned his back on his brothers and walked slowly toward the round hut where Pryth lay coughing and moaning, her life slipping away a little bit at a time.

As he walked, he left his mind open, "listening" for some kind of emotional reaction from his brothers. Telepathy was Loki's primary talent. Konner moved objects with his mind—the heavier the better. The first talent to manifest in Kim was precognition. He'd never have found the weird jump point to this planet without it. That weird jump point had been their only escape from the pursuing Judicial Crusier *Jupiter*. Commander Leonard had to break off the chase and go off on other errands and then come back several months later before her helmsman, Kat, had found the same jump point.

After the brothers had landed in this isolated system, Kim had discovered an ability to speed healing in others. He did not know how he did it, it just happened. Now he had to try to make the talent work on demand.

He'd studied hard over the last year to expand all of his talents and add new ones. Control over his talents increased daily. Except when he needed to heal. It either happened or it didn't. Even when he ate the addictive Tambootie leaves.

He reached inside his pocket for the fat leaves he always kept at hand. He licked the oil off the pink-and-green veins. Then he nibbled on the succulent flesh of a leaf. A surge of adrenaline filled his body. He looked out upon the night with new clarity. Vague shadows in the distance jumped into view as clearly defined objects.

Then he heard the shuffle of feet behind him and

mental grunts of agreement. His brothers had come to his aid after all.

Some of Kim's hesitation and fear evaporated.

They squeezed into Pryth's round hut one by one. The old woman with gray streaking her Rover-dark hair lay propped up against a makeshift bolster made up of a wolf hide draped over a basket filled with aromatic herbs and leaves. A small fire smoldered in the central hearth. More green smoke—born of the copper sulfate impregnated in the firewood—filled the room than escaped the hole in the conical roof. The smoke smelled sweet and astringent at the same time. Someone, probably Pryth, had sprinkled herbs over the coals.

Kim's sinuses cleared upon his first full breath inside the hut. The smoke might be doing some good for the patient, but not enough.

He handed the remaining Tambootie leaf to his brothers. Loki tore it in half and eagerly stuffed his portion into his mouth. Konner ate his more delicately, taking only as much as he needed to open his mind and his talent.

Kim felt their hands brush against his in rapport.

A coughing spasm racked Pryth's body. She leaned forward, hacking and choking until she could barely draw breath. Sweat poured off her brow. She shivered all the same.

The old woman began to gag. Alarmed, Kim knelt beside her. Instinctively, he reached into her mouth and pinched a wad of phlegm between his fingers. Slowly he drew out a long rope of greenish slime. He cast it into the fire. The flames sputtered and stank of garbage left out too long in the sun.

"Is that all you are going to do?" Loki snarled.

"You could do that without us. It's disgusting." He turned to exit.

"We need to do more, Loki. She needs magic as well as mundane cures. Without antibiotics, we have to find a way to kill the bacteria infecting her body."

"Pryth packs moss into open wounds to prevent infection. Maybe if we made an infusion with the moss and some willow bark," Konner suggested.

"After we try this. I'm getting some ideas," Kim said. He sat cross-legged on the packed-dirt floor. His rump turned cold almost immediately from the winter chill that had soaked into it. Summer heat had not yet had time to warm it, despite the fire.

No wonder half the village had contracted various forms of the disease that had felled Pryth.

Kim concentrated on breathing. His brothers sank to the floor on either side of him. Each placed a hand upon his shoulder. They matched their breaths to his.

In on three counts, hold three, exhale on the same three counts. "Breathe deep, exhale deeper. Purge your body of foreign thoughts, alien impurities. Breathe," Kim chanted.

Gradually, the three minds merged into one. Their talents and strength combined.

The world retreated from Kim's awareness. He knew only his breath and the power he inhaled. His vision tilted slightly and colors took on strange casts, as if the spectrum shifted slightly to the left toward ultraviolet.

A web of silvery-blue lines beneath the ground jumped into view.

Shadows retreated. He looked more deeply into himself and saw the essence of Pryth, saw the rampant infection that had invaded her body. He watched her will to live fade.

Panicked, he almost lost his trance. Konner squeezed

his shoulder, reaffirming the strength his brothers gave him.

One more deep breath and Kim concentrated on the red aura that surrounded Pryth, flowed in and out of her with her labored breathing. He reached out to touch the symbolic fire of infection. It burned his fingertips. He jerked his hand away, shaking it to dispel the heat.

Fortified with knowledge of the aura's nature he reached again and twined the fiery-red coils around his fingers and drew them away, as he had the phlegm. A section of red broke free of Pryth. Kim cast the pulsing red light into the hearth.

Sickly yellow-and-black smoke roiled up from the embers. It stank of rotten flesh, old sweat, and stale air.

Pryth heaved a sigh of relief. Then she began coughing again.

Kim sagged with exhaustion.

"I can't do anymore," he choked out.

"You have to," Konner urged him. "You have to get more of the infection out. Concentrate on her lungs."

"Use the ley lines," Pryth whispered.

"How?" Kim leaned forward eager for new knowledge.

Her answer was lost in another coughing spasm.

Kim took several more deep breaths. He thought he heard a rattle in his own lungs. Loki squeezed Kim's shoulder with both of his hands.

A little bit of strength trickled through Kim. He needed more of the Tambootie leaves.

He had no more with him. To leave to fetch more would break the trance. He might never achieve this level again.

Resolutely, he reached again to grasp the pulsing red aura of infection in the region of Pryth's lungs. The infection pushed his hand back. He pressed harder. His arm and shoulder ached as if he'd carried his own weight and more a long distance.

Loki supported Kim's overly heavy arm with his hand.

Kim tried again, feeling the strength drain out of him with every passing breath. At last he grasped a wad of the red light. It burned his palms.

"Hold on. The pain is not real," Konner whispered. He was sweating with the effort of maintaining the trance.

"Hold it tight and pull," Loki coached. His words came out on panting breaths.

Kim closed his fist and his eyes. He pulled. He had to lean back to extend the length of his retraction. In his mind he saw the infection drain out of Pryth. When he had as much as he could hold, he cast the long rope of it into the fire.

Rancid smoke filled his lungs. He coughed it out. Coughed again and again.

"Saint Bridget and all the angels," Loki breathed. "You've done it."

Kim sagged and coughed again, too weary to move. The pressure in his chest increased and he coughed again, and again. And again, until he could not breathe.

"Shite!" Konner exploded. "He's taken the disease into himself."

"You . . . must . . . take . . . it . . . out of him, now, before it spreads," Pryth whispered.

"I can barely lift my arms," Konner breathed. "I already worked magic tonight with the fuel cells. I've nothing left to give."

"Do it now," Kim whispered, afraid if he spoke aloud he'd cough again and never stop.

"We have to try together." Loki sounded as weary as Konner, almost as tired as Kim.

Kim felt his brothers each reach a hand to his chest and draw it away.

"Got it!" Konner said. Some of his fatigue had left his voice.

"Not all of it." Kim collapsed onto the cold floor, grateful that it leeched some of the fever heat from his face.

Then Pryth lifted a shaking hand and touched his chest, just above his heart.

The fever and pressure left him.

Kim opened his eyes. The fever pulsed again, raw and angry around Pryth.

"I cannot let you die for me," she whispered. She collapsed into unconsciousness.

CHAPTER 13

A VERY FAINT NOISE at the door to his private suite awakened Martin. He had not slept well, knowing his two new guards camped in his bedroom while he stretched out on the Lazy-former® in the main room. This latest intrusion on his rest sent his adrenaline rushing. He bounced out of his recliner and behind the chair without thought. The Lazy-former® shifted back to a standard upright position. He fished an illegal stunner from the folds of the furniture.

Before he could breathe again, a portion of the door slid back. The tall silhouette of a muscular man appeared, backlit by the lights in the corridor.

"Master Martin, we need to talk privately," Quinn whispered.

Martin remained still, listening to his heartbeat.

"You have no reason to trust me yet, Master Martin. I understand. I am here to help. But we need to talk where there is no chance of being overheard." Quinn took one step into Martin's living room. The door slid shut behind him. Only a residual glow from the solar collectors around the bioglass windows distinguished one shadow from another.

Martin crept out from his hiding place, keeping low, working his way around and behind Quinn.

"I offer you my word as an officer in His Majesty's

private service, and as a Sam Eyeam, I have come to help you, Master Martin."

"Not a word more," Martin whispered, pressing the stunner against Quinn's jugular. He had to stand on tiptoe and reach awkwardly to keep the weapon in place. "Out the windows into the walled garden." He pushed the Sam Eyeam toward the exit.

Ten steps for Quinn. Fifteen for Martin's shorter legs. He grabbed a robe and threw it over his shoulders as he went. He didn't want to get caught in only his underwear.

Martin pressed his hand against the sensor beside the long window. It slid open noiselessly. No one else could open this door. Not even his mother. Once outside in the garden, open to the night air within the city's dome, he closed the door by pressing against a second sensor that answered only to his palm print and DNA. Then he touched a third sensor. A faint static hummed and echoed around the small green space, fifteen meters to a side, within a tall brick wall. Grass and exotic flowering shrubs filled the space. Martin tended them himself rather than allow a gardener inside his security.

"We can talk now," Martin said. He kept the stunner aimed at Quinn's chest.

"That is some serious security," Quinn said. He glanced at his handheld and turned a tight circle, aiming it at the entire garden including upward toward the atmosphere dome three thousand meters up.

"My mother's people designed the security for her. I tweaked it so that even her stuff can't penetrate it. Another static field around the bedroom door alerts me if the guards in there stir."

"I'm guessing you have reason to be so paranoid."

Martin nodded, unable to voice his biggest fear. "Why are you here?" he asked instead.

"I need to know more about this quest to find your father. Why does your mother object so strongly to you going?"

"Melinda Fortesque sent a Sam Eyeam after him with an assassin's retainer and a locator beacon."

Quinn turned another tight circle that aimed his handheld at every possible shrub where Melinda could have secreted listening devices.

"Even the spy satellites can't see us," Martin advised him.

"Your mother owns the entire planet, including all of the industries and support businesses. Why does she need spy satellites?"

"Melinda doesn't trust anyone. And neither do I."

"My next logical question would be 'Who is your father?' "

Martin thought about it a moment. So Quinn had not overheard his earlier conversation.

What further harm could he do this mission by telling? If Melinda sent Quinn to spy on Martin, then the Sam Eyeam would tell her everything anyway. The name meant only a little more trouble.

"Martin Konner O'Hara."

Quinn whistled softly. "Curiouser and curiouser."

"What is that supposed to mean?"

"Only that we have bit off a lot more trouble than we can chew if we get caught. You and your mother aren't the only ones searching for that man and his brothers. There is a hefty reward for their capture."

"Brothers." For the second time that day he'd heard brothers associated with Konner O'Hara. For three years Martin and Konner had met each summer at camp. Konner acted as favored counselor to Jane,

Kurt, and Bruce as well. In all their long talks, Konner had never suggested that he might have a personal reason for befriending Martin. He had never mentioned his family or his history.

Martin had to discover much of that on his own.

"I have uncles?" Hope made Martin's voice squeak. "I have a family besides Melinda?"

"Yeah. Most of them are outlaws. But at this point, I'm guessing living on the run with the O'Hara brothers would be safer than angering your mother."

Another long pause while Martin thought about that piece of information. His mind raced and his heart sang.

"How did you find out your father's name, Martin?" Quinn asked. He still spoke softly. He probably didn't trust Martin's security fully.

That was okay. Martin didn't dare fully trust it either.

"Kurt found Melinda's marriage license on Meditcue II. So far we have no trace of an annulment or divorce."

"How'd he find that?"

"Bruce's father, Bruce Geralds, Sr., is also a Sam Eyeam. He deleted the record of the marriage. Kurt went looking for files that had been deleted on obscure bush planets."

"You kids have access to some kind of major software genius. Galactic Free Market?"

"Four heads are better than one. We do it ourselves."

"What else do you know?"

Suddenly liking this strange man, Martin decided to trust him. For now. He wouldn't grow up like his mother, afraid of everyone, with secrets she dared not expose to the light of day. Quinn had said he was one of the emperor's private agents. If so, he could get the information to the proper authorities and maybe . . . just maybe free Martin from Melinda.

Besides, once Quinn knew what Martin knew, his life was in as much danger from Melinda as any of her enemies, including Martin—her only child and heir.

"We found a dissenting report concerning the accident that killed my grandparents sixteen years ago. It said the ship did not blow up from an internal malfunction. Someone fired upon it. My grandparents were murdered. But the official report that was accepted as the 'true' cause of their deaths holds that the explosion was an accident. The dissenting report was suppressed. Very difficult to find."

"I've read the report."

"Is that why you came? A little late."

"I was sent for another reason, one that I cannot tell you at this moment, but one that is to your advantage. Getting Melinda out of the way can only help all parties concerned. Including your father."

"Did you know that Melinda hired a Sam Eyeam just before the 'accident'? Did you know she paid him more than double the annual salary of the average worker on Aurora? Only one small armed merchant vessel left Aurora on the same day as the accident. That vessel was the only one that could have fired upon my grandparents' cruiser just before they reached the jump point."

"I suspected as much, but I have no proof."

"I do."

"Will you share?"

"When we find my father and both of us are safe."

"Without the proof, neither of you will ever be safe."

"I know."

"Do you have any idea which Sam Eyeam your mother hired?"

Martin clamped his mouth shut and crossed his arms. That was one piece of information he could not allow free of his handheld—which he'd triple encrypted and keyed to his DNA.

"Fine. We'll deal with that later. Now I've cleared it with your mother to take you four kids on a tour of one of her industrial complexes day after tomorrow, the one that makes rides for amusement planets. What she does not know is that the air car I will fly is spaceworthy. We'll use it to dock with the vessel I have in orbit."

"How'd you manage that?" Excitement lit Martin's veins. He was going to get free. Day after tomorrow, he'd be free!

"Never mind. Let's just say it pays to be prepared for any emergency. I always plan an escape route before I commit to a mission. That's how we Sam Eyeams stay alive."

* * *

Just before dawn Kim crept up the path to the clearing. If M'Berra had returned his call, Kim had slept through it.

All he wanted was to crawl into bed, pull Hestiia close, and sleep for a week. Defeat as well as exhaustion weighed heavily on his spirit. How could Pryth waste all of his efforts to save her life?

Now the village would be lucky if she lived two more days.

He didn't know how they would cope without the old wisewoman.

And he'd lost his chance to compromise with the IMPs and gain access to the medic and medicine.

He neared the barrier and hummed his mother's favorite lullaby. A shimmer in the air showed him the portal. He stepped through to the seven-acre haven that sheltered Kim and his brothers, Hestiia, Dalleena, and Taneeo in rough cabins and lean-tos. A confusion field generated by the stolen crystal array from *Jupiter* kept the clearing invisible to the outside world.

Faint light from an oil lamp showed beneath the door to the one-room hut he shared with Hes. He paused a moment, wishing he could go to her right away. He needed to place his hand on her swelling belly and feel the life growing within. Sometimes he thought he could communicate with his son this way. Other times he rejoiced in just feeling the strong heartbeat.

Tonight he needed reassurance that Hes and the baby lived. But different duties called him first.

He tiptoed to the rough lean-to on the far side of the clearing. The crude shelter butted right up against the tree that marked the edge of the clearing and the beginning of the force field.

"Taneeo, it's Kim." He rattled the chains of beads hanging over one end of the lean-to.

The man inside remained quiet. Kim had not expected an answer, but politeness required he speak. In nine months, Taneeo had not uttered a word. When prompted, he would eat and drink if someone brought sustenance to his mouth. He could even walk after a fashion if someone held his hand and led him to the latrine or the hot springs for a bath. His eyes refused to focus. As far as Kim could tell, the former priest of the village had no thoughts of his own.

The spirit of the rogue dragon, Hanassa, had possessed Taneeo's mind and body. But Taneeo had proved himself stronger than the dragon. Still, the battle between them had left Taneeo witless, near catatonic.

Kim ducked into the shelter. Taneeo's eyes were closed. In sleep?

Kim did not know if his friend had truly slept in the last nine months or merely feigned it so that the O'Hara clan would leave him alone.

Kim ran his hands swiftly over Taneeo's slight arms and legs. The skin was smooth now, without trace of the exoskeleton he'd grown to accommodate the dragon. "That's an improvement," Kim said under his breath. Then he checked his patient's neck and spine. These, too, showed no trace of the hard cartilage.

"Physically, the spirit of Hanassa has departed, Taneeo. He no longer controls your body. But where has the rogue purple-tip dragon gone? He has to have a body, preferably one that carries his DNA. Which of his bastards does he haunt now?"

"A woman," Taneeo croaked. He turned intelligent eyes to his friend.

"Taneeo?" Kim stared at the man in surprise.

The priest nodded and swallowed deeply.

Kim offered him the nearby jug of water. He needed to prop Taneeo up and hold the vessel to his lips. The priest drank greedily, holding the liquid in his mouth for several seconds before swallowing.

"What happened? What brought you out of the catatonic trance?" Kim asked eagerly.

"Someone. Someone tempted Hanassa away."

"Who?"

"I do not know. You asked me a question. What question did you ask me?"

"Never mind about that. Let me help you up. You

need to regain strength and mobility. I'll rouse Hestiia and we'll get you some food."

"I need to . . . ah . . ."

"Yes, that first. Then food. Would you like to sit by the fire?"

"Yes. That would be nice. What question did you ask me?"

"I don't remember."

CHAPTER 14

"TIME AND TIDE wait for no man. Let's get that boat in the water!" Loki shouted. False dawn barely glimmered along the edge of the horizon far out in the bay. Too restless to stay abed any longer, he rattled the bead chains in front of every hut and cave in the village.

"The weather's fine, the tide is right, and the fish are running!" He marched around and around the central fire pit to the tune of sleepy grumbles and more than a few curses.

On his third circuit, he broadened his path to include the festival pylon, three slender trees stripped of branches and bark tilted into a narrow tripod. Every major event in village life took place at the pylon: marriages, funerals, harvest, planting, first presentation of babies.

After the villagers had fled the IMPs who now command their old home, they had migrated to the base of the cliff where the Stargods fortified and concealed their clearing. Pryth had demanded the pylon's erection before anyone selected a cave or cooked a meal. The pylon meant home more than meals and places to rest a head. On their journey they'd eaten and slept many places without a pylon. This was home. That meant a pylon first, food and sleep later.

Now Pryth lay dying.

Loki refused to think on that.

He looked around to see what was keeping the men from joining him for a day of pitting his mind and muscles against the sea and the fish.

The first shaft of sunlight glinted off the crystalline hide of a dragon parked on his haunches between the path up to the clearing and the path down to the cove.

Loki arrested his neat frantic progress through the village. He gulped in startlement. "Um . . . Loki here." He barely remembered the dragon protocol of introduction.

(Iianthe.) The voice rang through Loki's mind like the deep tolling of an ominous bell.

"Iianthe? The purple-tip?" A second shaft of sunlight revealed a hint of deep purple along the outlines of the dragon and in the series of horns marching from his forehead down his back to his tail.

(You needed me. I came.)

"I did? Um . . . I do?" He hadn't remembered calling a dragon.

(Come. The desert continent is a long way from here.)

"Yeah. Right. Paola and the snakes."

(You need to see the Krakatrice to understand their menace.)

"Krakatrice? Why do you call them that?" Loki modified his urgent steps to a casual stroll as he aimed for the dragon's side. Excitement gathered in his belly. He'd never ridden a dragon alone before. Never had one at his beck and call before. This was almost as thrilling as pushing *Rover* to its limits and evading hostile fire.

(Krakatrice is their name for themselves.)

"And what is the dragons' name for themselves?" Loki climbed up Iianthe's shoulder. He noted that the last vestige of silver had grown out of his short fur.

This dragon had matured well in the last year. Iianthe wasn't full size yet, from what he'd heard, but still more than large enough to fly him to the big continent and back without tiring.

(You could not pronounce our word.)

"May I at least hear your word for dragons?"

A mental chuckle tickled the back of Loki's mind. The dragon rose up on all fours and began running and flapping his wings in preparation for flight. As his feet lifted free of the ground, Iianthe loosed a mighty roar/screech/bellow that nearly shattered Loki's eardrums and certainly woke everyone in the village. A dribble of flame accompanied the dragon speech.

(That is our word for dragon,) Iianthe said. He sounded smug.

Loki ran the sound through his mind. "You're right, I couldn't pronounce it. I presume the bit of flame is part of the speech?"

(Of course.) Iianthe gained altitude and circled around to the east, flying directly into the rising sun.

Two hours later the coastline of the big continent came into view.

"You've been strangely quiet this trip, Iianthe," Loki said over the roar of wind in his ears. He looked all around him, noting the lack of islands, shoals, and reefs between here and the shore. Shipping would be a breeze, pun fully intended, if they could just open up those ports to the hinterland and its mineral resources.

Unfortunately, the deposits of ore were in the hills three-to-five-days' walk from the port city. The Krakatrice had made travel impossible. No one caught in the desert without the protection of stout walls survived the night.

(Your mind is preoccupied with thoughts of your lady and the problems of fighting the Krakatrice.)

"Well, thanks," Loki replied slightly affronted. This dragon seemed altogether too free with mind reading.

(Think on this next time you use your talent to read a mind.)

Loki stuttered and stammered a moment. "You don't like me very much, do you, Iianthe?"

(Like. Dislike. Two sides of the same Tambootie tree.)

Neither of them said a thing for several wing flaps that drew them ever closer to land.

"Tambootie tree. Poison and blessing."

(When two are alike, they see in the other what they do not like about themselves. Rather than admit the flaw, it is easier to despise it in the other twofold.)

Loki and the dragon chuckled together.

"So we are both arrogant, adventurous, and asinine."

(Responsible, reverent, and reasonable—upon occasion.)

Another laugh between them.

(Your lady awaits). Iianthe banked and descended, gliding on the air currents that took him closer and closer to the jumble of tightly packed buildings inside a three-point-five-meter-high wall that described a crescent along a small bay.

From this elevation the city looked like a waxing moon. Loki saw signs of construction of a new wall a kilometer outside the original.

Iianthe took a low pass above the city. All eyes turned upward in fear, then awe at the sight. One feminine figure ran through the gate of the new wall out toward an empty plain.

The dragon aimed for the woman and settled in front of her. He had to run the last hundred meters, digging his talons deep into the dirt and raising his wings high to slow his momentum.

Loki jumped free of the dragon's back even before Iianthe come to a complete stop.

He gathered Paola Sanchez into a tight hug and swung her around in joyful greeting. "Jaysus, I've missed you." Then he kissed her soundly.

She kissed him back. They lingered together for many long moments, oblivious to the crowd growing around them.

(Ahem.)

Loki couldn't ignore the dragon clearing his throat. He wondered how much flame had accompanied the sound.

(You have things to see and learn. Bring your lady,) Iianthe commanded.

"Today I am at your service, Iianthe." Loki described a sweeping bow, then scooped Paola up into his arms, deposited her on the dragon's back, and clambered up behind her.

"Loki? What is going on?" she asked inspecting the dragon with her eyes while she slapped her hips in search of the stun pistol and dagger she usually wore.

(You will not need weapons today. I will protect you.)

Paola shook her head. Her thick dark braid swung across her back.

"Kind of takes a little getting used to," Loki said, tugging the braid with affection.

"That was the dragon talking to me?"

"Not just any dragon. This is Iianthe, the only purple-tipped dragon in the nimbus. There can only be one purple-tip at a time. Say hello to him and give him your name. Dragons are big on names."

"Hello, Iianthe. I am Paola Sanchez, leader of the Amazon troops."

(Greetings, Paola Sanchez. Iianthe here. Hold tight. We have much to do before the sun sets.) Without further warning Iianthe took six running steps, sweeping his wings strongly to build lift and speed.

Loki barely got his butt settled between two spinal horns before they were airborne. He wrapped one arm around Paola in front of him and clung to a purple horn with the other.

A vast landscape of terrible beauty unrolled beneath them.

"I love this place," Paola said quietly. I've been on a dozen bush worlds and three civilized ones, but none of them compare to this place for sheer majesty."

Loki could only shrug his shoulders. Most places were the same to him. He liked this planet better than most, but home to him was aboard *Sirius* flying the vast distances between stars.

Within one hundred klicks of the port city, Iianthe brought them to a rough landing beside a shallow ravine. He rippled his back in invitation for his passengers to debark.

"What are we supposed to see and learn here?" Loki asked. He peered uneasily at the near barren gray-green dirt spotted with volcanic rocks of black and dark red. An occasional low and spiky shrub struggled to survive in the lee of those boulders.

(Dig,) Iianthe commanded.

"In case you didn't notice, we didn't bring any tools," Loki said. Hands on hips he stared defiantly at the dragon.

"In case you didn't notice, the temperature is near forty-five degrees centigrade," Paola added. "We didn't pack any water. Working in this heat could kill us."

(Dig.) Iianthe demonstrated by scratching the dirt with one huge paw, talons fully extended. He had a hole nearly a meter deep and two long at the head of the ravine by the time Loki and Paola managed to do more than scratch the surface. He looked as if he were trying to extend the ravine.

"Uh, Loki, the soil here is different than on the surface," Paola said, holding two handfuls, one the ubiquitous gray-green, the other darker and richer.

"It feels different, too. It's damp." Loki dug with more enthusiasm. "Kim should be the one you brought here, Iianthe. He's the professor who knows about dirt and planting and such."

(He would not come.)

"You're right. He won't leave Hestiia any longer than he has to until she gives birth." Loki dug some more.

(Step back!) Iianthe commanded.

Loki and Paola scrambled for the sides of the ravine and climbed out just as Iianthe pulled aside one last clump of dirt.

A trickle of water burst free, beneath one of the rocks. The tiny rivulet grew to a sizable stream as Loki watched, jaw hanging open.

"Where did that come from?" he asked no one in particular. "If there is this much water beneath the surface, why is this place a desert?"

(The Krakatrice. They cannot live near water. Over the centuries they have moved mountains to cover all the water on this continent.)

"I need a pump and a fire hose. We can take sea-water and spray the bloody snakes to keep them away from the city!" Paola chortled.

(Not enough.) Iianthe shook his mighty head. *(The matriarch can survive water. You must kill the matri-arch in order to subdue the rest. Come, there is more.)*

Once more Loki and Paola climbed atop the dragon's back and flew deeper into the desert.

Once they were fully airborne, Loki suffered a moment of dizzy disorientation. He had to cling tightly to Paola and the dragon to keep his balance. Closing his eyes helped.

When he opened them again, he noticed how the terrain below them changed. A great basin fell away from the surrounding broken and lumpy ground.

"Is that water?" Loki pointed toward a distant glint of silver against the gray-green background. She shook her head as if she, too, emerged from a few heartbeats of upset.

(Yes.)

In moments the dragon landed beside a small lake. Loki and Paolo dismounted slowly, cautiously.

"Must be spring fed to survive the dirt movement of the Krakatrice," Paolo scuffed the dirt with her boots. A small cloud of dust rose up.

"Barely enough water to support six low shrubs let alone any game," Loki mused. "Is this a meteor impact crater?"

(Look at the location. See what was a long time ago.)

Loki looked up toward the cliffs that defined a rough circle around the tiny lake. A full klick away in all directions. Cliffs that suddenly grew a lot closer.

And the entire basin filled with water.

"Run! We're going to drown."

CHAPTER 15

KAT AWOKE RESTED and aware. She only suffered a fuzzy transition between sleep and reality when she came out of *the* nightmare. This morning her body wanted to linger with the stranger's arms wrapped around her and his head upon her breast.

Sometime during the night she had scooched down and stretched out. The two of them had shared the narrow cot quite well, comfortable with the implied intimacy.

A stir of activity outside the med cabin convinced her she should not be found mussed and drowsy with an unknown man. If he'd been an officer from *Jupiter,* even a noncom, no one would have thought twice about her choice. A few moments of memorizing his face with her fingertips had revealed to her that this man had not come to the planet aboard *Jupiter.* Three hundred men and women trapped together on a mid-sized spaceship for months at a time were not too many for her to recognize everyone on sight.

She tested her weight on the injured ankle. It held, even if it did shoot lances of fire upward. After splashing water on her face from a basin and tidying her uniform, she limped out to join the mess crew at the cooking fire.

Today she needed to corner Commander Leonard about negotiating with her brothers. Konner had rescued her. He'd kept his promise to her. A niggle of family loyalty had crept into her thoughts during the night.

Surely they could find some compromise so that Loki, Konner, and Kim would allow Kat to get a message off to IMP Central for a rescue ship. Perhaps if the O'Haras declared themselves a free and sovereign planet of the Galactic Free Market they could avoid judicial punishment. They might also avoid droves of land-hungry colonists. But they'd never keep everyone out. Progress and contact with the rest of the galaxy were a given.

The mess chief handed her a mug of something that resembled coffee in both flavor and texture. They might call it coffee, but it did not give her the satisfying jolt of the real thing. This roasted root brew was all they had. They'd run out of the coffee beans four months ago. The hydroponics tanks were too small to waste precious space on coffee bushes.

And she'd lost the last tank that might have given them a little leeway in what they grew. Chances of salvaging the tank and the crashed lander were slim. They just did not have enough active fuel cells.

"Welcome back to the land of the living," Commander Leonard said. She smiled brightly and saluted the mess crew with her own mug of hot coffee. For once, she'd left off the dramatic black patch over her left eye. She kept her left lid closed though. The skin around the socket had lost the bruised look. All trace of broken bones around the damaged eye seemed healed.

Kat looked closely into Amanda Leonard's right eye, searching for signs of the harridan who had screamed at her over the comm unit to track *Jupiter*'s explosive demise. Today Commander Leonard looked sane and cheerful, ready and eager to tackle the chores of the day. The captain opened her left eye briefly, then squinted as light penetrated. The blue iris did not track properly and the pupil seemed unnaturally dilated in the morning sunshine.

"It's good to be back," Kat replied cautiously. She looked around suspiciously and found Lieutenant Commander M'Berra hovering close by, as if he didn't want to get too far from Leonard should she begin raving again.

"I look forward to your report, Kat. I think I'll go out with the foragers today. We need . . . things. Time to get to know our new home. Do you have any recommendations where I should start?"

Kat looked down at the shorter woman in surprise. Her captain had not left Base Camp once in the nine months they'd been here. She had not eaten native foods. She had insisted upon strict military discipline, patrols, and watches. And she wore the black patch like a badge of honor—a reminder to one and all that the O'Hara brothers who had wounded her were their enemy. Judicial protocol no longer seemed enough for her. She wanted revenge.

"Perhaps you should get to know the locals in the next village. If we make friends there, they can help us survive. They might even lead us to the O'Haras. It's only a three-hour hike," Kat said. That was a three-hour hike for her, with her long legs and boundless energy—when she didn't have a deep burn on her ankle. For Leonard, the walk would take closer to four or five, especially since she still wore soft ship boots with barely any protective sole.

"The locals. Yes. I have visited them. Perhaps we should renew our acquaintance before we conscript them to plow and plant for us."

"Renew your acquaintance, sir? Conscript?" Kat asked, startled. That sounded very much like a plot to enslave the locals. A plot that had been hatching in Leonard's brain for many months. When had she become acquainted with them in the first place?

"Certainly. Oh, and call me H . . . Amanda, Kat. We have to forge a new society now that *Jupiter* is gone. *My* Marines will help." The captain turned abruptly and ambled over to inspect the hydroponics tanks.

"What happened yesterday while I was gone?" Kat asked the air.

"Nothing unusual," M'Berra replied. He stretched and scratched as he yawned. "I need coffee."

Medic Lotski emerged from M'Berra's cabin. She looked sleep tousled and relaxed for the first time in weeks.

"Nice to see I wasn't the only one who shared a cot last night," Kat murmured.

Gentian emerged from the med cabin. He stretched forward to his full (and considerable) length on his front paws, with his rear and tail high. His talons dug deeply into the packed dirt. Then he slung forward, lowering his back, nose reaching for the sky while he stretched his back legs. This gymnastic maneuver complete he opened his mouth in a huge yawn, revealing very long and sharp teeth. More teeth than any normal cat had a right to have.

Kat watched in horror as the tips of his blue/black wings escaped their protective folds of skin. She didn't know why she had to keep the true nature of this beast secret, but she did.

"What in the nine hells of Perdition's rings is that?" Amanda Leonard screeched and pointed at the cat.

Gentian's wing tips disappeared and the cat slung

to the ground, ears flat against his head, and his nose working overtime.

"He's just a cat who followed me home last night," Kat said. She moved to stand between Gentian and the captain.

"Get out of here! No cats on my ship. No cats, ever, of any kind." Both of Leonard's eyes grew wild, riveted upon the cat. She began to pull at her neat black hair.

M'Berra moved faster than Kat thought possible for a human. He grabbed the captain by the shoulders and shook her. "Snap out of it, Amanda," he commanded in his deep voice that reverberated down Kat's spine.

Sanity returned to Leonard's eyes. She slumped beneath M'Berra's grasp. "My God, what did I do this time?" she whispered. Her left eye closed once more.

"I can't cover for you much longer, Amanda," M'Berra warned. "Let Cheney Lotski treat you."

Kat noted that the medic had worked her way around the campfire behind their captain. She held a hypo spray discreetly behind her back. She came up on Amanda's left, her blind side. How many times had this happened in the last nine months? Kat knew the captain had become increasingly erratic. Now she showed many symptoms of true insanity.

Without the commander, even as a figurehead, the crew had not a chance in the universe to unite and capture the O'Hara brothers' ship *Sirius* to get back to civilization.

Yet, all these months that the crew had been awaiting Amanda Leonard's orders to mount an expedition to capture the three brothers and gain access to *Sirius,* the captain had delayed, stalled, and prevaricated because if she ever did get back to civilization she would no longer have the O'Haras to blame for everything that had gone wrong in her life.

Nor would Kat.

Kat's breath came in short sharp pants. Her chest constricted. She had trouble swallowing that realization.

"No one is going to track down those men unless I lead them," Kat said under her breath. "I'm the only one who can find them. I've got to make plans now."

Would they believe her offer of compromise? Would they even accept her as a legitimate negotiator for *Jupiter*'s captain and crew?

* * *

Hanassa withdrew reluctantly from the Amanda woman. She had accepted his strength and insight without much struggle. But he could only push her so far before the black man and the medic drugged her body senseless. Perhaps Amanda Leonard was not the proper person to host his body.

He decided he'd like to be a woman this time. Their bodies responded to external stimulation with so much more awareness than a man's. Sex within one of them might prove very interesting and much more satisfying than the quick release granted to males.

He needed to look around some more, though. The Cyndi body still seemed the most likely person to help him regain control of this world. Not only did she have the cunning to succeed, the Stargods held her hostage. Hanassa wanted proximity to the three brothers.

They were first on his list to be sacrificed to the god Simurgh. He could almost taste their blood, sweetened by revenge.

* * *

"Why are you packing for an extended overland journey when there are aircraft of varying configurations sitting in the next meadow?" the stranger asked Kat. He scratched idly at the bandages where his IVs had penetrated his skin.

Kat looked up from stashing extra socks between other essential items in a survival pack. "Who are you and what business is it of yours?" she snarled at him.

She'd hoped to keep this reconnaissance mission secret from M'Berra and Leonard. But if the stranger knew, then everyone at Base Camp knew.

"Bruce Geralds, Senior." He held out his right hand in greeting while leaning heavily on a crude walking stick with the other.

"Nice to meet you, Geralds. Lieutenant JG Kat Talbot." Kat went back to finding a place for one more pair of clean underwear without shaking his hand.

"Thought you'd be more friendly after we slept together," Geralds said with a smirk.

"We did not . . . well, I guess we did. But that does not make us lovers, or friends, or buddies." She stood up and hefted the weight of the pack. Eighteen kilos. Too heavy. What could she toss?

"Your journey is my business because you are going after the O'Hara brothers. So am I."

"You aren't going anywhere real soon. I saw how cut up your feet are." Kat sank cross-legged to the packed-dirt floor of the cabin she shared with three other women. Resolutely, she began pulling everything out of the pack and inspecting it. Silently, she sorted the contents into three piles: essential, needful, and desirable. Unfortunately, the only thing that fell into the final category was the clean underwear which weighed nearly nothing.

One item at the bottom of the pack had to go with her, just as the braided hair bracelet she wore would always go with her.

"I was hired by Melinda Fortesque to retrieve her husband, Martin Konner O'Hara, in time for their son's fourteenth birthday," Geralds said quietly. "I've missed the due date, but the least I can do is take the man back to his wife so she knows he's not dead."

"Melinda Fortesque? The woman everyone in the galaxy loves to hate?"

"One and the same."

"I thought they were divorced, or the marriage was annulled or something." Kat tried to remember Loki's precise words when he told her they had a nephew.

He'd said that Konner had a son . . . nothing more. Now Konner claimed he'd married Dalleena. Kat had never questioned the legality of that union until now.

"No divorce. No annulment, according to Melinda Fortesque. She paid me very well to find the man she loves. I pride myself on completing my missions."

"You're a Sam Eyeam," Kat said flatly.

He nodded briefly.

"Where's your ship?"

"A dragon blasted my shuttle with fire. Destroyed it completely."

"What about your ship? A shuttle can't withstand a jump, doesn't have enough room inside for a crystal drive to take you through jump."

"I hid my solo merchant vessel behind the moon."

"I'd have found it when I scanned for the *Sirius* from *Jupiter*'s orbit,"

"No, you wouldn't. I stole some technology from

Konner O'Hara. *Son and Heir* is shielded with a confusion field."

"Just like Kim's clearing, and the *Sirius,*" Kat mused. "Come on." She sprang up in one smooth motion. "If you know the technology, then you know how to find a similar field and break through it." She grabbed her pack and his free hand and started marching.

"What's the hurry? You've waited nine months." He dug in his heels and refused to follow her. He had enough strength to keep her from dragging him.

"We are going to take a fighter five hundred klicks south of here. If we don't leave today, some other pilot will make an excuse to fly and use up our dwindling fuel."

"May I walk on my own to the fighter? Slowly?"

"Yes, of course." Her own ankle did not want to hurry either. "I'd better take some more supplies. We might be gone a couple of days."

"Good idea."

"You never said where you have been for nine months and why you came back raving about cannibals." Kat slowed her pace to match his painful hobble across Base Camp to the hydroponics tanks.

"Konner's pet dragon knocked me out and flew me to the extreme west of this island continent. He dumped me with a tribe of wanderers who call themselves Rovers." He clamped his mouth shut and refused to say more.

"How long have you been walking?" She slowed even more.

"Too long." He jerked his hand out of hers.

"Okay, I won't press you. But you have to talk about it sometime. If not to me, then to Lotski or

M'Berra. Or maybe even one of the dragons. You'd be surprised at the wisdom behind their cryptic words."

Irythros had pulled memories from Kat that shifted her entire perspective. Mum and Kat's brothers were not to blame for abandoning her. But if she released her anger toward them, then she had to shift the blame to someone else.

Herself.

"Let's get moving before M'Berra stops us." She forged ahead, leaving Geralds to catch up as best he could.

"You aren't going anywhere today, Kat Talbot." M'Berra stepped squarely between Kat and the food supplies. His black skin gleamed in the spring sunshine. He glared at her. "We mount this expedition as a team, with plans and backup. I've locked up the fuel supplies for all of the aircraft. No one goes off on their own. Even you, Kat."

"I was only going to do reconnaissance," she protested.

"Not alone and not without backup."

"But . . ."

"No buts. I am in charge now and we are going to do this right. I have my own plans for the O'Hara brothers. Now get your butt back to the med cabin. Neither of you are cleared for any activity until Lotski gives the okay."

Kat hesitated. Frantically, she sought an argument to convince her senior officer.

"Move it, Kat, or I'll carry you back to your bed and lock you in."

CHAPTER 16

"WHAT KIND OF SUMMER vacation is this? Your mom said you had homework. *Homework!*" Bruce exploded into Martin's suite followed closely by Jane, Kurt, and, of course, Quinn. They all looked damp, as if just emerging from the pool.

"Melinda never takes a vacation and doesn't see why I need one," Martin explained as he fiddled with the programming of his pet project.

Machine language marched across the holo screen in an arcane order that only Martin understood.

Kurt stared openmouthed at the symbols. "What in the name of the Holy Mother is that?"

Martin closed the programming window, then stood up from his Lazy-former®. "Scaramouch, show latest shipping route map," he told his personal computer.

"Scaramouch?" Quinn lifted one eyebrow in query.

"Personal hero," Bruce replied. His mouth worked as he suppressed a giggle. "Marty'd be a rated fencing champ in foil and epeé if Melinda ever let him off planet long enough to compete."

Martin smiled, too. He hadn't had much to laugh about these last nine months. Ever since he'd discovered just how long Bruce's father had worked for Melinda and how much he got paid. No wonder a Sam Eyeam had enough money to send Bruce to the most exclusive summer camp in the empire.

He turned his attention back to the holo screen where his friends stood silently while two fencing figures moved back and forth across it. Their blades thrust, parried, riposted, parried again, back and forth, back and forth. Quinn stepped closer and examined the silent images.

"Did you program this?" he asked Martin.

"Yes," the boy replied.

"I can't fault their technique, or yours." Quinn shook his head in amazement. "I would enjoy a bout with you, Master Martin, if we have time."

"Melinda will give us time. She postponed our tour of the amusement park factory."

"Indefinitely," Jane Q groused. "Do you think she suspects something?"

Martin glared at her. Despite all his security devices, he never knew when and if his mother would hack through them. Nothing in the palace was safe from her scrutiny.

"What is taking so long?" Quinn asked. He began pacing in front of the fencers, mimicking their moves with precision.

"The program is huge, constantly updating data. I had to pull memory and power from every system in the palace—except Melinda's."

At last one of the figures on the screen stabbed his opponent. Realistic blood burst upon the scene as the defeated fencer collapsed. The drops of blood spattered outward, spread, flashed, and became the stars in a three-dimensional, if not proportionally accurate, map of known space. Some of the stars remained red, others turned green or blue. The vast majority remained white.

Quinn walked through the map examining configurations. "Earth," he said pointing to the blue star at the center of the holograph.

Martin nodded.

"So the other blues are GTE." He continued examining the points of light. "That would make GFM green and the Kree Empire red."

"White is uninhabitable or no known valuable resource," Martin added.

They all watched as a group of stars changed from blue to red.

"I guess the war with the Kree is heating up in that sector." Quinn shook his head.

The stars in question flashed green, then blue, and back to red.

"I haven't accessed the map in a few weeks. The data is catching up. That cluster is the Murgatroyd Alliance. Each of the four star systems has a jump point and inhabitable planets. They change hands an average of three times a year," Martin explained. Then he slouched in his Lazy-former® and waited for his friends and Quinn to finish their inspection.

"What are we looking for?" Bruce asked. He traced a chain of green stars that seemed to penetrate GTE space. He whistled in amazement as another star, much closer to Earth, changed from blue to green. The war with the Kree wasn't the only war the GTE had to fight.

"There is a blank spot here," Quinn said pointing to the anomaly Martin had found when he first constructed the map. "It seems a logical extension to explore this area from adjoining sectors."

"What about jump points?" Jane Q asked, spinning around and watching everything in amazement.

"Scaramouch, show last known position of the O'Hara distress beacon," Martin called out.

An orange light appeared dead center in the anomaly.

Quinn whistled again.

"Two beacons were recorded broadcasting from that area. Both ceased to function within a few weeks of each other," Martin explained.

"How did they get in there?" Kurt asked. "That's a lot of empty space in between."

"A lot of unmapped space," Quinn corrected. "A lot of maps were lost three hundred years ago when the old republic collapsed. A lot of human colonies got lost at the same time. We haven't found half of them yet. I wonder . . ." He continued walking around and around the area.

All of them remained silent for several moments, puzzling out a number of questions. While they did, Martin noted that Aurora blinked from blue to green. His mother must be having fun with the diplomatic envoys from Earth.

"Scaramouch, show jump points," Quinn said. The bodyguard kept returning to the blank anomaly, tracing lines from other star systems toward the blinking light of the distress beacon.

Nothing happened.

Martin repeated the order. "The computer is locked on my voice print only."

"Good security. Won't keep a dedicated hacker out, though."

"It will slow them down long enough for the system to alert me to the attempt."

While they spoke, a number of purple lights began blinking. Delicate trails of violet mist connected them in an intricate web.

Jane traced one of the trails, eyes wide in awe at the amount of space the jump point had to fold between one end and the other.

At the edge of the vacant anomaly, a violet smudge wandered randomly around the sector.

Quinn's gaze riveted on the smudge.

"That isn't supposed to happen." He pointed at the weird jump point.

"Scientists haven't been able to explain the physics of jump points, let alone their existence, since the Kree first used them to invade Earth over five hundred years ago," Martin explained. "Why can't there be an unstable jump point? Why can't there be an entire sector that's been lost to human exploration because the jump point wanders and doesn't show on normal sensors very well?"

"How'd you program your system to find that thing?" Quinn took out his handheld and began making calculations.

"When you eliminate the impossible—like getting a beacon deep into that area without a jump point—what remains, no matter how improbable, must be the truth." Martin smiled.

The program shimmered. Melinda's holo image appeared in the middle of it, clear enough that she looked to be standing there.

"Martin. You will transfer this program to my system immediately," his mother said blandly. "I need to explain some things to my guests."

She disappeared as abruptly as she had appeared.

"Not even a please or thank you?" Quinn asked.

"Melinda gave up manners years ago. Have you got enough data to navigate to the area of the wandering jump point?"

"No. The program is huge. I'd like to copy it to my ship."

"Sorry. It won't copy. I don't know why." Martin did know why, but he could not explain that now. "It transfers in one lump or not all, erasing all trace of itself at its previous location." But the transfers to backup were always incomplete.

"How much time do you have before your mom returns?" Kurt asked. He, too, tapped data into his handheld.

Bruce and Jane whipped out their own instruments.

The door slid open. Melinda stood there, impatiently tapping her foot. "Martin, I know you want to show off for your friends. But I need this program now." She turned away and marched back toward her own quarters.

"She'll want to start seeing it download into her system by the time she gets back to her office."

"Damn. That's not enough time. I need more information." Quinn ran his hands across his scalp, leaving the straight brown hair standing on end in an unruly mass. He suddenly looked vulnerable . . . and more likable.

"I think I've got most of the important stuff memorized. But I've got to start transferring it now. Keep recording as long as possible." Martin moved to the wall controls and reluctantly punched in the codes to send the map to his mother.

* * *

Kat lay fuming on the cot in the med cabin. M'Berra had ordered restraints to keep Kat from taking off on her own. The first officer from *Jupiter* didn't trust her. With good cause. She had no intention of remaining in camp any longer than it would take her to find a way out of the webbed fabric straps holding her wrists to the cot.

If put to the choice, she wasn't sure she could

choose between the welfare of her crew or the freedom of her brothers. All she truly wanted was a chance to get back to civilization.

At the moment it looked as if she might have to do that all on her own.

Even Gentian had deserted her. The flywacket had curled up against Bruce Geralds' feet and started purring.

Kat worried the straps with her mind as well as friction against the smooth metal cot frame. Once she'd opened electronic force bracelets with her mind. That time, Loki O'Hara had used the criminal restraints on her to keep her from blocking his and his brothers' sabotage of *Jupiter.*

How had she done it? She stopped wiggling for a moment to think. Her mind whirled with a dozen images of that long day sitting in the passageway near the shuttle bays and cargo holds of *Jupiter.* The gravity had been uncomfortably heavy in the outer reaches of the spinning ship. She and Loki had talked quietly about their childhood together before the disaster that had separated them. Kim had sat with them, nursing a numb leg—she had shot him with a stunner. Konner had spent that time stealing the king stone from the crystal array. Without the king stone the ship's power grid went berserk, orbit had decayed, communications had been severed.

Later, Loki had stolen the rest of the array for some unknown purpose, further disrupting the ship's power. Discipline had broken down when Judge Balinakas had ordered evacuation, overriding commander Leonard's attempts to keep the ship working. He'd used the short time the captain had been unconscious as a result of a fight with Konner O'Hara—the fight that had cost her the use of her left eye—to assume control. The rivalry between the judicial personnel and ship's crew had plagued Leonard ever since she took command of the judicial cruiser. Balinakas had triumphed at that moment, but not totally.

He and his people—lawyers, clerks, and anthropologists—had never found their way to Base Camp to fully assume command over the crew. The Marines—the enforcement arm of both the ship's crew and the judiciary—had pledged their undying loyalty to Amanda Leonard. Now she had no one to answer to for her insanity other than Jetang M'Berra.

And Kat.

How had Kat managed to open the force bracelets? Why had strips of conductive plastic linked by an electrode responded to her wishes.

Somehow she must have found the precise frequency of the electronic key and then hummed it.

These straps had no electronics. Instead they were woven with spider silk that molded and clung to the skin, and fastened with a molecular bond. They needed a special solvent to open them for reuse. Or a sharp blade. Kat had neither.

In most tasks she had become ambidextrous, but her choice of dominant hand was always the left. Kat took a deep breath and turned her eyes and her mind to the left strap. She concentrated on the nearly invisible overlap and bond.

The longer she stared at the strap the deeper became a pain between her eyes.

(*Use the ley lines,*) the disembodied voice came into the back of her head. (*Ley lines power your magic as the omniscium powers crystals.*)

That was a new thought. Kat knew that omniscium was the key ingredient in the bath for forming the crystal matrix for star drives. But she did not realize that the elusive element also powered them.

Crystals had to be tuned. So, perhaps, did the ley lines. She lay still a moment and tried to open her senses to the "tune" of the mysterious silver-blue lines.

She heard only a faint disharmonic buzz between her ears. Not a buzz. Gentian's loud purr. It was out of harmony with Kat's inner senses.

"Mbbrt?" Gentian woke up with a start. The constant dull roar of his purring ceased abruptly. The big black cat yawned and stretched. Then he jumped off of Geralds' cot and ambled over to Kat's. He butted his head against Kat's fingers for an ear scratch.

"Sorry, Gentian. The fingers don't work right."

The cat reached up and sniffed the straps. He licked Kat's fingertips gently and sniffed some more. The tips of his wings protruded a tiny bit.

Satisfied he knew what to do, Gentian started gnawing at the webbing where it looped around the metal frame of the cot.

"Smart cat," Geralds whispered.

Kat watched the flywacket work at the tough fabric rather than reply.

Geralds sat up and inspected his feet. "What the . . . ?"

Kat watched him twist into new contortions to see his soles. "Care to share the strange phenomena?"

"The cuts are healed." He swung his legs over the side of the cot and tested his weight on his bare feet. "Some of them were quite deep and needed stitches. Now they are closed without traces of scarring. And the stitches fell out."

He bounced up and down on tiptoe then took three dancing steps toward Kat.

"What kind of miracle did your medic work?"

A strange sense of satisfaction radiated out from Gentian, engulfing Kat in goodwill.

Did you have something to do with that? she asked Gentian.

(Ultrasonic waves,) the flywacket replied.

Of course. The original U.S. healing unit was based upon a cat's purr.

"What are you two smiling at?" Geralds asked.

"Nothing important," Kat replied.

Gentian reached up and touched her nose with his. An image of the webbing dissolving flashed through her mind.

"How?"

He showed her again.

She concentrated.

"You want some help with those restraints?" Geralds bent over her.

"I think I have it." With the words came the thought. The strap flopped open.

"Uh . . . uh . . ." Geralds stammered. "How? How did you do that?" He backed away from her, hands at his sides. He looked ready to flee on his newly healed bare feet.

"Magic," she whispered. She tried it again with her right hand. The straps remained firm. Gentian slid under the cot and gnawed on it a bit. His drool coated the bond.

Kat tried concentrating on the strap again. She visualized the bond dissolving—as if the flywacket's saliva was a solvent. The restraint opened.

With a sigh of relief she sat up and worked her ankles free. "Don't suppose you could spare a few of those sonorous purrs on my ankle, Gentian?"

(Later. You need to leave here. Now.)

"Right. It's broad daylight. I suspect M'Berra has posted an armed guard."

The flywacket shook himself all over and poked his nose out the door. He scooted backward at twice the speed, seeking the safety of the shadows beneath Kat's cot.

Kat felt her companion's broadcast of alarm as a cold vibration up her spine. The fine hairs stood on end and her teeth ached from clenching.

Consciously, she relaxed her jaw and approached the doorway. She flattened herself beside the opening and peered out.

Amanda Leonard stood near the center of the village with a long whip in her hand. She snapped the flayed tip against the ground in agitation. Before her stood twenty locals in a loose clump. They faced her proudly, defiance written all over their faces.

"You will obey me," Leonard snarled. "I am master here and I command you to plow and plant my fields." The whip in her hand snaked out and lashed the arm of the nearest local.

Three Marines behind the locals shifted their stun rifles, pointedly removing the safeties.

"We obey only the Stargods and our consciences," a heavily muscled man of middle years said quietly. He did not even look at the welt on his arm. His comrades nodded in agreement.

"Then you will die." Leonard replied, equally calm and quiet. She raised her arm, preparing the whip.

"Stand down, Commander Leonard," Kat commanded. She marched out from the protection of the med cabin. "Slavery and corporal punishment went out with the dark ages. You have broken about six major GTE laws in the last two minutes." She grabbed

Leonard's wrist, controlling the captain's grip on the whip.

Kat's fingers sought the pressure point just below Leonard's thumb that would force her superior officer to open her hand.

"All life is sacred. We don't eat meat because it takes a life, even the life of a mere animal. Just to threaten death is punishable by mind-wipe," she added for emphasis.

"We make our own laws here, Lieutenant Talbot. Now you stand down or face the consequences." A Marine pressed his stun rifle against Kat's jugular.

CHAPTER 17

LOKI GRABBED PAOLA'S hand and lunged for the first foothold he could find. Together, they scrambled to the top of the cliff. Panting and bewildered, Loki searched for a trace of Iianthe, or the desert that had been here a few heartbeats before.

Wild cattle with their spreading horns and shaggy red coats ambled toward them across a verdant plain. Deer and a myriad variety of game dotted the landscape, grazing contentedly.

"Um, Loki," Paola gulped.

He turned around and saw the entire basin filled with clear water. What had been a cliff was now the defining edge of an inland sea.

All of the animals suddenly froze in place. Individuals lifted their muzzles to sniff the air. Some silent communication spread among them. Herds scattered in the blink of an eye. Only the cattle remained. The big bull turned and took a defensive stance while his ladies bunched together, taking turns drinking.

A huge cat—bigger than any wolf or gray cave bear Loki had seen in the land of the Coros—with yellow fur spotted with gray splotches slunk toward the water, alert, wary, predatory. It opened its mouth, revealing saber like teeth as long as Loki's forearm.

He and Paola each reached for daggers and stun guns.

(That will not be necessary,) Iianthe chuckled in the back of Loki's mind.

The lush landscape disappeared in the blink of an eye.

Loki stumbled to his knees. Paola kept her feet but had to extend her arms to find a new balance.

"What happened? We were somewhere else and then back here. What happened, Iianthe!" Loki demanded.

(I gave you a dragon dream of what was; what the Krakatrice have destroyed.)

"A dream?" Loki cocked his head and stared at the dragon, puzzled.

"No dream. I was there. I smelled the water and the grass and the animal musk. That bull was ready to mate. I could smell him five klicks away and so could every cow in the herd," Paola insisted.

(Thus is the power of a dragon dream. We do not give them lightly. The entire nimbus agreed that you needed to see what was in order to understand the true menace of the Krakatrice.)

"Okay, we saw what happens when you deprive a continent of water. Take me back to the city. It's time I organized my ladies into an offensive," Paola said.

"Wait." Loki held up his hand signaling a moment of quiet while he thought. "All animals need water to survive. How do the snakes continue without water?"

(They derive moisture from their prey.)

"But there isn't any prey left!"

Silence from the dragon for many long heartbeats.

(Come. You will see and understand.)

"I want some answers, Iianthe," Loki said. He remained in place, hands on hips, determined to be just as stubborn as the dragon.

(I have not the words. I must show you.)

Fuming, Loki and Paola climbed aboard once more. Iianthe took his time launching into the air and flying south and west. Not so very far, into another huge basin, this time without a lake at the center.

Instead, a tall finger of rock and soil poked up toward the heavens. Around the finger, the matriarch of the Krakatrice coiled her entire length. Her head rested atop the edifice, her tail at its base. She looked about her, a true monarch surveying her queendom.

Loki whistled. "She must be thirty meters long!"

"Wh . . . what is that on the ground?" Paola asked. She closed her eyes and gulped.

Loki looked more closely at the black tangle of snakes surrounding the matriarch's throne. He saw the glisten of white bone and bloody flesh. The Krakatrice had found prey.

Then he spotted a faint trace of silver wing and a blue horn. He gagged. "Jaysus, they've caught a young dragon."

(When our nestlings first learn to fly, they are vulnerable outside the nest,) Iianthe said. His mental voice choked on a sob.

"Those are big snakes. One dragonet will not fill their bellies for long," Paola pointed out. She sounded frightened.

Loki had never seen or heard of anything that could break through her courage. He held her more tightly until he could feel her heartbeat against his own chest. He tried to find comfort for them both in this little sign that they both lived.

(We guard our young carefully. But the matriarch is clever. She can fly. She seduces the young with adventure. She pushes them to fly beyond their strength to return home. Then she strikes. Our numbers grow thin because fewer and fewer of our young mature.)

"Oh, my God!" Paola gasped and turned her face away.

"What?" Loki searched for the source of her distress. He clamped his hand on his dagger, knowing full well the long knife would provide small and inadequate defense against the monsters below.

"Th . . . there." She pointed at the edge of the tangle of snakes without looking.

Loki gagged again as he watched the matriarch strangle with her tail one of the larger snakes. A bevy of her young slithered over the fallen elder and began devouring it.

(After a battle, no matter how many you kill, you will never find the corpse of a Krakatrice.)

"They can't keep this up for long. There aren't enough dragons to feed them for long. They can't cannibalize themselves without endangering their numbers. What then?" Horror began to eat away at Loki's insides. He had a feeling he knew what Iianthe would answer.

(Tomorrow night they will grow hungry again. They will attack the city. Your three-and-one-half-meter walls will not be high enough to keep them out for long.)

"Take me home, I have Amazons and defenses to organize. I think I can devise a manual pump. But a fire hose eludes me. Any idea how to kill the matriarch?" Paola said.

(If I knew I would not be allowed to tell you. Dragons may not kill one of their own.)

"The Krakatrice are not dragons," Loki insisted.

(They are our cousins. We have promised the God of All never to kill one of our own.)

"Then take me home, too. I have to settle the problem of the IMPs before I can divert more resources to help Paola and her Amazons. But I'll set Konner and Kim on the problem of the pump and fire hose. Will you take them to Paola, Iianthe?"

A mental nod of agreement. *(Knowledge is your best weapon. Use what I have shown you today wisely.)*

* * *

Cyndi marched restlessly around the festival pylon. She walked east to west. This was the path the primitives danced during their mating ritual in the early spring.

Cyndi wasn't in the mood to find a mate. She had one waiting for her back home. She thought longingly of her gentle Eric. He didn't have a lot of ambition or political acumen, but he loved her.

Right now she needed some of that quiet love, a soft touch of reassurance, and a listening ear. More than she needed a bath and clean clothes. She'd had more than enough "adventure" to last a lifetime.

She couldn't be sure, but she thought she'd seen a dragon this morning. A big one with royal purple on its wing veins and spinal horns. Only that colored outline had told her she wasn't imagining the shimmering light distortion.

"So, it's true. They do exist," she muttered as she walked.

Dimly, she was aware that the other women watched her warily as they went about their chores. The men had all left at dawn to go fishing.

Gods, she hated fish! But these people knew nothing about combining plants properly for a complete protein. She'd been forced to eat fish just to survive this last winter.

But thinking about slimy, disgusting, and foul fish didn't give her any clues as to how to use a dragon to get home.

They communicated telepathically. They flew high, higher than the human eye could see. Could they tap into the king stone aboard *Sirius* in orbit and get a message home to Eric?

She wiped away a tear of loneliness.

Eric would move the entire force of the empire to find her, once he knew where to look. She knew it in her heart.

So how did she convince a dragon to come to her aid?

If you can hear me, please talk to me, she thought as loud and as hard as she could.

Silence greeted her.

Now she couldn't suppress the tears she had not shed for nine months.

* * *

"Why do you resist me, Kat?" Amanda Leonard asked.

Kat stared back at her former captain. Once more, restraints held her to her cot. This time force bracelets immobilized her limbs rather than simple surgical tape. She forced herself to relax. As soon as Amanda left, Kat would break free. Until she had privacy, she needed to appear docile.

But she would not give this woman the satisfaction of an answer to her ridiculous questions.

Instead, she reached out with her mind to Gentian who cowered in the far corner, beyond Geralds' cot and out of sight of Amanda. Kat sent him reassuring thoughts. She wished she knew why her flywacket feared Amanda, and Amanda disliked—almost to the point of fear—Gentian.

"You know that I am destined to rule this planet." Amanda caressed Kat's face with a horny fingernail.

When had Amanda's fingernails grown so long? When had they become so strong and ugly?

"Interesting. Judge Balinakas thinks he's gong to rule the planet from his stronghold," Geralds remarked. He reclined on his cot, hands behind his head, and studied Amanda through slitted eyes. No force bracelets for him. But then he had not defied Amanda.

"Judge Balinakas!" Amanda screeched. "That bastard has tried to usurp my authority since the day I took command of *Jupiter.* He never acknowledged that a mere judge is an inferior creature to a *captain.*"

Kat bit her cheeks rather than laugh. The judicial branch of the crew aboard a judicial cruiser was supposed to be a self-contained unit. Judge, attorneys—prosecution and defense—clerks, recorders, and even two anthropologists to protect the cultural integrity of outlying planets, dealt with criminals after the Marines captured them. The ship's crew ran the ship. In theory, lines of authority never crossed. Judge Balinakas challenged those lines on a daily basis.

"Balinakas had no right to order evacuation after Konner O'Hara stole the king stone. He has no right to claim any part of this planet as his own. It is mine. All mine." Amanda advanced upon Geralds, claws extended as if to scratch him to death.

"You were in med bay, incapacitated and unable to issue orders," Kat reminded Amanda. "M'Berra was dirtside trying to capture the O'Haras. The judge had the right to evacuate his own people with a contingent of Marines for protection. The rest of the crew panicked and followed the Marines out the door." She kept her voice calm and matter-of-fact.

"Another reason to bring Konner O'Hara and his brothers to my justice. You must lead me to them, Kat." Amanda sat on Kat's cot and ran one hand affectionately through Kat's tangled curls.

"My brothers will face justice eventually." IMP justice, not Amanda's. But Kat would not say that right now. Her life depended upon keeping this woman reasonable and calm.

"We were friends once, Kat. My pretty Kat," Amanda crooned. "You obeyed my orders willingly until Konner O'Hara and his brothers stole your affections."

Kat raised her eyebrows at that. "You were my commanding officer. Of course I obeyed. And I have no affection for the biological family that abandoned me as a child. Governor Talbot and his daughters are my family."

"Remember that. I'll release you when you agree to lead me to Konner O'Hara. I know you know how to find him. I will have my revenge against him for the loss of my eye and the loss of my ship." Amanda stood up and began prowling the cabin restlessly. She picked up vials and instruments at random, abandoning them in different places for some new shiny toy.

"Your eye seems quite recovered," Geralds said from his cot.

"What do you know about it?" Amanda screeched. All traces of calm fled. She arched her taloned fingers menacingly.

"I observe that you have abandoned the patch and that your eye tracks correctly, even if the pupil is misshapen and enlarged," he replied.

"Define misshapen!" Amanda demanded. Her voice descended into reasonable tones once more. But she scrunched her hair with strong hands as if ready to begin tearing it out.

Kat looked a little more closely at Amanda's eyes as the captain passed her cot in her increasingly erratic circuits of the cabin.

Both her pupils had turned into vertical oblongs—much like Gentian's. Her once pale blue eyes had darkened into the same rich purple as the flywacket's.

CHAPTER 18

KIM PROPPED PRYTH higher on her makeshift bolster and offered her a cup of water liberally laced with willow bark and stewed moss. Her skin was hot to the touch, dry and crackly like fallen leaves in a drought.

The old woman turned her head away. "Let me die," she whispered.

"I can't." Kim pressed the water on his patient until she took a tiny sip. "We need you, Pryth. You have to get better. I don't know how this village would survive without you." He didn't add his fears for Hestiia's health and the safe delivery of their baby.

Guilt that he had not been able to heal her kept him at her side every moment that Hestiia did not need him. He'd moved his wife into the big cave here in the village so that she would not be alone if she went into labor.

"Another will rise to take my place. 'Tis always the way." She paused to cough weakly. She no longer had the strength to raise the fluid in her lungs that gradually drowned her.

"No one can take your place. No one has your wisdom and experience." Kim tried again to get her to take a sip.

She closed her eyes and drowsed in his arms.

Slowly, he placed her back against the bolster to let her rest in peace.

Her breathing grew louder and raspier. The labored sounds filled the round hut and pressed against Kim's sanity. The close confines amplified the noise.

Desperate to relieve Pryth of the killing disease, he threw a new handful of aromatic herbs onto the fire. The astringent smell barely masked the rancid odors of sickness and smoke.

He wanted to cough. Didn't dare, lest it rouse the old woman from her much needed rest.

She opened her mouth and coughed long and hard. Her lungs rattled and a gagging sound came from her throat.

Kim rushed to lift her higher and ease the pressures on her chest.

Spasms racked her. Her wasted body lay heavily against him.

He cradled her against his chest trying to impart some of his own strength to her.

At last she quieted.

Kim had to check to make certain she still breathed. Her chest rose and fell shallowly.

He was about to help her lay down again when she turned her big dark eyes on him. The pupils dilated more than usual in the dim room. The black irises seemed to fill the entire space available, even the whites.

Yet there was a strange awareness and intelligence there.

"Hestiia knows everything that I know. Let her grow. Love her enough to allow her the freedom to explore and expand her limits. The flywacket was once hers. She has the ear of the dragons." The old woman's voice took on the overtones of many voices speaking from the past.

"Don't talk, Pryth. You must rest and conserve your strength."

"I must pass on the mantle of my office. Bring Hestiia to me."

She collapsed, unconscious. Each intake of breath sounded loud, like a bell already tolling her death.

Kim crawled out of the hut and nearly ran to where Hestiia basked in the sunshine beside the central fire pit. She had chosen to sit upon a broad rock that seemed to fit her swollen bottom perfectly.

"Prtyth has asked for you, Hes. She has something important to tell you. But you can't go in there. We can't take a chance that you will catch her pneumonia."

"I must go to her." Hestiia levered and heaved herself off the low rock. Her belly seemed to have swollen overnight.

"You are too near your time. It's too dangerous."

"This is more important than the risk." Hestiia turned stubborn eyes upon him.

He tried to stare her down.

Within moments he capitulated and offered his wife his arm. She placed it around her waist to better support her in her rapid waddle across the village center.

"You'll have to help me," she said quietly at the door to Pryth's round hut.

"Are you sure you want to go in there, Hes?"

"I have to. The life of the village depends upon this."

"Upon what?"

"Women's secrets. Women's knowledge. Women's wisdom." Once again she gave him that stubborn look.

He knew better than to fight it. Carefully, he helped

her bend over through the low doorway. Once inside, she dropped to her knees beside the pallet. She placed one hand over Pryth's eyes and the other over her mouth.

The room seemed lighter, less smoky than before. Almost as if the stench of impending death no longer lingered here.

A shaft of sunlight broke through the smoke hole and bathed the two women in an eerie glow.

Kim wanted to back away in atavistic fear.

"You may stay, husband. But you must never repeat what you see, or hear, or feel to any other male. I keep you here because I need your help," Hes whispered.

Instinctively, Kim placed his hand upon her shoulder, imbuing her with whatever strength he could, much as his brothers had given of themselves during the aborted healing spell.

Guilt flooded him again.

Hestiia gave him an impatient glare. "There is no time to indulge in selfish emotions." She sounded a lot like Pryth in that moment.

Kim clamped down on his emotions and tried to concentrate on giving his wife whatever help he could.

Hestiia began to chant in low somber tones.

Kim could not catch the words or even the language. He leaned closer, trying to commit the syllables to memory. They eluded him like mercury globules floating in zero G.

Then the light shifted once more. The sun moved on. The glow around Pryth faded.

A deep aura of bright white and yellow surrounded and filled Hestiia.

Kim almost yanked his hand away, afraid of the eerie light burning his hand as well as his psyche.

Hestiia's chant turned joyful, raising from sonorous tones to a bright song. She lifted her hands from Pryth and raised them high, glorying in this arcane ritual.

Slowly, her aura dimmed to the normal layers of energies Kim detected around every living thing if he tried. He didn't have to work at seeing the pulsing orange, green, and brown of Hestiia's life.

She lowered her hands and her head. Her lips kept moving.

Kim realized that she chanted the prayer for the dead.

Pryth lay quiet, peaceful, and unmoving. Her eyes stared at Hestiia and Kim in love and blessing.

And then she was gone. From one eye blink to the next her life passed into another realm that Kim could not reach.

He braced himself for the terrible experience he had endured when another man had died at his hands many years ago. He'd felt echoes of it before, when others had passed away near him. The need to guide the loosed soul into the beyond remained dormant now. The need to follow that soul did not rise.

He breathed a sigh of relief.

Hestiia slumped against him in exhaustion.

"What happened, love?" he asked, gently caressing away the lines of fatigue on her face.

"She has passed to me the mantle of leadership and wisdom. Everything she knew is now mine, to help me build upon my own experience to guide this village. Everything she learned from her mentor and her mentor before that going back countless generations is mine to tap if I need it." She opened her eyes. They glowed strangely, the pupils huge, as if she still absorbed information through them and they could not open wide enough to accommodate the data.

"This is really strange." Kim's voice shook.

"This is the way of life. The way of women. Come. Help me up. We must prepare her pyre and mourn her properly. But she is not truly gone. She lives in our hearts."

Hestiia clutched her belly as she rose to her feet.

"The baby?"

"Will be fine. Come. We must give the sad news to the village. Tonight we will mourn her death and celebrate her life."

CHAPTER 19

"PRYTH WAS OLD, Konner. Well past the time for her to join her ancestors," Dalleena said quietly.

Konner did his best to ignore her and the sorrowful activity at the center of the village. If he had to dwell on the old wisewoman's death, he'd do it privately, not by gathering wood for her pyre and chanting her ballads and tales with the others.

He blanked his mind to all but the numbers piling up on his handheld. This fuel cell, the one he'd brought to the village last night remained full. The empty one was gone.

Who would steal an empty fuel cell?

"I think, that with the nine remaining cells, I have enough fuel for one trip to *Sirius,*" he said by way of reply to his wife. He reached up from his crouched position to hold Dalleena's hand. "I've got things aboard the mother ship I can use for a pump and fire hose for Paola's Amazons. Once aboard *Sirius* I can properly recharge the fuel cells. But then I have to go. I have to find my son."

"You must not forget your duties to the dead, Konner."

"And what about my duties to the living on the big continent and to my living son?" He could not look at her. The image of Martin, as he'd seen him last, two and one-half Terran years ago, tall for his age with chestnut-brown hair and vivid blue eyes. A softness about his nose and chin reminded Konner of Melinda, but not much else did. In intelligence, vivacity, posture, and stubbornness, Martin was all O'Hara.

Konner's heart ached with emptiness. Even if Dalleena announced right now that she carried his baby, he would always miss Martin, his firstborn. A child he had been forbidden to raise. A child left in the greedy and manipulative clutches of his mother.

Melinda had cheated Konner out of their prenuptial agreement and one million Adols. The Auroran currency was the most stable in the galaxy. She'd cheated Konner out of Martin's life. She had cheated when she bribed a port employee to implant one of Konner's own patented locator beacons aboard *Sirius* and then sold the unique frequency of that beacon to the IMPs.

He had to get Martin away from that woman, even if he had to kidnap the boy.

And yet he hated to leave this place. Hated the thought of abandoning his friends and neighbors, *his people* to the mercies of the IMPs trapped here and the Krakatrice that tyrannized the big continent.

"You will come with me when I leave?" Konner asked.

"Try to leave me behind, Stargod Konner." Dalleena bent to kiss him.

He rose up with her in his arms.

"It's time," Loki said softly. He'd looked worn and weary since he'd returned from his adventures with Paola and Iianthe, just a few hours ago.

Konner and Kim had had to greet him with the news of Pryth's death during his absence.

He stood at the base of the festival pylon. Hestiia

and Poolie, wife of the headman Raaskan, both heavily pregnant, draped vines laden with flowers from the junction at the top of the pylon. Three represented the fertility of the season, the unchanging cycle of birth, life, death: Maiden, Mother, and Crone.

The women seemed strangely calm and accepting of Pryth's passing. More so than Kim did.

"We gather to celebrate the life of one we loved," Taneeo placed a stick on the pyre where Pryth's body lay covered by a wolf pelt. The priest had made a remarkable recovery in the last day.

Except for a hollowness about his eyes and the fragile air of one just risen from a sickbed, Konner would not know from looking at Taneeo that he had lain in a coma for many months, possessed by an alien spirit.

Konner joined Loki and Kim at the base of the pylon, the place of honor to observe the funeral. The villagers expected their Stargods to preside over the ceremony. They'd done this too many times over the winter.

Beginning with Taneeo, each person in the village spoke in turn. "Thank you, Pryth, for your gift of sanity when mine fled," the young priest said and bowed his head. He placed a stick upon the pyre.

"Thank you for curing my child of the croup." That speaker also laid a stick on the pyre.

"Thank you for the love charm." A young man and his bride held hands as they added a bit of wood.

"Thank you . . ."

They all had a reason to thank Pryth for the giving of many gifts when she lived. She'd not be forgotten soon. They each had a reason to share in the grief.

"Thank you for accepting me as I am, and not trying to make me into a clone of someone else." Even Cyndi added a bit to the ritual.

Loki nodded to her with respect as she passed the brothers and moved into the shadows, out of the heart of the village.

"Thank you for making a joke out of my first hunt, which I believed to be a disaster. Now we remember the joy of the campfire rather than the empty bellies," a young warrior said. A chuckle went round the group.

"Thank you for making me a silly hat so that I would feel beautiful at the harvest festival," a scarred woman said as she slipped her hand into that of her husband.

Their mood lightened as they remembered the good times, the laughter, the joy of Pryth's life.

Konner's turn came last. What could he say? He'd known the old woman for less than a year. Others had already thanked Pryth for her courage and her wisdom. What he remembered most about her was the way she pranced about an evening campfire, reciting the legends and history of her people. "Thank you for the gift of song," he said quietly.

"Amen, so be it," Loki and Kim echoed.

Someone broke out a flute and began one of Pryth's favorite tunes, a sprightly march that accompanied the story of how the Stargods had rescued the villagers from Hanassa's sacrificial altar and then led them to a new life. A man took up a drum and added rhythm. A young couple began to dance about the pylon. Headman Raaskan broke out the last keg of beer left from happier and more prosperous times.

They all laughed and danced and celebrated the good things about the woman they had lost.

Almost as an afterthought, as the sun lowered toward night, Taneeo shoved a torch into the pyre.

As the first flames reached greedily for the next layer of branches, Hestiia placed both hands against her swollen belly. Her face turned pale and she bit her lip. "Out of death comes life," she whispered.

The women gathered around her, including Dalleena, hastily urging her toward the nearest cave. They shouted with joy. Kim trailed behind them, lost, anxious, shouting orders that they ignored. At the mouth of the largest cave, where several families dwelled in modest comfort, two women, one of them Yaakke's wife, turned and stopped Kim from entering.

Yaakke seemed to be missing. He, too, had disappeared into the shadows, along with Cyndi right after saying his bit and adding a bit of fuel to the pyre.

"This is women's work," the women said. "Go find something else to do." They backed into the cave and dropped the leather curtain in front of it.

"But . . . but . . ."

"Come, my friend. Let us drink to the birth of your son!" Raaskan clapped Kim on the shoulder and handed him a mug of beer.

"But . . ." Kim looked over his shoulder toward the cave. The men pushed him toward the keg where all the men gathered.

"What can you do that they can't?" Konner asked his brother. "They have a lot more experience with this than we do."

"Experience?" A strange look came over Kim's face. Then buried his expression in the act of taking a long drink. "Yeah, experience."

"Where's Loki?" Konner asked.

No one answered.

"I've read all the medical texts. I know what has to be done," Kim muttered. "I should be there. Experience or no."

"You will be in the way of women who have delivered hundreds of babies." Konner gently prodded his brother in the back. He wondered when it would be Kim's turn to ease Konner away from a birth. "Birth is one of the great mysteries of womanhood. They would be uncomfortable with you in their midst," he advised Kim.

"What if something goes wrong? Hestiia has already miscarried once. I don't know if we could bear to lose another child."

"Think about the positives. We have enough fuel to reach *Sirius*. In a few weeks we'll be telling Mum about her grandchild. I'll be telling Martin about his new cousin."

Inside the cave Hestiia screamed in pain. Poolie came rushing out, face lined with worry. She hurried as much as she could to her own hut where she gathered a bundle of supplies.

"I'm not waiting for her to die," Kim announced. "We're taking *Rover* to get the medic. I don't care if we have to kidnap her. Lotski is coming back to save my wife." He marched resolutely toward the shuttle.

Konner hastened in his wake, unable to deny his brother this small comfort. Even though it meant waiting another week or four to refuel again. He'd figure out something to cobble together a pump and fire hose for Paola.

He'd waited nine months to rescue his son. What difference could a few more weeks make?

But he wished he knew who had sabotaged the fuel cells and then stolen the empty one. That could delay him even longer if the thief got smart and struck again.

* * *

Kat made a point of limping heavily as a Marine escorted her back to the med cabin from the latrine.

She wanted them to underestimate her until she was ready to make a break.

Sergeant Kent Brewster, Kat's friend and the man who had kept their equipment running longer than anyone dared hope, stood at the edge of the camp with an armload of lily bulbs ready to be roasted for supper. An armed Marine stood next to him. Brewster paused and offered an arm for Kat to lean on. The guard prodded him forward with the butt of his stun rifle.

Brewster stumbled out of Kat's reach. He recovered clumsily, dropping half of the lilies. He shrugged at Kat and grinned on one side of his mouth. The other side seemed bruised and painful. He, too, had been forced to comply with Commander Leonard's new regime.

"Where is M'Berra?" Kat asked casually, within Brewster's hearing.

"Occupied," her Marine barked.

Brewster shook his head slightly.

So the second-in-command had opposed Leonard and found himself imprisoned or coerced.

What had happened to Leonard to make her snap? Her insanity had been growing for months. The explosion of *Jupiter* must have been the last straw.

But that didn't explain the changes in her eyes and horny hands.

"I never would have thought she'd become a despot," Kat muttered. "*My* captain was always fair and observed the rules and regs meticulously. Slavery is not legal, moral, or ethical."

"Shut your yap, or I'll shut it for you." The Marine prodded her with the muzzle of his stun rifle.

Kat marched forward, her mind numb. She knew

she had to do something to end this. She *should* do something. But what?

Inside the med cabin, Gentian cowered beneath Kat's cot. Geralds appeared to be sleeping. Her heart warmed at the thought of Gentian climbing into her lap and working his healing purrs. She'd only been with the creature a day and she already felt a part of him, lost when he didn't follow her out on the simple errand of a trip to the latrine. She'd really used the excuse to scout the progress of Amanda and her slaves. Gentian's sensitive nose and ears would have given her more information than her own limited senses.

Leonard's whip cut through the air with a teeth-grating snap. A man moaned.

"Work harder, every last dregging one of you, or you'll feel more of this," Leonard commanded, as she cracked the whip again. She sounded almost reasonable. "I need these fields cleared, plowed, and planted by sunset." Not a reasonable order.

The Marine clasped the force bracelets around Kat's wrists and ankles. Then he shut the door firmly behind him as he exited. "We'll feed you at sunset if you behave yourself," he growled.

She heard him latch it with the simple loop of rope around a peg.

"Presumptive of him to think that lock and those bracelets will keep you in," Geralds commented. He slid his hands behind his head and surveyed the cabin. A casual observer might think him nonchalant.

Kat saw the tension in his back and legs. He was ready to fly off the cot and into action in a heartbeat.

She found a note in the back of her throat and hummed it. Her mind pictured the force bracelets opening. They fell away from her hands and feet. This was easy compared to the medical restraints.

Amazing how easy this magic stuff came to her now that she didn't fight it. Now that she had Gentian's senses and perceptions linked to her own.

"Now what do we do?" Kat prowled the cabin, searching for answers as much as an escape. Gentian dogged her heels. But he kept his ideas to himself.

"What do you mean 'we'?" Geralds asked.

"You are as much a prisoner as I am. Don't you want out? Aren't you afraid Leonard will enslave you, too? You are a stranger to her with little or no value but the muscles in your back."

"I've done enough running for a while. I think I need to sleep some more. At least until dark."

Kat peered out the tiny window in the back wall. She watched the locals trudge through the fields dragging a plow, two men acting as draft animals while a third guided the plow. Five more men, with an armed guard, approached the far meadow beyond the wetlands. They carried ropes and stalked the wild cattle. A new bull had moved in and taken over the herd since last autumn. Brewster had shot the old bull after it charged him and Dallenna. Dallenna had been seriously hurt by the charging animal. Brewster—as usual—had avoided injury. Nothing seemed to touch that man.

Where was he?

"Leonard has close to one hundred men loyal to her. They are all heavily armed and eager for a fight," Kat muttered.

Gentian flashed her an image of every weapons stash in Base Camp. She instantly knew by smell who carried fully charged weapons and who had empty ones just for show. Recharging them had proved just as difficult as keeping any of the other equipment running. But those weapons had priority with Amanda Leonard. Gentian had seen fuel cells stolen from fighters and landers hooked up to spare weapons.

Grateful for the information, Kat reached down and scritched Gentian's ears.

"I wouldn't want to tackle those Marines in the *daylight*." Did Geralds put extra emphasis on the last word?

"Neither would I. I wonder if they are going to break some more taboos by killing and eating one of the cows." The previous bull had made several fine meals for the crew who rapidly lost all their inhibitions about eating meat. They seemed also to have lost their belief in the GTE law never to take a life, any life, even the life of an animal for food.

"If they eat a heavy meal full of meat they will be sleepy and sluggish," Geralds commented.

"So they will," Kat replied. The beginning of an idea tickled her mind.

She sank back onto her cot, checked to make certain her backpack was beneath it and stretched out. Gentian jumped into her lap. He didn't purr. He didn't make a sound. He just quivered in fear.

"We'll think of something, Gentian. I promise."

They both fell asleep.

CHAPTER 20

KIM FELT THE SUN set behind the mountains at his back. The rhythm of day shifting into night settled into his bones. His hearing sharpened as his eyesight closed down in the reduced light. He heard a few frogs croak in the wetlands south of Base Camp—nowhere near as many frogs as a year ago.

Last year, too many frogs had carried a plague. But Konner had seeded the swamp with selenium to neutralize the bioengineered disease. Another reason the locals had named the three brothers Stargods.

Now Kim and his brothers had to live up to their expectations and the responsibility.

Crickets joined the gentle chorus and a night bird added syncopation. Kim's heart beat in rhythm with the land. He shifted to a more comfortable position, lying prone at the edge of a rise just west of Base Camp.

At the back of his mind, a knot of worry threatened his need to meld with the planet. He knew Hestiia labored long and hard. The faint disquiet in his gut became a roiling cramp.

He clenched his teeth and breathed slowly, desperately trying to master the pain in himself and in his wife.

All his focus had to remain on liberating Medic Lotski and as many medical supplies as he and his brothers could. He hoped the ten warriors along with his brothers would be enough manpower.

Commander Leonard had one hundred Marines.

"Look!" Loki pointed toward the fields near the wetlands. "They're driving *our* villagers with stun weapons and whips." He gnashed his teeth.

"Are you saying only we can enslave those people?" Konner asked with wry amusement.

"No, I am saying that after we went to the trouble of liberating them, no one has the right to enslave our people," Loki reiterated.

"They have my father," Yaakke said. He half rose from his crouched position in the long meadow grasses. He'd inserted himself into the pack of men after the funeral. Kim didn't know how he'd occupied himself during the ceremony.

"Not for long." Kim pulled Hestiia's brother back down into hiding. "But it won't help our cause if they catch you, too. We have to think this through. There are more of them than of us. And they are better armed."

"But we are meaner," Loki said. A hard glint came into his eyes devoid of the mischief he usually exhibited before a brawl.

"I wouldn't count on that," Konner said. He pointed to the woman who drove the slaves with a whip. "That's Amanda Leonard. She has several grudges against me—and us."

"This could be a trap to lure us in," Kim mused. "Kat knows that we will feel honor bound to rescue our people." Trap or no, he had to get into camp tonight and get the medic out. Hes needed help from a professional, not just the accumulated experience of several women of childbearing age. He had trouble believing Pryth had transferred her wisdom to Hestiia, even though he'd witnessed the magical ritual and given the women enough of his bodily strength to complete the procedure.

"I don't think Kat would . . ."

"Wouldn't she?" Loki returned. "Last time I saw our sister, after the battle for the crystal array in the autumn, she had all the weapons of a lander loaded and ready to kill the three of us, if she could find us." Finally, he let loose his old familiar grin of mischief, eager for a fight.

"No, you aren't thinking what I think you're thinking." Konner's face also split in a big smile.

"Give our baby sister some comeuppance?" Loki was enjoying this too much, not focusing on the real problem of the enslaved locals and the need to take the medic back to the village.

"Chances are that Chaney Lotski will be in the med cabin," Kim changed the subject.

"*Our* cabin," Loki growled.

"So how do we get in?" Kim nibbled on a bit of Tambootie, willing the drug to enhance his night vision.

"We need to work around the perimeter to the east," Konner whispered. "Approach from the back."

"Patrols are heaviest there," Kim reminded him. As he spoke, he watched an armed Marine pace the east end of the village. He held his stun rifle restlessly, more than ready to shoot something.

"They are expecting an attack from the coastal village, to liberate the slaves," Loki surmised. "I would."

"How about the north end, from the river?" Kim watched one man leaning against a tree by the boat launch.

"Possible." Loki held his hand out to Kim for a bit of the Tambootie.

Kim gave him a leaf fragment, regretting immediately he had not brought more. He always needed more. Each dose had to be larger than the last to gain the same effect.

"Then again," Loki mused as he nibbled, "maybe we should just walk right in through the front door." He rose from his prone position to a crouch. Obscured by the long meadow grass, he dashed toward the end of the line of slaves.

Kim shrugged and followed. Why not? He and his brothers were as ragged and dirty as the exhausted men who trudged in from the fields.

"The rest of you stay put until the time is right. Keep *Rover* safe at all costs," Kim whispered to their gathered men.

"I doubt those arrogant Marines know every one of their slaves on sight," Konner whispered.

"They might even feed us," Loki said, now in line behind the last slave.

"Do not count on the bitch doing anything for our well-being. She is worse than Hanassa," said Yaaccob, the village headman and father to Hestiia and Yaakke, two places up the line from Loki and Kim.

"Hanassa?" Kim asked. He kept his head down as a guard wandered the length of the line of twenty-five, now twenty-nine, slaves. "Is it possible?" he whispered to his brothers once the guard had passed on.

"Anything is possible," Loki replied. "But my money is now on Cyndi as the dragon's host."

"Neither woman is of Hanassa's blood," Yaaccob reminded them.

"Is that required?" Kim asked. He wished Iianthe, the purple-tip dragon was around to answer some questions.

(You have but to ask,) a deep and melodic voice came into the back of his head.

"Does Hanassa need a body of his own lineage to transfer his spirit?" Kim asked subvocally.

(Trust no one who has touched the one we cannot name, or been touched by him.) An angry flurry of wings signaled the end of the conversation.

The wind from his passage swirled about them, gathering dust and dried leaves in its wake.

The entire line of slaves ducked and covered their heads with their arms. All of the guards scanned the skies with rifles aimed upward.

"When you decide to piss off a dragon, you do it in spades," Loki whistled through his teeth.

"I did not realize Iianthe was so near. I should have felt his presence in my mind," Kim said.

"Get back in line, all of you!" snapped the nearest guard.

Amanda Leonard snapped her whip to emphasize the order.

"Gather around the fire. All of you," she said, most pleasantly. "I have a little surprise for you."

"I don't like surprises," Kim muttered.

"Silence!" barked the guard. "You will listen and obey our beloved captain."

Kim grimaced. The Marine's eyes burned with the light of fanaticism. They'd have a hard time breaking the captain's hold on her followers.

"Bring out the women," Amanda Leonard ordered quite loudly, as if she wanted everyone within a kilometer's distance to hear and understand what she intended.

A growl of pained anger rose from the throats of twenty-five enslaved men.

"Silence!" Leonard cracked her whip. An older man slumped in the middle of the line, clutching his naked chest.

Kim stepped toward him. His hands ached to touch and heal the red welt running diagonal across the man's chest. Blood oozed from the top end of the wound. Kim's entire torso burned in sympathetic agony.

"Stay put," Loki hissed. He held Kim back with a fierce grip upon his elbow. "She'll recognize you."

"But . . ."

"Not yet. We have to think, have to come up with a plan."

"Where's Kat?" Konner asked.

"Haven't seen her," Kim replied. Scanning the Base Camp inhabitants gave him something to do other than fretting over the wounded man he dared not help.

"I can't find Lotski either," Loki said.

"We need Lotski. Hestiia can't last much longer. She's been in labor for hours. I don't know how to use my magic to help her."

Just then, three armed Marines led out seven local women, all stripped to the waist, wearing nothing but their summer sarongs slung about their hips. They kept their eyes lowered, away from their husbands, brothers, and fathers among the male slaves. One young woman, barely sixteen, trembled and blushed in shame.

"I understand that when my people first landed here, that you primitive barbarians enticed them with food, strong drink, and promises of sex." Amanda Leonard began pacing. She coiled her whip and tapped her leg with the handle in rhythm with her steps.

Kim blanched at the reminder of the subterfuge he and his brothers had concocted in order to strand the three hundred crew members on this planet, so they could never, ever reveal its location to the Galactic

Terran Empire. They could not risk that the GTE would leave the planet unpolluted or politically free.

Civilization and its conveniences carried a price.

"If my people are to be believed, and they always tell the truth," Leonard continued her pronouncements and her prowl. Behind her, an entire squad of Marines smirked at her statement, giving the lie to her words.

"None of them got lucky that night." Leonard whirled to face the slaves. Her eyes accused them of betrayal. "Not one of them got lucky. So tonight they will. With your women. While you watch."

"That is enough." The door to the big cabin flew open with a bang. Kat stalked out. Her eyes blazed greener than the green bonfire. Her long strides gobbled up the space between herself and her captain.

"Stand down, Lieutenant," Leonard barked.

"No. I renounce your authority to give illegal orders." She took a deep breath and speared the commander with the icy fire of her gaze. "I deny your sanity. I refuse to obey you, Commander Amanda Leonard. I, Lieutenant JG Mari Kathleen O'Hara Talbot order all those who still honor the laws and ideals of His Majesty's Imperial Military Police and the Galactic Terran Empire to lay down their weapons and lock you up until a rescue ship arrives or your wits and morals return."

As one, fifty stun rifles locked and loaded. As one, all fifty turned their aim toward Kat.

CHAPTER 21

"GENTIAN, YOU WANT to provide a distraction that will allow us to get out of here?" Kat asked. She tried to keep her eye on all of the Marines. There were too many of them.

(No,) Gentian squeaked. He scooted farther into the shadows.

"Please. I really need some help."

The flywacket sighed.

Kat sensed his fear. Finally, he emerged from the med cabin, body low, ears flat against his head, tail twitching nervously, Kat's pack in his mouth. One step outside he spread his magnificent black feathered wings, let loose a yowl, and launched himself into the air.

The pack dropped neatly at Kat's feet. The flywacket knew how much she treasured the item in the bottom.

The slave women dropped to the ground shrieking.

"Plague bringer!" Yaaccob, the village elder, shouted. "Shoot the plague bringer." He dove for the nearest Marine, trying to wrestle the stun rifle from his hands. He smiled hugely. "You must shoot the plague bringer!"

"What is happening here?" Amanda Leonard commanded. She sounded almost like her old self, rather than the insane despot she had become.

"I did not just see that." Geralds hugged himself in the doorway. "I have seen some mighty weird things since landing on this planet, but that takes the stardust."

His comments went unnoticed in the chaos that followed. Kat noted that the slave men all seemed to have engaged Marines in close combat, trying to take control of the weapons.

"That's a good enough distraction for me," Kat said. She grabbed her pack and then Geralds by the arm and ran toward the nearest aircraft south of Base Camp.

"Where's Lotski?" A voice rang out. It sounded very much like one of her brothers. Kim by the tenor quality.

"I should have known those three would be involved in this," she grumbled.

"Those three? The O'Haras?" Geralds stopped dead in his track. "If Konner is there . . ."

"We've got to get out of here. Capturing Konner is no good unless we are free to leave the planet." She yanked him into a stumbling jog. Not that she was sure she'd let anyone capture Konner. He and Dalleena had rescued her from the snake monsters. Then he had kept his promise to deliver her back to Base Camp.

She owed Konner.

Besides, Geralds hadn't earned her trust even if he was a dregging attractive man.

Ahead lay the shadowed mounds of several small aircraft at rest. Kat jumped into the first, a one-man fighter that could almost accommodate a second small person crouched behind the pilot's seat. She slammed her palm against the manual override and hit the ignition.

A red light blinked in silence. The engines remained dead. She tried the ignition again. The red light blinked faster—almost louder.

"No fuel!" she screamed at the inanimate machine.

"M'Berra said he'd locked up the fuel cells to keep you grounded," Geralds reminded her.

Kat let loose a string of curses she didn't realize she knew. And would never knowingly use in mixed company.

Geralds chuckled from the ground outside the cockpit. "I admire your independent spirit. But that won't fuel the plane."

"With me, Kat," Konner called. He let loose an indiscriminate spray of stunner fire.

Kat scrambled out of the fighter. "Have you got a dragon? she asked, taking the stun pistol he offered and blanketing Base Camp with energy bolts.

"Better, I've got *Rover,* the shuttle."

"Got room for two more?" she asked. Then she threw herself onto the ground, just beneath return fire from the Marines.

"We'll manage." Konner shot a wide blast and sprinted away from Base Camp.

Kat followed. She shoved Geralds hard to make him keep up with her.

She thought she saw a glimmer of a blue ley line in the moonlight. Desperate to get free of Amanda Leonard and her fanatical followers, Kat veered her path to stand upon the line. Then she turned and fired blindly four times.

Four Marines slumped to the ground.

She grinned and continued to run after her brother and Geralds.

Angry shouts and curses and the pounding of heavy feet against the land erupted behind her. Many booted feet. She risked a glance over her shoulder. Kim followed her, shooting at a phalanx of pursuing Marines, Amanda Leonard in the lead.

He, too, sought to stand upon the ley line for his next shot.

Kat watched as three blasts in a row from Kim's gun hit the captain square in the chest. Amanda Leonard should have fallen unconscious with the first.

She kept plowing forward, her whip in her hand and a murderous gleam in her eyes.

Kat shuddered in fear and disbelief.

Then Loki roared through the squad of uniformed men and women, the familiar figure of Medic Chaney Lotski thrown over his shoulder. Jetang M'Berra ran hot on their heels, also firing a weapon into the midst of their shipmates—now enemies.

Three natives armed with clubs and spears guarded the open hatch of the family shuttle. Kat did not question their presence; she dove onto the deck, then scrambled as far into the cabin as she could to make way for the others.

Gentian swooped in and landed beside Kat. He did his best to hide behind her along with the pack she had forgotten while trying to start the fighter.

One by one, Geralds and her brothers followed. Konner had the shuttle fired up and rolling before Loki threw his prisoner onto the deck and hopped aboard. M'Berra came last, still laying down cover fire while the natives took their places in the shuttle.

Kat slapped the hatch control before M'Berra had his feet all the way in. The portal irised closed, slowly. Too slowly.

A stunner blast shot through the partial opening. One of the natives slumped to the deck.

The engines roared louder. The shuttle lifted off,

leaving Amanda Leonard and her faithful followers jumping, screaming, and shooting uselessly at the cerama/metal hull.

"I guess this makes you one of us again," Kim said with a grin. "An outlaw on the run from the IMPs."

"I guess it does." Kat sank onto the cushioned bench of the cabin. All her hopes and dreams for military advancement, her happy, *civilized* life had just gone up in smoke.

If she ever got back to civilization and the people she called friends and family.

For good or ill, she was stuck with the brothers she had disowned for twenty years.

"I guess I'm back in the family again. For good or ill."

* * *

We have concerns about the flywacket who must prove himself. His courage lacks conviction. He reacts only when prodded by the one he must guide. He does not take action on his own. The one he must guide does not seek his advice. She follows her own path. We must make certain she stays on the correct one now that she has found it. We know now that the flywacket will not push her; he will not fulfill his destiny. Should we recall him now or later? Later might be too late.

* * *

Hanassa screamed curses long and fluently at the retreating glow from the shuttle's engines. The voice of his host body sounded harsh, cracking from overuse.

"Simurgh take you all. I will find you. I will follow you and I will kill you one and all!"

His body suddenly grew faint from hunger. Only blood would satisfy the dragon within.

He turned and examined the Marines who had failed to recapture Kat and the brothers.

"One of you will die."

They backed away, bringing their useless guns to bear.

"You failed me. I will have blood. Only blood will pay for your betrayal."

The mind of the one he possessed tried to claw her way through him, trying to put a halt to the bloodlust that drove him.

He recognized the logic behind her demand.

"Bring me a slave," Hanassa ordered the contingent of Marines. "For every day that Lieutenant Talbot remains at large, a slave will die. By day after tomorrow the natives will bring me all three of the Stargods and their treacherous sister and be glad to sacrifice them to me."

"We could send a fighter after them. Shoot them down," a corporal offered.

"Do not waste the fuel. The natives will bring the offenders to me."

The three men who stood closest to her smiled and their eyes lit with enthusiasm for the plan.

The others melted into the shadows.

Hanassa returned to Base Camp and retreated into the med cabin, the largest and finest of all the structures left behind by the O'Hara brothers. This building was now his home. From here he would rule.

But first he had to put Amanda's body to bed while he went hunting for a way to get closer to his enemies.

CHAPTER 22

"KEEP YOUR BACK turned to me while you watch the door, Bruce," Martin instructed his friend.

"I don't see why," Bruce grumbled. "We're friends. We're not supposed to have secrets from each other."

"Believe me, you do not want to know what I'm doing if Melinda ever gets hold of you." Martin sank his right arm up to the elbow into the guts of his computer. He'd had to put the entire system to sleep, including the systems he'd borrowed memory and power from, for this surgical operation. Otherwise, Melinda could monitor his activities too easily.

The wall panel lay at his feet. The bottom of the secret compartment was deep. He had only recently grown tall enough to reach it without a step stool.

He groped with his fingers, feeling for the treasure he'd secreted here months ago.

"That's another thing, Marty. You never call her 'Mom' or 'Mother.' You always use her name, like she was your sister or an impersonal guardian." Bruce shifted anxiously from foot to foot, gaze riveted on the door.

"Her rules. No reminder that she has blood or emotional ties to me. That would make her vulnerable through me. She also likes to thinks she is younger and therefore more attractive than the mother of a teenager."

Ah, there. His fingers brushed against the cool blue crystal he sought. A faint tingling progressed up his hand to his arm and shoulder. Suddenly, his eyes found a new focus as if seeing the crystal nestled into its bed of fiber optics as well as the scene in his room.

Dizzy for a moment, he lost his grip upon the crystal and grabbed something else. He withdrew a palm-sized clamp.

"Is that what I think it is?" Bruce whistled and grabbed the device.

"Yes. It's an illegal Klip. Melinda put it on my computer to drain power and monitor everything I do."

"Then how did you keep our correspondence secret?" Bruce examined the Klip closely, memorizing its construction.

Martin smiled and reached again into the wall compartment. "Will you get back to the door?"

"You mean you've got more in there than just this?" Bruce's eyes went wide with awe. He shook his head. "This is amazing. You've got a mind to match your m . . ."

Martin glared at his friend as he grasped the blue crystal—even more illegal than the Klip.

Bruce docilely returned to his vigil at the doorway. He slipped the Klip into his pocket and seemed to forget it.

Martin grabbed the crystal and yanked it free of its fiber optic connections. Without this, the star map only reached half its true potential. He didn't need the map anymore. He had the proximity coordinates of the wandering jump point firmly in his mind.

"Will you hurry up, Marty," Bruce said. He continued to peer into the hallway looking for potential intruders. "Jane and Kurt are waiting for us. We'll miss the best part of the factory tour. I really want to see how they program the virtual reality scenes into the rides without requiring headgear."

Bruce turned around again.

Martin slipped the crystal into his pocket. It was about as big around and as long as his index finger. He had to keep his hand around it to disguise the telltale shape in his formfitting synthleather slacks interlaced with heat deflector threads. They made his long legs look even longer and, he hoped, gave the illusion that he was taller than he already was.

Bruce always opted for the baggy pantaloons, which made his square body seem bulkier. But the drapes and folds of fabric could hide a myriad of secret pockets and gadgets.

Martin needed to find a better place to secrete the crystal—a gift from his father, Konner O'Hara. He rubbed it idly.

His focus shifted again. The room seemed to tilt to the left and colors took on new depth and brightness.

He stumbled, not certain where the floor truly was or which way was up.

Bruce jumped to hold his arm and keep him upright. "You feeling all right, Marty? You look kind of pale. Maybe we should postpone the tour of the factory."

"No. We have to go today. It's the only time Melinda will let me out of the palace without her. She's tied up with those dippos from Earth. We *have* to go today." He couldn't tolerate another day of being his mother's prisoner. In another day she might figure out just how incomplete the star map appeared on her system and come looking for answers.

They took two steps together, Martin leaning heavily on Bruce. Either the world righted or he got used to the strange slant to his perceptions. Then he shook himself free of his friend's support and marched to the hallway. They'd meet Quinn and the others at the side entrance near the garages. Just a short distance, then he could sit and think about the crystal and what it did to him. What the miniature king stone did to his computer. Did it have something to do with the way a full-sized king stone reacted with the rest of a crystal array to power spaceships and take them through jump points?

He almost giggled at the thought of flying through a jump point wearing nothing but an EVA suit and the little crystal that warmed to his touch and seemed to snuggle into his hand. Crystals were monopoles—no north or south to their magnetism, just their own internal forces. Perhaps he was a monopole, too. Separate, they were lost. Together, they were a family.

"Where are you going, Master Martin?" An armed security guard at the side door jerked Martin out of his strange looping thoughts and back to reality.

"My mother authorized a field trip to the amusement park factory." Melinda might not like being reminded that Martin was her son, but it never hurt to keep that in the front of any conversation with her employees.

"My orders say that trip was canceled. Ms. Fortesque wants you to join her for lunch with her guests from Earth. I'll just escort you to the formal dining room. Your friends are free to take the tour without you if they choose, or they may dine in the family parlor." The guard grabbed Martin by the elbow and propelled him back down the corridor the way they had come.

CHAPTER 23

"WHO ARE YOU REALLY, Sam Eyeam?" Konner asked the stranger who had followed Kat so faithfully into *Rover;* the man who had brought one of Melinda Fortesque's beacons to this planet and then disappeared. He almost did not recognize the man with his scraggly beard and hair. He'd know those straight white teeth, those perceptive hazel eyes, and that blade of a nose anywhere, though.

Konner made an adjustment to their altitude. The extra bodies in *Rover* made their flight home slow and ponderous. Too slow. The IMPs could probably fuel up one of their fighters and get it airborne before *Rover* landed and cloaked.

The Sam Eyeam shrugged. "I am who I am. I do what I do."

Kat almost doubled over in laughter at that answer. But her mirth carried the edge of hysteria. She held the flywacket too tightly, almost crushing the big cat with both arms wrapped around it. The flywacket didn't seem to object.

"What's the joke, baby sister?" Konner asked, only slightly pleased at the emergence of her sense of humor. He wanted answers before they reached the village at the base of the cliff. Answers to questions and solutions to dilemmas.

"You might as well tell him, Bruce. If he can't pry

the answers out of you, he'll turn Loki loose on your mind with his telepathy," Kat said. She sounded as if she only half believed her words.

"Take over the controls, Loki," Konner said. "And don't deviate from the flight plan. We can dispatch a dragon later to check on Paola and her Amazons." As soon as his older brother transferred the operation of the shuttle to his station, Konner swung his chair around to face his sister and the Sam Eyeam in the cockpit of the shuttle.

"There is no such thing as telepathy," the stranger said quietly.

Konner and Kat both cocked their left eyebrows at him.

"But on this planet, with flying cats and dragons and such, maybe . . ." His words drifted off as Konner and Kat continued to gaze at him fixedly.

"You mean . . . ?" he choked.

"Yes," Konner replied quietly. "Psi powers work here. Maybe not elsewhere, but on this planet they do."

"It's the ley lines," Kat added.

"My name is Bruce Geralds, Sr.," the Sam Eyeam gulped. "I was hired by your wife to find you and bring you back to Aurora for Martin's fourteenth birthday. We missed the date."

"Melinda Fortesque is my ex-wife. Dalleena Farseer is my wife," Konner corrected the man. Did Geralds truly believe the story he spouted? Had he memorized it at Melinda's command? If he believed it, he was too gullible to be a successful Sam Eyeam. But then, maybe that was why Melinda hired him, because he believed her lies and she could manipulate him.

"Not according to Ms. Fortesque," Geralds replied. "And not according to GTE law. In fact, by my reckoning you are a bigamist and the only way to straighten this out is to return to Aurora with me." Geralds grinned.

Konner's stomach sank abruptly. He knew Melinda's tricks. Why was she working so hard to get him back when she had gone to great lengths to get rid of him?

"Actually, Ms. Fortesque is guilty of lying to you." Konner leaned back, assuming an act of casual confidence he did not feel. Melinda was up to something and he did not trust her or her Sam Eyeam. "I have copies of the annulment papers, all properly signed and sealed."

"Then that makes Martin illegitimate and any claim you might have on him null and void," Geralds returned with a smile that did not reach his eyes.

"On certain worlds in the Galactic Free Market, that might be correct," Kim interjected. Leave it to the family professor to come up with the facts. "In the GTE, if the child is conceived within the bounds of a legal marriage, even if that marriage is later annulled, then the child is legitimate and both parents have claim to custody until settled irrevocably in court."

"And that court date has passed." Konner swung his chair back to his console. He did not want to think about it. If he concentrated on one thing at a time, he could hold off the bad thoughts that threatened his sanity. If he concentrated upon Dalleena, the future had hope. A future he planned to share with his son.

"While this conversation is very interesting, it does nothing to save the people Amanda Leonard enslaved on this planet," Jetang M'Berra said. His black skin gleamed with perspiration. "Nor does it explain why you kidnapped Chaney." He and the medic knelt beside the wounded Raaskan on the floor. She tested pulse and temperature and read off numbers to M'Berra who stayed within touching distance of her at all times. Her blonde fairness made an interesting contrast to his nearly blue-black skin and hair.

"We came specifically to persuade Dr. Lotski to come with us. My wife is in labor after a difficult pregnancy," Kim said. He held his hand across his middle as if he shared the birthing pains. Knowing Kim, he just might.

"Sheesh! I haven't delivered a baby since medical school. I'm a military medic not an OBGYN," Lotski protested. Still she crept closer to the cockpit. "What have you got in the way of medical databases?" She and Kim dissolved into a conversation about swollen ankles and back pain.

"I need to go back," M'Berra insisted. "Now that I know Chaney is safe, I need to do something about Amanda Leonard. I need to liberate her slaves and lock her up with reinforced force bracelets."

"You can't do anything behind a locked and guarded door," Konner reminded him. "Which is where her Marines will put you once you return."

"But . . ."

"Our villagers will be safe for a while. Most of them escaped in the fray created by the flywacket." Konner tried to keep the worry out of his voice. "Smart of Yaaccob to use that old superstition about flywackets being connected to the plague we cured. Now they know Gentian had nothing to do with the disease. But they created quite a diversion."

In the midst of the fray, Konner had whispered to Yaaccob that all from the village would be welcome in the south.

If they could find a way to feed them. If the villagers could travel five hundred klicks on foot.

The weight of responsibility pressed heavily against his mind. At this rate he'd never get away long enough to untangle the skein of lies Melinda had woven around their son Martin. He'd never regain custody of the boy within or outside the law.

He needed to use the Sam Eyeam, Bruce Geralds, to get to Martin, but how?

If only he had four pairs of fully charged fuel cells, he'd grab Dalleena and fly back to *Sirius* alone. With the mother ship he could get to Aurora in about four jumps, a little over a week's travel.

Without the fuel cells he was stranded, and they'd just used up most of their remaining reserves on this latest crazy mission.

* * *

Cyndi gasped for breath. Her lungs resisted life-giving air.

The pressure on her chest increased.

"Get off of me," she ordered. She had no breath to scream.

Setting her mind, she thrashed her arms at whatever tried to crush the life from her.

Her blows hit only cold night air.

She smelled sulfur over the salt that permeated the air of this coastal village.

Something hot breathed on her neck. *Do not resist me.* The words sounded raspy, nearly as breathless as she.

"No man rapes me," she said or thought with all of the formidable determination her father had instilled in her.

I have need of your body.

"So do I." With a tremendious heave, she rolled to her side. The pressure moved to her back. But that allowed her to grab some air.

Harder on both of us this way.

"I have no intention of making this easy for you or any other."

Why couldn't she hit the man? Why didn't she recognize his voice? After nine months in this filthy village she knew every one of the natives by their voice, their posture, their *smell.*

This assailant was a stranger.

How had he gotten past the guards? She could have sworn the warriors who prowled the perimeter by night could see in the dark. She'd never been able to sneak past them. And she had become an expert at eluding the best security systems in the galaxy when she thought she loved Loki. She'd managed to meet him in the most obscure and the most obvious places without detection.

You are weak. You grow weaker.

"Never!"

A sharp stab to the back of her neck felt like a medical probe. She twisted and shrugged and rammed backward with her elbow.

She met only air. Hot, rancid air.

Give in to me. I need your body.

"The seven rings of hell around Perdition take you," she screamed.

Cyndi got her knees under her and reared back. The pressure fell away. She panted for breath, head down, hands resting upon the floor of the cave where she slept with five other women.

Somehow she'd managed to roll all the way to the back of the cave. A little niche beneath a sandstone ledge offered her refuge. She squeezed in, confident that no one could reach her there.

Why hadn't anyone responded to her screams? In the dim glow from the fire outside she discerned the shapes of five other women where they sprawled awkwardly upon their mats in the areas each had staked out as her own. One snored.

Still they all remained deeply asleep.

They cannot help you. They cannot hear you.

The pressure came back, this time atop her skull. Her temples screamed with pain. Her eyes felt as if they would bulge out.

"You cannot have me." She rammed her head against the ledge above her. The pain felt almost good in contrast to the pressure.

Cease! I cannot use your body if you damage the skull.

"I will kill myself before I let you have me. I will smash my skull so badly my brains will leak out. You." Bang. "Will." Bang. "Not." Bang. "Have me," she breathed in relief as the pressure evaporated, leaving her with a monstrous headache.

She closed her eyes and fought to manage the new pain. If she concentrated just so, she could imagine the pain and bruises liquefying and draining out of her body and mind.

Some time later she came to her senses with a dull roar in her ears and a new, warm pressure upon her chest. She opened her eyes.

Daylight streamed into the cave. The other women stretched and yawned and prepared to start a new day.

Cyndi lay upon her own mat near the back of the cave, her meager possessions strewn about her. Her head ached and she felt a lump on her forehead that must have bruised into an ugly purple and black.

Then she became aware of a huge black cat sitting and purring upon her chest.

(You had need of me.) The cat levered itself off her chest, stretched and yawned, in mimicry of the humans who shared the cave.

Then it sauntered toward the entrance. Each of the women sharing the cave paused to scratch its ears. But it kept moving toward the cave mouth and the open air. At the arched opening it spread glossy feathered wings and took off.

Cyndi held her breath a moment, watching the magnificent animal.

"This place is getting to me. The nightmares are getting weirder. Or I am going insane. I have to find a way to leave. Soon. With or without Loki O'Hara. I don't care who wins possession of this place anymore. I want out. I want my husband who appreciates who and what I am."

CHAPTER 24

MARTIN DRAGGED HIS feet. The guard, a new man he did not know, hauled him along mercilessly.

Halfway to the cross corridor that led to Melinda's wing, Martin willed his knees to collapse. The guard merely stooped long enough to hoist him up with both hands.

But that gave Martin the chance to stick his left hand into his pocket and finger the blue crystal. Could he stash the thing somewhere along the way for later retrieval?

If Melinda found the treasure, she'd surely confiscate it and find some way to punish Martin for possessing it. That would not keep Melinda from using it—if she figured out what it could do.

Damn! He wished the guard had not been so diligent, had not recognized Martin.

The guard's hands went slack; he stared off into space. After a moment he touched the comm port embedded in his skull behind his left ear. Everyone who worked for Melinda had one so she could communicate with anyone at any time. Even Martin had a port, though Melinda rarely used it. She preferred to speak through a holo image on his computer.

"Master Martin did not pass my post, sir," the guard

said. "I have not see him." Still staring blankly, the man returned the way they had come.

Martin touched his own port to monitor communications. All the while he kept his other hand on the blue crystal.

"The boy must still be mucking about in his room," the authoritative voice of the security chief came over the comm system. "Roger, you are closest. Go see what he's up to. The boss is getting a bit antsy."

Martin didn't wait for a reply from Roger. He took off down the corridor at a run. Not quite understanding what was happening, he kept his hand on the miniature king stone and willed himself invisible. He slid to a halt outside the family parlor.

He'd guessed right. His friends were dining there, discussing how to spend the afternoon since Melinda had hijacked their plans.

"Good, you are all here," he panted as he nearly careened into the doorjamb.

Jane and Kurt looked around the room anxiously, their eyes never lighting on Martin.

Quinn squinted and stared at Martin, not quite focusing his eyes.

Bruce looked out the window, staring as blankly as the guard.

Belatedly, Martin released his death grip on the crystal while keeping his hand in his pocket.

His three friends and Quinn finally looked at him in bewilderment. Before they could voice their questions, he blurted out orders right and left.

"We have to go now. I mean right now. If we aren't halfway to orbit within ten digital minutes, Melinda will find us. But right now all is chaos and they aren't looking in the garage."

Quinn threw down his serviette and jumped up. He

punched data into his handheld. "No time to gather our luggage, time to move. Good thing I already stashed Jane's extra trunk with emergency provisions."

Jane grinned at Martin mischievously. All of her extra baggage did more than just serve her vanity.

Martin wanted to kiss her. Not now. They didn't have time for anything, let alone the explanations he'd have to give afterward.

"We'll take the servants' tunnel to the kitchen and then to the garage. Come on. Stop staring and get moving. Time for questions later." Quinn bounded for the exit on the other side of the dining parlor.

Martin followed Quinn through a doorway hidden within the rich wall paneling. He returned his hand to the crystal, praying that his new discovery worked as well with groups as himself.

"No one say a word and keep your steps quiet," he whispered.

"What . . ." Kurt began a protest.

"Shush," Martin commanded. "Later," he mouthed.

They hurried down the tunnel, letting the slight downslope speed their steps.

Martin wanted to run. He didn't trust the crystal to keep them invisible. He didn't dare hope that he might finally break free of Melinda's grasp.

But running would make noise and make it harder to keep the group together.

He forced himself to breathe calmly and evenly.

A waiter passed them bearing a laden tray with the second entrée. He looked at them curiously then passed on, too well trained to question his employer's son.

Inwardly, Martin cursed. He gripped the crystal tighter. *Concentrate,* he told himself. *Concentrate on the entire group being invisible.*

Giles, the family butler, strode purposefully up the tunnel.

Martin held his breath. This man was an old and loyal retainer. He reported everything to Melinda as part of his job.

Concentrate, concentrate. Martin forced himself to look where he placed his feet and not into Giles' eyes. He forced himself to think about being elsewhere with his friends and not in the tunnels.

Black stars burst before his vision.

Still he could not draw a breath. He had to concentrate.

Giles passed on and turned right into the connecting tunnel to Melinda's wing.

Martin released the breath he'd held too long. He gasped and bent over, hands on his knees while his lungs spasmed.

"Easy, Marty. Breathe," Bruce whispered. He grabbed Martin's arm and propelled him forward.

Jane and Kurt kept looking around in puzzlement. They both opened their mouths to ask questions.

Quinn pressed his index finger to his lips, signaling absolute quiet.

They moved on.

Servitors dashed about the kitchen, clanging trays, cursing each other and tripping over their own feet. The normal organized chaos of mealtime for a demanding employer.

Martin had spent far too many free moments ensconced in the cheerful warmth of these rooms when no one bothered to take notice of him, except the servants. He knew the most likely path through here without triggering inquiries.

He continued to stroke the crystal, but trusted more in the busyness of the place to pass through unnoticed.

At last they slipped into the garage. Six small air cars rested on mounts near the front. Melinda's huge limousine, and Martin's smaller, older one were parked nearer the rear.

All of the mechanics, driver, and maintenance people had gone to lunch.

Quinn waved the group over to a midsized boxy-looking vehicle that would seat six comfortably but not attract attention in traffic as the flashier limos would.

"It looks different," Martin whispered to Quinn. "Modified for orbital travel?" An extra layer of cerama/metal encased the vehicle, painted a modest gray to match the original van body. New seals about the windows and a bulky "something" attached to the undercarriage betrayed the true nature of the changes to a careful observer like Martin.

A passing glance showed a bulky passenger vehicle, nothing unusual.

The bodyguard shushed him and nodded.

Silently, they all settled into the van. Martin took the seat beside Quinn, the only licensed driver in the group. Martin drove frequently with his tutors because no one on Aurora would think of arresting him. This time they wanted anonymity, not the token police force watching for a teenage driver.

Jane and Bruce took the middle seat. Kurt happily stretched out his long legs on the rear seat well below window level. He'd learned how to maintain a low profile after the assassination attempt on his home planet.

Quinn fiddled with something below the dash. When he finally raised his head, a big grin split his face. "That should give us some privacy. I've disabled the GPS as well as the tracking device your mother had secreted here as soon as I asked permission to use this air van."

The bodyguard touched a couple of interfaces on the dash and the engines purred to life. He signaled for the garage door to open. It remained firmly shut.

Martin whipped out his handheld and keyed in an override. The door remained stubbornly closed.

"Try this, I found it somewhere, I don't remember where," Bruce said handing the Klip to Martin over the top of the seat.

Martin grinned and applied the clamp to a set of controls beneath the dash. Then he tried the override code again.

The door rose sluggishly.

A mechanic wandered in, wiping his mouth with his sleeve. A woman behind him, also in green mechanic overalls, yawned widely. She looked up and pointed toward the van. A questioning look crossed her face.

Her companion pressed his comm port and spoke urgently.

Martin did not need to hear his words to understand that he notified security of the breach in protocol. No one had scheduled the van for use today.

Quinn stepped on the accelerator and launched the vehicle out of the garage with the door only half open.

An alarm sounded inside the palace.

Sirens blared on the airways outside.

"Hang on tight. This is going to be close," Quinn said through gritted teeth. He pulled back on the controls and sent the van upward the moment the tail cleared the garage. Then a sharp ninety-degree turn left, another turn sixty degrees right.

Martin keyed his handheld to close the garage door. Then he tapped in Melinda's override code. No one would be opening that door soon.

The palace fell away behind them. Martin did not even take a last look at his home. His thoughts were all on the future and getting away.

Quinn pushed the air van higher and higher. He squeaked through heavy traffic above, below, and in front of them. Atmospheric forces screamed around them.

He pushed them higher yet.

A black air car with flashing red-and-white lights came up beside them, an unmarked police vehicle. "Descend and park. Repeat, descend and park, by order of the Aurora City Police," a voice broadcast through the interior comm system as well as loudspeakers outside.

Quinn put the van into a sharp dive. The police followed at a more leisurely pace. Then Quinn pulled out and accelerated upward once more.

Caught unaware, the police continued on their downward path for nearly a full digital minute before recovering. They sped up in full hot pursuit.

An energy pulse zinged past Quinn's side of the vehicle. He grinned tightly and swerved crazily, all the time pushing them closer and closer to orbital altitude.

Another shot sizzled along the roof.

Martin smelled burning cerama/metal and heard the hiss of escaping air. "We aren't going to make it, are we?"

"Never say never, Martin. I still have a few tricks up my sleeve." Quinn put the van through a couple more wild swings. "There should be a tube of caulk beneath your seat. Seal that leak before the atmosphere gets any thinner."

The police fell back.

Another shot pierced the rear window. Quinn sent the van into a wild dive.

The police car zoomed closer.

Quinn jammed controls upward and to the right.

A sharp jolt from the rear rocked them hard. Martin's safety restraints bit into his shoulders as he fell forward and to the side.

The van careened downward, out of control.

Martin shook his head and looked around. He had to grip the seat hard with both hands to keep himself from launching toward the windshield.

Quinn lay slumped forward, limp and unconscious, eyes closed. A bruise was already forming on his forehead.

Martin shook the man, pushing him back against the seat, away from the steering column. His head flopped backward. No response.

CHAPTER 25

MOVEMENT STIRRED around the entrance to the largest cave. Kim lifted his attention from the dying flames of the communal fire. He didn't dare hope that Hestiia's long labor was finally over.

The sun had risen over the bay an hour ago. Pryth's pyre smoldered. By tonight, it might be reduced to ash so that they could cast the remains to the four winds.

The villagers milled around, sharing breakfast, completing small chores, lingering while they all awaited news of a new life added to the village. Kim's brothers and Kat sat with him upon rocks placed conveniently to the fire for them. Kat yawned and looked longingly at the ground, as if she'd like to stretch out and fall asleep right there.

M'Berra and Geralds had found beds somewhere and gone off to them hours ago.

Loki jumped up and paced, unaware that people passed back and forth across the entrance to the big cave with some speed and urgency.

At last Chaney Lotski ducked out of the cave entrance and wandered toward them. Her eyes looked sunken and hollow with fatigue and her already pale skin seemed almost translucent in the early light.

But a grin split her face when she saw Kim. "Congratulations, Mark Kimmer O'Hara. You are the father of a healthy baby girl," she said, offering her hand.

Kim took it numbly. "A girl?" He gulped in shock. "We were sure it was a boy."

"Disappointed, little brother?" Konner asked. Then he jumped up and slapped Kim's back with enthusiasm. "I have a niece. Did you hear that everybody? I have a niece!"

Kat and Loki joined him in jumping up and down with excitement.

Slowly the fog lifted from Kim's mind. "A girl. It's a girl!" he shouted. Then he sobered. "Hestiia. What about Hes? Is she okay?" He anxiously searched Lotski's face for a clue.

"She will be fine." Lotski became serious. She seemed weighed down with responsibility. "She lost a lot of blood. She's weak and tired. But she's nursing. That will help slow the blood loss. The women here know more about childbirth than I do. If they hadn't come up with special herbs and moss to pack the bleeding, we might have lost her."

She took a deep breath and closed her eyes, heavy with fatigue. "Herbal remedies or not, I don't want her out of bed for three days and she shouldn't even think about another child for a couple of years. She needs to fully recover. And if that means celibacy to prevent another pregnancy, then so be it."

"I can't even think about that. As long as Hes is okay, I'll do anything, anything to keep her that way."

"It's what you don't do that's more important."

"Can I see her?" Kim started walking with long purposeful strides toward the cave before he had an answer.

"If the ladies have finished cleaning up and will let

you in. But don't stay too long. Hestiia needs her rest."

Kim hesitated at the cave mouth.

Poolie, as wife of the headman and therefore in a position of authority among the women, beckoned him in. Hugely pregnant herself, she rubbed under her belly in ever larger circles, as if soothing her own early labor pains. She held a finger to her lips, then pointed to the still, pale face of Hestiia beneath a mountain of sleeping furs on a pallet near the center of the cave.

Kim crept close to his wife and knelt beside her. A lump of emotion clogged his throat and his hands trembled. One of the other women twitched the edge of the furs aside to reveal a wrinkled pink lump cradled in the crook of Hestiia's arm.

"My daughter?" he breathed.

"Our daughter," Hestiia whispered. She raised a tired arm and caressed his face with one finger.

He caught her hand in his and kissed her palm. "She is beautiful, as light and fragile as the air." He didn't quite dare touch the little thing that opened vague blue eyes to stare at him. The pink fuzz on top of her head looked like it might turn red later, maybe blond. He didn't care.

"Then we must call her Ariel." Hestiia smiled as she gently uncovered the baby for Kim's inspection. "But remember that the wind can be a formidable force. Remember the storm last Solstice?" A bit of a smile touched her lips.

"Just like her mother," Kim agreed. He counted ten perfect fingers and ten wrinkled toes. Two arms. Two legs. A head atop a long skinny body. What more was necessary?

"Ariel she is. But she is also Pryth. She will carry

both names," he decided. The memory of the old wisewoman passing the mantle of experience and responsibility to Hestiia lingered in his mind.

"Yes. Thank you." Tears filled Hestiia's eyes. " 'Tis right and fitting that we honor our friend and mentor."

"Get some rest, love. I'll be right outside." Kim bent to kiss his wife on the brow.

Her eyes closed. Immediately, her breathing took on the slow steady rhythm of sleep.

Kim sat and watched her a long time, unwilling to accept even the little separation of leaving the cave.

* * *

"You know, Kim's going to be even more reluctant to leave this place with us when we return to civilization," Loki said quietly.

Kat stared at her oldest brother aghast. "How can you even think about separating them at a time like this!" She placed her clenched fists on her hips and stared at Loki, chin set as stubbornly as she knew how.

"We can't leave him behind," Loki protested. He matched her posture with equal belligerence.

"Now, now, don't fight. We just got reunited," Konner stepped between them.

"If anyone leaves this planet, it will be me," Kat insisted. She had a brief mental image of herself leading Loki in force bracelets off an IMP rescue ship. She shook her head.

No, she would not do that to her brothers. She had grown past the need for revenge. But she'd still like to slug all three of them for the twenty years of separation.

Well, maybe not Kim. He had been little more than a baby when the family broke up. And now he was a new father.

She couldn't help grinning. For twenty years she had been the adopted daughter, accepted and loved but just slightly outside the family dynamic in Governor Benedict Talbot's household. Now she had more family than she knew how to manage.

"Look, we can't settle the issue of who goes and who stays until we get the fuel cells recharged again," Konner said. The middle brother, the neutral one who always found ways to mediate among his siblings. Just as he had twenty years ago. "I'm as anxious to get back to civilization to claim my son as you are to get back to your lives. But we have to settle the problem of Hanassa and what he's doing to the people here. We have to find a way to kill the Krakatrice on the big continent."

Kat took a deep breath to settle herself. "We are all tired and jumpy. Any decision we make now will be based on flawed judgment. Let's get some sleep." She stretched her back. Then she yawned. It grew to encompass her entire body. And just kept growing until she thought her jaw would crack and she'd never be able to open her eyes again.

"Sleep sounds good. I'll take you up to the clearing and get you settled." Konner yawned, too.

An emptiness settled in Kat's belly that could only be filled with sleep. Sleep and something else.

"Where's Gentian?" she asked.

Konner shrugged.

"I saw him skulking around near dawn," Loki offered. "But not since."

Kat's emptiness became a knot of anxiety. She called the flywacket with her mind. He did not reply and he did not appear.

"He'll turn up when he's ready." Konner shrugged and led the way to the uphill path.

"Somehow, I don't think so." Kat shivered with a new loneliness.

* * *

The flywacket has gone into hiding. We cannot find him. We cannot recall him to the nimbus if we cannot find him. He may have his uses yet. But he has abandoned his chosen one. She will flounder without his guidance. We have no other to send to the aid of the humans. We dare not allow any more of our numbers to be corrupted by them. Their taint is potentially more damaging than the one we may not name gone rogue, or the threat of the Krakatrice to our way of life. The humans must blunder their own way now. We may not interfere further. The nimbus has decided.

CHAPTER 26

WITH THE GOOD NEWS that both Hestiia and baby Ariel would thrive, the village moved, as one, to go about their day. The men downed the last of their tay, a hot herbal infusion that sort of tasted like tea, and headed for the cove.

Loki held Yaakke back from the group headed down to the fishing boat. The tide was nearly full, and it was time to negotiate the treacherous cove and bring back food for the village.

"You don't seem yourself lately, my friend," Loki said. He didn't quite know how else to ask the man about his gloomy mood and how his eyes followed Cyndi wherever she went.

"I am more myself now than a few days ago." Yaakke looked affronted. At the same time he would not meet Loki's gaze.

"Has Cyndi done something . . . ?"

"She insulted my honor and the traditions of the Coros."

Loki breathed a little easier. "Then you are not likely to succumb to her seduction. I wanted to warn you."

"I lusted after the woman. She is beautiful." Yaakke flashed Loki a wide grin. "But no more. I have seen her kind before. She uses men and then discards them. We do not allow women like her to live among us.

We tolerate Lady Cyndi only because she is a prisoner of the Stargods."

At least the man knew in his head the dangers he faced. But had his heart caught up with the logic?

Loki didn't think so, not the way Yaakke searched the village for a glimpse of a bright blond head that wasn't there.

Loki let the man go off to his fishing. Then he went in search of the woman who had been missing for several hours. Who knew what mischief she was up to now.

He found her hiding a short distance west of the village. She sat in a pool of sunshine in the center of a lovely copse. Two empty leather buckets lay upon their sides at her feet. Eventually, she'd have to fill those buckets in the creek three meters away. But the longer she idled here, the fewer trips she could make before someone else did the job.

"Where'd you get that bruise, Cyndi?" Loki stood behind the woman he had once loved. Even from here he could see the black-and-purple mark on her temple and the swelling lump beneath it.

"I tripped. Not that it's any of your business." She did not look at him, continuing to bask like a cat.

"What did you trip over? Your conscience?"

She turned a malevolent glare upon him.

Loki shrugged it off.

"As much as I dislike you, you are my responsibility. I need to know if someone hit you." Loki sat on the grass beside her, his back against a sapling Tambootie tree. Proximity to the tree of magic might elevate his ability to pry secrets from her mind.

"You would not believe me if I told you." The sarcasm and contempt left her face. She hunched in upon herself.

"You look almost vulnerable. What happened, Cyndi?" He couldn't allow himself to sympathize with her. That way lay disaster. He deliberately pulled an image of Paola into his mind. A small secret smile began in the middle of his belly and moved upward.

She looked upward as if counting the leaves in the tree canopy above.

"You must have realized by this time that life on this planet is weird," Loki said quietly. "I've seen some pretty strange things since I came here, including dragons and flywackets. I've done stranger things. Things that you'd call magic and disbelieve until you thought deeply about it. I don't believe half of it yet myself."

"Have you seen any ghosts?" she asked, almost casually.

He caught a whiff of intensity in her posture.

"Sort of. There was man called Hanassa. Three times my brothers and I killed him. Twice he returned to plague us. And this third time . . ." Loki shook his head, not willing to voice to an outsider what they suspected Hanassa capable of. Last night's battle with Amanda Leonard was too reminiscent of their previous encounters with Hanassa.

"Hanassa." She rolled the name around her mouth as if tasting it. "What did he look like?"

"Middling height and coloring. Stocky. Vibrant. Very intense eyes."

"Did . . . did he have something to do with Taneeo?"

"Taneeo was his apprentice for a while. Then his slave. Then . . ." Loki clamped his mouth shut.

"Taneeo was in a coma. Now he's not. Did Hanassa do something to his mind?"

Loki gulped. "Yes."

"Did the ghost of Hanassa take possession of Taneeo's mind?" Cyndi rolled to her knees and stared fiercely into Loki's eyes.

For a few heartbeats her face took on the wild intensity that reminded Loki of Hanassa. Her mild blue eyes glowed and flared. Did he catch a glimpse of red in there?

"Did he?" she repeated. "Tell me, Loki. I need to know."

"Yes."

"How?"

"You wouldn't . . ."

"Try me."

"In the dragon nimbus, there are red-tipped, blue-tipped, green-tipped dragons, and maybe some other colors I haven't seen yet. But there can only be one purple-tipped dragon at a time. Purple-tips are always born twins. In this latest generation three purple-tips were born. The nimbus refuses to kill one of their own. Two of the purples had to become something else. Iianthe remains a dragon. Gentian shrank into a flywacket—a large black cat with wings."

Cyndi nodded at that, as if she'd sent the critter.

"Hanassa possessed the body of an ailing human boy child about two years of age. He grew up looking and acting like a human, he became a priest. But he was filled with anger at no longer being a dragon. He began forcing the Coros into war and took blood sacrifices. He enslaved many people until my brothers and I ended Hanassa's life."

"No wonder the locals worship you as a god."

"I am not a god. Merely a man with the technology to solve a few of their problems. But I'm running out of supplies and ideas." The problem of the Krakatrice hung heavy in his gut.

If anyone could handle those monsters, it was Paola. But he feared for her.

"When you killed Hanassa . . ."

Loki shuddered at the memories her words conjured. He'd pulled the trigger on a needle rifle and shot Hanassa. More than a little bit of himself had died at that moment. He'd tried to follow his enemy into death. Never again would he kill, man or animal.

"When you killed Hanassa, he didn't stay dead, did he?"

"We think—we think his spirit invaded Taneeo. He was physically weakened by months of privation and injured. Vulnerable." Taneeo had caught more than a few of the poisoned needles in the rifle spray. His body had taken a long time to recover, and when it did . . .

"We think Taneeo's will was stronger than Hanassa's. He fell into the coma because he fought Hanassa's possession of him."

"But Taneeo is awake now, showing no signs of inner struggle."

"That is correct."

"So where did the spirit of Hanassa go?" Her chin trembled as if she already knew.

Could this truly be Cyndi speaking? The woman Loki had known would never have accepted any of this discussion as more than horror stories, the product of an overactive imagination.

"Possibly into the body of Commander Amanda Leonard."

"You battled her last night. No, don't deny it. I heard the talk around the fire."

"Yes. Kim shot her four times, square in the chest with a fully charged stunner. The energy in *one* of those shots should have knocked her unconscious.

Possibly stopped her heart. She kept right on following us. Never missed a step."

"Afterward, what happened to Amanda?"

"We fled. I don't know. Where is this going, Cyndi? What does this have to do with the bruise on your forehead?"

"I had a bizarre nightmare in the middle of the night. I think Hanassa tried to take me. But I wouldn't let him. He fled when I threatened to kill myself rather than give in to his pressure."

"Cyndi, I don't know if I should believe you. Or if I should lock you in force bracelets until we know that slippery bastard hasn't invaded you." Loki sat up straighter.

"I'm clean, Loki. Believe me, I forced the bastard out. When I woke up this morning, the flywacket was on my chest purring. And then he flew away. I thought I was going insane until you told me about . . . about purple-tipped dragons." She sank back down in her half recline.

"The flywacket belongs to Kat."

"Who cares?"

"You should."

"Loki, you have to promise me, that when you leave this planet, you will take me with you. You can't leave me here. You can't take a chance that I will succumb to Hanassa."

"I can't promise anything. Right now we don't have enough fuel to leave. You wouldn't happen to know anything about some sabotaged fuel cells, would you?"

"If you won't take me with you, then be warned, I will do everything I can to escape to Base Camp and help the IMPs get off this miserable rock."

"Go ahead. But believe me, if Hanassa is in Amanda

Leonard's body, he isn't going anywhere. He's bound to this miserable rock by more than a lack of fuel."

How did he know that? He shook his head clear of the strange notions that kept invading his thoughts—like he'd touched more of a dragon than just its back when he rode one and experienced a dragon dream.

Loki climbed to his feet and returned to the village. His insides quivered and his hands shook. For the first time since the night he and Mum had escaped their burning home with Konner and Kim, he was scared. Truly frightened that his wits, his audacity, and his strength would not prevail over his foes: supernatural, monstrous, or human.

CHAPTER 27

"CAPTAIN?" one of the Marines addressed Hanassa.

He remembered to salute the man. Strange how cooperative the mind of his host had become. Especially when that mind realized that Hanassa's dragon strength had partially repaired the damaged left eye. Eventually, he would fully repair it, but such work took time and energy he did not have at the moment.

"Report," Hanassa barked. Amanda continued to supply him with the proper vocabulary.

"Captain, the village is empty. All of the natives have deserted." The Marine stood at full attention.

Hanassa sensed the fear, the loyalty, and the courage that kept the man in front of her and so rigid his body nearly hummed when the breeze struck him.

He wanted to lash out at the bearer of bad news. Amanda gripped his will and held tight. *Use his fear, do not abuse it,* she whispered.

"Explain," Hanassa spat. He began to pace, unable to contain the energy that wanted to lash out and draw blood.

"During the night they all slipped away. We have only two dozen men as slaves." The words came out clipped. The Marine's face glistened with a sheen of sweat.

"Two dozen? That is barely enough to work the

fields," Hanassa's anger flared again. He needed blood to calm himself.

His stomach roiled in revulsion. This Amanda person had a stronger influence on him than he thought.

If we kill any of those slaves, then we will lose them all. We will not have enough to work the fields and feed us. If we and our men starve to death, we will not have a base of power to achieve total control of the planet.

Amanda also had logic.

"Do you still wish me to select a sacrifice?" the Marine asked.

"Select one man for flogging. Send the rest into the fields. And keep a careful watch on them all. Oh, and, Sergeant?"

"Yes, Captain?" The man sagged with relief.

"After I have drawn blood with the whip, I will need . . . I will need two of my men to come to my cabin."

"For punishment, Captain?" He went rigid again.

"Not exactly." Hanassa allowed himself a wicked smile. "Though by the time I am sated, they may believe it to be so."

"Very well, Captain." The man saluted and backed off.

You are learning. Between the two of us we should go far. Now listen carefully while I show you how to field strip and recharge a stunner.

* * *

Late in the afternoon, Kat helped move Hestiia back to the family clearing. She carried the new baby while Kim carried Hestiia. She marveled at the tiny scrap of life in her arms and wondered if she'd ever have the courage to form a lasting bond with a man so that she, too, could have children.

She heaved a sigh of relief as she settled the baby next to her sister-in-law.

But she couldn't settle herself. She wandered randomly through the environs of the family clearing. About every tenth step she glanced over to the main cabin where Hestiia slept.

But the baby didn't sleep. She apparently didn't like the move and refused to nurse or sleep.

Kim walked his own path around the clearing, crooning to the tiny baby he carried, trying to keep her quiet while his wife slept.

A soft pinkish-blond fuzz crowned the baby's head and her eyes were the unfocused blue of a newborn. Hard to tell yet if she would grow into the family's bright red cap of curls or the midnight-blue eyes of her father and uncles.

Undoubtedly, she'd inherit the pale skin and cursed tendency to freckle.

Kat let her mind wander at will along with her feet. If she concentrated too hard on how to deal with Amanda Leonard, then all she could think about was the terrible injustice of enslaving the natives. She wondered if she could have prevented her captain's slide into insanity if she'd noticed the signs in time.

But then Jetang M'Berra had noticed the signs and covered for Amanda, tried to mitigate her actions for months.

She'd done it again, dwelled on the past rather than solutions. So she wandered and called to her flywacket. Since his disappearance the morning of Ariel's birth, the flying cat had not returned to Kat's side and had not communicated with her.

She missed him terribly. Not until he was gone had

she realized just how lonely she was. She might have found her family, but she was not yet one of them, did not share growing up with them, did not agree with them. She considered herself a civil. Her brothers disdained her culture and clung desperately to their bush origins. She had been taught to scorn them with equal fervor.

And then there was the little matter of their crimes against the GTE, transporting contraband, nonpayment of customs duties, escape from various jails, fleeing arrest, assault upon a judicial cruiser, and others, she was sure. They must answer for them eventually.

If they ever got off this planet.

Gentian come to me, please, she called. *I miss you.*

"Konner?" She paused by his "power farm," the array of fuel cells set out to collect solar energy augmented by brandy distilled from the Tambootie berries. The still burbled happily off in the woods somewhere, converting the toxic fruit to something the cells could use to recharge. "Konner, how did you know to call Gentian a flywacket?"

"Gentian? He's returned from the dragon nimbus?" Konner looked up from his endless fussing with the cells.

"You've met my flywacket before?"

"He belonged to Hestiia when we first arrived. Then he disappeared. The dragons said something about him not being worthy due to cowardice."

"Hestiia didn't miss him?" She'd only had the beast at her side one full day and she felt empty without him.

"Hestiia had Kim by that time." Konner grinned.

Kat had to match his expression. Their younger brother seemed to have found his soul mate, his other half, in Hestiia. He still stared blissfully at his daughter as he carried her around the clearing. He pointed out the wonders of the world to her as he walked and bounced. The baby seemed oddly alert and content for a newborn. No wonder Kim vowed never to return to civilization. He'd found a home here on this isolated planet beyond the back of beyond.

"You, too, seemed to have found happiness, Konner."

"Yeah, I have. I never thought I'd find a woman as comfortable around machines as I am, least of all on a primitive planet. Dalleena and I are better suited than I dreamed possible. She's coming with me when I leave here to find my son." He returned to his work.

The clearing seemed strangely empty without the bustle of a dozen people. Loki was in the village trying to cobble together some kind of pump and fire hose. Dalleena was in the village helping Lotski, M'Berra, and Geralds settle in to village life. They weren't family, so they did not get to live in the clearing.

Kat strolled by the lean-to she had claimed. It was well chinked with moss to keep out drafts and piled with furs for comfort. Still, she had not slept well, missing Gentian. And possibly Bruce Geralds.

She returned to her pacing and her thinking.

At the center of the clearing, where she and Konner had buried the king stone from *Jupiter* last autumn, she stopped abruptly. Something was wrong.

"Konner?"

Her brother barely looked up from his fuel cells.

"Konner, what happened to the ley lines that used to cross here?" Her steps had not been as random as she thought. Without realizing it, she had traced the path of the mysterious silver-blue lines.

"Ley lines?" He stood and brushed his hands against his buckskin trousers. "I placed the crystals according to predetermined ratios. Blue king stone at the center, surrounded by twelve green drivers, then one hundred forty-four red directionals at the rim of the force field. The ley lines had nothing to do with it."

"Oh, yeah?" She took a deep breath and allowed her eyes to lose focus. Three straight lines of magical power slid into her vision. Then she plotted the lines on a graph only she could see. "Three lines should converge and form a pool of power right where the king stone stands. There's a hole in the web where you dug."

"I can't see the lines from this angle." Konner paced a circle around where Kat stood. The disturbance in the dirt had settled beneath winter rains. It hardly showed at all.

And yet power filled Kat like an electrical current. She felt as if she were the energy flowing along fiber optics to the concentric circles of crystals that powered the confusion field around the clearing.

"Take a deep breath, Konner," Kim advised, coming closer. He cradled the now sleeping baby in one arm. He, too, pointed out the three lines with his free hand. Each gesture came to an abrupt stop short of the crossing point, directly beneath Kat's feet.

"Both of you, breathe deep and slow," Kim continued. He drew in a long breath himself.

Kat mimicked his rhythm, the world seemed to shift slightly to the left, colors intensified, her vision sharpened, then blurred as halos appeared around her brothers' heads and each object within the clearing. Strange how Kim's aura was bright yellow and green, the baby's only mild shades of blue and green, so pale they were almost white. She must be too young for definition.

Konner pulsed bright orange.

Kat held out her hand to see what colors she emanated. She saw only a layer of white.

She looked at the ley lines. Now she could see that the main lines had shot out small tendrils toward the junction point, repairing themselves.

"Do you see that?" Kat explained the phenomenon to her brothers. "I guess this means we should always look before we dig."

She thought back to the time last autumn when the dragon Irythros had flown her to the desert south of here to show her the ley lines and teach her how to use them. She had used the power to reach outward, to travel along the theoretical transactional gravitons, like a king stone seeking its mother crystal. Kat had sought her own mother and not liked what she had seen when she found a woman obsessed with amassing more and more wealth and power in order to find her daughter. But she'd never have enough. Never allow herself to have enough because if she tried to find Kat and failed she could not live with herself.

So why was Kat filled with the same kind of power now? The ley lines did not yet reach the spot where she stood, right over the king stone. She sent her vision diving down. Blades of grass and weeds, individual grains of dirt, tiny rocks, fat worms, all peeled back, layer after layer as she delved deeper and deeper. Down a full meter to the apex of the giant blue crystal.

Deeper yet she dove, down the two-meter length of the stone to the nest of fiber optics that spread outward to connect to the twelve green driver crystals, each one meter in length, and the one hundred forty-four red directional crystals, each only half a meter in length. The entire family of crystals hummed happily in harmony gathering nitrogen and other elements from the planet to fuel themselves. They spat energy outward in a dome to enclose the clearing in a shield that opened only to a combination of O'Hara DNA and music.

Kat withdrew with a jerk. She flailed for balance, totally disoriented from her rapid withdrawal of communion with the crystals.

"Breathe, Kat. Breathe deep. Don't panic. Crystal thrall is like that." Konner steadied her with words and physical strength.

"Konner, what did you use in the crystal baths to regrow the damaged array aboard *Sirius?*" She knew, but she needed confirmation.

"Our starter kit was outdated and useless. But we found a veritable soup of every known element and mineral in a creek spilling out of the blown-out volcano," Konner explained.

Both brothers eyed her warily.

"You found omniscium in the creek?" Impossible but they must have. The key ingredient to crystal growth for star travel was only found in gas giant planets and hard to mine. It turned to vapor upon contact with atmosphere.

"Yes, we found trace amounts of omniscium. Enough to complete a crystal bath," Kim confirmed. He wrapped both of his hands around the baby, cuddling her close. For warmth? Security?

"Do you still have the equipment to test for omniscium?" Kat began to tremble all over with the magnitude of her theory. She deliberately stepped away from proximity with the king stone and avoided touching any of the ley lines.

"I've got a gas chromatograph."

"Will it test dirt? With a probe?"

"I can adjust it."

"Then test the ley lines. I think we are dealing with rivers of omniscium. I think your theoretical transactional gravitons, the web of energy that holds the universe together and conspires to keep everything in place, are also rivers of omniscium. I think this planet is riddled with the stuff and that is why dragons are real and magic works."

* * *

The beginning place is in danger, the place where the web of ley lines begins and ends. These human invaders are smarter than we thought. We cannot allow them to proceed. We cannot allow this knowledge to spread. The one who harbors Hanassa can use this knowledge to wreak greater damage than all the others combined. That one has no conscience, no consideration for anything but violence and subjugation.

CHAPTER 28

MARTIN PLACED HIS hands flat on the steering controls of the van. Rapidly he touched in new commands. His stomach trembled and his teeth chattered in fear. Quinn was unconscious. Quinn, their only hope to escape Melinda.

"Drag Quinn into the back seat," he yelled at anyone who might hear. Crashing from this elevation was worse than getting caught. He didn't intend to do either.

"Someone get him out of my way." He scooted as far right as he could, trying to get a firmer grip on the column with its touch pad. Quinn's heavy body slumped against his shoulder, interfering with Martin's control.

Sluggishly, the van leveled out. He nosed it upward a notch. They were deep into the tangled grid of working class domiciles. Martin knew how to lose the police hot on his tail. But he had to have fine control of the screens.

Pressure on Martin's shoulder eased.

"Help me, Bruce. You, too, Kurt," Jane ordered.

Quinn moaned.

"He's alive!" Jane cried. "Come on, guys, help me move him. We've got to treat that wound and Marty's got to drive."

Somehow his friends hoisted Quinn into the center

seat. The man rolled his head and half opened his eyes. But he did not hold onto consciousness long.

Martin settled into the driver's place with ease. Now he could fly this thing the way Quinn had meant to. Maybe better. He knew this city. Quinn did not.

His body still shook with shock and nervousness. But he had a plan. He could do this. With help. They just had to stay free and alive until Quinn came to.

Bruce climbed over the seat and took the navigator's place beside him. He didn't know the city either, but he could look out for obstacles, like new constructions creating box ends.

Martin banked hard left, down into an alleyway, then hard right through a tunnel made by two buildings that had grown together by a skyway that expanded into more apartments.

"Barrier on the left-hand alleyway," Bruce warned.

Martin swung right and down.

The more maneuverable police car followed him, gained on him. "Jonesy must have hired some new officers. These guys know what they are doing," Martin muttered.

"Marty, I don't think that's a police vehicle," Kurt said, hesitating on the last words.

"He's right," Jane added. "Auroran police would never fire on a vehicle with you in it, Marty. You are too valuable to Melinda."

"Or too much of a liability," Martin said.

"I think it's the guys sent after me. They're trying to kill me and don't care about collateral damage," Kurt said. He slunk down deeper into his seat.

"Everyone gets out of this alive if I have anything to say about it," Martin said through gritted teeth. He sent the van into a steep climb, out of the maze. As he came level with the roofs of the dwelling complexes, his engines nearly stalled and he twisted into a tight spiral around the buildings. Within a few blocks he'd put a fair amount of insulated building foam between him and his pursuers. Their sensors should be mightily dusted. If they were using standard police equipment.

But what if they were hired assassins out to get Kurt?

Or Martin?

Or Quinn?

A few more twists and he came up behind the unmarked car.

"Hang on to Quinn," he called back to his comrades.

With a deep breath and a mumbled prayer he shot forward. His front end slammed against the black car. Their pursuer lurched and twisted, loosing altitude rapidly.

Martin shot upward, seeking orbital elevations. "We still losing air through the places those bastards shot us?"

"I sealed those that didn't self heal," Kurt replied. He pressed his hand against the three previous holes. "That's the good thing about the insulation foam between the normal hull and cerama/metal."

"Get my handheld out of my pocket, Bruce." Martin shifted his hips a little to give his friend better access.

"You could have worn pantaloons, buddy. These synthleather breeches are too tight," Bruce complained.

"Pantaloons don't attract the girls, though." Martin flashed a cheeky grin at Jane.

A few more mumbled protests and Bruce squeezed the device free. Martin placed his thumb on the screen to activate it.

"Punch in the following code to open the atmosphere dome." He spewed a string of numbers and letters, almost faster than Bruce could tap them in. The code should dissolve as fast as it entered the computer so no one could copy it. Unless they had an eidetic memory. Bruce probably did.

"Wow, how'd you get that code? Only the flight controllers at the orbital station are supposed to have it." Kurt craned his neck to watch the slightly cloudy distortion of the force field dissolve.

"Same place I got the Klip. I stole it from Melinda."

"You have your father's instincts," Quinn mumbled. "Let me take over from here." He tried to sit up, groaned, and flopped back with his head in Jane's lap.

"Just tell me how to find your ship, Quinn," Martin said. He and Bruce exchanged grins. In a similar situation either of them might have preferred to rest their heads in Jane's lap. She'd grown up a lot in the last two years. For the better.

"You mean, you haven't figured it out yet?" Quinn asked. He still slurred his words.

"Good thing that you had your safety harness on. You banged your head, probably got concussed, but you didn't crash through the windshield," Jane said. She stroked the man's straight hair lovingly. A dreamy look crossed her face.

Martin frowned. His face grew hot and his hands clenched on the drive panel. He forced himself to concentrate on the puzzle of where a Sam Eyeam could hide a ship in a closely patrolled planetary system.

He'd have to have brought the ship to the Aurora

system ahead of time, abandoned it while he returned to escort Kurt here. That meant several weeks had passed without being able to monitor the ship. Several weeks for patrols to accidentally stumble upon it.

"You hid it in plain sight, piggybacked to that derelict military cruiser in high orbit. Melinda leaves the cruiser there as a reminder to IMP officials of what she can do if anyone interferes with her absolute control over Aurora," Martin chortled.

"And conveniently near the jump point," Quinn added. He had better color in his face, but his eyes still looked glassy.

Martin set a course for the cruiser.

"I don't suppose any of you four have ever piloted a ship through jump?" Quinn asked. He struggled to sit up again. With a gentle push from Jane he made it this time though he held his head between both hands and kept his eyes closed.

"I know the theory for putting a ship in line with a jump point," Kurt said.

"Marty, here, is the only one of us who has ever driven anything," Bruce said grudgingly. "My mom insists I wait until I'm of age. If my dad were home more often, he'd teach me, though."

Martin refused to mention that Bruce's father had gone missing about the same time as the IMP judicial cruiser carrying an Earth diplomatic attaché in the same quadrant where the O'Hara brothers had disappeared. Bruce's father had a long history of employment with Melinda. He was probably responsible for a number of questionable projects.

"I've sat beside my mom's pilot when we went through a jump," Jane added. "I tried to keep my eyes open to see what jump really is, but I couldn't."

"Great—that means I'm going to have to do it on my own. I can't talk you through it. Not until one of you has had a *lot* more experience," Quinn moaned.

"Jane, there should be a first aid kit under your seat. See if there's a pain blocker in there," Martin said to hide his nervousness. Jumps were dangerous, and they'd be going through them fast, probably with Melinda's military on their tail to compound the dangers. As soon as they broke free of the cruiser, her people would spot the ship and pursue.

"Quinn, how did you know to park your ship here?" Martin asked. The timing was all wrong for him to have done it *after* Kurt's dad hired him.

"If I told you, I'd have to mind-wipe all four of you, and that would defeat the purpose of the mission."

"You're still working for the emperor. Only his private Sam Eyeam would have the authority to do that."

"I thought he was working for my dad," Kurt protested.

That statement met silence all around.

"You want me to give evidence against Melinda so you can break her control over Aurora." Martin didn't know if he should feel dirty, depressed, or elated. Maybe he just felt used. Manipulated by the emperor as badly as he had been by his mother.

He had the evidence to condemn Melinda. A lot of people would be hurt if that evidence ever became public. Including his friends. Would he ever use it?

"Believe what you want. Just dock with my ship so we can get out of here. Safely."

"Will I ever be safe again, Quinn?"

"I'm going to work very hard to make certain that all four of you remain safe." He placed a neural pain blocker against the back of his head and closed his eyes as well as the conversation.

* * *

"What do you mean, the ley lines are rivers of omniscium?" Loki burst through the clearing's barrier heedless of Bruce Geralds who followed him. All thoughts of a long soak in the hot spring fled in the wake of this exciting new development.

"Just what I said," Kat replied. "But it's only a theory."

"Your theory sounds plausible to me." Loki let a smile crease his face. "This could mean our salvation. We could buy seats in Parliament as well as our citizenship. We could change GTE policies if we control this much omniscium."

"But we won't," Kim said quietly. "If we let the GTE, the GFM, or the Kree know about the omniscium, then we open this place to destruction far faster than farming and industrialization would. A vote in Parliament won't change policy fast enough to save this planet from pollution, overpopulation, and any number of other ills inherent to the GTE."

"Believe it or not, the galaxy needs fresh food more than it needs more star drive crystals," Konner added. He pulled three gadgets out of the jumble of equipment around the power farm.

"But . . . but . . ." Loki protested. He knew his brother was right. But the wealth, the power, the *control* they would gain. No one would dare outlaw them again. They'd be free to go anywhere in the galaxy they chose. Even Cyndi would have to respect him—not that he cared anymore what she thought.

"We're going into war with the Kree. We are going to need more ships, that means more crystals. The GTE really needs this planet," Kat said. She lifted her chin in typical O'Hara stubbornness.

Loki wanted to object to her argument, just because he could not allow himself to agree with her. But he did agree with her.

"We don't have the equipment to mine omniscium, even if we agreed to do it," Kim said with a degree of finality.

"We don't even have enough fuel for *Rover* to get back to *Sirius,* so we can't market the stuff," Konner added. He stuck probes from his gadgets into three different places in the clearing. Then he whipped out a handheld and studied it.

"You are recharging the fuel cells," Kat countered. "You'll have enough fuel in a few weeks."

"It's taken me all winter to get that much and we wasted half of it rescuing you last night." Konner lifted his chin in stubbornness to equal his sister's.

"We are headed into summer, greater solar power to recharge the cells, more fruits and berries to distill. We'll have enough fuel in no time," Loki soothed. He couldn't help but rub his hands together in glee. "And I have some ideas about mining. Didn't the omniscium turn to a salt in the creek? If we can channel a ley line into a water source . . ."

"And poison the entire watershed of that creek?" Kim asked. "We don't know how toxic omniscium is in large amounts. No one has ever found enough in a single concentration to find out."

"Base Camp has a forge," Geralds offered. If we depose Amanda Leonard long enough to get access to the forge, we could make pipes to stick into the ley line junctions and funnel it into the water. Or vats of water if you insist."

"No," Kim and Konner said together. They both looked at the handheld and whistled.

Loki grabbed the device and watched numbers pile

up next to an obscure glyph he guessed represented omniscium. This find grew by orders of magnitude with each passing moment.

"Will pottery seal tight enough to contain the salt?" Loki asked the group. He moved closer to Kate. Geralds followed him. The three of them lined up against Konner and Kim.

Kat picked up one of the dozen water jugs resting near the path to the hot spring and the creek, ready for filling the next time someone went in that direction. "One beaker of omniscium salt this size would fill the baths for fifteen crystal arrays."

"No one leaves this planet, or comes back to it except Konner and Loki. We will not contaminate the land or the culture with outside influences," Kim reiterated.

"We agreed on this, Loki," Konner said. "The location of this planet must remain secret to protect the people as well as our resources."

"We can't keep this place a secret if we start marketing omniscium in large quantities," Kim added. "I won't have my daughter exposed to GTE influences." He cooed at the baby as she began to fuss.

"We can keep it secret," Loki insisted. "It's all in the marketing. We only release a little bit at a time, food and omniscium." Desperation fueled his mind with new ideas, new possibilities.

"The three of us vote as a family, as we always have," Kim said.

"Kat is family, too," Loki reminded them.

"So are Dalleena and Hestiia, and the new baby," Konner countered.

Control of the situation began slipping out of Loki's hands.

"Mum also must be consulted on something this

big." Surely Mum would agree with Loki. Mum would do anything to regain her citizenship, anything to regain her daughter. And her vote outweighed all the others combined.

At the moment Loki had Kat and Mum. That had to be enough to overrule his two bush-blind brothers.

"Mum cannot be consulted. She's too far away and we don't have the resources to set up communications," Konner said, almost with glee. He thought he had control of the question.

"I know how to contact Mum. I can show you how, Loki, with the king stone and the ley lines," Kat whispered.

Loki felt a smile and a plan growing in the back of his mind.

"Why don't we discuss this after we depose Amanda and gain access to our forge again." He had to stall. In the meantime, he and Kat and Geralds could begin experimenting with mining techniques and long-distance telepathy.

CHAPTER 29

"UH, QUINN, I'VE NEVER docked a van to an orbiting vessel before," Martin said hesitantly. The ramshackle solo vessel looked like a piece of mismatched junk thrown together with no regard for aesthetics. He was surprised any of the parts fit together well enough to maintain a seal. It looked to be just another piece of the derelict cruiser it perched under.

Quinn held his head in his hands and moaned.

The lack of gravity made Martin fight to maintain a horizon. His upside-down view of their world made the air car drift at unexpected angles. The darkness, barely alleviated by the van's headlights, didn't help matters.

"He's in pretty bad shape, Marty. Can't you figure it out?" Jane asked. She continued to stroke the bodyguard's hair and murmur soothing nonsense at him.

"Line up your headlights to the docking clamps, just like parking in a garage," Quinn said. His words slurred and his face looked pale. That concussion was probably more serious than he wanted to let on. But at least he was conscious.

Martin gulped and did his best to follow orders. Every time he'd parked an air car—a much smaller and more maneuverable air car—he'd had attendants guiding him and gravity anchoring him. He didn't like the proximity of the belly of the ship against the side of the van. He'd have to scrape the cerama/metal sides of both to line up with the clamps.

"I don't think this thing is going to fit. The clamps look too far apart." Martin slowed as much as possible, creeping forward one centimeter at a time. He had to fight the controls to keep the van in a straight line.

The van scraped the hull. He cringed and backed off a few centimeters.

"You can't hurt the hull with a van," Quinn said. "Unless you care about returning the van to your mother in pristine condition, go ahead and scrape. Just park the damn thing."

"Consider this learning under fire," Bruce added.

"That helps a lot, Bruce," Martin ground out. "Fire won't burn in vacuum and that's what we've got outside. And I think we are running out of air inside. This van was modified for suborbital travel, not built for it."

He eased forward a bit more and felt the docking clamp lock on to the front of the van. Martin breathed deeply. Perspiration drenched his back and brow worse than at the end of an extended fencing bout.

"Are you aligned properly for the air lock to secure tightly?" Kurt asked. He scanned the extending portal skeptically.

Tears prickled Martin's eyes. What if he had failed and they all died in the air lock because he had done a sloppy job? His mother would kill him for damaging the van . . .

She would murder him anyway for trying to escape her net of control. She'd murdered her parents. Or at least she had hired the assassin and then bribed the investigators to declare the incident a tragic accident. She had cheated Martin's father out of a prenuptial agreement. She had deprived Martin of a family and a normal home life, all so that she could manipulate and control everything and everyone around her.

Why hadn't she just arranged for Konner's death once she had confirmed her pregnancy?

Because Konner O'Hara had family who would ask questions.

If Martin and his friends died escaping her, she could blame it all on Giovanni political enemies from Nuevo Italia. Had she arranged that, too, to cover her tracks?

"What's the seal readout?" Quinn asked. His eyes still did not track properly.

"Where do I find the display?" Martin asked, jerked from his self-defeating loop of dismal thoughts.

"On the portal's arm, just outside your window."

Martin found the red display of digital numbers. "Does eighty-nine percent sound right?"

"Good enough if we hurry." Quinn handed Martin his handheld. "You'll have to authorize the lock to accept five bodies without EVA suits. Code sixteen alpha, twenty-three gamma, delta, delta, beta."

Martin tapped in the code. The portal creaked and shifted ominously.

"Okay, open the doors and scramble." Quinn didn't look as if he could move, let alone scramble.

Somehow, they dragged him into the air lock, closed the van doors, and engaged atmosphere. A lot of air leaked out of the faulty seal.

At last the inner door opened and they all stumbled gasping and careening into a storage bay onboard the saucer-shaped vessel.

"Help me to the bridge." Quinn looked as if he was about to vomit. But he held it in as he grasped a handhold and reached for the next. "We've got to get moving before Melinda figures out where we are."

"Flight control sensors will lock on as soon as we engage engines," Martin warned. He gulped, too. He hadn't much experience in free fall and still had trouble finding his horizon.

"You don't look like you can stay conscious long enough to get us through jump," Jane said. She planted herself directly in front of Quinn.

Martin had often seen that stubborn expression on her face at summer camp. Usually when she opposed Kurt's plans for some new mischief with the computers, or Bruce's practical jokes, or Martin's solo hikes deep into the wilderness. Rarely had any one of them won an argument with Jane when she put on her "den mother" face.

"All I have to do is get us to the jump. The ship's computers do the rest." Quinn plowed forward, pushing Jane aside. In null G, she floated to the opposite side of the bay before she found another handhold.

"We'll have to remember that move," Bruce whispered to Martin. In the echoey bay, Jane had to hear it.

She "hmpfed" and followed Quinn and the boys through a maze of gangways to the bridge, a bubble of viewscreens somewhere in the midsection of the ship.

"Anchor yourselves." Quinn sounded more alert. At least he did not slur his words. He followed his own orders, pulling his safety harness over his shoulders and anchoring it to the center of his seat before the pilot screens.

Martin took the copilot's seat, assuming he had a right to it after driving the van this far. His three friends pulled down "jump" seats from various parts of the bulkheads and strapped in as well. They all tried looking over Quinn's shoulders to watch how he took the vessel out of sleep mode and into full power.

"Jettisoning the van from the portal," Quinn said.

Martin scanned his screens and saw an icon drifting away from the ship. Jane peered out the porthole nearest her and nodded. One less encumbrance from Martin's past.

"Does this ship have a name?" Martin asked. He tapped a duplicate pattern to Quinn's on his blank screen. If he could just do it one more time, he'd have it memorized.

"All ships have names and ID codes. We are sailing aboard the *Margaret Kristine.*"

"Who is she named for?"

"You'll have to ask the emperor that. It was his ship before I bought it. I kept the name because I like it."

"What's that blinking yellow light over my head?" Kurt asked. He strained against his harness to see the beacon better.

"Jump warning," Quinn muttered.

"Already?" Bruce gulped. "We haven't even disengaged from the derelict yet."

"Then that red light flashing on the comm board is normal, too," Jane said. Her voice quaked a little.

Martin jerked his attention away from Quinn's screens to his own.

"Quinn, someone is trying to signal you. I bet it is flight control on the orbital station."

"Ignore it. We'll be out of here before they can send someone out to see what's going on." As he spoke, the ship moved. Acceleration gave them limited gravity.

A klaxon blared three times. Martin wanted to hold his ears and close his eyes against the noise. He didn't dare. He needed to say awake and alert. He had to make sure Quinn did, too.

"Entering jump," Quinn warned.

Reality blurred and dissolved.

Motion seemed to cease.

Time stopped.

Martin lost contact with his body.

And then they were into the jump. Martin looked down upon his inert body from somewhere . . . somewhen else. Time became a meaningless measure of existence.

Jane screamed. Kurt slipped his harness and dove through low G to shake Quinn's slumped form.

The klaxon sounded a proximity alert. "Unknown ship approaching," ship's computer said in a sweet, lilting feminine voice. "Proximity alert. Prepare for crash."

* * *

After a second lonely night of sleeping in the clearing alone, without Bruce Geralds at her side, Kat joined her brothers Kim and Konner as they marshaled every available hand and headed back to clear a new field in the village.

Kat toted rock after rock out of the west field until her back felt as if it would split in two and her hands were a swollen mess of cuts.

Her brothers expected a wave of refugees from near Base Camp. They needed several more acres cleared and planted before they arrived. The season had already progressed too far into summer for them to expect a full crop. Hopefully, they'd harvest enough to get them all through the next winter.

Food took precedence over mining omniscium.

Kat mopped sweat off her brow with her sleeve.

The remnants of her uniform looked as tattered and filthy as the clothing of everyone else in this village. She'd carried her fair share of rocks from the field to the borders where skilled stoneworkers piled them into low walls. Eventually, the walls would separate the various fields and keep the livestock from munching new crops.

She plopped down upon a good-sized boulder, one too big to carry, and took a swig of water from a nearby bucket. She'd seen others take brief rests here.

Everyone in the village and the clearing had been drafted to help—even the protesting and disdainful Lucinda Baines. Taneeo, the village priest, had told her that she would not eat unless she worked. The village would not survive without the crops.

Even the Stargods—the three O'Hara brothers—added their backs to the heavy labor.

Kat's shoulders and legs ached from the unaccustomed work. Her back itched where perspiration had dripped and dried.

Trying to look casual, Kat made her way to the festival pylon at the center of the village. She leaned against it, letting the poles support her weight. The three poles lashed together into a tripod and anchored deep in the ground marked more than the middle of the living area. It marked the junction of three ley lines.

She had some serious experimentation and research to do before Loki's plans for mining went any further.

Kat breathed deeply as Kim had showed her: in on three counts, hold three, exhale on three. She felt the now-familiar shift in orientation and spectrum. Power tingled in her feet, up her body, and into her mind. Her perspective shifted from inside her body to up above the top of the pylon. She looked down upon her body and up into the heavens. With just a little stretch she could reach . . . reach out to Gentian.

Her mind zeroed in on her errant flywacket directly into his body. The gray-green desert around him/them looked frighteningly familiar. Gentian clawed and twisted at something metallic and mechanical. Too close. She couldn't discern what the thing was from five centimeters' distance.

Forcibly, Kat removed herself from Gentian's mind and watched him from a slight distance. The metal "thing" resolved into the hydroponics tank inside the lander she'd had to abandon after *Jupiter* crashed. Gentian worked at freeing pumps and hoses from the innards of the contraption.

Kat chuckled. Gentian wasn't truly a coward, he just disagreed with nimbus definitions of courageous acts. Right now, he defied the nimbus to help Paola with a kind of weapon to defend the port city.

Loki would be glad when Kat told him.

She shifted her mental reaching upward. Up . . . up to the saucer-shaped *Sirius*. She drew its deep silence and patience into herself, understood the nuances of the sleeping crystal array, and listened to the computer running maintenance diagnostics.

For a femto of a second she flitted through the fiber optics to the computers. She became the ship, attuned to the crystal array.

She could now fly this ship no matter what booby traps and safety protocols Konner had installed.

Communication with Mum, or possibly even Kat's adopted father, Governor Talbot, should be an easy jump from here. Dad would not know how to respond to a telepathic call, might not even receive it. But Mum . . . all four of her children had psi powers. She probably did, too. For that matter, both Kat's blood parents probably had strong psi factors for their children to manifest their talents so strongly.

All she had to do was find the transactional graviton the king stone used to contact its mother stone. That web of energy should be a mere extension of the ley line she stood upon.

There. She grabbed hold of the energy with her metaphysical hand and began tracing it back toward Earth's moon and the crystal factory in orbit around it.

(Go back,) a deep voice, that might have been many voices, echoed in her mind. *(Do not venture beyond the realm of dragons.)*

"I have to," she told them. "Since you won't return Gentian to me, I want to talk to my mother," she lied. She did not *want* to talk to the obsessive woman her mother had become, but she needed to know how, to show Loki.

(You speak the truth only when you say you miss your flywacket. For the rest: You can lie to your brothers. You can lie to the stranger, the Sam Eyeam you want as a lover. You can lie to yourself. But you cannot lie to us.)

"Oh, yeah?" she sneered silently.

She sensed an equally private chuckle from the voices.

"Please let me do this. I need to know if I can talk to my Mum this way."

(Not until you have found your true home and know what you want from your mother and your brothers.)

"But . . ."

She fell abruptly back into her body. Her senses reeled and her stomach rebelled.

"Let's get you a cool drink and some shade," Bruce Geralds said. He took Kat's elbow and led her off to the nearest cave. "You should know better than to work out in the sun without a hat."

(You should know better than to deal with dragons before you are ready.)

CHAPTER 30

THE SUN SET upon the village at the base of the cliff. Weary workers trooped back into their caves and huts eager for a hot meal and sleep. Kim wanted nothing more than a soak in the hot spring and the chance to hold his wife and daughter in his arms again. But he had duties to this village and the one that Amanda Leonard had enslaved.

"Iianthe?" Kim called the purple-tip dragon with his mind as well as his voice. "Iianthe, we need to know what Amanda is up to. We need to know how the other villagers fare. But they are far away and we cannot fly to them right now. Can you help us?"

His mind and ears remained empty of any dragon presence.

"Maybe Irythros will answer me," Konner offered.

"Try. Irythros is more adventurous and eager to please than Iianthe. My dragon is serious and all too aware of his status as the only purple-tip in the nimbus." Kim sipped the herbal infusion the local women called tay. It tasted nuttier and sweeter than real tea. Still, it refreshed him and kept him occupied while the old women who had not been in the fields finished preparing the communal pot of stew.

Konner turned on his sitting rock and faced the bay. His brow furrowed in concentration.

"All I get is emptiness." He turned back to face the

evening bonfire, shaking his head. "It's like they are all occupied with something else."

"You both look as if you have a headache," Kat said, joining them. Her own face looked pale and her eyes squinted as if the campfire was too bright.

"Try some tay," Kim offered her a cup and the pottery jug filled with the hot brew. "What have you been doing to share our headache—besides working twice as hard as anyone else out in the bright sun?"

"Trying to contact Gentian. I really miss my flywacket. His purr cures any number of ailments, including headaches." She sipped at the tay, grimaced at the strange taste, then sipped again. A little of the strain eased from her face but not her hunched shoulders and scrunched neck muscles. "I stood at the festival pylon and reached out with my mind. I found him trying to dismantle the abandoned hydroponics tank for a pump and hoses. He's helping Paola without permission from the nimbus."

"Speaking of working too hard," Loki joined them. He carried a larger mug that smelled of beer. "What are we going to do about Ms. Lucinda Baines?" He folded his legs and sank onto his own rock. "I don't think she carried more than two handfuls of pebbles all day."

"Let her go hungry," Konner muttered. He stretched his back. He'd spent the day wrestling a pair of oxen into a yoke and then plowing. His ability to lift heavy objects with his mind should have made the job easier. Psi powers drained more energy from the body than hard physical work.

Only the Tambootie eased the burden. Konner rarely indulged in the drug.

Kim had a hard time fighting his constant need to

lick the oils from the leaves and then chew them, even when he wasn't working magic.

The old women and young children passed plates of stew around to one and all. Kim ate hungrily, barely noticing the chunks of fish that had gone into the mix. The men had not had a chance to hunt today. He and his brothers had eased their refusal to eat meat enough to consider fish edible. The addition of shell-fish from the shore made a nice change in their diet.

Yaakke picked up a reed flute and began playing a lilting ballad about a lover lost at sea. One of the women picked up the tune in a husky alto. A tenor voice added harmony.

And then, miracle of miracles, Cyndi added her clear soprano. She sang the sweet lyrics with passion while the village as a group hummed along in a quiet resonance until the last poignant chorus where the dragons returned the lost sailor to his lover.

Loki sat with his mouth open in wonder. "She actually joined the group!"

"I wish I could sing as well as she does," Kat said around a yawn. "Might ease the long lonely nights aboard ship."

"Did she sing while aboard *Jupiter?*" Loki asked.

"Once. She got a little tipsy during a poker game. She sang as she cleaned us all out of chips. I could have sworn she cheated, but I never figured out how."

"I thought if we gave Cyndi enough freedom, she might try to escape to Base Camp," Loki muttered. "Now she seems to be fitting in a bit, she might prove an asset. Our people do love their music."

"I don't think we need to worry about Cyndi harboring Hanassa's spirit. Amanda Leonard's insanity and attempt to enslave the locals is more typical of the rogue dragon than Cyndi singing love ballads," Kim said.

"I agree," Loki said quietly. Then he related Cyndi's strange dream.

"Sounds like Hanassa tried to gain a foothold here to work mischief against us," Kim admitted.

"We need a spy at Base Camp, but I wouldn't ask anyone to volunteer for that dangerous job," Konner said.

"*S'murghit,* we need to find out what is happening at Base Camp." Kim slammed his cup against his sitting rock, sloshing tay on the ground and onto his buckskin breeches. Just one more stain among many.

Kat's head jerked up. She stared at the rising moon in intense concentration. All traces of the earlier headache vanished from her expression and posture.

"What is it?" Kim whispered.

"Gentian," she breathed. "He's coming back." Her shoulders relaxed and a smile crossed her face. "He's certainly a chatterbox tonight."

"What's he saying?" Kim asked. He hoped that Gentian had messages from the dragons.

"Right now he's flooding my mind with images of his hunt. Yuck, I didn't need to know the fine details of gutting a squirrel." She grimaced as if the images had left a bad taste in her mouth.

"Wait a minute." She held up her hand to hold off Loki's sarcastic comment. "Paola now has the parts to make a pump and hose to fight off the snakes." She paused another moment while she listened. "He saw a line of people walking this way from the big river—I think they are the slaves who escaped from Amanda. They are weary but safe, about a week's walk from here."

"How many?" Kim asked. He whipped out a handheld and began plotting the number of acres they would need to feed additional mouths.

"Gentian doesn't think in numbers," Kat replied. She stood up, eyes still on the moon.

A shadow crossed the pale surface. Villages stood to look as well. Some of them crossed themselves in superstitious fear. Many more crossed their wrists and flapped their hands in a ward against Simurgh, the bloodthirsty demon dragon they used to worship.

"There he is," Kat sighed in relief. Then her face and body stiffened.

"What, Kat?" Kim asked. He did not dare imagine what new worry replaced his sister's joy at the return of her flywacket.

"Amanda and her Marines have fired up the forge. They are making weapons to replace their stunners. Lethal weapons. This time they mean to kill all those who resist."

* * *

"Solo merchant vessel, this is Imperial Military Police Cruiser *Hercules*. Identify yourself," a crisp male voice announced over Quinn's comm system.

Martin sank back into his body from the jump with a stomach lurching jolt. He shook his head to clear it.

Jane shook Quinn's shoulder to rouse him.

"What do we do?" Bruce whispered, as if the vessel outside could hear them.

Martin slapped the comm unit. "*Hercules,* this is Imperial Scout *Margaret Kristine,* piloted by Adam Jonathan Quinnsellia," Martin said in his deepest voice. Was that how Quinn would introduce himself?

"State the nature of your mission, Pilot Quinnsellia."

"I'm on a private mission for His Imperial Majesty."

"Not enough info, Quinnsellia. You could be anybody trying to bluff your way past this blockade."

Aurora blockaded? Martin's head spun with questions. No time for speculation. He had to convince this IMP cruiser that they were on a legitimate mission or risk being sent back to Aurora and Melinda's wrath.

"Secrecy code," Quinn mumbled. "Alpha, alpha, alpha, one, one, one, zeta, two, quantum, three."

Martin repeated the code out loud to the IMP cruiser.

"Good hunting, Agent Quinnsellia," the voice from *Hercules* replied. "Let us know if you find any trace of the *Jupiter* in your travels. Politics are heating up over the loss of that ship and the dippo they carried as a passenger. His Majesty, in particular, wants that ship found."

"Will do," Martin replied. He shut off the comm link and stared at the pilot's screens. "Now how do I get this thing underway?"

Quinn touched a few places on his screen. "You have control. Steer by the touch screen."

Martin placed one finger on the dark rectangle at the center of his controls. An icon of the ship appeared on the viewscreen along with a glyph representing the IMP cruiser.

"Now ease your way around the other ship. Very light touch," Quinn directed. His eyes crossed and he looked close to losing consciousness again.

Martin complied. The icon careened a long way toward starboard.

"You having problems, Quinnsellia?" The voice from the IMP cruiser overrode Martin's cut off of the comm system.

"Too broad a stroke. This isn't a VR game. Little movements," Quinn advised.

"Let me do that," Jane eased into position next to Martin. She placed her smaller fingers on the screen and barely moved them. The icon of the ship straightened up and moved slowly around the cruiser. "You talk to the man and make it sound like you really are Quinn."

"Um . . . *Hercules,* that last jump was rough," Martin said. "Left me a little dazed at first. I'm okay now."

"You flying solo? Sounds like you need some help. I'll gladly lend you a navigator."

"Don't let him. He just wants to monitor my mission," Quinn protested. "IMPs don't like the fact that His Majesty employs solo agents."

Martin nodded and returned his attention to the comm. "If I let your navigator aboard, I'd have to mind-wipe him. That would defeat the purpose of his presence. Thanks for the offer anyway, *Hercules. Margaret Kristine* out."

This time Quinn turned off the comm unit and added a few extra commands. "He won't override that again."

"You look better, but still shaky, Quinn," Jane said, as she steered the ship into space beyond the IMP.

"Can you navigate us to the next jump?" Quinn asked. He posted coordinates on the upper left-hand corner of Martin's screen. Their current position appeared in the upper right-hand corner.

"I think so." Jane bumped Martin with her hip, indicating he should move.

He scooted out of the chair and let her take his place. She settled comfortably, never letting up her control of the steering. "Just a matter of watching the numbers until they match. I've worked similar exercises at home manipulating robotic arms for virtual dissections in biology."

"I've worked robotic arms when I rebuilt my dad's home security system," Kurt chimed in. "If I could shadow Jane's moves for a little while, I'm sure I could spell her."

Good idea." Quinn tumbled out of his own chair so that Kurt could take it. "I'll be in my quarters with the med kit. Holler if you run into any problems bigger than space dust. The galley is fully stocked, help yourselves. Oh, and Martin, why don't you see if you can load your star map into my system."

"The only copy is on Melinda's computer."

"Is it?"

Martin fingered the blue crystal in his pocket and wondered the same thing.

CHAPTER 31

KAT HELD GENTIAN close in her lap, cherishing their togetherness. After everyone had eaten, she had slipped away and now sat on the ground overlooking the cove at slack tide. She blanked her mind a moment, trying to center herself. Maybe then she could figure out what was important, where she belonged, who to trust.

Amanda Leonard, her *captain,* had gone insane and now apparently hosted an alien spirit. The brothers she had blamed for abandoning her twenty years ago now seemed honest men, victims of a corrupt judicial system. Her own thoughts and perceptions had gone awry, affected more by new psi powers that gave her information without hard evidence.

She communicated with a flying cat more readily than she did Bruce Geralds, an attractive man she considered a potential lover.

She had some sorting out to do.

"Will you spy for me again, Gentian?" she asked quietly, stroking the silky fur around his ears.

(*I am afraid. But I must or my nimbus will take me away from you. I do not know how they will punish me for cowardice.*)

"It is okay to be afraid, my friend." Kat continued her loving caress of the flywacket, reassuring him and herself of their bond. "I am often afraid. My duty is stronger than my fear, though. I need you to help me stop Amanda from doing more damage to herself and the people around her."

(Your brothers will do it. You must remain safe, so that I may remain safe.)

"My brothers need you to spy for us as well. The dragons do not respond to our request for aid. You alone can travel the distance between here and Base Camp and back again safely. You alone can help us. I need you to help me put my world in order. I have many new emotions and situations to sort through. I need to take care of Amanda and the world I came from before I can accept my brothers as family."

(For you I will do this thing, though I do not like it. I fear the spirit that moves your Amanda.)

"We all fear her. And I promise that when I leave this place for good, I will take you with me. I will protect you from the nimbus. I will keep you safe."

The flywacket settled deeper into her lap with a sigh. Kat thought the conversation ended. Then her companion spoke again.

(My nimbus may not allow you to protect me from them.)

"Your nimbus has never run up against Mari Kathleen O'Hara Talbot before." Kat laughed a little and ruffled his ears with rough affection.

They both yawned hugely, reminding them that a very long day was nearing an end.

Her brothers prepared to climb the hill to return to their wives and their beds. The villagers wound down their celebration of a hard day's work successfully completed. Their songs had dwindled away along with their chatter. A few women nursed mugs of hot drinks and men finished off their beers, as one by one they sought their night's rest.

Teenagers patrolled the perimeter of the village, taking the first watch.

She heard a hesitant step behind her and stiffened her back, prepared to defend herself.

"Don't go back up the hill tonight, Kat," Bruce Geralds said quietly. He wrapped his arms around her shoulders.

Kat leaned back a little, welcoming his warmth. Sleeping snuggled against him, waking with him close would be nice.

"Bruce, I'm not ready for a relationship. I've just found my family after a twenty-year search. They aren't the monsters I believed them to be. They aren't angels either. Until I figure out what they are, and what I want from them, I can't really accept them as family. It's all too new. I've too many emotions to sort through to risk an entanglement."

"I'm not asking for a long-term commitment, Kat—unless we never get off this rock. For now, I just don't want to sleep alone." He kissed the back of her neck.

Tingles of pleasure radiated down Kat's spine and through her shoulders. She basked a moment within his caress.

Gentian jumped off her lap and began circling her. He made a point of coming between her and Geralds.

"I guess that damn cat has a voice in this matter." He broke contact with Kat.

"I guess he does. Maybe later, Bruce. Just not tonight." She stood and brushed off her crumpled and filthy uniform. "We might be able to find a few moments of privacy tomorrow in the hot spring." She lifted her eyebrows in speculation. She realized she needed more from him than just sex if she were ever to truly trust him.

"I'll hold you to that. I haven't had a proper bath in months."

"None of us have." She laughed, too. "We all smell a little musky and ripe. But if we all do, then we don't offend anyone."

"Kat, what are we going to do about the omniscium? We can't just leave it. The GTE needs it. With the money from it, I could break free of Melinda Fortesque. Konner could buy custody of his son. You could buy yourself three promotions." He stood beside her and looked her squarely in the eyes by the light of a cloud-covered moon.

"Not very likely. The emperor is trying to reinstitute merit promotions. If we ever get back, I'll have one heck of a lot of explaining to do." Something about his last statement bothered her. Her thoughts scattered as he kissed her full on the mouth.

"All nice speculation. I'll dream about it in my cold lonely bed. I'll dream of you, too." He pushed her away and walked back toward the jumble of caves and huts.

"What did he mean by breaking free of Melinda Fortesque?"

Gentian did not have an opinion. She stropped her ankles and butted his head against her so that she stumbled toward the path uphill to the clearing.

"Ready for bed, Kat?" Konner asked. He carried a small lantern that burned fish oil. It stank.

So did she.

"Can I get a bath tonight?" she asked, moving close to her brother's side and the circle of inviting light.

"Maybe in the morning, when the light is better."

Loki and Kim joined them. Companionably, they

all climbed the hill together. For the space of an hour Kat felt almost as if she belonged with them, almost as if she were a part of the family and not an outsider.

How long could it last?

"Why would you have to buy custody of your son if Melinda sent Geralds to bring you back to become a family again?" she asked quietly. "Why would you have to buy custody if you are still married to her as she claims?"

"Melinda is full of lies. Our marriage was annulled, and our prenuptial agreement destroyed—except for my carefully guarded copy," Konner said bitterly. "Melinda no more wants a family than she wants to share control of Aurora with anyone. She's blinded Geralds with stardust."

"Or maybe he's lying to get on your good side, Kat," Loki added.

"Or to get into my bed."

"Be careful, baby sister. Don't let your emotions blind you to people's faults," Konner warned.

"Use your magic to see who tells the truth and who lies," Kim added. "I'll show you how to use the Tambootie tomorrow."

"Can I practice on you three, see how much of the truth you are telling me?"

They all found something else to look at rather than answer her.

That was answer enough. She turned her back on them and walked back down the hill.

"Kat, remember that trust has to be given before it can be received," Kim called after her.

She almost stopped. A deep ache in her heart kept her moving back to the village and a lonely bed in the women's dormitory.

* * *

Noon sunshine sparkled on the water of the bathing pool. Kat stood in the pool at the base of the falls. Warm water swirled about her legs while a cool splash from the falls refreshed her face. For the first time in months she felt truly clean. Her clothes lay out on rocks, equally clean and drying in the summer sunshine.

Bruce Geralds swam lazy circles around her. His clothes were spread out next to hers.

He probably expected physical intimacies from her special invitation to enjoy the family hot spring.

She intended a different kind of intimacy—probes into his memories of his time before he showed up at Base Camp.

"Don't hunch your shoulders," Geralds whispered in her ear as he came up behind her. He grabbed her at the base of her neck and began massaging twenty years of knotted muscles.

Her head lolled forward accepting his closeness.

The current around her legs changed. She realized that he stood behind her, feet braced in the mud, while he gently pulled her body backward into a float.

She dug her toes into the soft streambed.

"Let me work on your neck for a while." She eased away from him enough to turn him so that he faced away from the bank on the clearing side of the pool. The force field ended just beyond the stream.

Kat now knew that Konner had had to make the force field quite large to accommodate the full crystal array in proper proportions. The king stone resided in the middle of the clearing with twelve green drivers in a circle at a specified distance. One hundred forty-four red directionals stood out from there in another circle, spaced proportionally. Every measurement came down to an exact ratio of twelve to one.

The whole encompassed enough land for a large garden, the hut, and this pool, with acres of trees to shade and shelter it.

With strong hands, she worked on the cords of Geralds' neck, then spread out to his shoulders and back. He had firm, lean muscles, a long body, and not much body hair. He seemed a perfect compromise between the short, compact body of the civilized planets and the taller, leaner body of the bush planets. Genetic manipulation had determined the differences many generations ago.

She liked his body. She wanted to like the man inside.

"There's an ugly scar here." She ran her fingertips diagonally down his back from right shoulder to left hip. "You should have Lotski look at it. Maybe she has something to reduce it."

"It's old. Too late for cosmetic repair." He moved her hands back up to his shoulders.

"How'd you get it?" She wanted to ask why he hadn't been able to get medical help soon enough to seal the wound without the ridge of thickened flesh.

"Accident. Too near an exploding ship in space. I had enough air and sense to climb into an EVA suit until the authorities picked out my life signs among all the debris."

"Still . . ." Any inhabited planet connected to the trade routes had decent medical care. He'd only have the scar if he had been in hiding after the accident with nothing more than rudimentary first aid.

Why would he have to hide? Unless he caused the accident.

"Leave it, Kat. It's history. Let's talk about something important. Like the omniscium."

"What's to talk about?" Kat returned her attention to the tightening cords of his neck. "We can't do anything until we figure out how to mine it. Then we have to figure out how to get it and us off this planet."

"I got a peek at the stash of fuel cells at Base Camp. Lots of partials, few full. I think if we put all of them in one of the fighters, you and I can get back to my ship." Geralds turned to face her, placing his hands upon her shoulders. His thumbs traced her jaw in a gentle caress.

"What about my brothers?" A chill ran up Kat's legs that had nothing to do with the currents in the pool.

"Let them fend for themselves. They'll recharge some cells eventually. But you and I can be free. Once we've sold a single beaker of omniscium, we can come back here. We can build a palace in the west and rule our own kingdom." He twirled in the water to face her, grabbing her about the waist in his enthusiasm.

"I—ah—thought cannibals lived in the west; that it was truly barbaric over there." She backed up through the tight whirlpool he had created with his move. Her balance was off as well as her ideas about controlling this conversation. "You had nightmares of cannibals."

"Only in the mountains between here and there."

"You had to walk through their territory to get to Base Camp. How did you survive?" Kat tried to put winsome admiration into her expression. She'd never been very good at flirting. She liked her relationships honest and open.

"I guess I'm too ornery to eat. They captured me in a blind pit. Left me there for a day and a night." His face fell and his enthusiasm faded. "I just barely escaped when they pulled me out. They chased me for days."

"Why? They must be desperate for food if they have resorted to eating other humans."

"On the contrary. They eat humans in a very solemn ritual. It's a rite of passage and a way of honoring an enemy they respect for his prowess in battle." He gulped and turned his face away.

"I'm sorry you had to go through that. No wonder you had nightmares."

"That part isn't important. I escaped," he said firmly. "What matters is that Judge Balinakas and his entire judiciary crew managed to get their escape pods to land together on a river near the far west coast of this continent. They've set up their own little city already, gotten the locals to build for them, organized crops and trade and communications . . . everything. The land is incredibly lush, full of everything, including mineral deposits. We could settle there, make it our base for mining and selling omniscium. We wouldn't have to put up with Amanda Leonard or her megalomaniac ideas." His face lit up again and he hugged her tight.

"Judge Balinakas won't accept rivals to his power," Kat hedged.

"Then we'll make our home someplace else. Someplace new and untouched. This planet is practically empty. Plenty of room for separate kingdoms. Please say yes. Say you'll join me."

"What about your wife and children?"

"Who ever said . . ." He did not deny that he already had a family. "I'll divorce her as soon as we get back to civilization. But I'll bring my son here. I want Bruce, Jr. with me. He's my son and heir."

"Just like the name of your ship."

Kat pointedly removed his hands from her waist and stepped back toward shore.

"Sorry, Bruce. I don't think I can desert my brothers. The omniscium belongs to the entire family. I can't and won't go it alone." She waded back to the embankment and began to dress in her nearly dry clothing.

"I trust my brothers more than I trust you," she said to herself and suddenly felt a lot better.

CHAPTER 32

KIM AND HESTIIA, perched upon their usual sitting rock, watching Medic Chaney Lotski progress through the village with half a dozen young women trailing after her. All of them wore flowers in their hair, in strings around their necks, wrists, and ankles. Chaney carried more flowers.

Jetang M'Berra and Taneeo awaited her at the festival pylon.

"I am glad we can celebrate a new marriage after so many have died," Hes murmured. She snuggled her face next to their sleeping daughter in her arms.

"We also celebrate new life. We present Ariel to the world today," Kim added. He draped an arm about them. Warmth born of love and pride blossomed in his belly. Today was the first day his wife and daughter had ventured out of the clearing since he'd carried them up there over a week ago, the day after Ariel's birth.

Taneeo evoked promises from Chaney and Jetang. To work together as one, to trust each other, to love each other, to support each other in times of trial, and rejoice together during good times.

Kim looked deeply into Hestiia's eyes, reliving the moment Taneeo had spoken the same words over them. His heart swelled. "I love you," he whispered to her.

She smiled up at him and leaned in a little closer. "You are my life," she replied.

"Marrying you was the best thing I ever did."

They gloried within their own private world a moment.

And then the gathered village erupted in shouts of joy and applause as M'Berra bent his tall African frame to kiss his petite blonde bride.

"I'm glad they did this," Kat said plunking herself down on the rock next to Kim and Hestiia. Gentian stropped her ankles and wove a purring path between and around the two rocks.

"Military authorities frown upon marriage between officers. They don't mind if they sleep together, but they don't want them committed. Too much work to make sure they are posted together." She frowned slightly.

"Is there someone you regret not committing to?" Hestiia asked quietly, almost shyly.

"Not me. I've yet to meet a man I can respect, trust, and like enough to commit to." Kat kept looking down at the pack she had placed at her feet.

Kim allowed her the space to follow through whatever deep thoughts troubled her.

"I want you to have something, Kim." Kat finally reached into the pack. She lifted her face and made certain she met and matched his gaze. Then she placed something soft and furry in his lap.

He looked down in surprise.

"What?"

"The reason I ran back into the house while it was burning," Kat almost choked on the words.

Kim couldn't tell what strong emotion welled up within her.

"Murphy!" His own fragmented memories brought tears to his eyes. He fondled the very threadbare green teddy bear.

"He was mine before I gave him to you the day you were born. Konner had him before me, and Loki before that. He's old enough maybe Mum or Dad had him originally. I really wanted to be a responsible big sister and pass it on properly."

"I used to sleep with him," Kim gasped. He'd only been four when Mum fled the family compound with her three boys. Kat—Katie then—had run back into the house and become lost.

"You . . . you risked your life to bring me my teddy bear."

"Mum forgot him. I heard you crying for him. I couldn't leave him behind. He's one of the family."

"The only family you had for a long time."

Kat nodded, swallowing deeply. Still, two tears trickled down her cheeks.

"He kept me company until Governor Mitchell's storm troopers found me. They fed me and then threw me into a cell. Mitchell didn't last long. He was too much a tyrant even for a bush planet. Governor Talbot replaced him within a month or two. He found me in the prison and rescued me and Murphy. Talbot adopted me, raised, and educated me as if I were one of his own."

"You needed Murphy then. You've kept him safe all these years. Maybe you should keep him."

"That's okay. I think Ariel needs him now." Kat reached over to caress the baby's cheek.

For the first time Kim noticed the bracelet of braided hair on her right wrist.

"Is that what I think it is?"

"Mum's. She made it from locks of each of our hair." She touched the fairest of the four strands. "That's Loki, he was almost strawberry blond as a kid."

"This dark chestnut has to be Konner's."

"Actually that's yours. You got brighter as you grew. This bright one is Konner's. He got darker as he matured."

"Then this flaming one must be yours." Kim caressed the silky strands.

"And this one, almost identical but a little lighter is Mum's. That makes the dark brown one our dad's. Did Mum ever find him? He disappeared just weeks before we had to flee."

"I don't know that Mum ever looked for Dad," Kim said sadly. "I would have liked to have known him."

"He was a great pilot. He started to teach me how to fly just before he left."

"You were, what, seven?"

"Yeah."

They shared a big grin.

"Can I come back to the clearing? I'd like to get to know my brothers, and my niece, and my sisters-in-law."

"You trust us enough?"

"I trust you with my life."

"But not your secrets," Hestiia added.

"In time, Hes. Give her time. We've been apart a long time."

"I've been lonely a long time. I didn't realize that until . . . Gentian invaded my life. He showed me how much I need my family."

"Then, welcome, Sister. Welcome home." Kim hugged her close, unable to check the tears of joy that flooded his eyes. His sense of completeness expanded and redoubled.

* * *

"I don't see why he did it." Cyndi watched the simple wedding between the tall African and the properly civil-sized medic. She didn't want to admit that this bush ceremony actually moved her more than an expensive legal union with all the trappings of gowns and flowers and lavish reception back home. "M'Berra could have gone places, but no, he had to throw away his career to be with her," she continued her litany of complaint.

She shuddered to think how close she had come, two years ago, to throwing away her own career, her place at court, and any chance of inheriting money from her parents when she had the opportunity to marry Loki.

She might well have already thrown away everything in boarding *Jupiter*. She reminded herself that she wanted to personally supervise Loki's arrest, trial, and punishment. In truth, she had the stupid, romantic, foolish need to do the right thing and break off her engagement to Loki in person. Her conscience had gotten her stranded here.

"Love is blind," Geralds finished the thought for her.

"Thank the stars I shredded the veil of inappropriate love before I made the same mistake."

"Did you?" he asked coming up behind her. He stood so close she could feel his body heat. "Just why did you hop a ride aboard *Jupiter?* Did you know that Captain Leonard was chasing the O'Hara brothers? Had you ferreted out the information that Kat Talbot is really their long lost sister?"

Cyndi gulped in horror that this man might have read her mind.

"Imagine the nerve of M'Berra, asking Loki to stand up for him." Cyndi decided to changed the subject rather than venture into the space debris of her true motives. "Can you imagine the nerve, the audacity of asking a known outlaw to be his best man? He should have asked you, or the headman. What's his name? Raaskan?"

"You don't know that I'm any better than Loki." Geralds smirked.

Cyndi almost imagined him laughing at her. He wouldn't dare. He still had prospects of a life back in civilization.

"You have to be better than Loki. More law-abiding. Anyone would be better than Loki."

"Except his brothers."

"I think his brothers have more honor than he does."

"Strange word, 'honor.' "

More shattering asteroids in that statement.

"You'd think that Chaney Lotski would have enough sense to ask me to be her maid of honor rather than Kat Talbot. I have more status, and I no longer have the taint of O'Hara associations." Cyndi wanted to give the medic a piece of her mind. She took two steps toward the knot of celebrants beginning to dance around the festival pylon.

"I think I know how to get you and me off this barbaric planet," Geralds said quietly.

Cyndi froze in place.

"Is that an invitation to go with you?"

"Could be. Can you help me steal some fuel cells from the O'Haras?"

"I have one already. I could have had two, but I couldn't lift one of them. So I took the lighter one and hid it."

"Right idea. Wrong fuel cell. You stole an empty one. We need six to get one of the fighters from Base Camp up to my ship."

"Fighters only require two."

"Two that are properly charged from the crystal array, under pressure. The patch job Konner has set up isn't enough. I'm not taking off with less than two sets of backups."

"The fighters are at Base Camp. How do we get ourselves and six fuel cells back there?"

"We get Captain Leonard to come here with one."

Cyndi fought the urge to run away screaming. The nightmare of fighting off the creature that Leonard had become frightened her more than losing her place at court.

"I think I can get into the clearing to steal the cells," Geralds continued. "But I need you to distract Loki while I cart them outside the force field."

"Plenty of places to hide them." She knew that for certain. No one had found the cell she'd stolen—even if it was empty. "But how do we get Leonard to fly one of the fighters here?"

"We call her and offer her the one thing she wants most—the heads of the O'Hara brothers on a plate."

CHAPTER 33

KAT WATCHED CAREFULLY as Chaney Lotski deftly wove a series of knots in a torn fishnet.

"Where'd you learn to do that?" Kat asked. She looked at the hopeless tangle in her own net.

"My own version of surgeon's knots." Chaney shrugged and smiled. She glowed in the summer sunshine. Marriage to Jetang M'Berra seemed to agree with her.

The big black man planed the outside edges of a new boat with a primitive tool. His bare back glistened with sweat as he concentrated on the task. The sweet scent of freshly worked wood drifted on the morning breeze.

"You two certainly seem happy." Kat needed to explore the topic of leaving with these potential allies.

"Never thought I'd be glad to land in the bush again," M'Berra laughed. He rested on his bare heels, knees in the dirt, one hand possessively on the boat.

"I always wanted to retire to the bush, just didn't think it would be this soon," Chaney added. Her hands flew as she continued working her net.

"Will you stay here when we have enough fuel to leave?" Kat shifted uneasily. Her brothers would certainly object if they knew she discussed the possibility of anyone leaving their precious planet and spreading the news of its existence.

"We've talked about it, Kat." M'Berra ran his

hands up and down the length of the boat looking for uneven places that might eventually leak. "Frankly, we both feel we've come to a dead end in the military."

"Surely you are up for a promotion. Maybe your own ship . . ."

"I'm bush. The only way I can get my own ship is to steal one and become a pirate or smuggler. Like your brothers. You'll run into the same prejudice if you go back, Kat. You can only rise so far, then the inbred nobles will put impossible barriers around promotions. Here I can be my own man, make my own decisions. Own my own land." He dropped the plane and picked up a bag of wet sand and began rubbing an imperfection his fingers had found.

"If you want to own land, why did you join the IMP service?" Kat just didn't understand this.

"On Meditcue II all the land is owned by two families. The rest of us worked for them. My only chance at an education was to join the military. My only chance to learn a skill other than farming or fishing was to join the military. Now it's time to move on and do something else."

"What about you, Chaney? Why do you want to retire to the bush?"

"Because everything I learned in medical school points toward a basic incompatibility of the human body with overcrowded domed cities, canned air, and bioengineered tank food. We're setting ourselves up for either some serious mutation or vulnerability to new diseases created by those overcrowded domed cities, canned air, and bioengineered tank food. The answer to the salvation of our bodies is here in the bush with fresh air, natural food, and space to be human." She smiled at M'Berra with love and longing.

"We've decided to raise our children here. The GTE and the IMPs be damned," M'Berra said, still concentrating on sanding the boat.

"We want our children free of GTE restrictions, pollution, and exploitation." Chaney touched her belly with tender fingers. "We agree with your brothers, Kat. This planet must be kept secret from the rest of the world. You might as well accept the fact that you will live out the rest of your days here."

"Not if I can help it." Kat threw her tangled fishnet aside and stalked away.

A week passed, then two. Kat watched the skies impatiently. She and her brothers heard sporadic reports from Paola Sanchez on the continent. The Amazons had killed many of the black snakes, but the matriarch eluded them. Construction of the second wall outside the port city grew slowly. The workers kept having to rebuild what the snakes knocked down during their nightly attacks. The pump worked to keep the snakes at bay, but the water also damaged the mud-brick walls.

Kat paced the clearing and the village. She completed the chores assigned to her while she thought and fretted. She had decisions to make and could find no answers to her questions.

Gentian frequently flew over Base Camp and reported back to her. Each time she had to spend an hour or more cuddling him to calm his fearful quivers and his need to run and hide.

Each day she ground her teeth in frustration as Amanda Leonard and her Marines ranged farther and farther afield on slave hunts. They captured large contingents of men and women who worked the fields a few days and then managed to escape.

"Amanda doesn't have the power of religious fear

to keep her slaves in awe and afraid. The natives know that most of the Marines carry empty weapons. They no longer have the power to recharge them," Loki mused.

Then he told Kat how Hanassa as a priest of Simurgh had maintained absolute control over vast tracts of the lush river valley. The former purple-tip dragon had threatened retribution on the entire populace from their god Simurgh. The awesome terror of a dragon attack forced the Coros to give themselves as slaves and sacrifices.

Until the O'Hara brothers landed in search of raw materials to repair their ship. In outrage, they deposed Hanassa. The Coros named the three red-haired brothers Stargods and followed them instead. Kim had invented a kind and gentle religion modified from his mother's beliefs for the locals.

"No wonder almost half of Amanda's original crew has deserted," Kat gasped. "Only the core of one hundred bloodthirsty Marines puts up with Amanda/Hanassa's harsh regime that breaks every law of the GTE and the Imperial Military Police."

Kat didn't report that Amanda kept her Marines enthralled with sex and vicious punishments. She didn't want to think how far her honorable captain had sunk in her quest for power.

Gentian reported that Amanda and her Marines weren't having a lot of luck forging proper weapons. They didn't have the secrets of working with iron that Konner had discovered.

And then Amanda managed to capture and enslave a true blacksmith. He and his apprentices turned out blade after blade of strong steel. Swords. Daggers. Spear tips. Arrowheads.

Kat clenched her fists and cursed at the stories she

heard of Amanda killing and torturing any who defied her.

Then the first refugees arrived at the village of the Stargods at the base of the cliff. The time had come to find safe homes for them. Either that or attack and kill Amanda Leonard.

The dragons remained strangely quiet.

On the night of the full moon, Kat waited until Loki patrolled the far side of the clearing with his back to the portal. Then she crept out and sneaked halfway down the path to the village. Gentian followed her on silent cat feet. But she felt his distress at her new plan to stop Amanda. She halted at a large outcropping of rock that provided a clear view of the valley below.

"Gentian, please help me. I need a dragon tonight," she said as she settled cross-legged on the rock.

(This is too dangerous. To you and your brothers.)

"But our cause is worth fighting for. It is worth the risk to free this place of Hanassa, or Amanda, or whoever tyrannizes the people." She petted the flywacket with long strokes from ears to tail. "Only when we are free of Hanassa can I leave this planet with good conscience. I'll take you with me. I promised. I always keep my promises."

He leaned into her hand. But his tail remained fat and bristled like a sea brush—a prickly animal that floated into fish traps and pricked the unwary with its poisonous spines.

"Gentian, if you ever want to redeem yourself in the eyes of the nimbus, you must help me. This is an act of bravery. Please help me call a dragon."

Gentian drew away from her, ears flat, tail now tucked tightly around him. *(If I must.)*

"You must."

(Why do humans have to lie to each other?)

"Because honesty is sometimes more dangerous than those lies."

* * *

Loki paced the clearing as part of his evening watch. He'd spent the last two weeks impatiently observing everyone; trying to find solutions to impossible situations.

Cyndi avoided him, always looking the other way when they passed in the village. She was up to something. He knew it. He just couldn't figure out what.

Over these last two weeks, no one had come up with a good idea on how to mine the omniscium, or power up the fuel cells faster. Loki's temper grew shorter than usual.

And so he paced, and thought, and paced some more.

He knew what he had to do, the one thing he had vowed never to do again. He had to kill Amanda, the host for Hanassa, a worse enemy to this world than the GTE, the GFM, and the Kree combined. Then he had to find a way to take out the matriarch of the Krakatrice to stabilize the rest of this planet.

Then maybe his brothers would see reason about mining the ley lines and getting off this rock in the middle of nowhere.

Resigned to his decision, he wearily crawled into his bunk in one of the lean-tos scattered about the clearing. During the coldest months, they had all crowded into the single cabin. Now in early summer only Kim and Hestiia slept there—when Ariel allowed them to sleep at all.

The roll of sleeping furs cushioned his body. He stretched and turned onto his side, ready to welcome a few hours of sleep.

"Loki," Kat hissed, barely audibly.

"What?" He was instantly awake, fearing . . . he did not know what. Mostly he feared his own memories of the time he had to pull the trigger on a needle rifle aimed at the heart of the man they had known as Hanassa. Every night when he closed his eyes, he relived that awful moment as his soul tried to wrench free of his body and follow Hanassa into death.

"Come with me," Kat whispered urgently. "I finally convinced a dragon to take me to Base Camp. But she won't take me alone. She said it's too dangerous."

"You defecting?" Loki pulled his boots back on.

"Usurping. I'm going to take command of Base Camp and get the forge working properly." She held up one of Kim's readers.

Loki knew the thing was stuffed with books and data. This one probably had Konner's notes on working iron.

"Then what?" Loki stuffed his knife back into his belt and sorted through the essential supplies he always kept near to hand.

"We start mining. I think if we combine all the fuel cells from Base Camp and here we can get one of the fighters to Geralds' ship *Son and Heir*. Then the three of us can return to civilization with the first load of omniscium."

"I figured you wouldn't leave the spy behind." Loki didn't trust the man who asked too many personal questions of others and never revealed a thing about himself. Kat spent altogether too much time with the Sam Eyeam. But she repulsed his touch and kept him at arm's length. And she never allowed him into the clearing, not even to use the hot spring.

"Bruce is an innocent, trapped here by mistake." She wouldn't meet Loki's gaze. A sure sign she hid something.

"We're all trapped here by mistake. One mistake after another." Loki crawled out of his lean-to and stood beside his sister. "We take *Sirius,* not Geralds' ship. I will command it, not him."

"What about Kim and Konner? We have to leave *Sirius* for them, if they ever get enough fuel to fly *Rover* again."

"We'll come back for them later. But I will not let Geralds take command. I command or we do not go." He set his jaw.

Kat set hers. They stared at each other a long moment in silent stubbornness.

CHAPTER 34

"ALL RIGHT. We take *Sirius*. But we leave a coded message so Kim and Konner can find and break into *Son and Heir,*" Kat said meekly.

Loki nodded his acceptance.

"Which dragon came to you?" he asked.

"A different one. The female. She calls herself Irisey."

"Is she big enough to carry three adults?"

"Irythros carried Konner, Dalleena, and me and he's only a juvenile. Irisey is fully grown—mother to both Irythros and Iianthe, and mighty proud of it." She grinned hugely.

"What about Gentian? Is he coming, too."

"He . . . he's too afraid." She wouldn't meet his gaze. Which meant she wasn't telling the whole truth.

Loki was almost willing to bet a fully charged fuel cell that Gentian disapproved of Kat's plans. He decided he'd be leery and watchful. He couldn't pull Kat's secrets from her mind, but he knew her well enough now to know she was up to something very sneaky.

They tiptoed to the barrier by the light of a setting moon and the glowing embers of the central campfire.

"Where's the dragon?" Loki asked quietly the moment they cleared the barrier. Bodies might not be able to penetrate the confusion field, but sound did.

"In the village, keeping Bruce from bolting. The last time he flew with a dragon, Irythros dumped him on the extreme western coast. It took him months to walk to Base Camp."

"He doesn't talk about his experience there." That bothered Loki. He'd grown used to communal adventure stories around the campfire each evening.

"He doesn't want to think about it," Kat said quietly. She knew more. Loki knew that by the tightness of her mouth and the way her shoulders reached for her ears.

A few paces farther and Loki lit a small lamp to guide their way. In recent weeks he'd noticed a marked improvement in his night vision, but he was reluctant to reveal that to Kat.

"Do you think the dragon would swing over to the big continent and pick up Paola?" Loki asked. He hadn't seen his lover in weeks and he missed her terribly. He also wanted a firsthand account of her attempts to deal with the snake monster. "We could use her strategic thinking."

"You will have to ask Irisey yourself."

They descended the last switchback in silence, aware how easily sound carried. No need to wake the villagers tonight. In the dim starlight, Loki caught a whisper of glow off a translucent dragon wing.

"She's gorgeous," he gasped in awe. In his mind he traced the curve of the wing back to the body. The size of the beast staggered him.

A faint chuckle brushed across his mind.

"Good evening, Irisey, Loki here," he introduced himself to the dragon on a whisper.

(Good evening, Loki. I am Irisey, matriarch of the nimbus.) Her lilting voice danced across his mind.

He bowed slightly, feeling himself in the presence

of true majesty. Cyndi could learn a lot from this lady dragon.

"We've got to get going, before someone misses us," Kat hissed in his ear.

"Introduce yourself," he hissed back. "Dragon protocol."

"We've already met," Kat pouted.

"In person, or only in your mind? Do it, baby sister. We want to keep the nimbus happy and pleased with us."

Kat glowered at him a moment.

He met her stubbornness with his own.

"Irisey, I am Kat Talbot," she said. But she did not bow, she kept her shoulders straight, her spine stiff, and her chin up. She approached the dragon, equal to equal.

Maybe they were.

A flicker of prescient vision rocked Loki's balance. For a single heartbeat he saw his sister as a matriarch presiding over a brood of children; power radiated from her aura, and ease with that power as if long accustomed to it.

He reached out and braced himself. His hand brushed the dragon's muzzle.

(Easy, Loki. The time is not yet for your sister to step into that role. Many dangers await your entire family before that can happen.)

Loki nodded and gulped. "She has a lot of growing up to do first."

"Who does?" Kat asked.

A flash of mental agreement crossed Loki's mind from the dragon.

"Cyndi," he lied. But it was the truth.

Kat scrambled atop the dragon. Loki followed as

soon as she settled between two spinal horns. He took a long moment to caress the dragon's crystal fur.

"Your wing tips and spinal horns are iridescent?" he asked quietly.

(All colors, and yet no color at all.)

"Where is Bruce?" Kat asked, querulous and cranky. "What are we waiting for?"

(An other.)

At that moment Bruce appeared out of the darkness. He held the hand of someone . . . someone with bright blonde hair.

"Cyndi," Loki breathed. "Why did he drag her along?"

(She is needed.)

"For what?"

(To remind you of what you fight for and against.)

"Enigmatic as usual," Loki muttered.

Cyndi followed Bruce eagerly until she spotted their transport. "You can't expect me to believe this isn't a nightmare," she protested, her voice rising into the now familiar whine. "Another nightmare." She stared at Loki.

He didn't know how to ease her misgivings. Her last encounter with a dragon had been Hanassa trying to force his spirit into her body.

"It'll be fun," Geralds cajoled her, unaware of her fears. "Think of it as sneaking out of your father's house to meet your friends and riding in a really sporty flitter."

"But . . . but I'm hardly dressed for an adventure." She waved her hand vaguely at her usual tunic and leggings.

"Don't worry about it, Cyndi. We don't have dress codes on this planet," Loki said flatly.

"Obviously. People still eat *meat* here. And they wear animal leather. And they bathe in," shudder, "water."

"Just get onboard. The dragon won't fly without you," Loki ordered. "We have important things to do."

"Like what?" Cyndi stood rock still, hands on hips, mouth set to disagree with whatever they planned.

"Like saving this planet from degenerating into civil war that will plunge it back into the stone age."

"Bruce?" Kat gestured toward the man.

Gleefully, he lifted Cyndi off her feet and threw her over his shoulder. She squealed and kicked him. He swatted her bottom. She cried out again.

A cry of alarm rose from the village.

Geralds climbed partway up the dragon's leg, then plunked Cyndi behind Loki.

"Hold on tight, little lady," Geralds said as he positioned himself behind Cyndi. Spinal horns braced them fore and aft. Cyndi squirmed restlessly.

"I don't have to obey any mere dragon. And I don't have to obey you, Loki," Cyndi pouted.

"Just what I need, two women in sour moods. Irisey, may I please leave one or both of them behind?"

(No.) The dragon took three lumbering steps toward the cliff, flapping her wings.

"Do I have to touch it?" Cyndi held her hands away from the spinal horn.

"You do unless you want to fall off onto the rocks in the cove," Loki replied. He gritted his teeth, forcing himself to watch as they approached the drop off. Would Irisey have enough air beneath her wings to fly? Or would she plummet onto the jagged beach, impaling her passengers?

Cyndi yelped and grabbed Loki fiercely around the waist. She buried her face into his back.

Sounds of alarm died away behind them.

Irisey took one last step off the cliff . . . and flew.

Loki breathed easier. He did his best to ignore the warmth that spread along his ribs from Cyndi's grip.

He threw his head back and let the wind play with his hair and beard. He opened himself to the chill air and savored the contrast between the cold penetrating his bones and the warmth of the woman clinging so desperately to his back.

In an amazingly short period of time, the dragon had flown along the coast and swung inward at the great river. Just a few wing flaps later she circled Base Camp. The watch fires glowed in the darkness along with two or three oil lanterns leading toward the latrine.

Irisey circled and banked a second time, selecting a landing place just south of the camp, away from the tilled and planted fields. She came down gracefully, running the last few steps to shed speed.

Kat dropped off the dragon's back before she came to a complete stop. "My thanks, Irisey." This time Kat bowed to the dragon.

Irisey dipped her head until the long spiral horn growing from her forehead nearly touched Kat's chest. Kat grabbed the tip and rubbed it gently.

Some private communication passed between them.

Loki strained to listen while Geralds helped a shaking Cyndi onto the ground, then supported her for several steps until she got her land legs again.

At last Loki slid down Irisey's haunch and faced his sister. "What was that all about?"

"Stand clear," Kat called.

Loki moved away from the dragon. Irisey's fur shimmered in the starlight and then . . . she disappeared. He heard her steps and wing flaps, but saw nothing of her form.

"I should be used to that by now." He wiped sweat from his brow, not liking his reaction to the mysterious dragon. "What's the plan, Kat?" he asked firmly.

Kat whipped out a needle pistol and aimed it at Loki's heart. "The plan is that you surrender to me and I turn you over to Her Majesty, Queen Amanda."

CHAPTER 35

MARTIN CHECKED the sensor monitor in the lounge aboard *Margaret Kristine* for occupants. He knew his companions had all stayed on the bridge. Still, he had to be certain before he called up his star map. Quinn already suspected that Martin had done something special to his computer back home to create the massive program and maintain it.

Seeing the glyphs indicating four warm bodies on the bridge, Martin withdrew the miniature blue crystal from his pocket. The facets sparkled in the artificial light of the lounge. It grew warm in his hand. He fancied it hummed at a special frequency in harmony with his own brain synapses.

He stared at it several long moments, enthralled.

"Martin, have you found coordinates for the jump point yet?" Quinn asked over the intercom.

Martin shook himself free of the crystal's enchanting voice. "Working on it," he called back.

Carefully, he opened a panel on the bulkhead and inserted the crystal into a nest of fiber optics that ran to the central computer. "Star map, please," he whispered to the crystal.

Instantly, the air swirled and sparkled in the middle of the lounge. Pinpoints of red, blue, and green light burst forth from the swirling hologram.

Martin walked through the three-dimensional map

to stand before the anomalous blank space and waited for the program to settle. It drew new data from the central computer and updated.

Aurora blinked from blue to green to red three times before it returned to a steady blue. Melinda had been busy in the last two weeks since Martin had escaped her clutches. Six green lights belonging to the Galactic Free Market switched to the blue of the Galactic Terran Empire in the immediate environs of Aurora.

Melinda *had* been busy for the Terran government to forcibly retake those six key systems in Melinda's trading empire. She must have pissed off the diplomatic envoys significantly for them to use that leverage. Melinda would have a hard time making much profit off those planets now that the GTE controlled their economy and tariffs.

Finally the lights stopped blinking and changing with updated information.

"Display jump points, please," Martin requested.

Purple lights popped into place in a seemingly random pattern. Martin blinked. The ship and the map seemed to tilt slightly to the left. If he looked at it just so . . .

Gone. He'd lost his brief glimpse into the pattern of jump point placement. No one had ever been able to determine where the jump points were until someone stumbled upon one and then charted its entry and exit points. Jump points always appeared either near a star system or near another jump point. He wondered why scientists had considered the wandering jump point near the *Margaret Kristine*'s current location the only dead end in the known galaxy.

"What's taking so long?" Bruce asked from the bridge. "We've been sitting out here for three days looking for the frigging jump point. I want to find it *now*."

"Just a femto. The map isn't as complete as it was back home." That was a lie, but Martin hadn't let any of them see it during their voyage to this point. He needed to keep the secret of the crystal, and the fact that it retained the entire massive program within its depths, just a little longer.

While he spoke, the pale lavender light indicating their wandering jump point came into view. He had to look carefully to make certain he truly saw it rather than imagined the pale pinpoint of light.

"Coordinates of jump point, please," he requested.

Strings of numbers appeared above or below every jump point except the one he watched.

Martin sighed in disappointment. Maybe he did imagine that pale lavender smudge.

"Crystal, please show me where the wanderer is at this moment."

Three strings of numbers appeared around the smudge.

"Quinn, this doesn't make any sense."

"Nothing about that jump point makes sense," Quinn said from the other side of the lounge.

Martin jumped back from peering at the smudge of light. "I didn't hear you come in," he gasped.

"I didn't intend for you to hear me. I wondered why you were so secretive about this map." He strode heavily to the open bulkhead panel and the crystal interface. A low whistle escaped his pursed lips at sight of the blue crystal.

"Don't touch it," Martin warned.

"I have no intention of touching it. I know what a full-sized king stone can do to a man who tries to disconnect it abruptly or incorrectly. I imagine this little guy can deliver quite a jolt." Quinn fingered the still bruised lump near his right temple.

"You need to see this, Quinn." Martin coaxed Quinn away from the crystal over to the jump point coordinates.

'Quinn bent his tall frame to peer at the numbers. "Does it mean that it will be at each of those points or that it has been there?"

"Your guess is as good as mine."

"Why don't you ask it."

"I didn't program it to do that."

"You didn't program it to do this." Quinn swept his hand around the room indicating the map that filled the lounge and spread into three gangways.

"Computer, explain the imprecise numbers at the wanderer."

Silence.

"*Margaret Kristine,* please explain the three coordinates given for the wanderer," Quinn asked.

Silence.

"I think it must be where the jump point has *been.* It has no way of plotting the future, only past data. Kurt, bring yourself and your math genius down here," Martin ordered.

In moments Kurt's big feet and lanky frame clanked into the lounge.

Quinn quietly closed the bulkhead panel before Kurt reached the last step.

"I see you got it up and running," Kurt said. He pulled out his handheld. "What do you need?"

"Look at these three coordinates and extrapolate a pattern."

Kurt punched numbers and formulae into his handheld. "Time interval?"

"Unknown."

Kurt shrugged and kept playing with numbers and formulae. Finally, he held up the mini computer. "According to this, the next time it appears it will be here." He pointed to the string of coordinates. "When that will be I have no idea."

"Good enough for me." Quinn shrugged. "I'll get us there. Martin, you do some refining on the sensors. This thing may not register normal energy fluxes. Whose turn is it to cook? We might as well get comfortable. We could be in for a long wait."

* * *

"About time you came to your senses, Kat," Cyndi said, arching her back and stretching her arms over her head. "I'm glad you came on board with Bruce's plan. Maybe now we can get something done about getting off this hunk of rock and back to civilization."

"We work on Her Majesty's timeline now," Kat replied. She fought to keep her tone level and her mind blank. She really did not want Loki rummaging around her thoughts with his telepathy. "Everybody march. We're late for our appointment with Queen Amanda."

"I can't believe the dragons went along with this plan, Kat," Loki said quietly. He had his hands in the air in surrender, but his eyes twitched as if a dozen plans ran through his mind at once.

"The dragons don't know everything," Kat replied, still forcing her mind to remain blank. Those eye twitches could be her brother's attempt to probe her mind as Irisey had probed her heart.

"Your heart isn't in this, Kat," Loki said. His voice took on a peculiar lilting quality, as if he tried to lull her suspicions. Or plant ideas in her head.

"I always knew you had a mercenary heart, Kat," Bruce Geralds chortled. "Queen Amanda will be much more open to mining the omniscium than your hidebound brothers. We'll be rich in no time. Richer than Melinda Fortesque." He hugged her briefly and began the short trek to Base Camp.

Queen Amanda, indeed. Kat almost snorted. Amanda Leonard's new title grated on Kat's nerves. But she had to go through with the plan. This was the only way she could hope to get close enough to the woman to subdue her. And if necessary, she'd kill her captain. Civilized people never took a life, not even animals for food. But Amanda had stepped way over the line of civilization. She had violated every moral and ethical code Kat could remember. Amanda's punishment—if she ever came to trial—would be imprisonment and mind-wipe. By any other words, death of the soul and personality if not the body.

"Konner and Kim will come after me," Loki continued his litany of advice.

"No, they won't. Kim won't leave Hestiia and the baby for more than a few hours and Konner won't use the fuel to come get you in the *Rover.*"

"The dragons . . ."

"Obey me."

Loki slumped his shoulders. Kat hated to see him looking so defeated. But she couldn't trust him to stay that way. Her oldest brother was resourceful if nothing else.

"Walk." She prodded his back with the needle pistol.

Loki took a few slow steps. "No comment from you, Cyndi?"

"I will go along with any plan to get me home and see you punished, Loki." She tossed her head and walked ahead of them. She greeted the Marines as old friends and made her way to the central fire pit and a cup of something hot.

Bruce joined her. Two armed guards stepped forward from the perimeter of their patrols. They took up positions on either side of Loki and matched him step for step into Base Camp.

Kat sighed gratefully that neither of them was Kent Brewster, the one Marine who might see through her facade—or glare at her in true disappointment. He'd be easier to recruit to her plan if he did not gain wrong first impressions.

"Kat, you know that the person wearing Amanda Leonard's body is no longer the captain you respected and admired. You do not owe her any kind of loyalty," Loki said.

"I don't want to talk about it with you, Loki." She jabbed the muzzle of her needle pistol sharply into his back.

Loki stumbled to his knees.

"Open your hands before you stand," Kat ordered. "You won't be flinging dirt in my eyes."

Loki obeyed her, shaking his head. "Who taught you to fight dirty, Kat? I thought you were a law-abiding officer in His Majesty's military."

"Never mind. Now stand up and walk, hands up, palms empty." She nudged his backside with her boot.

"Well, well, well. The prodigal lieutenant returns," Amanda said.

Her voice slithered over Kat and nearly made her shudder in revulsion. Kat suppressed her involuntary reaction.

"I've brought you a prisoner, Your Majesty, just as I promised. Konner O'Hara is now at your mercy."

Loki looked at her sharply, lowering his brows in puzzlement. He opened his mouth to say something.

Kat cuffed him alongside the head with the butt of her pistol. "Keep your mouth shut and show some respect for Her Majesty," she growled. Kat wanted to scream into his mind to trust her. She didn't dare. Amanda might overhear the telepathic communication. Kat had no idea what powers Amanda had acquired since coming to this place. For all Kat knew, her former captain could have as many magical skills and talents as all four O'Haras combined.

"Take Mr. Konner O'Hara to the new prison cell I built just for him. It's as close to sensory deprivation as I could make it, given the primitive technology and limited resources," Amanda purred. "I am so going to love hearing you scream when the darkness and silence press against your brain."

"How . . . ?" Kat started.

"Never mind how I contrived the cell. I have another one for you."

"Majesty . . . I . . ."

"You deserve punishment for running away from me, Kat. You should know better than to defy me." Amanda caressed Kat's cheek with an extremely long fingernail that had begun to curve downward, like a talon.

Three more Marines appeared out of the darkness. Two of them each grabbed Kat by an elbow. The third cut the air menacingly with a primitive sword.

"You won't be in your cell as long as your brother, Kat. I do reward people who bring me presents. But punishment always comes first."

•

CHAPTER 36

KONNER WOKE UP in the dead of night. Something nagged at his mind. He rolled over and ran his hands lightly over Dalleena's body. She breathed evenly, resting comfortably.

Satisfied that she was not the source of his disquiet, he slid from beneath their sleeping furs and peered out of their lean-to.

The campfire embers glowed, ready to be stoked into brightness with fresh tinder and wood. The surrounding trees and shrubbery rustled faintly in the night breeze.

He listened closely. Perhaps the baby?

Even Ariel, the two-week-old infant, slept quietly for a change.

Pressure in his mind sent Konner prowling around the perimeter of their clearing. He knew there was something wrong, something out of place. What?

Finally, he checked the other lean-tos. Taneeo had moved back to the village once he'd freed himself of Hanassa's possession. That left two more sleeping places.

"Loki," Konner whispered outside his brother's shelter. "Loki?" he said a little louder.

He rapped upon the side of the structure and crouched to peer inside. The sleeping furs lay in disarray. Both Loki and his boots were gone.

Konner stood up in alarm. He searched the clearing with all of his senses. Maybe Loki had just stepped out to the latrine. Maybe, but not likely. He would not have bothered with his boots for such a mundane errand.

"Kat?" Konner stepped over to his sister's lean-to. He skipped politeness and peered in as soon as he spoke. Her bed looked undisturbed, or neatly made up. Her boots were missing, too.

Where could they have gone?

Konner stoked the fire for light and searched the clearing one more time.

The pressure in his mind increased.

Wake up, a voice nagged him. He listened more closely. *Wake up and pay attention.*

Some of the pressure decreased, as if the speaker paused to draw breath.

Traitor. Kat betrayed us.

Not so much words as an impression of guns and Marines and Kat and Amanda together.

"Loki?" Konner asked the pressure in his mind.

The only reply was a vague sense of assent.

"Let me get Kim. He's better at this than I am." Konner ran the few steps to the one-room cabin Kim shared with Hestiia and the baby.

Abandoning politeness, he crashed through the doorway. He paused only a moment to orient himself and then felt his way to the far wall. "Kim," he whispered as he shook his brother's shoulder.

"Jaysus, I just got to sleep," Kim mumbled.

Ariel whimpered in her basket beside the bed. Kim picked her up and stumbled toward the doorway, a patch of slightly lighter darkness than the dim interior. He aimed for the central fire pit, holding Ariel against his shoulder, patting her back and murmuring soothing words.

"Now what is so all-fired important you had to wake me," he demanded querulously. "I swear I haven't slept more than ten minutes all night between a fussing baby and Hestiia's restlessness.

"Loki's in trouble. He says Kat betrayed him to Amanda."

Kim swung around to face the lean-tos.

"They're both gone. Took their boots."

"How?"

"There is this pressure in my mind. When I stopped to listen to it, Loki contacted me telepathically. You're better at this than I am."

"Not on no sleep. I need Tambootie to concentrate."

"You need that drug for everything."

"Do you want to clear up this mess tonight or not?"

"Okay. You get Ariel settled and I'll find you some fresh leaves." Fortunately, Konner did not have to go more than a few steps beyond the edge of the clearing. The first rays of dawn showed the distinctive umbrella outline of the deciduous tree with aromatic bark and toxic sap. The green leaves grew fat with pink veins. The moment he touched the first one, it dripped oil onto the back of his hand. It tingled immediately.

Before he could stop himself he licked the essential oils off the leaf.

His mind brightened. Every object in the clearing took on auras, highlighting their silhouettes. He wanted to study each rock and blade of grass, delving into the secrets contained in those subdued coronas of living light.

Another lick of Tambootie oil. Just one more. Well, maybe another a well.

Suddenly the pressure in his mind eased and became coherent communication.

They locked me in the fuel bay of a lander. Strapped me down so I can't move more than my eyelids. Insulated the hull so I can't hear anything. No light. Makes it easier to concentrate.

"Loki, we'll get you out."

No! The word sounded loud inside Konner's skull. *They think I am you. As long as Amanda is under that delusion, we have leverage. She hates us all, but you more than any of us.*

"How did she get the impression you are me?"

Kat . . . Oh, Saint Bridget. She deliberately misled Amanda. She's laid a trap of her own. But Amanda decided to punish her before rewarding her. Kat's locked in another lander.

"How did you get to Base Camp?" Konner tried to fume over the misuse of his precious fuel.

The female dragon, Irisey.

"If the dragons cooperated, then they have to agree with Kat. She didn't betray us, she used us to further her own stupid plan. Was Gentian with her?"

No.

Kat, how stupid can you get? Konner asked himself as much as his absent sister. *Couldn't you have confided in me?* Of all three brothers, Kat seemed to have bonded most closely with Konner. They had sat for hours these last few weeks just talking. He had rescued her from the snake monster.

She blamed him for abandoning her at the burning house back home when she was seven.

"Have you got some of those leaves for me?" Kim asked. He'd stopped long enough to put on his trousers.

Konner still wandered the clearing in his underwear. Strangely, with the Tambootie coursing through his system he did not need clothing for warmth.

He handed Kim a fistful of leaves. His hand nearly burned with the power they gave him.

Briefly, he outlined the situation to Kim as his younger brother licked and nibbled his Tambootie.

"Can you get out of your restraints, Loki?" Kim asked. His eyes crossed as he focused on something inside him. He stared blankly into the now burning central fire.

That's Konner's talent.

"And telepathy is yours, but he heard you. Now concentrate, both of you."

"Loki, you must have seen the restraints when they put you in there. What do they look like?" Konner asked. He dragged his thoughts away from the need for more Tambootie. The drug would help him blot out his disappointment in Kat.

He concentrated on the fire and what needed to be done.

Sticky webbing from med supplies.

"Good, they aren't force bracelets. Now picture the webbing in minute detail in your mind." Konner waited a moment to allow Loki to get the image firmly fixed.

The trail of Loki's thoughts, like a brightness in Konner's mind faded. He hadn't known it was there or what it looked like until it was gone.

"Once you can see it clearly in your mind, think about the stickiness dissolving. Watch each molecule of glue separating and becoming inert."

I can't.

"You can. Concentrate. Forget about talking to me. Forget everything but the webbing. Watch it dissolve." Konner waited a few more moments. "Now, the two layers that overlap are no longer sticking together. All you have to do is lift your wrists and the restraints will fall away."

A few more moments passed. The fire burned down. Kim added more fuel.

When it flared up again, Konner thought he saw a holo image within the flames of Loki lying in the darkness fighting the webbing.

In a few moments the restraints flew off Loki's wrists and legs. Nearly sobbing with relief, Loki released the head and throat bands.

"He's free," Konner breathed.

"Loki, you have to get out of there quickly. Dawn is just breaking." Had only a few moments passed? Konner felt as if he'd been staring at the fire for hours.

Where?

"Get to the village at the confluence of the river and the bay. Hide there. We'll come to pick you up."

What about Kat?

"I think we have to leave her to Amanda's not so tender mercies for a while."

"Ask him to steal a fuel cell or two," Kim prompted. He already nibbled on more Tambootie, as if the first dose had worn off and dropped him out of rapport with Loki.

Konner began to shiver. His own dose of Tambootie grew thin in his blood. He conveyed Kim's message quickly and received a tentative reply.

Then his hands began to shake and his stomach revolted. He dashed to the nearest bush and vomited up the shreds of the leaves he didn't remember eating.

* * *

"Try it now, Kurt," Martin called from under a control panel on the bridge of *Margaret Kristine.*

"No change in any of the sensor readings," Kurt called back.

"Maybe if you up the UV sensitivity," Jane said. She stood behind Kurt, watching his screens as closely as he did.

"We've tried UV, how about tachyon emissions?" Bruce offered. He swiveled idly in the copilot's chair.

"These instruments can't go any higher on either read," Martin spat, disgusted with the whole process.

"Martin, there is something else you have not tried," Quinn said quietly. He watched the viewscreen directly in front of them at the real-time display, as if he'd get to see a jump point open.

As far as Martin knew, no one had actually seen a jump point. They appeared as energy fluxes in the data stream.

"What?" Jane, Bruce, and Kurt all asked at the same time.

So much for keeping the illegal miniature king stone secret.

Martin scooted out from his supine position beneath the panel. He had to stand up to fish the crystal out of his pocket. Maybe Bruce had a point in wearing pantaloons. But he couldn't change clothes now; they had only the limited luggage Quinn had stashed in the van ahead of time—mostly changes of underwear and personal hygiene items.

He tried to keep the crystal in his palm, hidden from the others as it emerged from its hiding place.

Jane was on him in a flash, opening his hand. "By Gaia, its beautiful. Perfect," she gasped. She stroked the crystal as if it were a living being.

Perhaps it was.

Quinn swung around in his chair to observe the scene.

Kurt and Bruce reached simultaneously to grab the thing from Martin for closer examination. A spark lashed from the crystal to their fingers.

Instinctively, Martin closed his finger around it protectively.

"Acts just like a real king stone, too," Quinn remarked. A half smile quirked his mouth. "It seems that Martin here is attuned to the crystal. I'm surprised it doesn't hum."

"It does. It's in harmony with your crystal drive." Martin didn't know what else to say.

"All crystals are monopoles. They seek a crystal family to complete them, just as a bipolar magnet is attracted to its opposite," Quinn said casually.

"Where'd you get it?" Bruce asked. He kept his hands safely in his voluminous pockets as he peered at the little bits of blue light that were visible between Martin's fingers.

"My dad. Two summers ago."

"Where'd he get it?" Bruce acted offended that their favorite camp counselor hadn't honored each of them with something similar.

"Why didn't it reject Jane?" Kurt asked.

"She only touched it, she didn't try to take possession of it."

"It burned my fingers a little," Jane added trying to mollify her comrades. She shook her finger as if to emphasize the crystal's reaction to her.

"Enough speculation. Plug that into the computer matrix before we lose the jump point," Quinn ordered.

Grateful for the excuse to avoid further discussion of the crystal, Martin slid back beneath the panel. He fished around for a suitable nest of fiber optics to accept the crystal. At last he found a place deep into the sensor wiring.

"No map this time. Just a look at where the jump point is," he whispered to the crystal as he attached three fiber optics to it.

"Nothing happening to the sensor array," Kurt called back to him, a little too loudly, as if the panel and bulkhead muffled more sound now that Martin had the crystal in hand.

"King stones like multiples of twelve," Quinn reminded him.

"I know. I've studied crystal drives intensively since I started using this," Martin muttered, not caring if anyone heard him.

The next thee connections came easy. Then he had to seriously look for the next five. The last was the most elusive of all.

"I've used up all the fiber optics, and I still need one more," he complained.

Look deeper, someone said.

Martin thought the deep voice might be Quinn's. Yet it didn't sound exactly like the Imperial agent. Who could tell for certain halfway between the bulkhead and the hull?

"I am looking deeper." Blindly, he reached above his head and grabbed whatever came to hand.

Three fiber optic cables broke free of their connections. Which one was best? They all looked great. Two of the ones already connected came from secondary systems.

Martin sighed and began rearranging.

As he touched the final cable to the crystal, before he had firmly attached it to the facet, the miniature king stone began to glow. Flames seemed to shoot from the deep heart out along the cables. Quickly, he finished the last connection and nestled the crystal into a safe niche.

Jubilant music burst upon his ears.

"Are all the crystals singing?" Jane asked.

Martin clawed his way free of the dim bulkhead and blinked in the sudden brightness of the bridge. More than the usual change of contrast brightness. Every screen sparkled with new light.

"Wow," Quinn said, leaning back in his chair to take it all in. "That is some enhancement. Don't suppose I could persuade you to leave that crystal onboard?"

"Not on your life. My dad will need it when we find him. More than you," Martin said. He turned a full circle, trying to take in all of the new data that blazed across the screens.

"Jump point coordinates on screen!" Kurt nearly jumped up and down with excitement.

"Strap in, now!" Quinn called. "It's practically on top of us."

Martin fumbled for the nearest seat and found Jane already there. The klaxon blared its three-note warning. The ship tilted. Martin slid across the floor, flailing for balance. He slammed into Bruce in the other chair. He landed flat on his back on the deck.

The klaxon sounded again.

"So soon?" Less than twenty seconds had passed between warning and jump.

Martin grabbed whatever was handy. One hand wrapped around the support column of the copilot's seat. The other lay flat upon the deck, clawing at the cerama/metal for purchase. He stretched a foot to brace against the same place as his left hand.

The deck thinned to transparency, then disappeared. Martin held his breath. The ship dissolved. Only his mind kept the killing vacuum of space at bay.

CHAPTER 37

"YOUR MAJESTY." Bruce Geralds bowed low before Amanda.

Cyndi made a graceful curtsy, worthy of a ball gown, tiara, and the emperor's palace. She kept her eyes carefully lowered, all the while scoping out Amanda's body language and expression.

"We have information of great benefit to you," Geralds continued the moment Amanda waved him upright. He explained the significance of the ley lines and the amount of wealth that could be gained from mining it.

"Treasure?" Amanda's eyes brightened a moment. "I have no need of treasure. I require power." That voice was huskier and raspier than the voice Cyndi remembered from onboard *Jupiter*.

Then Amanda went silent a moment and her eyes cleared, willing to listen once more.

"Treasure is power," Cyndi reminded the former captain. Something had changed about the woman's eyes and posture. She sat hunched forward, as if her back hurt. She opened both eyes wide, yet her lids seemed hooded, leaving shadows upon Amanda's face. Cyndi could not capture her gaze, no matter how hard she tried.

Would she, Cyndi, show the same hardening of the

skin, the talon nails, and the hunched posture if she had given it to the spirit of Hanassa?

Would she exhibit the same insanity and cruelty? She swallowed deeply, trying to rid her mouth of a bad taste. She, the granddaughter of a previous emperor, wife to an heir of the current emperor, and daughter of a planetary governor would never allow her body and posture to become so ugly. Power also lay in beauty, if one knew how to use it.

"Explain how treasure can be power. Treasure is the useless accumulation of pretty objects that have value only to the frivolous."

"May I?" Cyndi asked, gesturing toward the camp stool beside Amanda.

Amanda glared in hostility.

Cyndi returned her stare with equal stubbornness.

Finally, Amanda nodded. Cyndi smiled to herself. Information was also power and she had a lot of it. She had to remember that the entity that now inhabited Amanda's body was still primitive. It did not have the sophistication and education that Cyndi did. It had bits and pieces of Amanda's technical knowledge, maybe a few of her memories, but not the understanding of how to use it.

She seated herself and settled her back against the big cabin before speaking. "On other worlds, money governs every action. Those with money can buy treasure. They can also buy people, influence, prestige, status. They can buy votes in Parliament."

"Money buys transportation to and from planets throughout the galaxy," Bruce added. "Money buys safety from those who have the power of coercion and blackmail."

Both Cyndi and Amanda glared at him.

"Go away, silly man," Amanda ordered. "I have no use for you at the moment."

Geralds blustered.

"Men have only one use. I do not need servicing at the moment," Amanda said mildly.

A great guffaw rose from the armed Marines waiting in attendance.

"Don't worry, you'll get your chance soon enough. She's insatiable," one of the Marines called. That met with another round of laughter.

Geralds stalked off.

"Now tell me how to gain access to this treasure you allude to but do not address directly," Amanda said in a raspy tone that implied intimacy.

"The O'Haras speak of a web of energy beneath the ground," Cyndi tried to visualize what Geralds had explained to her. She still didn't understand how the planet could be filled with omniscium. The most valuable element in the galaxy had only been found in uninhabitable gas giants.

"The ley lines. Yes, I know about them."

"They are made up of omniscium. That's an element that powers our starships." Not exactly true but close enough. She didn't know how to explain about crystals and star drives. She barely understood the basic principles herself. "A very small amount commands large sums of money outside this planet."

"If I control this omniscium, then people will come to me? They will worship and attend me as I deserve?"

"Ye . . . es."

Amanda fell silent a moment. "If people from afar will worship me, then I will have no need to cater to dragon needs for plentiful food and clean water," she mused.

"With our technology, we can clean the air and water of any pollution generated from mining the omniscium. We can grow food in tanks, no need to preserve the land." Cyndi imagined a domed city replacing the hovels of Base Camp. She smiled.

"Go away. I must think on this. This is information I can use."

A Marine grabbed Cyndi by the elbow and dragged her off to the other side of Base Camp. They left her nowhere near where Geralds prowled with two more Marines watching his every move.

* * *

Loki carefully placed his purloined fuel cell in the hollow of a tree and sank down gratefully beside it. He mopped perspiration from his brow with the back of his arm.

"Steal a fuel cell or two, Konner says," he muttered. The power source was nearly a meter cubed and weighed about thirty kilos.

The missing fuel cells from the power farm had been empty, easy for the thief to carry. Anyone who visited the clearing could have taken it.

Getting out of Base Camp in the sleepy hour before dawn was easy. Carrying a fully powered fuel cell five klicks before breakfast was a different proposition altogether.

"Speaking of breakfast . . ." He reached over and yanked a fading flower out of the ground. Dirt clung damply to the fat bulb at its base. He gathered his energy a moment before taking the plant to the nearest stream to wash it. This close to the braided delta of islands fresh water was the least of his problems.

He ate the bulb raw, then went searching for another. This time of year they were plentiful, not as nutritious as in the autumn but still sweet and tasty.

Eventually, he left the fuel cell in its hiding place and proceeded toward the village at the confluence of the river and the Great Bay. He stepped cautiously, mindful of the various swamps and how easily he left a trail in the damp ground.

Less than half of the village's one hundred families had found their way to the new habitat five hundred klicks to the south. He did not know if the remainder had shifted allegiance to the newcomers. They'd done it before to survive. They'd do it again. Survival mattered more to them than honor or freedom.

At the edge of the lines of huts and substantial houses, Loki paused to reconnoiter. The one street and many lanes seemed deserted. He looked and sniffed for smoke from cooking fires and communal gathering points. The air remained fresh and clean. Even the midden smelled stale and old.

If the villagers had not gone south, where had they gone? Surely the few slaves he'd seen at Base Camp were not the only ones left?

Then he heard the one sound that could chill him to the bones. Marines cocking stun rifles.

Loki did his best to fade into the tree line without betraying his presence.

Still facing the village he spotted two armed men, wearing heat-vision VR gear, as they emerged from a side lane. They marched purposefully toward his hiding place. Two more men joined them from the opposite side of the street.

Loki turned and ran. He hopped over fallen logs, skirted sharp saber ferns, dodged the biggest trees he could find, anything to put distance and obstacles between himself and the enemy.

Every hundred meters or so he paused behind a tall everblue to catch his breath and listen. The four men plodded on, relentlessly. They moved like robots on autopilot.

He wondered if Amanda had stolen their minds as well as their integrity.

He took off again and again. He didn't remember jumping two creeks or splashing through shallow channels of the river. Then he abruptly came to a very broad and deep arm of the river, sluggish at full tide, just before ebbing. A few meters to the west he spotted a causeway to the next island. He dashed across it and dove behind a broad cairn of tumbled boulders.

The ground beneath him tingled against his skin. He must have landed flush upon a ley line.

"Saint Bridget, make me invisible," he willed and closed his eyes. Maybe if he could not see his pursuers, they could not see him.

Kim, where in the saint's name are you? He broadcast the mental call on a wide band, using only the image of his youngest brother to drive his message rather than a direction.

Konner, are you out there?

The entire island seemed to vibrate with the rhythm of his words. Power surged through his body. He had to look down to make certain he did not float above his hiding place.

Opening his eyes, he knew where the four Marines had lost his trail. He watched them in his mind as they wandered aimlessly all around his island, never quite noticing the causeway.

And then he looked, really looked at where he lay. The land pulsed with silvery-blue light. He bathed in the glow from the merging ley lines. A deep well, or lake of power engulfed him.

(Welcome to the beginning place,) the dragons shouted at him.

He had to cover his ears to protect himself from the cacophony of their mingled voices.

Colors assaulted his eyes from the grass and rocks and dirt. The bay and the sky became as intensely blue as the power beneath him. He watched sap rising in the surrounding trees and heard worms and bugs burrowing beneath him.

"We're coming. Delays finding active fuel cells and pairing them up in the bay," Kim's voice and mind bounced off the rock and the well of ley lines. It echoed against the sky and the bay.

About time, Loki complained. He had to step off the pool. Too much power, too many sensations. He hadn't had time or practice to assimilate it all.

A mighty roar defended him. He looked up, expecting to see the entire nimbus of dragons spitting flame at him.

He saw only a swirl of energy far up in the sky, at the edge of the solar system, and a tiny ship jumping through the center.

Konner, Kim, jump point just opened. I have no idea who is coming to plague us now.

CHAPTER 38

"KONNER," DALLEENA SAID through the comm system. Konner opened a frequency to match hers. "What, Dalleena?" She sounded anxious. She wouldn't contact him on an open line while he was flying unless something terrible had happened.

"A jump point opened." Her voice shook. The last time her tracking sense had pinpointed the jump, Amanda Leonard and her IMPs aboard *Jupiter* had descended upon the planet.

"They're right," Kim said quietly. "Sensors just picked it up."

"We're on it, Dalleena. We'll contact the new ship and find out who they are." He hoped. Running everything on reduced power to conserve fuel also reduced their signal strength.

"Do we really want to tell strangers who we are and where we are?" Kim asked.

"Not really. Can you get any readings on what kind of ship?"

"Too far out."

The ship is small, Loki whispered into Konner's mind.

"Loki, I hope you aren't doped up on Tambootie. That stuff is addictive and toxic." Even as Konner spoke, he remembered both the revulsion of his reaction to the leaves and craved the wondrous power that surged through him.

No Tambootie on this island. I have found the beginning place. It is the tenth wonder of the universe and all ours.

"What?"

The confluence of all the ley lines. I can't imagine the amount of omniscium in this pool. Enough to create a million crystal arrays and then some.

"Loki, you are coming through as clearly as if you were sitting right next to me," Konner shivered at the amount of power behind his brother's psychic talent.

I feel as if I could fly with dragons!

"Well, don't try," Kim ordered.

"You hearing him, too?" Konner asked.

"Clear and clean."

I sense five people aboard the new ship.

"Some kind of IMP scout?" Konner asked.

They do not taste of officialdom, but I sense authority in at least one of them.

"Dalleena, can you sense anything about the people or the ship?" Konner opened the comm line again.

"They are too far away." Dalleena's voice was less clear and more distant than Loki's mental contact. That must be some pool of ley lines he had found.

(It is the center of the universe!)

Was that every dragon in the nimbus shouting?

* * *

Hanassa prowled Base Camp while Amanda gave him information. In the hour since Lucinda Baines had told him about the value of the ley lines, he had learned the basic principles of the star drives, about the extent of the GTE, about their new war with creatures called the Kree—winged beings not so different from dragons.

For the first time since assuming his first human body, he felt the urge to grow wings and fly.

Amanda inserted a memory.

A much younger Amanda encased in a flight suit barking commands into a helmet comm. Soaring above the atmosphere in a small fighter. Twisting and turning to avoid enemy fire. Laser cannons pulsing around her as she dodged the pirate ship with its cargo of food and medical supplies stolen from a relief convoy.

Her mind melded seamlessly with each new command that sent the tiny ship in a tight spiral around the enemy. Too close for them to aim. Just far enough away from the hull to drop a pulse torpedo into its engines. Then accelerating away, fighting six, maybe seven G's.

An explosion behind her.

Glorious triumph as her comrades back on the cruiser shouted success.

"I do not need the clumsy limitations of dragon wings. I shall fly again as you flew, Amanda," Hanassa whispered to himself and his otherself.

We need to help destroy the Kree. They are kin to the dragons. They must fall to our power as the dragons will fall once we make this planet unlivable for them. Without the dragons to protect them, the O'Hara brothers will succumb to our power as well.

"Yes, we must destroy the dragons and all their kin. We will mine the omniscium. Then the galaxy will bow to us as a god." A secret smile played over Hanassa's face. He knew just how to accomplish all of his goals at once.

We need Kat. She is the key. She has knowledge we do not.

"Kat is an O'Hara."

Then we destroy her after she releases the knowledge we need.

* * *

"Why do people keep running away from me? I want only the best for them," Amanda Leonard said quietly into the darkness that surrounded Kat.

Kat kept her mouth shut. No matter what she said, Amanda would find fault and lengthen the punishment. During the long night Kat had conceived and abandoned countless plans for escape. If she ran away now, she'd never again get close enough to Amanda to overthrow her.

"Your brother Konner ran away before I could exact his proper punishment. He does not love justice. But you did not run away from me, Kat. You know justice and love it as I do." Amanda ran her long fingers through Kat's tangled curls. "You could have run away, but you stayed because you know I am right. You know that I am the only one who can make this land the shining center of my empire. You want to stand by my side when the galaxy bows to me and my power."

Kat had managed to loosen her restraints enough to nod. She did and felt Amanda's talons—there was no other word to describe those horny fingernails—scrape her scalp. She cringed beneath the brief but fierce pain.

"People learn through pain, Kat. You know that and I know that. You shall be my chancellor, my chief adviser. I trust you to mete out the punishments I declare." Gently Amanda loosened the strap across Kat's forehead and the one around her neck. "Your Mr. Geralds tells me that there is a treasure trove of omniscium beneath the surface of this land. He wants to mine it to sell across the galaxy. I have plans, too."

Kat nodded again. Her throat went drier than it had been. Bruce seemed quite capable of selling his loyalty to the highest bidder. What more could she expect from a Sam Eyeam?

She'd kept him at arm's length for weeks because she didn't trust him. Her instincts had proved right.

"I have been studying Konner's notes on black-smithing, the ones you so thoughtfully brought me. I captured a blacksmith, but he knows only copper and bronze. The few good pieces of iron he turned out were happy accidents. Now I can force him to work properly in iron. Before the day is out, I will have pipes to channel the omniscium into the river. There I shall capture it in its salt form. I shall allow you to join in the celebration." Amanda opened an exit hatch. Blessed daylight flooded the fuel bay.

Kat had to blink rapidly against the sudden transition from absolute darkness to dim sunlight.

"You need to rest here a little longer. I need you strong. Learn from this, Kat."

The hatch slammed shut again.

Kat saw stars and afterimages as her retinas shifted once more to darkness. She cursed long and fluently.

* * *

"Where am I?" Martin asked the universe. If he had a body, he thought he'd be floating in open space far beyond anything known. He should panic. But he couldn't. The space around him was too beautiful. Distant glowing stars and nebulas against a blacker-than-black background, energy fluxes, and transactional gravitons pulsed around him in every color imaginable, and some quite beyond his imagination.

(Welcome, child of the Stargods.)

"Who said that?"

(We welcome you.)

"But who are you?"

(We are what we are. Who are you?)

That required some thought. He had trouble remembering anything beyond the vast starscape around him.

"I am Martin Fotesque-O'Hara," he proclaimed.

(You are who you want to be.)

"Am I?"

(A wise question from a child. You have much to learn, many to meet, and experience to gain. You have come to the right place to find answers to your questions.)

"I don't think I know enough to ask those kinds of questions."

(You will.)

Abruptly, Martin fell through time and space and lurched back into his body. His bones ached. His eyes ached. He thought he was going to throw up from the abrupt transition from the vision world to reality.

Or was his vision real and his body but an illusion?

No, an illusion wouldn't hurt this much.

Slowly, he opened his eyes to find the deck solid, and hard, beneath him. He wiggled his toes and fingers, grateful they were still attached to his body. Then he looked around. His friends seemed safe, if a little dazed.

"Was that jump longer than normal?" Bruce asked. His hands shook as he tried to adjust his screens.

"Seemed like it lasted a week," Jane replied. She wrapped her arms around herself, shivering, though the temperature on the bridge was a perfect twenty-one degrees Celsius

"Chronometers read that jump lasted seven-point-three-six seconds," Kurt said. "Within normal parameters." His glasses hung askew from one ear and his perfect politician's son's hair stuck out at odd angles.

"Time is distorted in jump," Martin croaked. "Chronometers are useless. That jump could have lasted seven-and-one-half seconds, or an hour. We'll never know for certain until chronos record how long they were stopped."

How did he know that? An hour seemed about the right amount of time that Martin had hung in space conversing with . . . the universe was as good a term as any.

"I need some water." Martin rolled to his knees and consulted his body before moving further. Nothing seemed broken or ill, just out of sync with reality.

"You okay, kid?" Quinn asked. "You weren't strapped in, and that was a rough jump."

"Nothing wrong with me now," Martin replied. To prove his statement, to them if not himself, he bounced to his feet and slid down the railing of the gangway to the galley.

Later, he'd ask if anyone else had weird experiences during that jump. Much later. When he had time to think about what really happened and what he imagined.

* * *

Danger, danger, danger. These foolish humans do not realize that iron is scarce and copper plentiful for a reason. Iron and power combined are volatile. Iron will be the death of our home. And the humans, led by Hanassa, will be our undoing.

Hanassa should know this. He should remember our lessons. But he left the nimbus when quite young. Perhaps he never learned that iron and power are poison; just as he never learned honor, dignity, and the value of promises kept.

CHAPTER 39

KAT AWOKE TO WATER dribbling across her face. She opened her mouth to capture a few drops of the precious moisture.

Not enough. Not nearly enough to satisfy her thirst. The air in the dark fuel bay had gone stale hours ago. The sun must be high or waning. It beat down on her prison mercilessly.

She ached all over from hours trapped in the same position. Lights danced before her eyes in tantalizing illusion that freedom lay just beyond her reach.

Sweat dripped off her face. She ran her tongue around her mouth as far as it would reach to reabsorb as much as she could.

Another stream of cool water hit her upper lip.

"Is it raining out?" Her voice sounded weak and raspy and loud to her own numbed ears.

(Soon. It takes time to convince the air to move from there to here.)

"Gentian?" she asked with new hope.

(Yes.)

Kat lifted her head a little. A tiny sliver of light shone at her feet, near the hatch to the cabin of the lander. Amanda had exited by a closer hatch. It remained sealed.

"How did you get in?"

(Through the main entrance.)

An image of the central cabin of the lander appeared in Kat's head. She barely recognized it stripped of seats and webbing for securing crew and cargo.

(You must come. Now.) Gentian began ripping at the sticky webbing with teeth and claws. He found the overlap and pulled. With a ripping sound, Kat's left hand came free of the restraints.

She reached and quickly dispatched the one on her right wrist, then the one around her waist.

By this time the trickle of light around the hatch had allowed her eyes to adjust. She could just barely see the outlines of fuel cells and her flywacket.

Careful of the low ceiling she sat up and dispatched her ankle straps. Blood rushed into her limbs with sharp prickles. Her head ached and every joint felt inflamed.

(You must leave this place. Now. The air is bad.) Gentian spat.

His drool hit her hand and she wondered if that was the life-giving moisture she had drunk so greedily. Her mouth and body were so parched she didn't care.

"Water," she croaked.

Gentian made his way to the hatch leading back up into the main cabin. He began digging at the lower edge with his talons.

Kat crawled after him and reached her heavy arm up to the latch. She barely had enough strength to pull the lever down. It protested with a loud groan of metal rusted in place. Impossible. The alloys couldn't rust. Maybe Amanda had coated the device with something caustic to seal her prison.

Gentian leaped at the hatch, snagged the latch, and combined his weight with Kat's. Together, they pulled the portal open. It swung inward. Kat fell backward, banging her head on a spent fuel cell. Better a minor cracked head than a bashed-in face. That hatch was heavy.

Rubbing the hurt with both hands, she managed to right herself and drag her body up the two steps to the main cabin. A hasty glance around showed the place had been stripped of all supplies and anything that could be used in Base Camp. Her footsteps echoed hollowly in the bare vessel. Even the pilot's emergency kit was gone from the cockpit.

She stumbled out of the lander into cloudy daylight in search of water. Even that hazy light was too bright. Everything appeared as white on white afterimages with fuzzy outlines. She squinted and blinked rapidly, willing her vision to adjust and her headache to go away.

(Get water,) Gentian urged her from the safety of the lander.

"Come with me."

(If the one you call Amanda sees us together, she will murder us both.)

"And if she sees only one of us?"

(She will accept your escape.)

"What if she spots you?"

(Then my existence will cease. I will not earn another opportunity to atone for my cowardice.)

"Then stay hidden. And thank you for helping me. I think you are very brave. Fear is a good thing if it keeps you safe." She stumbled toward the center of camp and the jug of water kept beside the fire pit. She drank greedily at first. Then she slowed down and allowed the water to linger in her mouth, bathing the parched tissues and restoring some of her equilibrium.

"About time you figured out how to escape," Amanda said sharply behind Kat.

"I gave up waiting for you to decide when to end

my punishment. I am of no use to you dehydrated, starving, and ill from heat prostration," Kat snapped back. She didn't care if she antagonized the woman. All she wanted was water, a light meal, and a hat with a wide brim to shield her eyes.

"Your timing is perfect, Kat," Amanda gazed at the northwest corner of Base Camp and the abandoned forge. Only it wasn't abandoned anymore. A stout man alternately worked the bellows and hammered at a sheet of red-hot metal. Nearby lay a circular clay mold about fifteen centimeters in diameter and a full two meters in length.

As Kat watched the blacksmith shouted something and two young assistants carried the long mold and rested it across two sawhorses and poured several jugs of water onto the clay. The blacksmith transferred the sheet of iron to the mold with tongs. A sharp sizzle and steam rose up when the two met. Then, with other tools Kat could not identify, he shaped the metal around the mold to make a piece of pipe.

Amanda jumped up and down, clapping her hands with joy. "I've done it," she crowed. "I've made the first length of pipe. Tomorrow, we begin mining the omniscium."

Kat glared at the woman out of the corner of her eye. Amanda had not done any of the work, but she took the credit for fashioning the iron treasure.

Something outside Kat prompted her to ask the question no one had yet put forth. "Why wouldn't a copper or bronze pipe work as well? Much easier to work with, and copper is much more readily available."

"Not enough strength. The omniscium will corrode copper."

"How do we know that? No one has ever found

omniscium in large enough quantities to test it against various substances. I think gas giant miners use glass or cerama/metal to capture the elusive elements."

"We can't make fires hot enough to burn all the impurities out of sand to make good glass. All we can get is something quite useless, too brittle. Trust me, Kat. I know that iron serves *me* best."

A great chill ran through Kat's overheated body. The world tilted and all the bright green of early summer seemed to shrivel and turn brown before her eyes.

She forced herself to breathe deeply and ignore the prescient vision. If it came true, Amanda could turn the entire planet into a barren prison.

* * *

Loki peered over the top of his rock barricade to scout for any sign of *Rover*. One of the IMPs stared directly at him through his heat-seeking VR gear. The cursed soldier stood less than ten meters away.

The soldier fired his lethal needle rifle.

Three neurotoxic needles scraped Loki's scalp. The top of his head instantly grew numb.

Loki pressed himself flat upon the ground, soaking up the power of the ley line lake.

"Saint Bridget, I wish I were anywhere but here." In his mind he saw himself standing next to Paola. He added the details of the black-and-red boulders surrounded by gray-green sand on the continental desert. Why not a battle with the snake monsters, too. Killing monsters had to be easier than avoiding IMPs with heat-seeking VR gear.

He imagined himself there two heartbeats before he had lifted his head.

His perspective shifted ninety degrees. White sparkles filled his vision. He lost contact with his body for one heartbeat—did his heart actually stop beating?

Then heat and grit blasted his face. A mighty roar filled his ears.

And Paola's strong arm wrapped around his waist.

"Take the stunner," she shouted at him.

All around them other women in tattered IMP uniforms fought off a tangle of big—extremely big—black snakes with stunners, bows and arrows, lances, and clubs. Another contingent worked furiously cranking a hand pump that sprayed the snakes and the sand before them with seawater. The women let loose long ululations of victory each time a serpent succumbed to their attack.

The Amazons held their ground against the oozing advance.

Behind the coil of slithering black muscle, a giant serpent, fully as big around as a pulse torpedo and too long to measure, rose up a full four meters. Six pairs of bat wings fluttered along her back. The matriarch roared protests of anger and pain.

Too stunned to object, Loki took the gun from Paola and fired into the open mouth of a snake. It swallowed the burst of energy, gulped, opened its red eyes wide in surprise, and fell backward.

Sweat poured off Loki's brow as he fired again. This time his blast took a smaller snake directly in its venom gland. Poison exploded in all directions.

Everyone, including the snakes, hit the dirt and covered eyes, ears, and mouths until the spray subsided.

The pump workers cranked harder and directed their spray upon the Amazons. The venom sizzled a femto in contact with seawater and then diluted and washed free.

"Dangerous move, Loki," Paola snarled as she slung an arrow into a bow as long as she was tall. "But thanks for the diversion. Now we know that the venom is toxic to them as well."

Even before she finished speaking, she loosed an arrow. It arched high and flew long.

Loki almost lost track of it against the glare from the dying sun at his back.

And, miraculously, he watched it descend directly into the sagging red pouch beneath the open jaw of the matriarch.

"Hit the dirt!" Paola screamed.

Loki didn't wait for the venom to explode. He suspected a single drop on the skin could eat away at flesh like acid. Grabbing Paola by the hand, he imagined them back in the pool of ley lines. He felt himself drawing in the awesome power.

Again, his perspective shifted ninety degrees. He saw a myriad of white stars. His feet hit the ground and he fired the stunner directly into the heart of the IMP who took aim at where he had hidden moments before.

"What the hell just happened?" Paola demanded, blinking. She shifted her feet, fighting for balance, lost the battle and sank to the ground, legs neatly folded, head in hands, bow discarded.

"I'm not exactly certain." Heat and disorientation rose from deep within Loki. He needed to sit.

But first he needed to make sure the IMP was unconscious and any other enemies far away.

Then he saw the mangled remains of one of the snakes wrapped around his leg. More than just a stunner blast had turned the viper's body inside out and scattered bits of it around the lake of power.

He took one tentative step away from the gore and

crumpled to the ground. His bare feet ached and stung. He took one glance at the monster venom burning the flesh around his anklebone and lost his battle to remain conscious.

CHAPTER 40

KIM SCANNED THE GROUND anxiously from *Rover*'s cockpit. He and Konner had heard nothing from Loki for over an hour. He didn't like the shiver at his nape that told him something was wrong.

"There!" He pointed at a red blob on his heat sensor panel. "Just beyond the causeway between two islands."

"I know the place," Konner replied and shifted direction slightly to port. "Hestiia led us across that causeway on foot the day we landed. Too bad we didn't know about ley lines and psi powers back then."

Kim switched his attention between the heat seeker and real-time views out the windscreen. The heat sensors left him with afterimages too similar to the symbols he saw during a prescient vision. But he needed the accuracy of those sensors to find his brother.

"Brace yourself. This landing could be a bit rough," Konner warned. He toggled the VTOL jets to set the shuttle down as close to the causeway as possible, without damaging the natural bridge.

The moment Konner gave the all clear, Kim threw off his safety harness and dashed for the exit at the center of the vessel. It irised open too slowly. He jumped clear before the portal completed the cycle and lowered the steps.

Loki sat in a lopsided huddle with his left foot dangling in a nearby creek. Paola stood in the creek, bathing his foot. Her round face looked tired with care lines radiating out from her eyes and below her mouth. An ominous yellow tinge marred her near perfect olive skin.

"What?" Kim asked, sliding into the creek beside Paola. He lifted Loki's foot in both of his hands and examined the wound.

"I'll bring the med kit," Konner called from a few steps away and dashed back to *Rover*.

"I think I got all the venom off," Paola said. Her voice shook. "But fresh water doesn't neutralize it anywhere near as well as seawater."

Kim had never seen or heard anything faze the Amazon before.

"Is the snake still around?" Kim asked. He looked anxiously at the water and nearby banks, not eager to be bitten himself.

"Sort of," Loki whispered. His face looked paler than Paola's. Kim thought he must be in terrible pain.

"What is that supposed to mean?"

"I killed it," Loki said. "I killed it with magic."

Kim gulped. "How?" he asked as he checked Loki's eyes for signs of vacancy, and his aura for leakage into death.

"I . . . I'm not sure how, but I willed myself into the middle of Paola's battle with the serpents. *On the other continent.*" He gulped and closed his eyes. "Then I willed us back here. But the snake was coiled around my ankle. It . . . it . . . turned itself inside out and exploded in transport." Loki gagged and held a hand over his mouth.

"By Saint Bridget, that's not possible," Kim breathed. If he could master that spell, a lot of their problems with fuel would vanish.

"I am afraid that it is possible," Paola replied. "One femto I'm in the battle of my life with fifteen of my ladies. The next femto Loki is beside me. We shot a few times. Took out a few more snakes, then he and I are back here with snake gore scattered all over the island."

She shivered and climbed out of the creek. She sat beside Loki and gently eased his head into her lap.

"I've got to get back to my ladies, Loki," she said softly. "I have to see if we took out the matriarch and how many of my Amazons are hurt. Please send me back."

"Can't." Loki's teeth chattered. "Too weak." His eyes rolled up in his head.

"I don't think any of us should try magical transport until we figure out what went wrong with the snake," Konner said, handing Kim the med kit. "I took a quick look around. That snake wasn't killed by any weapon I know of." He shook his head and looked more pale and worried than Paola.

"We'll worry about the transport later. Right now, Loki's foot is a mess."

It had swollen to about three times normal size and the venom had eaten into the muscle nearly to the bone before Paola was able to get it all washed out. Dead skin and muscle sloughed off in chunks.

"I don't have enough Tambootie with me to heal it." Grief and pain and guilt ate away at Kim. He should have thought ahead and brought a basketful of leaves. He couldn't see any of the trees in the immediate vicinity.

What could he do?

"The pool of ley lines," Loki said weakly. He'd barely regained consciousness. The pain must be incredible.

"The what?" Paola asked.

Kim squinted slightly and looked at the ground through his peripheral vision. Hundreds of silvery-blue rivers of power poured into the island. Their brightness nearly blinded him.

Then he saw it. A great lake of converged ley lines.

His jaw dropped in awe. "This truly is the beginning place," he whispered.

"The center of the universe," Konner added. He dropped the med kit and ran to the center of the pool. "This is the well. This is where all the transactional gravitons begin their web that holds the universe together!" he shouted. He raised his arms and turned circles in homage to the power.

"Help me carry Loki over there," Kim called.

Reluctantly, Konner returned to the creek. Together, he and Kim lifted Loki. The vast amount of power emanating from the land gave them strength beyond measure. Kim felt as if he could have tossed his oldest brother into the center of the well. But that would have been uncomfortable for Loki who groaned in pain at every movement.

They set him down behind the tumble of boulders.

"Check the IMP, Paola. Make sure he doesn't rouse and cause trouble," Konner said.

"Already done," the Amazon replied. She paused long enough to test the fallen soldier's pulse and the twisted vines she'd used to bind his hands and feet. "This devil's vine is a powerful restraint. It twines on its own and every movement by the prisoner makes the thorns jab deeper. Almost as good as force bracelets."

"Bloodthirsty wench," Kim muttered.

"That's what I love about her," Loki whispered. He tried to grin, but it turned into a grimace.

Kim returned the grin. Hestiia could be as fierce as any woman on the planet. As could Dalleena. "Looks like we've all found fitting partners," he said.

"Except Kat." Loki frowned. "Amanda still has her."

"We'll worry about our sister when I've fixed this." Kim looked more closely at Loki's wound, trying to figure out what needed to be done.

He took three deep breaths, exhaling each fully. With each intake he pulled power from the ground through his system, just as the dragons had taught him.

Eldritch light pulsed around him, encapsulating all three brothers in the magic of healing.

Kim's head seemed to disconnect from his body, feeling lighter than air. From this new perspective above his body, he looked more deeply into Loki. He saw damaged blood vessels.

With a thought he reconnected them.

He added fiber to the absent muscle, tendons, and ligaments from other parts of Loki's body. He took bits and pieces from the strong shoulders and back. Loki would reforge those areas quickly.

With only a tiny bit of the power available to him, he encouraged bonding and regrowth at one hundred times the speed normal to a body.

As they watched, the swelling reduced and the wound closed. Loki's facial color improved, though he still looked pale and exhausted.

Now for the skin. Kim needed to find seven layers the size of his fist to cover the raw flesh.

His strength flagged. The healing faltered and the glow surrounding him diminished. No matter how much power Kim drew from the ground, he needed his own strength to use it.

He dropped to his knees, still holding Loki's foot.

His neck did not want to hold his head up and his eyes closed of their own volition.

Konner placed his hand upon Kim's shoulder. For an instant they shared memories, emotions, and energy.

Kim stared at his bother, fully understanding him for the first time.

"That should do you for the finishing touches," Konner said. He looked as if he'd wilt, or fall over in a strong breeze.

"Take him, Paola. Feed him," Kim ordered.

Fully restored, he began the delicate job of building up tissue in layers to cover the gaping wound.

He funneled more power into his eyes and his hands. Blue light grew out of his fingers. With infinite care he molded and wove the power into the wound, forcing new skin to grow from the inside out.

At last he laid Loki's foot down as gently as possible. "I can't think of anything else to do. I don't know if it will even work," he said on a sigh.

"Loki has been telling me about the miracles you three can work. I only half believed. Now I know," Paola said. She examined the injury with a critical eye. "Not even a scar. We've never been able to save anyone if the venom gets below the skin." She folded her legs and sat beside Loki's head. She smoothed sweat-dampened hair off his brow.

Loki leaned into her caress and kissed her palm.

"You should probably stay off that foot for a couple of days," Konner added. He didn't seemed inclined to move from his spot a few feet to Kim's left.

"I can't sit idly by while Amanda has our sister. It's my responsibility to look out for all of you." Loki struggled to sit up, despite Paola's restraining hand on his chest. "And I don't think we should allow Amanda to mine the omniscium."

"That's a change of tune," Konner said.

Kim was too tired to talk. But he, too, was surprised by Loki's decision. Loki rarely if ever changed his mind once he took a position.

"This pool has to be protected," Loki insisted. "I saw some things in transit between here and the continent and back again. I didn't understand them then, just thought it was part of the . . . spell for lack of another word. This well of power is connected to the transactional gravitons. It might not be the center of the universe. There are probably hundreds of such wells scattered about the galaxies, maybe thousands. But disturbing any one of them could disrupt the entire web of energy."

"Mining here could begin the unraveling of the web," Konner mused. "I'd never thought about it before, but that sense of oneness with the universe we achieve when we work . . . magic for lack of another word . . . is because of the omniscium in the ley lines. It's connected to the web."

"You three are the Stargods. Can't you just declare this a holy spot?" Paola asked.

"That will work with the locals, but not with Amanda. The spirit of Hanassa that has possessed her doesn't respect us or anything holy. He . . . it . . . only respects his own personal power" Kim said.

"Loki is right. We have to stop Amanda before she mines," he added. "We need a plan. And we need the transportation spell. But do we dare use it before Loki figures out what he did and how he did it?"

"It's too risky." Konner shook his head and pointed to the pieces of snake that had begun to stink.

"I've got to get back to my Amazons," Paola insisted.

"We need help," Loki said. He tried to get his legs

under him, then thought better of it. He sank back against Paola's strong body. "You have to do this without me."

"We need to bring our warriors here," Kim said. We need to take back our land and our villages from the IMPs.

How could they without fuel; without the transportation spell? How could they defeat Amanda and save the planet without killing *people?*

And they had to do it all before the new ship arrived and complicated things.

CHAPTER 41

THE PROXIMITY ALARMS blared suddenly. The *Margaret Kristine* shuddered and veered sharply down, relative to the artificial gravity field.

"Pulse cannons, port and starboard!" Quinn yelled.

Viewscreens showed a dense asteroid field dead ahead and closing fast.

Bruce called up the tiny weapon to port. Martin took starboard. "Just like in the games! Better than steering. I like gross movements over minute any day," Bruce chortled. He blasted three small chunks of debris before he finished speaking.

"Only this is for real," Quinn reminded him. "One of those gets by you and I can't steer around it, we are all dead, exposed to vacuum. It's not a pretty or comfortable way to die."

Martin held back his own shout of triumph as he nudged aside an asteroid at least three kilometers long and two wide. The enhanced sensors showed it a miner's dream of minerals and ores.

Quinn veered sharply to port before Martin had time to think. He blasted the detritus of an exploded planetoid in every direction as quickly as he could swivel and aim the little cannon.

The next hour passed in a blur of concentration, aim, fire, aim again. Martin wished fervently that he had the crystal in his pocket and not nestled among the sensors. Maybe it enhanced his screens to give him time to aim properly. Maybe he only thought it helped.

At long last he loosed a big sigh of relief. He couldn't see any more asteroids or planetary debris in their path. Their route toward the inner planets of this system had been circuitous at best.

"I estimate travel time to the second planet roughly fifteen hours at reduced speed with sensors running at full capacity," Quinn said. He yawned hugely. "Wake me if anything strange comes our way." He stood and stretched.

Martin made a brief sensor scan. Two hours later he hit the comm unit. "Uh, Quinn, I think I see something strange."

"What?" Quinn's voice sounded groggy.

"Cerama/metal. Megatons of it spread between here and . . . and the orbit of the second planet," Martin replied. He continued staring at his screens in wonder. He'd never seen anything like it, even in simulation.

"Approximately fifty thousand megatons," Kurt corrected. He perched his useless glasses atop his head and looked more closely at his screens. "That's almost enough for a small cruiser." He whistled at the end of his sentence, a clear sign that the numbers presented an awesome picture.

Quinn appeared in the cockpit a femto later, hair mussed and eyes heavy. He swung into his chair and scrutinized his own screens. "Saints preserve us, that could be a judicial cruiser." He ran some hurried calculations.

"Kurt, get a reading on that big chunk." Bruce pointed to an object on the front screen that displayed real-time views of their path.

"I don't like the looks of this," Jane whispered. She

sat firmly in her jump seat staring wide-eyed at the front screen. "Those dippos on Aurora were looking for a missing judicial cruiser and its passenger, a planetary governor's daughter."

"So was the ship just outside Aurora's jump point." Martin chilled in memory of the scare the ship had given them.

"I've got a signature signal from the black box," Kurt said.

"Run it through my screen," Quinn ordered. He pulled up another screen.

"Registry marks that frequency as the *Jupiter,* the ship that's missing," he said quietly. "We've got to retrieve the black box."

"Any chance we can crack the box and find out what happened?" Martin asked. "The crew might have made it to the second planet. It's habitable."

"But there aren't any signs of civilization coming from there," Bruce protested. "No signals, no pollution, and definitely no doming. How would they survive?"

"The black box has to go back to GTE authorities. They are the only ones with the codes to crack it," Quinn said, his face stern.

A big grin spread over Martin's face. "When has a lack of codes ever stopped us? And we've got the mini king stone to help. Besides, this is an uncharted system. Who's to say that the GTE and their IMPs have jurisdiction?"

"If the IMPs are here, then they have jurisdiction. That makes opening the box illegal . . ." Quinn said.

"Like I said. When has that ever stopped us?"

"Your father is an O'Hara. He and his brothers have been redefining 'legal' for twenty years." Quinn shook his head and took a bearing on the black box.

"How would they survive?" Bruce asked again.

Martin shrugged. "They have to be alive. My dad's down, there, I know it."

"Don't get your hopes up" Quinn advised. "Have any of you ever seen an undeveloped planet?"

"Our summer camp was on a bush planet," Jane said. "It was pretty primitive."

"Summer camp with food shipped in, or fields already planted for harvesting, shelters, and plumbing; all that is luxury compared to what we are likely to find on the second planet from this star. Better think about what we need to take dirtside." Quinn set his jaw and went about retrieving the back box.

Martin sent out a broad signal, hoping against hope someone had salvaged basic communications from *Jupiter*.

Within an hour, they had homed in on the black box.

Kurt spent a long time concentrating with the robotic arm at an air lock in the belly of the ship. Martin watched him work in real time through a porthole. Kurt reached out and grabbed the box three times only to have it slip out of the claws. The fourth time he managed to retract the arm, with the box firmly clutched, into an air lock.

Martin waited impatiently while the air lock cycled through and allowed him entrance. He pounced on the black box a femto later. He ran his hands over the solid cube, one meter square, seeking a seam or the source of the signal.

"Quinn?" he asked through the comm. "Have you ever seen the inside of one of these?"

"No. And no one I know has. Not even the emperor. IMPs keep the workings top secret to avoid sabotage."

Martin walked around the thing. It offered no clues.

"Let's get it up onto the bridge. I need proximity to the mini king stone." He tried lifting the box by himself. He couldn't budge it.

"Maybe it's magnetic and stuck to the hull," Kurt offered. He pushed his glasses further up his long nose and scrutinized the box.

"Or it's extremely heavy," Bruce joined them. "Let me try. I've been lifting weights in heavy gravity back home."

Martin and Kurt looked at him skeptically. Bruce had always been the lazy one, more content to read about exercise than actually do it. He rarely swam at camp because that meant revealing his pudgy body to the scrutiny of counselors and girls.

"Hey, I can disguise a lot of muscle under these pantaloons!"

"Yeah, right." Kurt adjusted his glasses on his nose and peered through them as if examining a bug.

"So I'll prove it!" Bruce crouched down and wrapped his arms around the box. Using the thick muscles in his thighs he heaved upward, grunting and moaning.

The cube shifted a few centimeters, then plunked back into place.

"Well, he did move it more than we did," Martin said with a shrug.

"This requires some creative thinking," Bruce said, surveying the cargo hold. His eyes brightened and he grabbed an antigrav sled. I'll shift it, you two cram the sled under it. You should have thought of this in the first place."

"Didn't think we'd find one on a private vessel." Kurt looked mystified. "What would Quinn need an antigrav sled for?"

"Shifting heavy objects when he's alone." Bruce crouched down again.

"Why doesn't he just turn off the artificial gravity?" Kurt replied.

"We can do that?" Bruce stood up again without moving the box.

"But gravity takes over again as soon as we reach the bridge," Martin said.

"So we turn it off there, too."

"Reducing gravity to ten percent of normal," Quinn called through the comm. He chuckled. "Took you long enough to figure it out."

Within a few femtos Martin felt the tension leave his face and the weight of gravity leave his shoulders. He shuffled one step forward and nearly lifted himself across the hold.

Bruce jumped up and turned a somersault in the air.

Kurt frowned and shook his head at the frivolity.

Martin returned to the box and hoisted it to his shoulder. Cautiously, he proceeded up the gangway and onto the bridge.

With the box securely in place next to the bulkhead where the miniature king stone presided, he set about examining it more thoroughly.

"Mind if I get some weight back?" Quinn asked. "I really prefer to navigate with better control of my hands than this."

"Sure," Martin replied absently. He turned his entire focus onto the box. A faint pressure nagged at the back of his neck.

"I almost hear something," Jane said. She slid onto the deck and put her ear up to the box. Then she took it away, shaking her head.

"The king stone is humming," Martin said. Once Jane had brought his attention to the sound, he realized the source of the pressure. The vibrations changed pitch. "I think the king stone is trying to talk to the box."

The pitch changed again, became louder. The box responded with a major third down from the king stone.

The king stone adjusted its note again, this time pulling harmony from the primary crystal array and matching the box with a major fifth chord.

Quinn spun around in his chair and stared at the box. "Is there anything that stone can't do?"

"I don't hear anything," Bruce said. He assumed a posture and expression of affront.

"I'm attuned to the primary array. Martin is attuned to the miniature. When you have your own ship, you'll develop your own empathy with your crystals," Quinn explained.

The box let forth with another note, complementary to the crystal but up a major third. Then the crystal found the right response. The box split open along an invisible seam right around the center.

Martin jumped on the box and pried it open. Inside he found a holographic replay system. He pressed the start button.

A map of the *Jupiter* displayed itself in the air above the black box. Onboard sensors noted two human heat sources.

Martin tracked the two bodies. One exited in a solo scout craft. The other continued to move awkwardly to a different bay and a large troop or cargo lander.

An explosion of light and sound burst along the gangways of the ship.

"Get out of there, Kat. Get out now," a man's deep voice screamed. Then silence.

The system played the same explosion and vocal command over and over.

"What happened to them?" Jane asked.

"Three hundred people aboard that ship. Some of them had to survive." Quinn pounded his fist against his thigh.

"I hope my dad was dirtside when that happened." Martin blinked back tears. "Two people aboard. Only two people. That meant the rest evacuated. Right?"

"Let's hope they were all dirtside when the ship blew. Otherwise they are all dead, including the planetary governor's daughter. The GTE will move heaven and earth to find her," Quinn added.

CHAPTER 42

KAT WATCHED the captive blacksmith with awe. He heated and pounded the iron into a sheet ready to wrap around a clay mold. She matched the blacksmith's actions to the words on the reader she had stolen from Kim. At the very end of Konner's notes she saw a reference to purifying the coal until the smoke billowed nearly clear. Otherwise the fire couldn't raise enough heat to burn impurities out of the iron. The resulting metal would be too brittle to withstand ordinary stresses.

The smoke from the forge looked oily and yellow.

How much stress would the pipe undergo in channeling the omniscium?

The secret smile on the blacksmith's face told Kat that he knew he forged an inferior product. Why did Amanda let him get away with it?

Did she even know?

Amanda hovered around the forge, urging the smith to hurry. Her own impatience doomed her pet project before it fully started.

"Wonderful day, love," Geralds said, snaking his arms about Kat's waist.

She started within his embrace. She'd been so intent upon the forge, she hadn't noticed his approach. A dangerous lapse, considering her plans.

"Jumpy today, aren't you, love." Geralds tightened

his grip on her, pulling her back against his chest. He nuzzled her hair.

Kat resisted the urge to slam her elbow into his gut. She had to make him believe she agreed with Amanda about the slavery and the exploitation of all the planet's resources, including people.

"Amanda, I'm not certain iron will work. It's so impure. Copper or bronze, now . . ."

"No!" Amanda screeched.

Everyone at the forge froze in place.

Amanda looked around, wild-eyed, fists clenched, and shoulders hunched.

Then quite suddenly her posture softened, a bit of the old, logical, and reasonable captain peeked through her expression. "Believe me, Kat, I know that iron is the only metal that is proper. Trust me. All will work out in the end."

"Something feels wrong."

"Don't you want to provide the GTE with the means to destroy the Kree? Have you switched loyalties since you found your *outlaw* family, Kat?"

"No. I still respect the GTE. I want them to win the war with the Kree. But I'm not certain this is the way."

"The Kree must be destroyed!" Amanda's eyes turned black and she nearly tore her hair in desperation. "The Kree cannot be allowed to prevail. They must be destroyed once and for all."

As all dragons must be destroyed.

Kat wasn't sure whether she truly heard that last statement or not. She needed to stop this mining operation until she had a chance to think it through, maybe consult Irisey or one of the other dragons. Gentian would know if he hadn't disappeared again.

She made to close the reader and back away from the project.

"Let me see that." Geralds grabbed the reader away from her. "The smith is doing it wrong," he said quietly.

"Careful," Kat warned him. "I'm not sure we should . . ."

"Kat, I need the money from the omniscium. I need to buy the safety of my wife and son from Melinda Fortesque."

Kat raised her eyebrows at him. He truly did look desperate.

He stared at her long and hard for a moment, then his posture slackened a bit as he finally relented. "Melinda Fortesque held my pregnant wife hostage with a needle pistol at her head until I agreed to do . . . some very bad things for her. Then she held exposure of those deeds over my head for sixteen years." He gulped, keeping silent a moment as he mastered the strong emotions playing across his face.

Then he straightened out of his loop of bad memories. "Money is the only thing that Melinda understands. But with money I can hide my wife and son so that she can never find them, or me again."

"There has to be another way . . ."

"No. There isn't. Captain Leonard, I'd like to try my hand at pounding the iron." He held the reader out to Amanda. "Someone other than one lone blacksmith, who just happens to be a slave with no vested interest in the project, needs to know how to do this."

Amanda calculated something in her head while she looked Geralds up and down.

"You may proceed."

Geralds spoke slowly and distinctly to the smith. Either he had figured out that the local dialect was a lingering drawl, or he thought the man stupid. Then

Geralds pulled the heavy hammer out of the man's hands.

The smith backed off, hands at his sides. He still had that secret smile on his face.

Kat was willing to bet Geralds' first or second blow would shatter the iron. Blame for the disaster would fall on the Sam Eyeam's shoulders and not the slave's.

But Geralds consulted the reader and dumped a half bucket of water onto the greasy looking coals.

"What are you doing to my fire!" Amanda demanded.

"Purifying the coal so that it will burn hotter," Kat explained.

"Help him," Amanda commanded.

Kat backed up, unwilling to assist in this project that felt more and more wrong with each consideration.

A Marine leveled a stunner at Kat.

She shrugged and worked the bellows under the coals. The smoke billowed up dark and oily. Another dose of water and air cleared the forge of the stench of burning salt. One more dose made the smoke clear and white. The coals glowed green, just like every other fire on the planet.

Konner's notes had said the copper sulfate wouldn't hurt the forging, just the salt and other minerals found in sea coal.

"I need to reheat the iron before pounding it again," Geralds said.

The smith scowled and backed away. "Might as well start over with new slag," he said in his rough accent.

"That will take too long. We have to get these pipes made," Amanda ordered. She paced around and around the forge, wringing her hands.

The old Amanda, before Konner O'Hara sabotaged

Jupiter, before Amanda went insane and became vulnerable to the ravaging spirit of Hanassa, never reacted so nervously.

Geralds gestured the smith to reheat the metal.

Reluctantly, the big man grabbed the flattened iron with a pair of tongs and thrust the piece into the fire.

Kat kept working the bellows, keeping the fire hotter than before.

Amanda continued to pace and shout and speak nonsense words to the sky.

Kat owed this Amanda no loyalty.

Hanassa, what do you want of us? She projected her thoughts outward, wondering who, if anyone, she would contact.

Amanda jerked her head up and stopped pacing. She looked all around her, eyes narrowed.

Who dares speak? a thick masculine voice hissed back at Kat. She fought to keep her body and expression passive.

Another dragon, Kat replied. She averted her eyes from Amanda, pretending only to monitor the fire. *One who wishes to see an end to your tyranny.*

The iron glowed white hot now. The smith removed it from the coals and began pounding and folding it again. This time the iron looked brighter, resisted the hammer more. This time it would make a good length of pipe.

"I will see all of the dragons dead before I let you harm me. I will rule you all," Hanassa/Amanda said aloud and projected telepathically.

Watch your back, Hanassa. Your death comes from behind, above, below, and face on. You will give up this mad plan or die.

Never! I am immortal!

"We'll see about that," Kat muttered.

"Captain!" Sergeant Kent Brewster ran toward the forge from the center of the village. He'd retreated to playing with the comms rather than come under Amanda's too close scrutiny. "Captain, a ship has answered our distress signal. A ship, Captain. We're going to be rescued," the sergeant crowed. He did a little victory dance.

"Get that pipe ready. We've got some mining to do before the ship arrives," Amanda snarled. "I don't want anyone but me claiming the rights to the omniscium."

"We share the profits," Geralds insisted. He approached Amanda with clenched fists. "You promised, Captain."

"Lock this man up," she ordered the Marines that always hovered around her. "No one gets the omniscium but me. Kill the newcomers when they land and take possession of their ship."

CHAPTER 43

LOKI STARED AT the magnificent pool of blue at his feet. "Come back a femto," he called to his brothers.

"We need to get back to the village, start making plans," Konner protested.

"Just wait a bit while I think something through." Loki couldn't take his eyes off the well of ley lines. "If this omniscium is so powerful, if it fuels our psi talents by remote contact, why can't it refuel one of the cells?"

"What?" Konner's eyes lost focus.

Loki didn't need to read his mind to know that Konner ran calculations and physics probabilities through his head.

"Well, let's test it." Ever practical, Paola started in the direction where Loki had stashed the fuel cell he stole from the IMPs.

Loki followed her, dragging his feet. The moment he stepped off the well onto normal ground, heaviness returned to his body. In contrast, his mind was lighter and freer than ever before. He felt as if he'd just awoken from a long night's sleep filled with vivid dreams and had not yet coordinated his mind and body with reality. His ankle still ached, like the last few days of a sprain, but it supported him well enough.

His perspective was off, though, and he had to place

each foot carefully. Before he'd reached the causeway, Paola had returned with the half full fuel cell in her strong arms. Kim and Konner relieved her of the awkward and heavy burden. They toted it back to the well and placed the cube in the center.

Loki considered following them. Then he decided that if he touched the well again, he might not ever leave.

Within moments, Konner had one of his testing and monitoring gadgets out and pointed at the fuel cell. "I don't believe it." He shook his head, tapped the instrument, then peered closely at the fuel cell.

"It's regenerating! I've got to figure out how." Kim nearly danced across the well of power.

"Come on, Paola, let's get the rest of the cells from *Rover* and get them charged." Loki took her arm as if escorting her to a ball.

"Then can you take me back. I've got to find out about my ladies, and those snakes. There was venom flying everywhere when we left. I can't believe I took out the matriarch with a single arrow." She tripped alongside him.

Loki kissed her temple. "I can believe you did it. You are the finest warrior of your entire army of Amazons."

She paused a moment to snuggle up to him. "Now that you can recharge the cells, will you come visit me?"

"As often as I can. But with a fully fueled *Rover,* Konner's going to want to leave. He has to go to his son."

"I'm staying here." Paola stopped, hands on hips in a defiant pose. A pose that showed off her magnificent proportions and her stubborn pride.

"I know you are. You give me reason to come back

as often as I can." He kissed her again. Never would he try to tame her. He had dealt with a "tame" Cyndi and learned to despise her. He wanted Paola just the way she was. He wanted a regular lover who demanded no commitment from him; who had no more use for hearth and home than he did.

"I love you, Loki O'Hara." Paola rose up on tiptoe to kiss him. "And don't you dare take that as any kind of commitment."

"I won't." He kissed her back. "Let's get those fuel cells charged so we can get on with our lives.

"Good plan. So, if we've taken out the snake monsters, what's our first move in expanding the port?"

"Building boats."

"No timber near the port."

"Farther north on the continent?"

"What about cutting it here in Coronnan and transporting it to the big continent for building?" Paola grabbed a nearly empty fuel cell from *Rover*'s interior and handed it to Loki.

"Easier to build the boats here and sail them across. That will establish connections between the two." Loki set the meter-square cube on the ground and took the second cell from Paola.

She jumped down from the fuel bay and hefted the first cell into her arms before replying. "The people here are fearful of the water beyond the bay. Will they take the risk of sailing beyond it?"

"If one of us goes with them."

"Not Konner. He's too anxious to head out and see his son. Kim's fearful of leaving Hestiia and the baby until they both get stronger. That leaves you, and I know you are as anxious to leave as anyone."

They began walking.

"Not much sense in working to establish markets

for our produce until we have a surplus and a port to lift off from."

They nearly tripped over the now conscious and struggling body of the restrained IMP.

"And we have to take care of Amanda and her pet Marines before this place can grow."

"All before the new ship arrives."

"Let's get to work." Loki increased his pace, determined to finish what he started.

"I'll kill Captain Leonard for you," Paola said quietly. "I know how you feel about taking a human life."

Loki's insides chilled. For half a femto he relived the time he had shot Hanassa with a needle rifle. He'd died a little bit inside himself and needed to follow the tyrant into death. Only Kim and Konner had pulled him back.

"It's my job to secure this planet. I'll do it." All of the euphoria from the well of ley lines and discovering how to refuel the shuttle drained out of him. "But I'd rather capture Amanda Leonard and let the dragons punish her. Maybe they can free your captain of Hanassa's possession."

"If it works. But I will never go back to taking orders from anyone, not Amanda Leonard, and not you, Loki O'Hara."

* * *

The Krakatrice are subdued. Another matriarch will rise, in time. Until then we must break their earth dams and begin the water flowing again. Only water will contain them. Only water will restore the land to life. We need that land to grow and expand our nimbus.

Our Stargods recognize the importance of the beginning place. They have not yet eliminated the danger.

They must work quickly or all will be lost. Removing the menace of the Krakatrice was a minor battle compared to what they face now.

* * *

"I'm getting a signal from the planet!" Martin cried out to his companions. They'd scattered about the ship for food and rest. Except for him and Quinn who rarely needed to rest or eat.

Jane, Bruce, and Kurt scrambled up the gangway to peer over his shoulder.

Quinn kept a close watch on the debris field, both real time and computer enhanced.

Martin took the mini speaker out of his ear and turned on the full comm system.

"This is Lieutenant JG MK Talbot of His Majesty's Imperial Military Police. Please identify yourself." A woman's voice came through the static and background interference.

"That's a pretty weak signal. Let me boost it." Bruce took over Martin's place and began fiddling with the interface.

"Captain Adam Jonathan Quinnsellia of the *Margaret Kristine,* at your service Lieutenant Talbot," Quinn announced. "We are happy to find someone alive down there."

"You found the remains of *Jupiter,* then. We are happy that someone found us." Lieutenant Talbot's voice was a little clearer, but not much.

"What's she using for a comm, a handheld?" Bruce scratched his head and fiddled some more.

"We've been down here for nine Terran months. We only have one comm unit left with any power," she explained. Then she gave them landing coordinates. "What's your ETA?"

Martin checked the chrono and the nav plot. "Twenty hours," he replied.

Quinn looked at him strangely.

Martin placed his hand over the speaker to muffle his words. "Give us a chance to scout the place before we land," Martin whispered.

Quinn nodded his acceptance of the twelve-hour addition to their ETA.

"Strange name for a ship." Talbot's voice came in clearer than expected.

Bruce smiled and fiddled some more.

"Your signal is breaking up, Lieutenant. I'll explain when we meet in person." Quinn killed the signal.

"What?" Bruce protested. He ran his fingers over the controls again. "I was just getting through the static."

"Don't want to give too much info until we scout the situation."

"You didn't ask about Martin's dad," Jane said.

"Martin Konner O'Hara has at least seven warrants posted for his arrest," Martin explained sadly. "If we tell IMPs that we suspect he's on the planet, they'd go after him in a hurry. Any chance we have of getting him out before they bring him to trial and mind-wipe him and his brothers depends upon secrecy."

"Getting another signal," Bruce said.

"From Lieutenant Talbot?" Martin asked.

"Different location, different signature."

"Answer it, Martin. It might be from your family." Quinn said.

"What . . . what if it isn't? Maybe you should do it. Officially. In case there's trouble later." Martin couldn't explain why he was so reluctant to finally talk to Konner. His dad. He'd waited so long. If it turned out to be someone else at the other end of the comm . . . someone like Bruce's dad . . . he didn't think he could stand the disappointment.

Quinn sighed and opened the link. "Private merchanter *Margaret Kristine* here."

"Who?" the startled voice over the system was stronger and clearer than Lieutenant Talbot's.

"That sounds like him," Jane whispered.

"Not quite," Martin replied just as quietly.

Quinn spilled out his ident numbers and the name again.

"Strange name for a private merchant," the anonymous voice said.

That was the second time within the hour strangers had questioned the name of Quinn's ship.

"To whom do I have the honor of speaking?" Quinn's tone went cold and formal.

"Sorry. We're a little out of touch with protocols here. Mark Kimmer O'Hara, citizenship number Alpha George Cat Zebra niner eight two seven Omega Prime niner eight two seven."

"And your ship?"

"You don't want to know."

"That's the youngest brother," Quinn mouthed. "Very well, why did you hail me?"

"Looking for a little rescue down here. We've been stranded for over a year, running low on supplies and fuel."

Martin signaled for Quinn to cut the speaker. "Why don't I believe him?"

Quinn shrugged and turned the speaker back on. "ETA in twenty-five hours. Do you have landing coordinates?"

Martin's uncle gave them a string of numbers.

Bruce shook his head rapidly and pointed to the coordinates Lieutenant Talbot had given them. The sets of coordinates were nearly five hundred klicks apart. But the signal source from O'Hara was the landing place designated by Lieutenant Talbot.

What was going on down there?

Quinn raised his eyebrows. Then he read back the numbers deliberately transposing the first two.

"No, you don't want to land there. That will put you in the middle of the bay in about two hundred meters of water." Then the uncle read off the same set of numbers he had before.

Quinn confirmed them. "How many in your party, Mr. O'Hara? I'm a small ship, haven't got room for many."

"At least three, possibly as many as six. We just need a lift to our mother ship in orbit."

"I don't scan any ship in orbit."

Bruce did something else to the scanners. Another small ship appeared in the vicinity of the moon. "It's cloaked," he whispered.

"You probably won't find it. We're pretty good at hiding where you least expect to find us. See you when you get here. O'Hara out."

The comm went dead.

"My dad uses a cloaking field," Bruce explained. I knew how to adjust the sensors to find it. Wonder if these people stole the program from my dad."

"More likely, your dad stole it from Konner O'Hara. I've been hearing tall tales about that man's genius for a decade. At least some of the rumors should be true," Quinn replied.

"We need detailed sensor data," Martin said. "I'm going to do some adjustments to the system. Bruce, you program that cloak into the landing shuttle. We don't want them to know we're coming until we get there."

Martin opened a bulkhead and rolled onto his back. Then he pulled himself into the guts of the ship. "Jane, hand me a light."

"Not unless you show me what you are doing."

"Only room for one in here."

"I'll look on my own when you are done."

"I want that cloaking program on the *Margaret Kristine* as well," Quinn said. "I have the feeling we are headed into a mess worse than a nest of armed Kree."

CHAPTER 44

HANASSA HAD to keep moving. Had to keep all of his people in sight at once. So much depended upon that crucial length of pipe. He could not fail now. Amanda had shown him the way. The way to eliminate all of his enemies at once.

Mundane copper or bronze would not do the job properly. The dragons would survive if he used those common metals. He could not mine the omniscium properly with copper or bronze. He would not have the glorious opportunity to save the world by opening it to the Galactic Terran Empire. He needed the doming technology.

Amanda had shown him.

Amanda was the best host he could have chosen. He graciously bowed to her expertise in this.

Iron, the pipe must be. And Kat must be the one to insert it into the conjunction of two ley lines.

* * *

Kat carried one end of the heavy iron pipe. Geralds carried the other. Two meters of silence grew between them. He'd stopped asking why she resisted Amanda's plan and had to be compelled to carry the pipe under the duress of two stunners and three needle rifles aimed at her.

During the forging and shaping of the pipe she'd clenched her jaw so tight for so long that her entire face ached and her temples throbbed.

Amanda danced around them, crowing at the triumph of the pipe and glowering at the lack of communication from the approaching ship.

"Here, here, here." She finally pointed to the ground a full klick upriver from Base Camp.

Kat gratefully dropped her end of the pipe. Why hadn't Amanda commandeered a couple of Marines with muscles to carry the blamed thing?

Because Amanda trusted no one except her Marines and had them "guarding" the precious pipe and mining operation.

"Aren't we a little close to the river?" Kat asked. "We don't know what will happen when we release the omniscium."

"We have to be close to water so the omniscium will turn into a salt," Geralds said. He dropped his end just as heavily.

The pipe began to roll toward the river.

"Stop it!" Amanda screeched. She didn't seem to have any other volume lately.

"If she's not possessed, then she is insane," Kat muttered to herself.

"Then why did you betray your brothers to come back here?"

"Because it seemed the only way to get what I want." Like Amanda/Hanassa subdued, confined, possibly even dead.

She shivered with cold dread.

"I thought you and your brothers were the ones who say there is always another way."

Kat just glared at him.

The Marine contingent brought up five slaves with

shovels made from the shoulder blades of slaughtered cattle.

"Careful, just a few millimeters at a time," Amanda cautioned.

Kat allowed her eyes to cross while she studied the ground. The slaves dug at the precise center of a conjunction of two ley lines. The hub would provide a fair amount of omniscium, not nearly as much as if they had dug near the festival pylon at the center of Base Camp.

She dismissed the nagging alarm at that thought. She had other things on her mind.

If she wrestled a stunner away from one of the Marines, how much time would she have to shoot Amanda before the rest of the guards felled her with the needle rifles?

Since that plan would not work, she had to think of something else.

"The ship that's coming in, a private merchanter," she addressed Geralds. "Could Melinda Fortesque have sent another Sam Eyeam to complete your mission?"

He shrugged. "I haven't communicated with her in over nine moths. I believe both homing beacons she sent disappeared—deactivated or destroyed by Konner O'Hara. He's the only one who could figure out how to do it—since he invented them. Amanda probably believes me dead, and might send someone else. I don't know that she has leverage over anyone else like she does me."

"What crime did she force you to commit that she knows you won't disobey her orders?"

"What?" Geralds jerked away from Kat.

She had her answer. The explanation was more complex than he'd said. Melinda Fortesque—the richest woman in the galaxy—had blackmailed Bruce Geralds, Sr. into doing something heinous so that he could not betray his boss. Or risk the incriminating evidence sending him to prison and mind-wipe. Otherwise, he might confess to the GTE and accuse Melinda of blackmail. Why hadn't he and his family simply disappeared into the Galactic Free Market?

Melinda Fortesque's arms were long, but not that long.

"Kat, time for the pipe," Amanda called.

"What, is she afraid the slaves will sabotage seventy-five kilos of iron?" Geralds growled.

"Probably," Kat mumbled. She crouched to lift one end of the heavy pipe. Slowly she rose, feeling the burn in her thighs and lower back. "Help me, Geralds. I can't do this alone."

"I thought you were superwoman," he replied sarcastically. "Why can't you just maneuver it into place with the power of your mind?" He stood, hands on hips, feet braced, daring her to show off her psi talents.

"Do you really want me to open that nest of Kree in front of her?" Kat set her load back down and matched his stance, stubbornness for stubbornness.

"Do it, Kat. Show us why you are so special and why I have made you my heir," Amanda said. She almost panted in anticipation.

A glimmer of an idea. If she could pull it off . . .

"Oh, come on, you don't truly believe that stuff?" Cyndi asked from the sidelines. She'd come up on them very quietly.

"You are a menace and a failure. Why do you question me?" Amanda whirled to face Cyndi.

A true daughter of politicians and diplomats, Cyndi held her ground and replied with aplomb. "I asked a simple question. No one in their *right* minds believes in this so-called magic." She kept her eyes hooded, hiding something.

Kat raised a quick probe. This close to a ley line, she had enough power to catch a glimpse of a phantom dragon digging at Cyndi's mind. She believed all right, but still felt compelled to goad Amanda for a reason. She wasn't willing to give total power to a madwoman.

"And I am not a failure. I am a highly respected diplomatic attaché and wife to an heir to the Imperial throne."

"Errand runner," Geralds muttered. "Eric Findlatter is nothing more than a flunky and never will be."

"Not a failure?" Amanda laughed loud and long. "You have failed every time you tried to sabotage the O'Hara brothers, my enemies. You failed to find a way to gain fuel for an escape. The fuel cell you stole was empty. You failed to seduce any of the natives. You bore me. Take her away and lock her up." Amanda dismissed Cyndi with a gesture and turned her back on the woman.

Two Marines dragged Cyndi away. She spluttered and resisted the entire way.

"Now, back to work. Kat, show us your talents."

Kat looked around at the expectation on everyone's faces. If she showed the possibilities of the mind to these hard-nosed military types, born and raised into a technological society, she would alter their culture forever. Was that such a bad thing?

Only if she ever intended to allow Amanda and her pet Marines to return to the GTE.

Before she could do anything about that, she needed the omniscium.

Dared she begin the mining process without further research?

Without a word she placed her feet on either side of the shallow hole dug by the local slaves. At least half of them had melted away into the underbrush while the guards were preoccupied with Cyndi, Kat, and Amanda.

Kat rested her worn boots upon the ley lines coming together beneath the hole. She closed her eyes and took three deep breaths.

When her body felt lighter and her mind clearer, she recalled the image of the pipe resting on the ground. With each new breath she pictured the heavy iron lifting free of the ground. When she knew she could reach down and grab the pipe, she raised it with her mind and sent it swinging directly at Amanda's head.

Amanda screamed.

Kat opened her eyes and watched her enemy duck and bury her head in her hands. The Marines stared in confusion at the pipe, at their commander, at Kat.

Fatigue tugged at Kat's shoulders and her mind. Her control of the pipe began to slip. It careened wildly. She let it slam into the backs of knees and then tipped it up to mow the Marines down with unplanned clips to jaws and guts.

"Enough!" Amanda ordered. She lifted one hand, palm out, and grabbed the end of the pipe. She slammed it into the ground so that the base rested directly on the hole prepared for it.

A lucky strike? Or did the dragon within her give her amazing strength?

"Prop it up and anchor it," Amanda ordered.

Three marines jumped to hold the pipe upright while kicking dirt back into the hole and stomping on it until the length of iron stood on its own.

"Cap it," Kat whispered. "Cap the pipe or we lose the omniscium to the air."

"Push it deeper, Kat," Amanda said. "Push it into the ley lines."

"Not until you cap it."

Amanda continued to glare at her.

"Or give me something to cap it."

A slave handed her a clay bowl that fit precisely over the top. She tied it in place with a length of vine. The slave scuttled away.

"Push it the last three centimeters, now. Or die. Your choice." Amanda snapped her fingers.

The full contingent of Marines leveled their rifles at Kat.

"Saint Bridget help me," she prayed on a whisper. She gulped and stepped away.

"For heaven's sake. Let's just do it." Geralds wrapped his hands around the pipe and shoved it downward twisting the bottom end of the pipe down, down into the ground.

Kat closed her eyes and with her mind fully attuned to the pipe watched it move beneath the ground. She saw in the back of her head how it pushed the dirt aside a grain at a time. With the power of the ley line where she still stood she gently displaced plants, roots, seeds, worms, and insects so that they would not be trapped in the storm of elements about to occur.

Then Geralds gave the pipe one final push, letting it penetrate the knot of silvery-blue omniscium.

A ruffle of power along her back told Kat that the pipe had done its deed. She stepped away, uncomfortable with the new sensations. One step. Then five. Then another six steps.

She felt more than herd the other scurrying around her.

"Look out!" Geralds yelled. His strong hands yanked Kat away from the pipe.

She opened her eyes to see the upright tube of iron glowing. A blue aura pulsed along the full length of the upright. The pipe swelled and the glow burned ever brighter until she had to clamp her eyes shut again to avoid burning holes in her retinas.

Then she tumbled to the ground and rolled, Geralds on top of her. His hands and body shielded her from the increasing heat.

"What is happening?" Kat demanded. "I have to see what is happening." She twisted and opened her eyes to find Marines and slaves running desperately in all directions.

The clay cap blew upward fifty meters or more. Streams and sparks of unleashed omniscium gushed up and out like a volcanic explosion. The blue-and-silver sparks seared and withered all that they touched in a growing circle.

Amanda cavorted gaily around a shooting fountain of omniscium fire.

The fire poured into the river. The water boiled and smelled of dead fish. Birds screamed, their feathers burned in mid-flight. Animals fled, awful burns boring through their flesh.

Kat scrambled to her feet, grabbed Geralds' hand, and fled the growing destruction.

CHAPTER 45

HANASSA STOOD BENEATH the fountain of blue flame shooting from the wondrous iron pipe.

"Yes!" he shouted to the sky. "The dragons cannot live on this world now. I am the only dragon left. I rule this place. *Hanassa!* I name this world Hanassa."

His skin burned. The hot, sharp pain, thrilled his brain. His female body convulsed in ecstasy.

At each place a spark burned him, new dragon hide and hard cartilage grew. His bones pushed through to form an armored exoskeleton.

"The dragons must all die. But people will thrive to worship me because people know how to protect themselves from destructive air and water. Humans are smarter than dragons."

(But are humans as wise?)

"You know nothing!" Hanassa shouted.

(Will the protective domes and false air protect them from themselves?)

"That does not matter as long as they worship me. Me, Hanassa, god of this world and the only one who controls the omniscium."

(Do you control it, or does it control you?)

* * *

"Does anyone find it strange that this newcomer flies a ship named for our mother and his ident code is Mum's birth date?" Kim asked his brothers as they landed at the edge of their village.

"Coincidence?" Konner asked. "There must be millions of women in the GTE named Margaret Kristine."

"With Mum's birth date?" Kim protested. He opened the hatch to find a contingent of armed warriors led by Yaakke and M'Berra awaiting them. Dalleena had obviously roused them to action.

"Less likely a coincidence. Maybe we'd better find out if Mum sent this guy," Loki suggested.

"Only after we determine that my ex-wife did not send him. She did place the homing beacon inside *Sirius,* and sent the Sam Eyeam with a second beacon," Konner said.

"We have wasted enough time with discussions," M'Berra grumbled. "I'm more than ready to mutiny. Amanda Leonard is going down today." He stepped into the shuttle with dignity and resolve set into his face. He carried a spear and a club, much as his distant African ancestors had.

"The time has come to free my people forever from the monster Hanassa," Yaakke added. He entered the shuttle wearing a fierce expression, carrying his own spear.

A dozen other native warriors followed them.

"I want the needle rifle," M'Berra said quietly.

"The what?" Kim asked, trying for innocence. "Those are illegal."

"I know you have one. The evening storytelling session may exaggerate some things, make you three into gods. But I find them remarkably accurate on details. Where is your needle rifle?"

"Melted in the lava core at the heart of a volcano," Loki said. "I destroyed it after I shot Hanassa with it.

I only wish it had killed him." His face went pale with the memory.

Kim let the tale of the needle rifle rest with that lie. He knew that Konner had personally stuffed it into the storage locker beneath the bench where M'Berra sat.

"Let's fly," Konner said grimly. He brought *Rover*'s engines up from idle to full power.

Kim slapped the hatch mechanism. He watched the faces of anxious wives and mothers and the rest of the villagers left behind as they rolled forward before the hatch fully irised closed.

Silence filled *Rover* like a living entity no one dared breach during the entire journey north to Base Camp.

Konner set the little shuttle down just east of their destination.

"Saint Bridget and all the angels, what is that?" Kim stared at the magnified screens at his station in the cockpit. Seared black ground covered everything for a square klick west and north of Base Camp.

* * *

Screams of pain. The sharp acrid smell of burning flesh and plants invaded Cyndi's mind. She dug in her heels to stop the two Marines who marched her back to Base Camp.

They loosed her and stared in wonder at the mass destruction exploding from Amanda Leonard's precious pipe.

"Oh, my God!" She, too, stared as her mind gibbered in panic. She had to run. Run away. Hide.

The Marines seemed just as shocked as she. They stood frozen in place, jaws flapping.

Then all of her training to be the perfect hostess, an effective diplomat, and a successful politician slammed into place.

"Back to Base Camp," she commanded to all of the fleeing Marines and slaves. "Grab what you can and rendezvous at the big village. Take food, water vessels, and med supplies. Quickly. Move it, soldier."

The Marines gulped, stared at her for one heartbeat, and obeyed. She followed as rapidly as she could and retain her dignity. A princess did not flee; she retreated.

Along the way she pushed and urged others into action. "Food and medical supplies. All that you can carry," she urged again and again.

About every ten meters she risked a quick look over her shoulder. The fire spread. The swath of black ash encircling the still erupting pipe grew faster than she could walk.

Taking her pride and dignity in hand she broke into a run.

The air grew hotter. It burned her lungs with every breath.

She kept running, making certain everyone still mobile continued on to the big village. At the sight of burned and blackened people writhing on the ground she had to bite her lip and continue onward. They were beyond the help of any mere mortal. Stopping to ease their pains or comfort them in their extreme would only jeopardize the retreat of those who could be saved.

She stumbled onward, weeping in pain and agony for herself and everyone else.

"God, I wish I could go home."

* * *

"Our village," Loki gulped. "It's gone. Nothing but a pile of ashes." He leaned forward, peering out the windscreen at the real-time view. "Who would do that?"

"I can't believe it." Tears crept down Konner's cheeks. "All our hard work, the fields, our homes, even the wild cattle are all incinerated. What could do this?"

"That!" Kim pointed toward the fountain of fire pouring out of the ground.

And then they saw the river, the lifeline for the land and the people. The water bubbled and steamed. Thousands of fish, boiled alive, floated on the surface.

Loki crossed himself. Somehow Mum's universal ward and invocation seemed the only appropriate response. Konner followed suit.

Kim, however crossed his wrists, right over left, and flapped his hands in the local ward against the evil demon Simurgh, the first dragon to develop a taste for human flesh.

"We've got to find out how this happened," Loki said. His jaw trembled and his hands shook on the sensor array.

"Do we dare step outside *Rover?*" Konner asked.

"Please, Stargods, please take us to see if our old village, where the river meets the bay, has also been visited by this demon of destruction," Yaakke asked. He sank to his knees in the doorway to the cabin of the shuttle.

Loki hated to see his strong, adventuresome friend reduced to abject pleading.

"The village was deserted when I was there this morning," Loki tried to console the man.

"We hope to return to our homes when the intruders are eradicated. Please. Take us there. We were all born there. Our ancestors are buried there. We worshipped in the temple we built with our own hands. Please. Let us see how far this destruction stretches."

Kim gulped and nodded.

Loki knew the fierce attachment Kim and these people had for the land. He felt it himself though he hated to admit he loved this place as much or more than he did the wandering life he hoped to return to.

"We need to see the extent of the destruction," Konner agreed.

"But what is that artificial volcano? What fuels it?" M'Berra asked. He ran a series of equations through a handheld.

Loki looked back toward the blue-and-silver fire shooting out of the ground and the bizarre figure cavorting around it, impervious to the sparks and flames that did not drown in the water or the dirt.

"I'm guessing that Amanda Leonard began her mining operation with iron pipes," Konner said. "The iron may have acted as a catalyst, turning the omniscium volatile."

"Maybe there's a reason why there is so little iron on this planet. It can't exist in the presence of omniscium," M'Berra added.

"Why didn't we know this?" Kim asked.

Kim called up any and all records in storage. Loki read them over his shoulder. Nothing. The only references to omniscium at all stated that it could only be found in gas giant planets, that it was rare and fragile with a short half-life—less than ten years. The only use found so far was in the growth bath of star drive crystals. Nothing else. Nothing about its properties or behavior in the presence of other elements except those that went into the crystal baths.

"How can something so vital to our technology remain so elusive to our scientists?" Kim asked.

Loki had to stare at the scrolling information. He couldn't bear to watch the acres of black rolling by beneath *Rover*.

"There's the village." Konner pointed to the one hundred substantial, thatched homes along a major street and several alleys.

One thing Hanassa had done for these people, perhaps the only good thing the rogue dragon had done at all, was to organize the village along straight lines.

"There are the Marines from Base Camp," Loki said on a sigh of relief. The armed men and women along with the few remaining slaves huddled together in front of the temple. He spotted Kat's mop of red curls as she paced around them, seemingly giving orders.

So far the land remained ordinary green and brown. The damage spread toward and along the river from the artificial volcano.

"Look at the ley lines," Kim nearly shouted. "The damage stops in straight lines every time it encounters another river of omniscium. It's policing itself."

"Thank whatever gods who might listen for small favors," Loki breathed. He didn't feel as if Mum's God was interested in this place right now. Otherwise He shouldn't have let it happen.

"But the destruction flows back up every stream and rivulet to the headwaters and out from there. Without the river system, the land will die," Konner pointed out.

"We have to stop it," Loki said as much to himself as to his brothers.

"We will take care of this Amanda person. You

deal with the fountain of fire," Yaakke said. "Only a god can handle that."

What if we are not gods, only men? Mortal and fallible, Loki asked himself. He felt totally inadequate and did not know how to lead his people.

CHAPTER 46

"OKAY, MARTIN, this is your family, your call. Where do we land?" Quinn asked.

"I . . . I don't know. All our options look bad," Martin replied.

Jane, Bruce, and Kurt remained ominously silent. This was indeed Martin's decision.

"Let's go with the coordinates Lieutenant Talbot gave us. That seems to be the center of activity and I think they need our help," Martin said all in one breath. He prayed he was right and that the IMPs had not laid a trap for them.

"We've only made one pass . . ." Jane finally ventured.

"I know," Martin said. He couldn't look her in the eye.

"Those coordinates would have been my call, too, Martin. Had it been my choice," Quinn reassured him. He banked the small shuttle—the passenger area was not much bigger than the van—circled around the scenes of destruction, and dropped the nose for a touchdown just outside the village beside the bay.

"Should we all wear EVA suits until we know what is happening?" Martin asked.

"Sensors read normal atmosphere," Kurt put in.

"Normal atmosphere doesn't scorch everything in sight along geometrical grid lines," Bruce grumbled.

"You kids know the protocol. When it doubt, suit up. Anaphylactic shock due to alien pollens and microbes can kill you in minutes. I've got an implanted filter. You four don't." Quinn waved toward the compartment at the rear of the shuttle.

Jane dragged out five EVA suits and passed them around. In the tight confines they struggled into the bulky equipment and secured the helmets. They were now all linked by comms.

Quinn began the routine to close down controls of the shuttle. "This is keyed to me and Martin. No one else will be able to hack or jump the ignition," Quinn added as he stood and checked the cockpit. "We've been through a lot together. Remember to back each other up and we'll get through this one, too." He jerked his head into a single nod of approval to all four of them. Then he checked their seals and air supplies before donning his own EVA suit.

A morsel of pride swelled in Martin. He only hoped his own father appreciated him as much as this new friend did.

Quinn led the way as the five of them stepped out of the cabin of the shuttle.

"I thought a volcano would make more noise," Martin whispered over the comm system.

"I don't think that's a volcano," Kurt said. He moved his lanky body awkwardly in the ill-fitting EVA suit.

"Who knows what volcanoes are like on this planet." Bruce shrugged. "Every planet is different."

"But those mountains to the south are definitely volcanic," Jane protested. "They erupted along normal patterns spilling magma and ash, building through repeated eruptions and normal plate tectonic lifting."

"Quiet," Martin ordered. "I think I hear something . . . someone crying."

A high-pitched wail pierced the air and the sensors of Martin's suit.

Quinn increased his pace. Martin kept up with him. The others followed more cautiously, scouting the terrain carefully, watching Martin's and Quinn's backs, like the good friends they were.

Ash crunched under their boots. Rocks split at the barest touch. Martin guessed that the large mounds of crumbling black matter might have been trees. From the size of the mounds, this planet grew trees on a grand scale.

Heat radiated up from the seared ground. The ash billowed with each step, soon clogging their atmosphere filters.

Martin labored for each breath. Bruce and Kurt fared worse.

"Quinn, we have to shed the helmets," Martin said. Each word came out heavily. He had to pause and cough at the end of the simple sentence.

"You guys don't have filter implants." Quinn lifted his helmet free of his head, and shook his sweat-darkened hair. "I don't know if you will be able to tolerate the foreign pollens and impurities."

"An allergic reaction is better than not breathing at all." Bruce lifted his helmet free of his head.

"I have allergy meds on the ship." Kurt followed suit.

Martin and Jane exchanged looks and brief nods. Then they, too, shed their helmets. Martin inhaled deeply, got a mouthful of ash and coughed it back out.

Over it all, the sounds of someone wailing in pain and grief kept rising.

They hurried forward.

Then the roar of another shuttle overhead made them all duck.

"That's one big shuttle," Bruce gasped.

"It's *Rover*. That's my dad's shuttle!" Martin jumped up and began running in the same direction as the shuttle.

"Martin, come back. We don't know . . ." Quinn called after him.

"My dad's there. I know it." Martin kept on going, marking in his mind the short track of level ground at the edge of the village where the shuttle set down using its VTOL jets.

Three tall, red-haired men and a dozen or more people armed with primitive weapons spilled out of the shuttle mere femtos after it settled to the ground. The engines continued to run. The shortest of the men began shouting orders.

Martin's heart beat so hard and so fast in his ears he had trouble hearing every word. But he understood.

"Kim, check on the well. Konner, you and M'Berra fetch Taneeo and Chaney Lotski. Tell them to bring every remedy they know and a few they haven't thought of before. I'll sort out and triage."

"Wait," Martin gasped. "Dad, wait."

All three men froze in place.

"Martin?" Konner took one step forward.

Martin skidded to a halt a hair's breath away from him. They fell into a tight hug. Martin clung to his father with all the desperation of a two-year-old and a lifetime of separation.

Tears pricked at the back of his eyes.

The piercing wail of grief and pain rose behind them.

"Dad, what can we do to help?" Martin couldn't

let go of Konner, but he had to do his best to stop the awful destruction all around them.

"We?" Konner stood back a moment, keeping his hands on Martin's shoulders, also unable to let go.

His fingers dug tightly into Martin's flesh. The pain was nothing compared to the joy of seeing his father again, feeling his strength, being a part of his life once more.

Konner stared at Martin with hungry eyes.

"I ran away from Melinda. My friends helped. We've come to rescue you. What can we do to help?" Martin gushed as he pulled his dad close once more.

"You're the people aboard the *Margaret Kristine?*" The tallest and youngest came up beside Konner.

Martin guessed he was Mark Kimmer—Kim to the family.

"AJ Quinnsellia, pilot of the *Margaret Kristine,* at your service." Quinn held out his hand.

"Introductions and reunions later. We've got a crisis on our hands." A tall woman disengaged from the wailing crowd of ragged people in the village. She, too, had red hair and bore a marked resemblance to the three brothers, to Martin himself.

He wondered where she fit into the family tree. He'd never heard of a sister, even in the official records he'd stolen from Quinn's shipboard database.

"Are you okay, Kat?" all three brothers asked at once.

"For now. But we've got to get that iron pipe out of the ground *now*."

"I have a shuttle, what can I do?" Quinn stepped forward, keeping Bruce, Kurt, and Jane behind him. "I have four teenagers in my custody. I'd rather fetch the people you need from distant places than have my charges endangered by proximity to that . . . volcano."

"Good plan," Kim said. "Take the kids to the coordinates I gave you originally. Ask for Taneeo, he's the village priest and a healer. Lotski is a real medic from the IMP cruiser. Martin, tell the villagers that you are the son of Stargod Konner. They'll take care of you and your friends."

"I want to stay with my dad," Martin insisted.

Konner's fingers tightened on his shoulders once more. Neither of them dared separate right now. They might never see each other again.

"He knows?" Kim raised an eyebrow at Konner.

"He's my kid." Konner shrugged. "He's smart enough to figure it out. I presume there are no IMPs or agents of Fortesque Industries on your tail."

"None," Quinn reassured them.

"I can help you, Dad. Let me stay here." Martin's gut tightened. He had a feeling something terrible would happen to both himself and his father if he let Konner out of his sight.

"As much as I want you here with me always, I have to insist. Go with your friends. For your own safety. You will also be my representative in the village. Your family resemblance is the only way they will recognize your authority and not capture all of you and impound your shuttle. My wife Dalleena will help you. Now go." Konner gave Martin one last brief and fierce hug.

"Dad, please."

"You have to go. Martin, I can't do my job if I'm worried about you. Besides, you need to introduce yourself and your friends to the locals. They won't believe Quinn without you."

Martin turned around with a sniff. Then he straightened his shoulders and marched back to the shuttle. He had to blink back his tears. He had a mission to accomplish for his father. He'd do it. But he was coming back with Quinn and this Taneeo person. No one would stop him.

"I'm the son of a Stargod." He smiled and hastened his steps.

CHAPTER 47

"BREWSTER, YOU'RE in charge," Kat called over her shoulder as Quinn's shuttle roared off into the southern distance. Interesting coincidence. But she didn't have time to mull this over right now.

She joined Loki as he marched toward *Rover*.

"No one leaves this planet without me, and I'm taking this one hostage," Cyndi called. She stood on the top step of the temple, a needle pistol aimed at Geralds' throat.

Kat sighed in disgust.

Kat gauged the distance between herself and where the refugees crowded around the entrance to the temple with its silver bloodwood columns and carved dragon capitals.

She cursed fluently. Loki raised his eyebrow at her creativity.

"No way we can take her out from here. Too many people in the way," Loki said quietly.

"Fine," Kat yelled at the planetary governor's daughter and close kin to the emperor. "I don't care what you do to him. He's a murderer. I planned to take him back for trial and mind-wipe. Go ahead and kill him. That's one less worry." Kat turned her back on Cyndi. "I've got a planet to save." She gestured Loki back toward the shuttle.

"How dare you turn your back on me, Lieutenant!"

Cyndi said as she ran for Kat, hands extended like claws. "I'll have your commission for this."

Loki didn't even try to come between the enraged woman and his sister.

Kat glared at him as she prepared herself for attack.

"Listen to me when I talk to you!" Cyndi launched herself onto Kat's back, reaching to gouge her eyes with her broken fingernails. She breathed in hysterical pants.

Today's trauma had finally broken her control over her emotions.

Kat bent double and flipped Cyndi onto the ground. In two moves she had twisted Cyndi's arm into an impossible position and planted her foot on the smaller woman's waist. "No one attacks my back." Kat dropped to plant her knee on Cyndi's chest and hold a wicked knife at her throat. The knife Konner had made and then given to Kat for defense when they were first reunited nine months ago.

"What did you mean 'you don't care' what this trollop does to me?" Geralds added his own invective to the noise and confusion. "I thought we meant something to each other, Kat."

"Here your rank and connections mean nothing, Ms. Baines," Loki said quietly. Too quietly.

Kat wouldn't want to be on the receiving end of his wrath when he spoke like that.

"Now, see here, Kat. There's no call for violence." Geralds made to grab Kat by the collar.

"Oh, what the hell." Loki planted his fist in Geralds' jaw. "I've wanted to do that for a long time."

The man went down in a spluttering rage, blood trickling from a split lip. He started to get up.

"I'd stay down and stay out of the way if I were you," Konner added with menace.

"Saint Bridget, I wish we could leave them both here," Loki muttered.

"We'll deal with them later. Brewster," Kat called to the Marine who'd tried to hide himself in the crowd.

"Brewster, get your sorry ass over here. I want force bracelets on these two and you organizing these people. Do some triage until we get a medic."

"What about . . ." Kent Brewster jerked his head toward the still armed Marines mingling with the crowd, just as confused and panicked as the locals.

"I said, you're in charge. Anyone questions that has to deal with me." She glared at the contingent of Marines.

They all nodded acceptance of her authority.

Happily, she noted that they all placed their weapons at their feet and saluted her.

"Fickle bastards," she muttered to herself. After the stunt she had pulled with the iron pipe, they probably figured she had more power than crazy Amanda. They sided with her now.

She trusted them about as far as she could throw an asteroid out of a gravity well.

"Now what is this well that so desperately needs checking?" she turned to her brothers.

"The place where all the ley lines begin and end," Loki said quietly. "It takes up almost an entire island in the delta."

Kat froze at the implications. "It's feeding that volcano," she whispered her conclusion.

"We've got to take out Amanda and cap that . . . fountain of fire. The well will wait," Loki said. "Paola, you are with me. The rest of you help the refugees and begin evacuation. Find an escape route to higher, rocky ground." Then he and his lady climbed into *Rover.*

"This chore is not yours alone," Yaakke, the warrior leader from the village, stood firm, facing Kat. "We will come with you."

"Some of you," Kat agreed. "Half of you stay with the refugees." She marched toward *Rover.*

"I'll fly," Konner said right behind her.

"Amanda is mine," M'Berra said, hopping into the shuttle.

"If I don't get her first," Kat announced through gritted teeth.

(She belongs to the dragons.) Gentian flew above and around Kat for the first time in hours.

"Where have you been, friend?" She pointed out the soaring flywacket to her brothers—the only living creature left for many square kilometers.

(You may not meddle in the affairs of dragons.) With that, the flywacket disappeared into the sky that grew as gray and black as the ash beneath their feet.

"I will meddle with whomever I choose! With or without your permission, Gentian."

Within moments Konner set *Rover* down just beyond the circle of sparks from the eruption.

"Paola and I will circle around, try to approach Amanda from the rear," Loki said. He and his Amazon slid through the fuel bay and out the belly of the vessel.

"Yaakke and I will come at her from the other side." M'Berra and the local man followed Loki out the hidden exit.

Amanda greeted Kat, Kim, and Konner with a needle rifle. Her skin had blackened from innumerable burns. Bony ridges pushed through to form a hard exoskeleton. Long talons had replaced her fingernails. Her once lustrous black hair stood up in horny spikes. A hump on her back could be vestigial wings.

"She really is turning into a dragon," Kim breathed.

"The person you knew as Amanda is no more," Yaakke, said from behind a mound of ash that had once been a tree or a wild animal, no way to tell now. "Hanassa has taken both her body and her mind."

Kat could no longer think of the figure before them as a person. It was a *thing*. Taking its life did not violate any laws, ethics, or morals among civilized people.

She stepped ahead of the others, hoping some residual of the favoritism this *thing* had shown her a few hours before might allow her to get close enough to disarm it.

"You knew what the iron would do to the omniscium, didn't you?" Kat accused. "You've never valued life, only your own power. You would willingly destroy the entire planet rather than let someone else have power over you."

"My pretty Kat, you know me so well," the thing said in a wildly fluctuating singsong. The voice had deepened to masculine tones and came out in the volume of a dull roar. "Step out of the way so I may remove the menace of these others."

"I can't let you kill my brothers." Out of the corner of her eye, Kat saw Yaakke and M'Berra and two others working around to the *thing's* back.

"But your brothers have already killed me three times. It is about time I evened the score. Pity I can only kill each of them once."

"What makes you think that?" Konner asked. He sidestepped in the opposite direction, drawing attention away from Yaakke and the others.

Kat had no idea where Kim had gotten to. She hoped he stayed out of range as long as the *thing* kept the needle rifle locked and loaded. Did Hanassa have enough of Amanda's memories to know how to use it?

For answer, the thing laid down a spread of lethally drugged needles at Kat's and Konner's feet.

Kat froze in place, hands out to the side. Konner did the same.

"We are the Stargods, Hanassa. You cannot kill us." Konner edged a little farther around the circle.

Silver-blue sparks continued to spray the ground and Hanassa, just beyond Konner's feet. Rather than burning, the thing seemed to absorb the fire, growing more and more like a dragon with each blast of heat.

"Gods? I see only one of you, and your sister who is no god. She isn't anything but a bad little soldier who thinks too much and shows off." Another round of needles flew from the rifle.

Kat dove into the powdery ash. Dozens of drugged needles sprayed over the top of her embedding harmlessly into the dust. She sweated freely, from the fire and from her own fear. How had the others fared? Where the hell were Loki and Paola?

Konner held his ground. The needles aimed at him lay in a neat pile at his feet. He'd called upon some kind of magic to shield himself.

"Saint Bridget I wish I'd thought of that." With so much omniscium loose in the ground and in the air, she should be able to draw on it for power.

Konner took a step forward. A spark landed upon his "bubble" of protection and fizzled. He took another step forward.

Hanassa fired the rifle again. "This is how you killed me the third time!" it screamed.

The needles bounced off the shielding.

Kat scrambled backward toward a discarded needle handgun. The omniscium hadn't melted the cerama/metal housing yet. The gun didn't have the range of the rifle. But in Kat's hands it should have more accuracy.

Yaakke chose that moment to dash through the rain of fire, his spear leveled at the *thing's* gut. A wild ululation erupted from his throat. "You die, Hanassa. In the name of all the Coros, I kill you!"

He lunged forward. The spearhead pierced Hanassa's side.

"And what do you think you are doing, little man?" Hanassa loosed a full volley of needles directly into the man's gut.

He fell forward, dead before the next spark burned through his flesh to his bones.

His dead weight pushed the spear deep into his quarry.

Hanassa seemed not to notice the spear or the blood that flowed from its side.

Kat choked. A terrible pain filled her gut. White light filled her vision. The silhouette of a man appeared in the center of the light. He walked calmly away from her.

Sweet longing pulled Kat in his wake. Lassitude drained her body of strength and will.

CHAPTER 48

"YAAKKE, NO!" Loki reached to stop his friend as Yaakke went down under a spray of needles. His entire body flinched in shared pain.

"You can't save him." Paola held him back with a fierce grip. "You'll only burn up as fast as he did." She clenched her jaw.

Loki had to close his eyes. He couldn't watch the horror of the blue fire eating away at the man's flesh. His gut ached and the siren song of death lured his soul away from his consciousness. He pinched his thigh hard, concentrating on his own pain rather than the silhouette of a man walking into a vast tunnel of white. Yaakke's wandering soul invited Loki to cast aside his worries and cares—permanently.

The lure was too strong. The need to guide his friend into the light, to linger, to leave behind his pain and responsibilities . . .

Paola slugged him in the gut.

The physical pain jerked him back to reality.

With each deep breath he separated himself a little further from his need to die alongside his friend.

Then he saw Kat, curled into a fetal ball, wrapped around a pistol as if she needed to fire the thing into her own belly.

"Not yet. I can't lose you yet, Kat." He grabbed her hand and wrenched the gun away from her. Then he held her hand so tightly he felt her bones though his fingers. "Come back to your family, Katie. Come back to me."

"I won't die yet," she whispered with her eyes clamped shut. "I refuse to die before I have freed this world of Hanassa." Her breathing evened and color crept into her cheeks. "Guess working magic, tapping ley lines, has awakened the family curse in me."

Loki put his arms around Kat's shoulders and helped her to stand. He handed the pistol back to her. Emotions and thoughts flowed between them. They shared the awesome emptiness of losing a friend to death. Grief became a living ache within them both.

"That is the last innocent you will kill, Hanassa," Konner said. He stalked another dozen meters toward their foe. Anger poked holes in his bubble. Sparks penetrated to his skin.

They had to act quickly. Kat broke away from Loki. She whirled, aimed, and fired at Hanassa in one smooth movement.

Loki braced himself to share the rogue dragon's death as he had a year ago, the first time he'd killed him.

Hanassa held up a horny hand, talons arched to gouge out an opponent's eyes. The entire load of needles bounced against the palm and dropped harmlessly to the ground.

"You cannot kill me, O'Hara. No one can kill me. I am Hanassa. I am immortal!"

* * *

Kim saw his chance.

Kat distracted Hanassa with her pistol.

Yaakke's spear was still embedded in Hanassa's gut. The wound bled hideously.

Kim wanted to gag on the stench of fresh blood pouring down on the burned landscape.

With a great shout of defiance, he dashed into the circle of blue fire. Ten long strides and he leaped, drawing both his legs up to chest level. He kicked out on his downward arc. Both feet connected with the iron pipe. He slapped the ground to break his fall, and rolled to his knees in one movement.

The pipe tube tilted toward the river, away from the land. Not good enough.

"My cannon?" Hanassa wailed. He had to be growing weaker. No creature could not feel the loss of so much blood. "You can't destroy my cannon." He whirled, rifle leveled toward Kim's chest.

Kim stood. Most of the rivers of fire now flew away from him, toward the river. Stray sparks burned his face and through his clothing.

He screwed up his courage and attacked the pipe with all of his weight. Searing burns took their toll upon his strength.

Konner tackled Hanassa. The rifle spewed more lethal needles as it flew from Hanassa's hands.

A needle penetrated his arm. Another caught his leg. Instant numbness. But he had to keep pushing. He had to topple Hanassa's cannon of total destruction.

Ignoring that fray, Kim leaned his entire weight against the iron pipe. The flames lessened. He kicked again. And again. And again.

The pipe broke free of the ground and landed with a thud. Long cracks grew up and down its length.

The opening to the omniscium bubbled, belched one last flame into Kim's face, and died.

Kim reared back, arms across his face. The pain ate at his sanity, his will, and his consciousness. He collapsed and rolled into a fetal ball, praying he would die and the pain would go away.

But he'd destroyed the horrible weapon. He'd ended Hanassa's plans for total destruction of the planet.

CHAPTER 49

THE AIR SCREECHED and groaned. Kat wanted to cover her ears and eyes. She didn't have time.

"Get out of the way, Konner. I need to shoot this creature and end our misery," Kat called. Her middle brother held Hanassa in a wrestling position that unbalanced their enemy and kept its hands separated.

Konner's greater height gave him the leverage to keep Hanassa from gaining a solid foothold on the ground.

The spear stuck in Hanassa's torso waggled obscenely, threatening to overbalance them both.

Loki tackled Kat from behind. They fell to the ground together.

Kat clung to her pistol like a lifeline.

"I can't let you kill, Kat. You'll die, too. Or want to. I won't lose you now. We've come to love you. All of us have." He continued mumbling the same nonsense into her back as he pinned her to the ground with his greater height and weight.

Kat tried to throw him off. He braced himself and clung tighter.

"I have to do this." She almost wept with frustration. Perhaps Hanassa was right. Perhaps it was now more dragon than human, immune to attack with mundane weapons.

Immortal.

The gray sky turned darker. Thunder echoed around them. It rumbled on and on. It grew louder with each peal. Came closer and closer until the sound filled Kat's mind and blotted out all other thoughts.

Hanassa craned its neck away from Konner's pinning hold and stared at the growing darkness. "You have no command over me. I am no longer a dragon," it shouted.

Kat followed Hanassa's gaze. Hundreds of nearly invisible dragons hovered above them. Dragons with red wing tips and horns, blue-tipped and green-tipped dragons, and five iridescent all color/no color female dragons.

Their crystal fur refracted the weird and uncertain light beneath the ash cloud. Edges and outlines blurred together into one huge confusion field.

But only one purple-tipped dragon stood out among them. Iianthe hovered below the nimbus, smaller than his fellows, his colors brighter and more complete. All of the dragons faced Hanassa, eyes whirling in anger.

Gentian landed on the ground beside where Kat lay with her elbows braced to fire the pistol. The flywacket stood on his hind legs and placed both front paws upon her wrists.

She had to drop her arms in the dusty ash from his weight. Her body went slack and Loki eased his weight off her.

The gun dangled from her limp hands. The drive to kill drained out of her.

(Hold,) the flywacket whispered into her ear. *(Our laws prevail here. Justice is ours to exact.)*

Kat tried to formulate an argument. She dropped her head onto her arms. She had to think.

She was so tired logic deserted her.

The thunder of hundreds of wings flapping drove out all coherence.

"I've been running and fighting so long I just want it to be over. I just want to go home."

(What if you are home?)

"Go away and just let me finish this, Gentian. Then I can think."

(We can no longer tolerate the rebellion of one of our own.) The full nimbus of dragons spoke as one voice, deafening Kat's ears and mind. *(We have judged Hanassa guilty of wanton destruction of our home. Let him be exiled and his name no longer spoken among us.)*

"Never! I am not subject to your laws anymore," Hanassa proclaimed.

It wrenched free of Konner and raised a fist in defiance to the nimbus. Then it wrenched the spear out of its body and cast it aside. A fresh spate of blood flowed to the ground.

Could nothing weaken it?

"There is no place on this planet you can send me that I can't escape." Hanassa emptied the needle rifle upward into the bellies of a dozen dragons.

If any of the needles penetrated thick dragon hide and crystalline fur, the gigantic creatures did not react.

Kat covered her head and neck with her hands to protect herself from any falling projectiles.

(You need not fear the weapon of Hanassa. We have stopped this attack as we should have stopped every other attack.)

With that, Iianthe, the purple-tipped dragon, swooped down from the sky, talons extended and steam escaping his muzzle.

(This responsibility is mine,) he said sadly. His deep voice reverberated along Kat's spine.

Gentian launched himself up to join his brother as they both grabbed Hanassa by the shoulders and flew back to the gray clouds of ash that filled the sky. Hanassa flailed and twisted, screeching in protest. Its cries faded in the distance as the dragon and the flywacket disappeared.

"Where will you take Hanassa?" Kat called up to the dragons. The downdraft from hundreds of massive wings stirred square kilometers of ash into a dense miasma.

(We take the exiled one to the caldera of the volcano in the south. If ever he leaves that place, he will die.)

"What about the dragongate?" Konner asked.

(The warp in time and space will kill one of dragon blood. Neither the exiled one nor his descendants will ever leave that place by that exit.)

"A mere dragon taboo or curse will not confine Hanassa for long." Kat coughed and buried her face in her arms. When the wind of dragons passing eased, the ash still hung in the air.

"It's over, Kat," Loki said. "The dragons found a better way for us. We have to remember that there are always alternatives to violence and death."

"At the cost of our baby brother." She gulped deeply and blinked back her tears. As quickly as she could in the dense air, she made her way over to the fallen pipe. "Saint Bridget, I wish I'd known what would happen before." She kicked at the pipe. The cracks widened and it crumbled into four pieces.

Kim groaned.

Kat joined Konner and Loki in a crouch around him. She placed her fingers lightly on his neck pulse. He winced at her touch. The fluttering beat against her fingertips was faint and too rapid.

"Let me die here," Kim whispered. "I beg you. Let

me die here on Kardia Hodos, the path of my heart, my home. Bury me here."

The air screeched and groaned as if the very elements along with the dragons mourned his passing.

* * *

The roar of an incoming shuttle only slightly registered with Konner.

"We've got to get him to the well. Between us, we can heal him there," he said.

"The well is reduced by almost half," Loki said. "Will that be enough power? You and I don't have the healing talent."

Konner's mind spun, refusing to alight upon any answers. He couldn't lose Kim. He couldn't watch his brother die.

Kat stood up and began looking around, as if searching for an ambulance and stretcher. "We can't let him die."

Konner looked around, too. Then he remembered the returning shuttle. Quinn had come back. Did he have Taneeo or Lotski with him? Or had he left them at the village? Martin ran toward them with a knapsack bulging with packets of herbs and a few crude surgical instruments.

Right behind him came Hestiia and Dalleena. Thank Saint Bridget and all the angels. He gathered Dalleena to him even as Hestiia threw herself across Kim's chest. Tears and wails poured from her.

Konner wished he could join her. His gut ached with the emptiness of grief. What could they do? How could they save Kim when he was so horribly burned that he wanted to die?

Dalleena's steadiness gave him the courage to begin thinking again.

"Quinn, what have you got in your shuttle that we can use as a stretcher?"

"Not much, but I've got a portable stasis unit," Quinn replied. "If we get him into suspended animation, we can get him to a hospital in less than a week."

"I'll get it!" Martin reversed course and in just a few heartbeats he leaped free of the shuttle, carrying the rolled-up metallic blankets and cryo-generator.

Konner's heart warmed with pride for his son. But he had to be the boy's father now, not just his friend and camp counselor. "I told you to stay in the village, Martin."

"I'm needed here."

"Your mother . . ."

"Has nothing to say about this. I have chosen my custodial parent."

"The courts . . ."

"Since when have you paid attention to the courts?" Martin gave him a cocky grin that reminded Konner too much of Kim at age fifteen.

"Don't let them take me away, Hes," Kim said. "Let me die here. Bury me on the island where I first saw you, Hes. Bury me in my home, Kardia Hodos." He gripped her hand with his remaining strength.

"Save him!" Hes demanded. "You must save him. No matter what it takes." Tears spilled down her face. Great sobs racked her too thin body. "Even if you must take him from me and our daughter, you must save him!"

"She's right, Loki," Konner said. "We can't let our baby brother die. If there is even a breath of a prayer that he might live, we have to get him to a hospital."

"What about the well? We can heal him there," Loki insisted.

"Gentian says no." Kat cocked her head, listening to some distant advice only she could hear. "He says that the well of life is the same as the well of death. The beginning place will only make his wounds worse."

"Martin, give me the stasis unit." Konner took the cumbersome bundle from his son. "Help your Uncle Loki roll out the blankets while I make sure the cryogenerator works."

"I'll fire up *Rover*," Kat said.

Hestiia put a delicate hand upon Konner's arm to stop him from beginning the process of taking her husband away from her and their home. Chin trembling and eyes brimming, she peeled back the metallic blanket and tucked it gently beneath Kim's chin.

He forced a tentative smile. "I love you, Hes," Kim said, voice painfully weak.

"I love you, Stargod Kim. Come back to me and our daughter." Hestiia kissed his mouth, his cheeks, and his brow in solemn farewell.

Then she rose and walked back to the shuttle, spine straight, dignity and pride keeping her moving.

Konner dashed away his own tears as he pressed the start-up sequence on the stasis unit.

Kim closed his eyes and fell into a forced cold sleep.

Martin and Dalleena slipped their hands into Konner's. He held them both tightly, praying he would never have to separate from them like this. Praying they were doing the right thing in taking Kim away from his beloved planet. Kardia Hodos he had named it.

Kardia Hodos, the pathway of the heart.

* * *

"Perhaps I should take Kim back to civilization aboard the *Margaret Kristine,*" Quinn said, monitoring the controls of the cryo-generator. "I have some diplomatic clearances. Kim has a citizenship number. I can arrange for questions to be squashed," he offered as they flew the frozen bundle that was once an honorable man toward the gathering of refugees.

Kat was about to ask the next question, but Konner beat her to it. "That is another question that has to be answered before we do anything. Why is your ship named for our mother and why is the identification number the same as Mum's birthday?' He worked to keep the metallic blankets in a bubble so they didn't adhere to Kim's skin and damage him further. The rig had come without a frame.

"Your *mother!*" Quinn asked. He sounded almost accusatory.

"Yes, our Mum," Kat chimed in.

"The ship had that name when I bought it. I liked the name." Quinn closed his mouth and lowered his eyes.

Kat knew that look. The man had secrets. Well, she and her brothers had secrets, too, like mind reading.

She looked calmly at Quinn. A bright green layer of energy lay atop his aura. She peered close, seeking to unfold the physical barriers between his mind and hers.

She met a blank wall, not so much a wall as a mist. Her mental probe sped right through. But she caught a glimmer of an image. A man saying good-bye to the love of his life and their children.

"Who did you buy the ship from?" Could it be her father? Was there a way to find out if Dad still lived? Perhaps he thought them all dead. Perhaps that was why he had never come looking for them.

"That is information I cannot and will not give you." Quinn turned his head away and looked pointedly out the portal toward his own shuttle flying alongside them, piloted by Martin.

No more information leaked out of him.

Frustrated, Kat looked to Loki for help. He piloted *Rover* and kept his eyes forward. But he shrugged.

I tried several times and couldn't get into his mind. I have no idea who he is or what he is thinking.

So much for that strategy.

"I'll use Geralds' ship to take Kim back to civilization," Kat said. "I'm blood kin and can get him into any hospital, even the best military facility. That way I can concoct some story about Amanda Fortesque's brave Sam Eyeam rescuing me and dying in the process. Konner and Loki won't be endangered at all."

"Geralds?" Martin gasped over the comm unit from Quinn's shuttle. Konner had insisted he keep the comm open in case he ran into trouble. Quinn had assured him he wouldn't. "Bruce Geralds, Senior? Captain of the *Son and Heir?*"

"What do you know about Geralds?" Kat demanded. She moved to the copilot's seat and set the comm to privacy.

"His son is my best friend. He's at the village with Kurt and Jane," Martin explained to his aunt. He lowered his voice as if he knew she needed this information kept between them. "He's a criminal who needs to be brought to justice. But it will devastate my friend if he finds out."

"Let me worry about that for now. Do you have evidence?"

"Yes, Aunt Kat. In my handheld and on an encrypted database aboard the *Margaret Kristine.*"

"Keep it safe and don't let anyone else know you have it until I tell you different."

"He killed my grandparents on my mother's orders."

Kat gulped. Somehow she'd known the man couldn't be trusted. As much as she liked him, enjoyed his company, she had never let her guard down in his presence. Now she knew why.

But Amanda had coerced him into committing that crime.

So why did he stay employed by her? What other hold did she have on him to keep him from running off to the Galactic Free Market with his family?

"Coming in for a landing, folks," Loki announced. "I'll try to keep it gentle. Martin, you copy my every move one hundred meters to starboard."

"Aye, aye, Captain."

"Cheeky kid. I like him."

"So do I," Kat admitted.

"He's going to be a better pilot than I am!" Loki said as he watched Martin set down the smaller shuttle with ease.

"It's a smaller vessel than *Rover,* state of the art controls," Kat said wistfully.

"Here's the plan. We evacuate as many people as want to go south. Then Konner and I take Kim back to *Sirius* and on to the nearest medical facility. We have contacts in the GFM that aren't afraid to try something new and experimental if it will work on his wounds. Kat, you take the kids back to their parents on *Son and Heir*."

"What about me?" Quinn asked.

"You are stranded here along with everyone else. This planet has to remain secret from the rest of civilization," Loki insisted.

"I'm taking Kim," Kat protested, ignoring Quinn's spluttering comments.

Loki jumped down to the ground at the north end of the village without replying.

"Stubborn O'Hara won't listen to anyone," Kat muttered.

"Just like you, Kat," Konner almost chuckled as she passed.

"Lieutenant Talbot," Quinn said quietly at her shoulder. "Is that Lucinda Baines, the diplomatic attaché?" He pointed toward the glaring and defiant woman sitting on the temple steps with force bracelets on her wrists and ankles.

"Yes," she replied cautiously.

"Half the galaxy is out looking for her. You need to take her back to civilization. The patrols will find the jump point near the coordinates of *Jupiter*'s last transmission sooner or later. And when they do, this paradise will no longer be a secret. The devastation Hanassa caused will be nothing compared to what GTE miners will do to get that much omniscium. And if I don't return, the emperor himself will come looking for the *Margaret Kristine*."

CHAPTER 50

"STARDUST TAKE THEM all," Loki cursed. "I wish this mess would just go away." He stared in turn at Quinn and Cyndi across the evening gathering at the home village. They'd evacuated every warm body, injured and hale, that they could find from the region of Hanassa's omniscium canon. Quinn and Martin had worked tirelessly side by side with Konner, Kat, and Paola.

M'Berra had suffered burns from the omniscium to his arms and legs. He might lose the use of his left arm. Chaney Lotski, his wife and the only true medic, worked on him with desperation. The village women added their herbal knowledge to all of the injuries.

And Yaakke had died a hero's death. Loki wanted to choke with grief at the loss this represented to himself as well as the village.

A song in tribute to Yaakke's valiant act tickled the back of Loki's mind. By the end of the night he hoped to eulogize his friend. He wished Paola could stand at his side as he sang the song that would make a historical legend of the man. But Paola had gone back to her Amazons to clean up after the death of the matriarch Krakatrice as soon as they could spare a trip aboard *Rover*.

Jane, Kurt, and Bruce, the other three teenagers, had pitched in at the village end. For some reason,

Loki hadn't bothered to think things through; he'd deliberately kept Bruce Geralds, Sr. away from his son until the last minute,

Now they all sat in shocked and exhausted silence nursing hot cups of tay and wondering what would happen next.

Did they dare trust the end of the day to be the end of the horror?

Hestiia and Ariel sat in *Rover,* quietly grieving with Kim's body, telling him of their love for him, though he lay in stasis, unable to respond. Could he hear?

Loki and his siblings, along with Martin, gathered for a private conference at the far end of the circle of firelight, close to *Rover*'s parking place and the illusion of escape. "We can't leave Cyndi, Quinn, Geralds, and Martin's friends . . . and we can't let them escape," Loki continued his litany of grief. He didn't trust his former lover and he didn't know Quinn well enough to trust him—though Martin did and that spoke well of him.

"I wish I knew who Quinn had bought his ship from. If I could pry that secret from his mind, or his mouth, I'd trust him more." Kat stood up and brushed her trousers free of a few specks of dirt, as if dealing with this thorny question soiled them more than nine months of living rough on a primitive planet had.

"Quinn might swear to keep this planet a secret, but I'm not willing to take the chance. He doesn't have a vested interest in keeping this place secret. He does have a vested interest in reporting to the emperor." Kat sighed and shrugged. "I've been betrayed too often by those I thought I could trust and saved by those I knew I could not." She grinned at her brothers.

Loki hugged her. He needed to make sure she was still here, still allied with them.

"Martin likes and trusts him," Konner offered. He hugged his son as if afraid the boy would slip away forever if he didn't keep him close.

"But apparently, Quinn's got the ear of the emperor," Kat said. "Don't ask me how or in what capacity. I barely understand it myself. That opens more jump points into the unknown."

"If the ley lines here are a part of the transactional graviton web, then we can't disrupt the balance any more than we already have," Konner said. "Star travel, communications, even planetary gravities might be disrupted." He and Martin studied a handheld, trying to puzzle it all out.

"Omniscium is too valuable. The emperor couldn't ignore this source, even if Quinn swore him to secrecy," Loki added.

"What are we going to do?" Kat banged her fist against her thigh. "All of these people have connections to important people who will come looking for them eventually."

(May I help?) Gentian asked them all.

"Who said that?" Martin jumped.

"He's never spoken to me before!" Loki said as he scanned the night sky in wonder.

"Or me," Konner echoed.

Then the flywacket dove below the clouds and came to a flapping halt at Kat's feet. He neatly tucked his wings beneath their protective flap of skin and rubbed his face against Kat's leg. She bent to scratch his ears and his purr rumbled loud and full.

Martin's jaw dropped in wonder as he, too, reached a tentative hand to pet the flywacket. Maybe he needed to make certain the beast was real.

"How can you help, my friend?" Kat asked.

(Take me with you when you leave Kardia Hodos,) Gentian begged. His eyes engaged each of them in turn.

"If that's what you wish. But we aren't certain how we can leave without the outsiders."

Loki's heart swelled to hear her refer to the others as outsiders—as if she finally felt she belonged here. With her family.

(I can give them each a dragon dream. They will each believe the story I send them, with no memory of this place.)

"A dragon dream is a powerful weapon." Loki crouched down to stare the flywacket in the eye. "Do you dare do this without the consent of the entire nimbus?" He'd had firsthand experience with one of the dreams. The image of a spotted saber cat leaping to attack him remained as vivid in his mind as if he'd actually lived through the experience.

"I've heard of dragon dreams," Kat whispered in wonder. "Irisey, the female dragon, said something about wishing she had the authority to give Amanda a dragon dream so she would banish the spirit that possessed her. But all of the dragons must agree before a dream may be given."

"How complete is a dragon dream?" Konner asked Gentian.

Hope began to lift Loki's spirits. "A dragon dream is more real than reality."

(Yes. Kardia Hodos will become to these people less than a dream, only an occasional flicker of the imagination. Ask the one called Brewster if he remembers setting a spark inside the ship that brought Kat.)

"Brewster," Loki called the sergeant over to him. He looked closely at the man's aura. Shades of innocent green looked open and vulnerable. Loki set his mind to probe the man. "When was the last time you were aboard *Jupiter?*"

"I went back once with Lieutenant Talbot right after we evacuated nine moons ago. I helped her salvage comm units and a hydroponics tank right after you stole the crystal array. Lot of good that did. Everything at Base Camp is ash." The man frowned deeply. "I sure hope a rescue ship comes soon. I don't see how any of us can survive without hydro tanks."

"You'll learn," Kat said. "You didn't go back the day *Jupiter* exploded?"

"Are you kidding? Once was enough. That ship was spooky, all empty and silent." He visibly shuddered all over.

Kat sent him back to help Taneeo and Lotski care for the frightened and wounded.

"His mind is vacant of any sense of lying," Loki said quietly as soon as Brewster was out of earshot.

(I assure you, he set the spark that destroyed the intruding ship. I watched him do it.)

"Why?" Kat asked the flywacket.

(The ship presented a danger to the nimbus. It had to die. One of its own had to perform the act.)

"And most of the debris went outward, outside the planet's gravity." Kat shook her head in wonder.

"I . . . I retrieved the black box," Martin said quietly.

The adults looked at him skeptically.

"We cracked it," he affirmed and met their gazes with confidence. "I showed a small fighter leaving the ship's schematic just before the explosion. The bigger lander left in the wake of the blast."

"Why am I not surprised that you alone in the GTE figured out how to crack a black box without the codes?" Konner hugged his son again.

"Can Brewster pilot a fighter?" Loki asked his sister.

"I coached him on flying a lander a couple of times." She shrugged. "If he's as bright as I think he is, he could figure it out, but his piloting wouldn't be pretty."

They all looked at each other in silence.

"Okay, so we give these people a dragon dream. They forget this place," Loki said with resolve.

"There is something else we have to do," Kat faced her brothers with her jaw set in O'Hara determination. "A dragon taboo won't keep Hanassa confined for long. He . . . she . . . it will find a way out of the volcano sooner rather than later."

"Any ideas?" Loki asked her. He wasn't too happy about leaving the problem in dragon hands either.

"If we had any crystals, we could set up a force field like the one around the clearing. Opposite to it, designed to keep one person in but open to all others," Konner offered. "But the only spare crystals we have are aboard Geralds' ship and we need that to get everyone off this planet who has to go."

"Crystal? Like a king stone?" Martin asked.

The adults all looked at him questioningly. Something stirred in Loki's mind. Something akin to hope.

"Will this help?" Martin fished a glowing blue stone from his pocket.

Loki gasped in wonder. "A mini king! Where'd you get that? You know they are illegal?"

"Dad gave it to me two years ago. And I know how illegal they are and how powerful."

"Where'd you get it?" Loki demanded of his younger brother.

"A very talented craftsman in the GFM." Konner shrugged. "He helped me figure out the physics of the cloaking field using that crystal."

"Will that little king stone be enough? Don't we

need a bunch more crystals to complete the array?" Loki asked. He wanted to reach out and grab the magnificent stone but forced himself to keep his hands at his sides. The stone wasn't his. He wasn't attuned to it. It would reject him as assuredly as its big brothers would aboard a ship.

"There are lots of native crystals," Kat said, whipping out her handheld.

"But are they monopoles?" Konner looked over her shoulder, making adjustments to her scans.

"Martin, would you please place the mini king on the ground behind the rock you are sitting on?" Konner asked.

The boy looked at his father skeptically but obeyed. Then Konner took his own handheld over to the stone and attached some kind of probe to it.

"We have a match!" he crowed. "This little guy is so hungry for a task to complete it is already bonding with the crystal matrix in this ordinary granite."

(We must hurry,) Gentian reminded them. *(We must work your magic and mine very quickly, before the dragons find out. They do not like their judgment questioned or interference in their decisions.)*

"Then let's do it. We gather crystals at dawn." Loki sat back on his rock and relaxed, happy to have a plan for him to direct. Happy to have his family working together.

* * *

Martin stared at his king stone. It rested comfortably in his hand. In the back of his mind he heard it humming quite happily.

Through the stone, Martin was aware of every rock chip and boulder within the ancient volcano caldera as if they were living beings instead of inanimate lumps of mineral. He could explore all of the caves leading off of the bowl of this dry and dusty place. He even knew the cycle of the mysterious dragongate that overlooked the lava core deep within the blown-out mountain.

He smiled to himself as he memorized the workings of the dragongate. A jump point. Only this one was limited to locations on the planet rather than distant star systems. The dragongate also had many termini. A true jump point only had one.

"You ready to bury the king stone?" his father asked him gently. "We've got the rest of the array spread around the exterior of the mountain, including one at the opening to the dragongate." He looked around at the dirty and dusty crew of locals they had drafted for the dirty work of burying the crystals at precise intervals.

"I think so." Martin remembered all the times the king stone made him feel special when no one truly loved him. Now he had his dad and a wonderful, if weird stepmother who could track anything on planet or off. He also had uncles and an aunt and a cousin.

"I don't need the crystal anymore, Dad. I've got family." He didn't need the stone anymore. But the stone needed a family of crystals to be happy.

Konner hugged him tightly. Then together they connected a handheld to the base of the crystal with fiber optics and placed the king stone upright in the deep hole Gentian had dug for it.

* * *

"I used to admire you, Captain Leonard," Kat said to the huddled figure before her.

Hanassa had retreated into one of the caves to nurse its hurts. The wound in its side had scabbed over, but it must still give pain and the blood loss had left the rogue dragon weak and resentful.

Now it hunkered into a throne carved of silver bloodwood on a dais one hundred meters inside the labyrinth of caves. The toxins in the sap would poison anything else that touched the raw wood. But Hanassa seemed impervious to the beautiful carving.

The only light came from Kat's torch. Hanassa didn't seem to need illumination.

Only one more thing remained to do before Kat could blast off from this planet and return to her life and her career. She had few regrets.

Kat still hated the thought of leaving all of her shipmates stranded on this primitive world. Fortunately, most of them, led by M'Berra's example, had settled in and begun to forge a new life.

A brief check on Judge Balinakas' city to the far west revealed a thriving society. They'd begun building massive government buildings and temples. They'd even begun a campaign to tame the cannibals in the mountains.

Only Amanda's seventy-eight remaining Marines objected to being left. M'Berra held them in a separate cave by force of arms until the force field was in place. His useless left arm cradled in a sling served as a powerful reminder of the crimes those Marines had committed and helped Amanda commit. The Marines would be able to come and go from the caldera, to serve their captain, and bring in supplies. But they were exiled from the villages. They faced a miserable existence in this barren volcano with only one small area on the plateau capable of growing food.

"I know you are in that body somewhere, Amanda

Leonard," Kat continued. "I know that some bit of your psyche still lingers. You deserve to know what is happening here."

Carefully, Kat outlined the purpose of the force field, a reverse of the one that protected the family clearing. This one was keyed so that Hanassa alone could not penetrate the field, others could come and go without triggering the energies bonded to the king stone and its family of native crystals.

Presumably the dragongate was similarly keyed to not allow Hanassa passage. But no one truly understood that weird exit point except the dragons. Kat had to trust Gentian's assurances that Hanassa would not leave by that portal.

"I learned a lot from you, Amanda. I learned what it means to be a good captain. I also learned how easy it is to let personal obsessions get in the way of leadership. Thank you for those lessons." She turned to go but paused at the narrow passageway to the outside. "Thank you, Captain Leonard."

"You will fail," Hanassa snarled. "You don't have the courage to put aside your personal desires and your 'love' for your family. They will always get in the way of your career. You should kill them now."

"My family will not get in my way. They will support me. They love me. You never loved anything except your ship and yourself. That got in the way of your success."

Kat left before the *thing* behind her could offer any more "advice" that she would not take.

She still hadn't decided what to do about the outstanding arrest warrants on her brothers. And her mother.

"She's right, you know," Bruce Geralds said at the cave entrance. He'd volunteered to help set the force field since he understood it well enough to steal the cloaking configuration for his own ship with a similar setup.

"How so?" Kat held back from coming too close to him. Given half a logical explanation for his actions, she just might allow her attraction to him to overcome her good judgment.

"Your brothers are still criminals. They will drag you down, keep you from getting deserved promotions." He had the decency to keep his eyes on his feet.

"And what about you? What about your criminal actions? Why did you continue to work for Melinda Fortesque? Do her dirty work. Make life miserable for my brother Konner. You lied, cheated, stole. You arranged the murder of her *parents*. What about your crimes?"

Geralds gulped and looked away. "My sister held a seat in the planetary Parliament of Enigma VI when Melinda first hired me. She's in the GTE Parliament now. She's a good politician. And an honest one. She cares about people and she won't be bribed. But her husband's family has connections." His eyes met Kat's gaze briefly then darted away again.

"What kind of connections?" she probed. Good connections could make or break a political career.

"With the pirates of Palaleeze II." He named a notorious group of raiders. They nominally held membership in the Galactic Free Market so the GTE couldn't go in and clean out the nest of murderers, slavers, and thieves.

"Ouch," Kat whispered.

"Ouch, yes. One whisper of those connections and Pat's career is dead. Her husband would be arrested and their kids taken from them. Jim's a good man.

He's broken from his family. But the association is enough to send him to prison and mind-wipe."

"Melinda threatened to expose your brother-in-law if you didn't do her dirty work."

"Over and over again. She may have already ruined my family since I didn't return with Konner, dead or alive."

"If she had, then your son would have known about it, suffered for it."

"That's my only hope. That he never finds out the truth about me."

"That can't be helped, Geralds," Quinn said, coming up behind them. "We're ready to set things in motion and leave, Kat." He looked her in the eye with frank appraisal. But he still had too many secrets for Kat's liking.

"What can we do for Geralds?" Kat asked. "He was coerced. He's not likely to repeat his crimes once he's freed from Melinda."

"Will you testify against her?" Quinn asked.

"Gladly." Geralds sighed as if relieved of a heavy burden. "As long as you keep my brother-in-law's family connections a secret."

"You'll probably have to do some prison time, but I think we can plea-bargain you out of mind-wipe."

"Does Bruce have to know?"

'I can't see a way around it," Kat said. "But in bringing Melinda down, we set Martin up as her heir. He can do a lot for Bruce and your wife. That's better than staying here for the rest of your life. Letting them wonder if you are dead or alive."

Geralds gulped. "I surrender to you, Quinn, as a fellow Sam Eyeam. I trust you to treat me and my family squarely." Geralds bowed his head.

"You do know what we plan to do to you?" Kat

stopped Geralds and Quinn from exiting with a tense hand on each of their arms.

"It is for the best," Geralds sighed. "I don't want to remember a lot of what happened here."

"You can make me forget this place, Mari Kathleen O'Hara Talbot," Quinn said quietly. "But I don't think I'm capable of forgetting you." He took Geralds by the elbow and led him out to the relentless sunshine and the waiting shuttles.

"Now what did he mean by that?" Kat stared after them a moment, then looked back one last time on the pitiful remains of her once proud captain. "Goodbye, Amanda. I know you will never be happy. You never could be happy even before Hanassa invaded you. But I do hope you find peace here on Kardia Hodos."

"This place is Hanassa!" Amanda insisted.

"Very well, then, you rule this volcanic crater called Hanassa. But we give a different name to the rest of this world." She turned her back on Hanassa, knowing that her captain had died inside the crabbed and twisted body.

Sadly, she joined the others for the last trip back to the family clearing and the village.

Then she could go home at last.

If home was out there, beyond the stars, then what would she call this place?

(Kardia Hodos, the pathway of the heart.)

EPILOGUE

"DO WHAT YOU must," Kat said, petting Gentian. All those who were leaving had gathered around *Rover* and Quinn's shuttle.

(You must promise to take me away with you.) Gentian leaned his considerable weight against Kat's ankles.

"I promise. You will leave with me, Gentian. You will be my companion henceforth, wherever I happen to roam."

"Let's do it," Loki ordered. "Do it now and we will all be free of the burden of this place." He looked anxiously into *Rover,* checking on Kim's stasis, ready to take off.

(But you will never be free of Kardia Hodos. This home will remain with you forever.)

Kat smiled at each of her brothers, her sisters-in-law, her niece, and her nephew. "We will come back. Each of us in our turn, if nothing else, to return Kim to his wife and daughter."

Hestiia cuddled her infant daughter close as she gave each of the family a tight hug. Then she moved off to join the villagers. She had shed her tears and now she entrusted the love of her life to his family. Her family. They'd enlarged the coding on the family clearing so that she could come and go without Kim.

(Each of you will come here in turn for your own

reasons. In your own time you must make peace with this place,) Gentian continued. *(Then it will be your home forever, no matter where you roam.)*

"Amen, so be it," Kat whispered. Her family echoed her sentiment.

Gentian turned to face those selected for the dragon dream. He spread his wings and flapped them once, commanding attention.

Then, one by one, the faces of his victims went slack, their eyes vacant. As one, they turned their backs on Kardia Hodos and retreated to their assigned shuttles.

* * *

Loki and Konner dropped Kat and her two passengers aboard *Son and Heir*.

With their help Kat strapped a sleeping Geralds onto the lounge bench and Cyndi into the narrow bunk aboard *Son and Heir*.

Then her brothers departed with brief but intense hugs.

Kat blinked away her tears before these two strong men could see them. She suspected they shared her emotions, but she refused to reach out with her psi talents to eavesdrop.

She envied the diplomatic attaché the smile on her face. Whatever she dreamed pleased her.

Kat would report to her superiors in the Imperial Military Police that she and Cyndi had barely escaped the explosion of *Jupiter*. All hands were dead or missing. Geralds, already strapped into another bunk, had rescued them from certain death as their escape pod drifted in void beyond the jump point.

The nine-month delay in their return to civilization

resulted from a king stone damaged in a battle with the O'Hara brothers who escaped.

Back on the planet, Hestiia grieved over Kim's injuries but fully expected her Stargod to return. Dalleena accompanied Konner along with Martin.

Kat stooped to scratch Gentian's ears just as the comm system beeped. She answered it in the gangway so as not to awaken Cyndi.

"Yes, Loki?' she asked recognizing *Sirius'* signature on the screen.

"All secure over there?" His face on the screen showed him running departure protocols on his bridge. Konner sat beside him as copilot.

"Getting there. Just tucked in my passengers. Gentian says they'll sleep for another day."

"The *Margaret Kristine* just blasted off without so much as a good-bye." Loki looked a little miffed at the impoliteness.

"Why should Quinn say good-bye when he doesn't know he's been here? He or the kids?" But he had promised to remember Kat. She was beginning to look forward to their next meeting. Not soon, but someday.

"Will they be all right, Aunt Kat?" Martin asked from the third console aboard *Sirius*.

"Gentian says so. They believe you bailed out before they left Aurora. The weeks they've been in space were just idle travel to keep Kurt away from assassins until his father is elected again. Truth drugs and electric probes shouldn't pry any different information from them."

"That's a relief. I want to call them as soon as I safely can."

"You can stay with your dad until Geralds and I can present evidence of your mother's crimes to the GTE. I have the documents from your database. I'll leave a message at the rendezvous point when Melinda is arrested and you can claim your inheritance."

Kat switched the signal to the bridge of the tiny ship and made her way there to continue the conversation as she prepared for launch.

"We'll let Mum know you're alive," Konner said. "If she agrees to see you, we'll have her leave messages at the same rendezvous."

"I'll look for it." Kat stroked the braided hair bracelet. What would Mum live for if she acknowledged that her lost daughter wasn't lost anymore? Would she know where to find the man who had sold his ship *Margaret Kristine* to Quinn? Would the family be able to find their father and finally all be together again?

"Let me know how Kim fares and when he's ready to go back home. I'd like to be on that flight." Kat shifted to the more immediate problem rather than dwell on "what ifs."

"Will do. We'll wait for you to launch, then follow you through the jump point. Good luck, baby sister."

Kat familiarized herself with the bridge controls, ran her safety checks and fired up the crystal drive. Only then did she look through her viewscreen. Two very large male dragons, one green, one blue, hovered in front of her.

How did they survive in the vacuum of space?

She paused with her hands on the controls.

Gentian slunk down in the copilot's seat as far as his safety harness would let him.

(You must return the flywacket to the nimbus,) the dragons said in chorus. *(He must answer to us for his crime of cowardice and disobedience.)*

"Cowardice?" Kat asked incredulously. "Gentian acted with more courage than the entire nimbus combined. He helped me and my family when you all would only stand back and watch!"

"Is everything okay, Kat?" Konner asked over the open comm.

"Everything will be." She glared at the image of the dragons in the viewscreen. They had not moved, but she sensed they consulted each other along a private line of thought.

(Gentian is one of us. He must remain with us.)

"Sorry, gang. He's part of my family now." Kat's heart warmed. She had a family; brothers, sisters-in-law, a nephew, and a niece. Even Murphy, the green teddy bear, had a new home and a new child to love. She swallowed a lump in her throat.

And she had Gentian. A friend and companion. She also had a place to call home, a place outside her career in the Imperial Military Police. She wasn't lonely anymore.

She reached over and reassured Gentian with a lingering caress. He leaned into her hand and purred.

(Can you guard the flywacket as we would?) the dragons asked Kat.

"I can do better. I can love him as part of my family."

(Then he is yours until he realizes that humans are less than perfect companions for kin of a dragon.)

"I trust Gentian to let me know if he's ever dissatisfied with me as a companion."

(I will love you as my own until you no longer need me. Then I will return to the nimbus if no other of your family needs me. And not before.)

When Kat looked back at the viewscreen the dragons had vanished.

"Jump point coordinates plotted in and ready for launch," she announced to her brothers.

She activated the controls and began the flight to the rest of her life.

"Kardia Hodos," she mused. "The pathway of the heart. Kim named this place correctly."

Irene Radford

"A mesmerizing storyteller." —*Romantic Times*

THE DRAGON NIMBUS

THE GLASS DRAGON
0-88677-634-1

THE PERFECT PRINCESS
0-88677-678-3

THE LONELIEST MAGICIAN
0-88677-709-7

THE WIZARD'S TREASURE
0-88677-913-8

THE DRAGON NIMBUS HISTORY

THE DRAGON'S TOUCHSTONE
0-88677-744-5

THE LAST BATTLEMAGE
0-88677-774-7

THE RENEGADE DRAGON
0-88677-855-7

THE STAR GODS

THE HIDDEN DRAGON
0-7564-0051-1

To Order Call: 1-800-788-6262

Irene Radford

Merlin's Descendants

"Entertaining blend of fantasy and history, which invites comparisons with Mary Stewart and Marion Zimmer Bradley" —*Publishers Weekly*

GUARDIAN OF THE PROMISE

This fourth novel in the series follows the children of Donovan and Griffin, in a magic-fueled struggle to protect Elizabethan England from enemies—both mortal and demonic. *0-7564-0108-9*

And don't miss the first three books in this exciting series:

GUARDIAN OF THE BALANCE

0-88677-875-1

GUARDIAN OF THE TRUST

0-88677-995-2

GUARDIAN OF THE VISION

0-7564-0071-6

To Order Call: 1-800-788-6262

DAW 32

Mickey Zucker Reichert

The Books of Barakhai

THE BEASTS OF BARAKHAI 0-7564-0040-6
THE LOST DRAGONS OF BARAKHAI 0-7564-0106-2

The Renshai Trilogy

THE LAST OF THE RENSHAI 0-88677-503-5
THE WESTERN WIZARD 0-88677-520-5
CHILD OF THUNDER 0-88677-549-3

The Renshai Chronicles

BEYOND RAGNAROK 0-88677-701-1
PRINCE OF DEMONS 0-88677-759-3
THE CHILDREN OF WRATH 0-88677-860-3

The Bifrost Guardians

VOLUME ONE: *Godslayer; Shadow Climber; Dragonrank Master* 0-88677-919-7
VOLUME TWO: *Shadow's Realm; By Chaos Cursed* 0-88677-934-0

Other Novels

FLIGHTLESS FALCON 0-88677-900-6
THE LEGEND OF NIGHTFALL 0-88677-587-6

To Order Call: 1-800-788-6262

DAW 35

Tanya Huff

The Finest in Fantasy

SING THE FOUR QUARTERS	0-88677-628-7
FIFTH QUARTER	0-88677-651-1
NO QUARTER	0-88677-698-8
THE QUARTERED SEA	0-88677-839-5

The Keeper's Chronicles

SUMMON THE KEEPER	0-88677-784-4
THE SECOND SUMMONING	0-88677-975-8
LONG HOT SUMMONING	0-7564-0136-4

Omnibus Editions:

WIZARD OF THE GROVE 0-88677-819-0
(Child of the Grove & The Last Wizard)
OF DARKNESS, LIGHT & FIRE 0-7564-0038-4
(Gate of Darkness, Circle of Light & The Fire's Stone)

To Order Call: 1-800-788-6262

DAW 21

Melanie Rawn

"Rawn's talent for lush descriptions and complex characterizations provides a broad range of drama, intrigue, romance and adventure."
—*Library Journal*

EXILES

THE RUINS OF AMBRAI	0-88677-668-6
THE MAGEBORN TRAITOR	0-88677-731-3

DRAGON PRINCE

DRAGON PRINCE	0-88677-450-0
THE STAR SCROLL	0-88677-349-0
SUNRUNNER'S FIRE	0-88677-403-9

DRAGON STAR

STRONGHOLD	0-88677-482-9
THE DRAGON TOKEN	0-88677-542-6
SKYBOWL	0-88677-595-7

To Order Call: 1-800-788-6262